The
# CONTINUING
# SAGA
of
# EFFIE FARRADAY

## L.A. Williams

## ALSO IN THE EFFIE FARRADAY TRILOGY...

The Life and Dreams of Effie Farraday

The Loves and Sorrows of Effie Farraday

**Available on Amazon**

\*\*\*\*\*

Book cover design by Lynn Williams

I dedicate this book to my parents

**Copyright © 2018 Lynn Williams**

This is a work of fiction. Names and characters are the product of the author's imagination and any resemblance to actual persons, living or dead, is entirely coincidental.
The views expressed in this work are solely those of the author and do not necessarily reflect the views of the publisher, and the publisher hereby disclaims any responsibility for them.

ISBN 978-1-9995832-1-7

# Chapter 1

I was soaring through the clouds like a great, powerful bird with wings as strong as iron. The wind blew fiercely into my face and through my hair, causing it to obscure my vision; instinctively I reached up to brush it out the way, only to find my hands were prevented from doing so by my feathered wings; realising I'd taken on the form of a bird I found my hair no longer hampered me and my view ahead was clear. Glancing down I gasped at the altitude, but my alarm was only temporary and in no time at all I was quite calm and happy, for it seemed I'd been this incredible avian for all the long, wondrous days of my life. It was a privilege and a gift to roam these skies without restraint, to proudly survey the land below, devoid of thoughts and spared the burden of human emotion; what a joy, what a blessing it was to live as this particular creature and possess such freedom.

I passed over endless fields, carpeted in many shades of deep and contrasting greens that only the most accomplished artist could capture; then there were rivers of purest blue, so vivid and inviting that I yearned to dive into their watery depths. As I flew further there were thick forests and woodlands of old, with seemingly unchanging landscape stretching forever onwards, making me wonder if it covered the entire land.

Almost immediately I started to descend and to my delight was swooping down towards golden cornfields, their brightness intensified magnificently by the sunny day. With ease and grace, I effortlessly glided to the ground and found myself standing near a tiny church, almost lost from sight by the ancient yews that smothered the structure in all its wisdom. I'd taken on human form now and was slowly walking ˙er to the heavy front doors of the church, and without fear ˙tation I entered.

In the flickering candlelight the old building took on a ghostly feeling, casting shadows all about. Although the church was still and quiet, I could see the congregation seated in their pews, gazing ahead at the dimly lit altar where three figures stood. I imagined everyone would turn and stare at me as I made my way down the aisle, they would hear the soft tapping of my shoes as I went by. But it seemed they were all oblivious of my presence, I was invisible. As I approached the altar it became apparent that a wedding ceremony was in progress, and the bride and groom were standing there patiently before the vicar; what a romantic setting it was with the soft glow of the candlelight and with the abundance of delicate looking floral arrangements encircling them. I stared at the couple for a few moments in bewilderment, wondering why they were waiting in silence rather than saying their vows.

Out of the blue I happened to glance down at myself, and was shocked to discover that I was wearing a flowing wedding gown, literally caked in mud.

Without thinking I let out a cry of laughter.

It seemed I wasn't invisible anymore, for the groom swung round and glared at me. The man's face was impressive and remarkably familiar; I knew this person from somewhere, and I had the distinct feeling he was very dear to me. But as I returned his unwavering stare a chill ran through me, for there was something wrong with his eyes: there was no warmth behind them, no tenderness, no expression at all, they were blank eyes. With a rising feeling of sickness, I turned my attention to the bride, who was clinging protectively to her groom: she was almost beautiful with her long, dark hair and striking eyes, but her hair lacked lustre and hung lank over her shoulders and her eyes looked over me with such malice and contempt that I hurriedly adverted my gaze.

It seemed time stood still as we all stared curiously at one another, and as I peered round at the congregation, they remained there motionless, like dummies waiting to be brought to life.

Unexpectedly I heard a sudden great bellow from outside the building and shuddered. At first, I believed it to be thunder but then the doors of the church came crashing open to reveal a tangled mass of branches. It was one of the ancient yews from outside in the churchyard, but its life hadn't come to an end as nature had intended, no, a strange power had enveloped the great tree, uplifting its roots; spreading the gnarled, creaking branches unnaturally into the church and up the aisle. The bride let out a scornful laugh as several of the huge branches reached over to my feet and formed a talon like grip around my ankle, causing me to fall forwards onto the cold, stone floor, and without hesitation it began to haul me backwards towards the entrance of the church; desperately I attempted to grasp onto something or somebody but only managed to painfully scrape my nails along the floor. Feeling a surge of terror, I weakly cried out for help, hoping in vain that someone would come to my aid. The congregation had shifted their gaze now and were staring at me like spectators at a show, watching in hideous fascination as I struggled to break free from my enemy. Approaching the door, I desperately attempted to cling onto it with my weakened fingers. A powerful surge of strength was all I required to remove the branches from my ankle, this was only a dream after all, and in our dreams, anything is possible, but this dream had turned sour and the likelihood of a happy ending was rapidly diminishing. Just before my hands were roughly wrenched away from the door, I briefly caught the eye of the groom, who was now standing before me. For one brief moment I wondered if he was going to help, but hope quickly faded as I saw him snigger cruelly at me.

'Farewell Effie Farraday. Please return from whence you came.' He uttered coldly.

Looking at him in alarm I noticed how he peered down at me disdainfully as if I was an unwanted stranger who meant nothing to him. But I was far from a stranger, for at that moment it dawned on me who he actually was.

When I uttered his name, it was but a whisper. 'Gideon?'

But it was too late, too late to confront him, and it was of little use to try and struggle now, the tree had won. The land surrounding the church had vanished and all that remained was an immense void, a bottomless pit of darkness. Realising the relentless claw was unwavering in its purpose, I vaguely clung to the hope that my body would once more transform into a magnificent bird, making it easier to escape the clutches of this evil thing. But it was not to be. With ease the tree dragged me down into a black hole of hell and I plummeted for what seemed like an entire lifetime. Thankfully my foot was eventually released and I sensed someone grasping my hand, rather tightly, and when I opened my eyes my heart was glad to the sweet face of my Aunt peering down upon me.

'Effie, Effie, are you feeling better? She asked, with an agonised look of concern etched across her face.

My Aunt's voice sounded muffled and far away.

I stared tearfully into her eyes and smiled feebly. 'II think so.'

How it eased my mind to know my Aunt was clutching my hand rather than some unnatural being, however my relief was somewhat short lived as I suddenly remembered how just a while ago, I'd fainted at the altar in front of all the guests.

In the distance I heard the sound of muffled voices.

Not ready to face the world, I instinctively closed my eyes and allowed myself time to gather my thoughts. But even in my befuddled state it was clear that delaying the inevitable was not the answer, and very shortly I would have to face everyone.

'Constance, we cannot stall a moment longer. If there's any chance of saving this ceremony we must get Effelia up.' Isaiah's gruff voice had a hint of irritation in its tone.

With my eyes half open I discreetly glanced at Isaiah, noticing his red face and disgruntled expression. To my surprise I almost felt sorry for him: he'd spent endless hours planning this day in the hope it would run smoothly and without a hitch; then I decide to pass out, minutes before my wedding vows, ruining everything. Of course, it could never be proved if I collapsed through my failing to have breakfast that morning or because of him, the mysterious man who had made his grand entrance at a most inopportune moment. I remember the stranger standing there, his hair blowing across his face in the breeze from the open door. On reflection, when

4

our eyes briefly locked, there may have been a vague recognition of some sorts, but it was all rather hazy.

My Aunt began stroking my hair. 'Just give Effie a moment Isaiah, she's in shock.' Her voice was stern. 'Does it not bother you that your daughters just fainted?'

I heard someone groan.

Duncan's deep voice came drifting across the room.

'Perhaps we should cancel the ceremony.'

I heard Isaiah's distinguished sounding voice. 'Oh no Duncan, there's no need for that. Please don't concern yourself with what's just occurred. Effelia faints all the time; it has nothing to do with that man. As soon as she wakes up properly let's put this nonsense behind us and proceed with the ceremony.'

Unable to bear it any longer I opened my eyes. My Aunt, Isaiah and Duncan were looming over me with peculiar looks on their faces, but what struck me most odd was how Isaiah was holding Duncan's arm as if he was frightened of him scurrying off.

'There see.' He exclaimed rather loudly. 'Effelia is ready to proceed.'

I frowned at Isaiah, riled by his sanctimonious and domineering attitude towards the whole situation. He was so righteous in his beliefs and so desperately eager in his pursuit to have me marry Duncan that he seemed blind to the involvement of others. He would endeavour to ignore the doubts of the groom and assume the docile bride would do as she was told. It seemed to me the one mission in Isaiah's life was to have me marry Duncan. I've of little doubt he had our entire future mapped out in front of us like a patchwork quilt of life, and Isaiah would be there in the very centre.

A sickening dread came over me as I tried to contemplate what to do. Seeing how dejected Duncan appeared made my heart sink, it was a complete contrast from earlier when our auspicious day lay before us in all its glory. And now the dilemma was deciding if we should still take that giant step into married life; would he still want me after the embarrassing fainting episode, was he serious about

5

cancelling the wedding? So little time had passed but much had changed: during my brief interlude something or someone had had a profound effect on me, and my mind had shifted direction, the route along the path of life was no longer clear, I had become lost along the way, unsure if becoming Mrs Bartholomew was now my ultimate destination.

Duncan came closer. 'Effie, what's going on?'

I gulped.

The heavy curtain that was draped over the doorway leading to the chapel was suddenly drawn back and Reverend Cosgrove entered, looking rather agitated. He was a kind, softly spoken man who I'd know most of my life, and although he was probably used to dealing with predicaments such as this before a wedding, I still felt guilty.

'Please, please lower your voices, you are in a place of worship. Quarrelling between yourselves surely will not help.' Reverend Cosgrove exclaimed, trying to pacify the situation. 'May I suggest allowing Effie and Duncan a few moments alone, so they can discuss the matter in peace with one another.' He uttered in his soft, genial voice.

Isaiah threw him a scowl, then glanced over towards me. I was sitting up now, perched on the very edge of the sofa. Inadvertently I put my arm out and disturbed a pile of hymn sheets on a nearby table, sending them flying all over the floor.

'Oh, so you've decided to get up at last have you?' Isaiah snapped at me.

It wasn't hard for me to totally ignore Isaiah's remark and speak directly to Reverend Cosgrove, who at this precise moment appeared much more amicable than my belligerent looking father.

'Yes, please Reverend Cosgrove, it... it shouldn't take too long to resolve the matter.' I said in a weak voice, glancing towards a sullen looking Duncan and wondering what on earth we were going to do.

Isaiah had released his arm now and was striding up and down the room.

My Aunt came over towards me. 'Oh Effie, I'm so glad you've recovered from your fainting spell,' She exclaimed. 'Are you feeling a little like your old self again?'

I smiled endearingly at her. 'Yes, yes Aunt, as well as can be expected.

She smiled nervously at me. 'You have a short chat with Duncan then we can resume the ceremony.' She spoke in a hopeful sounding voice, nodding reassuringly at me. 'You have your fiancée to thank you know, he caught you before you fell. If it wasn't for his quick reaction you would have collapsed onto that hard, cold floor.'

I tentatively glanced at Duncan, muttering a thank you to him before swiftly looking back at my Aunt and taking her arm. 'Are you alright Aunt?' I mumbled.

She had appeared so joyful earlier on today and now her face was strained and confused, and it was all my doing.

'Why yes dear, what's a wedding without a little drama,' she chuckled.

Isaiah huffed. 'Please be quick you two, there's a lot of unhappy guests out there waiting patiently.' He turned to look at my Aunt. 'How beastly it must be for all your friends Constance, having to sit there for so long in that drafty old chapel.'

My Aunt stood there contemplating what Isaiah had just said. 'Yes, how right you are Isaiah, and some have made a great effort to be here today, especially Mrs Winstanley, she rarely travels out these days.

It wasn't hard to picture all of my Aunt's friends huddled together in the pews, whispering amongst themselves. Whatever happened now I was sure to be the subject of great gossip and speculation for some time to come, and I imagine they would greatly embellish the events of this day with relish.

With an exasperated sigh my Aunt briskly headed over to where Reverend Cosgrove was waiting patiently by the curtained entrance. With a sideway glance she looked my way and spoke to me in a stern sounding voice. 'Just promise to be quick Effie, this isn't the time to dilly-dally.

How I wanted to laugh at her quaint way of asking me to hurry, but I could see by the expression on her face that she wouldn't thank me, her mood was far too cheerless.

'Of course, Aunt, I promise.' I said, trying to sound sincere.

Isaiah stood there and appeared reluctant to leave. 'I shall return shortly.' He said briskly. 'Meanwhile, I shall go and placate our poor forgotten congregation.' He strode over to Duncan and fleetingly placed a hand on his shoulder, mumbling in his ear. 'Remember what I told you Duncan, the gentleman who interrupted the ceremony so rudely was just a mere stranger, and was entirely unconnected with Effelia passing out.' He threw me a dubious look and followed my Aunt and the Reverend into the chapel, leaving me alone with Duncan.

I gazed over at Duncan, who was sitting slouched forward in a chair with his hands tightly clasped together. His faced looked rigid and unfriendly as he glared at me. Unable to meet his gaze a moment longer I turned away and went over to the far side of the room where a long table was laid out, displaying an array of ornate looking vases filled with dried flowers and several decanters of drink with mismatched crystal glasses.

Feeling rather giddy I grabbed the front of the table in an effort to steady myself.

'Whilst you were unconscious, I heard you mutter the name Gideon.' Duncan said in a subdued tone.

I was silent for a moment, unable to know how to respond.

'Effie, at least look at me.'

I swung round to face him, immediately noticing the pained expression in his eyes.

'Well, who is this Gideon?' Duncan uttered in a slightly raised voice.

My eyes glazed over as I attempted to remember my strange dream, but as is often the way with dreams it had greatly faded from my mind; and now my only clear recollection was of meeting someone named Gideon and then being dragged away by a monstrous tree.

I put my hand up to my brow as a sharp pain shot through my temple. 'Duncan, please give me a minute.'

With a big sigh I slowly walked over towards the small window at the back of the room. Drawing up the blinds I peered out at the blustery weather, and saw how the white delphiniums were swaying vigorously in the breeze, desperately trying to remain upright. It was then I noticed a lone figure sitting on the wall that ran the perimeter of the small chapel garden. It was Duncan's sister Charlotte. Her bridesmaids dress was partially hidden by a fur coat, which she had tightly wrapped around herself to keep warm. At first it struck me odd that she wasn't in the chapel with everyone else, but then it occurred to me that Duncan had already told Charlotte that the wedding wasn't going ahead and asked her to wait outside for him.

I turned to stare at him in alarm.

'Was it Gideon at the chapel door today?' Duncan uttered impatiently.

Biting my lip, I yet again stared out of the window.

For a while I stood there, deliberating over his question. In my muddled state of mind, I felt unable to think straight and couldn't really say for certain whether the mysterious visitor who'd interrupted our wedding and the man from my dream was indeed the same person. And had I fainted because the figure standing in the chapel doorway was known to me?

'Effie, Effie, are you listening to me?'

The urgency of his voice startled me and I swiftly turned around to face him.

'No, I don't think so.' I said, my voice sounding uncertain. 'I'm sure I'd not met the man before.' I gulped. 'But perhaps he knew me. It…. it is peculiar that he shouted for us to stop the wedding.

'Yes, indeed.' Duncan said vaguely, deep in his own thoughts. He glared at me for what seemed like an eternity then strolled over to the long table. His voice was low as he spoke. 'I did wonder if the man knew you, as he did give you an odd look.' He paused. 'But after Isaiah had a word with him, he seemed happy to leave.

'Didn't Isaiah say what the stranger wanted? I asked, trying to glean as much as I could from the conversation.

'No, he only said the man had turned up at the chapel by accident, that's all.' Duncan shrugged his shoulders and let out a small laugh. 'Of course, I don't think anyone really believed his explanation.'

I pictured Isaiah having words with the stranger, and how with his powers of persuasion he'd hurry the poor man out of the chapel. Isaiah would then face the congregation like a conquering hero and take great joy in telling all the guests how he'd bravely wrestled with the stranger and marched him outside. He would then gloss over the entire episode as if it was a matter of no importance, and would simply say that the stranger had made a mistake. But however clever Isaiah might think he's being by divulging very little information, he hadn't got the power to prevent inquisitive minds; I'm sure many of the guests would not be content with some mundane explanation, even if it were the truth. Curiously intrigued, they would sit in their homes later on today and painstakingly go over the events, conjuring up their very own wild theories of how and why the day went so horribly wrong. However, in time I knew it would pass over, and they would become absorbed by another enthralling subject, allowing me to once again fade into the background, where I would be quite happy to remain.

I sighed, and looked over to see Duncan glaring at me. Being so wrapped up in my thoughts I'd almost forgotten he was in the room.

'We'll probably look back on all of this and laugh.' I grinned at him. 'When we're old and grey.'

I wasn't sure if my comment was supposed to make light of the situation or if it was just one of those pointless and unnecessary things I had the habit of saying in an awkward situation. Either way I could see by the furious look on his face that he wasn't amused.

My eyes followed him as he moved across the room.

'No, no I don't think so Effie.' He declared solemnly.

Seeing how agitated he'd become I tried to rectify the situation by reverting back to being sensible. 'I suppose the stranger mistook me for someone else.' I murmured. 'He most likely realised as soon as he entered the chapel, and that's why he left.'

Duncan narrowed his eyes 'Yes, I suppose so.' He snapped. 'But putting that aside it doesn't explain who Gideon is, does it?'

For a moment I gaped at Duncan blankly, then went and flopped down onto the sofa, looking soul searchingly at the floor. Trying to find the right words to explain what had happened seemed like an impossible task, and unlike myself Duncan had an extremely logical mind, and would no doubt find my dream utterly preposterous. I deliberated whether or not to tell him that the dream was mere nonsense, and calling out the name Gideon didn't necessary mean I knew such a person, but in my heart this felt like a betrayal, as not only would I be deceiving Duncan I would be deceiving myself too.

As I looked up, I saw Duncan crouching down beside me, staring intently into my eyes. 'Do you love this Gideon?'

It was an innocent enough question, and Duncan certainly had the right to know the answer, it's the least he deserved. Whether I liked it or not perhaps my fainting spell had inadvertently served as a reminder of this Gideon; had my strange and disturbing vision lit a candle of recognition in my head on purpose, a flickering light to guide me to those shadowy recesses of my mind which were shrouded in a grey mist of forgetfulness, a place only I could locate. But did I have the power to retrieve this memory and pull Gideon out into the vivid sunshine? Or would he languish in the shadows because he wasn't real, just a character I'd conjured up in my dream. Suddenly my mind became clear and I could hear my heart pounding in my chest as I realised what I must do.

Duncan took my hand and squeezed it. 'Just be honest with me Effie.'

I stared into his face. 'It's not easy for me to say this Duncan but there's...' my lips started to quiver with nerves. 'There's a possibility I am in love with Gideon.'

He looked unwaveringly at me, then without saying a word he tore his hand from mine and rose up from the floor, striding across the room, cursing under his breath.

'A possibility?' His voice thundered across the room at me. 'So, you may love him or you may not.' He began to shake with laughter. 'And you choose our wedding day to announce it to me.'

'I'm so dreadfully sorry Duncan, but I didn't realise until this day.' The room was eerily quiet apart from the dull, monotonous ticking of the clock. I jumped as it suddenly chimed. 'All that has happened this morning has caused me to question my future.' For a moment I felt myself holding my breath, not wanting to say another word but deep down knowing I must. 'And I can't go through with the ceremony with such doubt in my mind.' I briefly caught his eye then looked away. 'It wouldn't be fair on you.'

I felt so ashamed that I could hardly bear to look at him. How awful he must think me, how despicable and cruel, and he would be right.

Lowering his eyes to the ground he sighed heavily. 'I see.' A strange smile appeared on his face, as he looked me in the eye. 'And does this Gideon love you?' Duncan said in a solemn voice

'Well, I...I'm not sure.' I said vaguely. 'I think that he might.'

Duncan's face was gradually becoming redder. 'Where is he then, why isn't Gideon here now? He shouted at the top of his voice.

'I have absolutely no idea.' I exclaimed with a nervous laugh.

Grimacing, he bent his head. 'Unbelievable.' He said, loosening his tie and throwing it on the floor. 'You are unbelievable.'

All I could do was stand there opened mouthed and watch as he poured a rather large whisky from the decanter, swigging it back in one go. Any notion of a happy, contented life with Duncan had all but dissipated now, like the last leaves falling from a tree on a chilly autumn's day. Perhaps I should have attempted to rectify the situation, to try and salvage what was left, but both of us knew it was far too late for that. The autumnal leaves had been blown far away on a gust of wind, and like our future they were lost forever.

'Well, it seems I've had a lucky escape then doesn't it? He uttered in a curt voice. 'You've not changed one bit have you

Effie Farraday, even after all these years you're still the same strange girl that I remember from school.' He began to laugh hysterically. 'With that faraway look in your eyes, as if you were living in some kind of fantasy world.'

I wanted to cry out to him that he was mistaken, that I'd changed, but then I knew how mendacious that answer would be.

'Yes, yes, you're right, I am still that girl, but I thought you were aware of that. Anyway, what's wrong with having a harmless daydream, life would be pretty mundane if we didn't.' I paused. 'And perhaps I do tend to be preoccupied with my thoughts on occasions, but that's hardly a criminal offence now is it.'

Disregarding my sentence Duncan stood there sniggering. 'Even your old friend Mace ran away from you, I bet he became tired of your erratic behaviour.'

I clenched my hands together tightly, digging my fingernails into my palms. 'You know very well Mace didn't run away, he moved away because he was getting married.'

'Don't you find it strange that he didn't invite you to his wedding?'

I began to stammer. 'Isaiah explained the reason why. Mace found it too difficult...difficult to....' my words faltered.

'See, you can't acknowledge the truth. You won't accept the fact that Mace is tired of you and that he doesn't want to see you again.' Duncan said, pointing his finger at me. 'It's probably a similar story with this Gideon.'

I got up and stumbled forward. 'I know you're upset, and I understand that, but please do not pretend to know my own mind better than me. I would appreciate it if you would keep your opinions about Mace to yourself, especially when your views are totally unfounded. As for Gideon...well you don't know anything whatsoever about him.'

I glared at Duncan - my arms folded. Of course, I was also at a complete loss when it came to Gideon, a fact I found quite amusing: my only knowledge of him was a few exceedingly sketchy details from my dream of today and a vague realisation that perhaps I loved him; it was entirely feasible

13

that this man was simply a mere figment of my overzealous imagination. But to confess this to Duncan would not only make me appear extremely foolish but also validate his belief that I was still the same scatter-brained girl from school who didn't know her own mind.

The sudden noise of someone clearing their throat caused me to abruptly swing round towards the small curtained door. Reverend Cosgrove was standing there, looking rather sheepish.

'Apologies for the interruption but time is ticking away.' The Reverend uttered in a soft voice. He looked down and tapped his watch. 'Are you both ready to proceed?'

I sensed a note of uncertainty in the Reverend's voice. No doubt he'd overheard the two of us bickering to one another.

An uncomfortable silence followed. I stood there open mouthed for a moment, and then took a quick sideways glance at Duncan, who was standing beside the back door that led out to the graveyard.

'Well Effie, why don't you tell the Reverend, why don't you explain to him why we can no longer be married?'

Although it was clear the wedding was to be no more, to actually hear Duncan utter the words made it seem so final and real. I could feel the colour rising in my cheeks as I faced Reverend Cosgrove, knowing it was my duty to tell him the bad news. Of course, I could pin the blame on the stranger at the chapel door, or the peculiar dream that made no sense, or the mysterious Gideon, or even the poor groom, but ultimately it was me, I ruined the wedding.

I nodded and looked at Reverend Cosgrove. 'Duncan and I have decided not to go ahead with the ceremony. I'm so sorry to have wasted your time Reverend.'

A fleeting look of alarm crossed over Reverend Cosgrove's face and then he gradually smiled. 'That's completely acceptable.' He clasped his hands together. 'You'd be surprised at how common occurrence it is for the bride and groom to change their minds right at the last moment.

I looked over at Duncan, praying he wouldn't ask me to elaborate as to why we weren't marrying. He smirked at me as he spoke to the Reverend. 'Effie is going to make an announcement to the congregation, aren't you Effie?'

I glared at him with a look of complete horror, and found myself too shocked to reply. My eyes flicked to the Reverend, who looked rather taken aback.

'Oh, very well then I shall go and tell the congregation that you are coming out to speak to them Effie.'

The Reverend hovered for a moment as if he was going to speak again then disappeared from view.

I turned to look at Duncan, who was staring at me with a mixture of pity and sorrow. 'Goodbye Effie, and good luck with Gideon, I hope for your sake he turns out to be the one for you.' He laughed for a minute then his face became serious. 'It's a shame Effie, you and I could have been happy together.'

'Yes, perhaps we might have.' I said, smiling gently at him. I took one more glance at his face, knowing it would be for the last time. 'I wish you well Duncan.'

I felt a gust of air come into the room as Duncan opened the door, and with a brief smile, he was gone from my life.

For a while I could only stand there, staring into space. But then a distinct feeling of dread washed over me as I remembered what I had to do. I knew I shouldn't shirk my responsibilities but the temptation to sneak out the back was overwhelming, so much so that I found myself unconsciously gravitating towards the door. It would be easy; no one need know, no one would think lesser of me. Reverend Cosgrove would make the announcement to the congregation, a duty he was completely comfortable with. But then I thought of my Aunt, and how she would feel if I sauntered out the back entrance like a coward. I had no wish to add to my woes by becoming a feeble specimen of a person with absolutely no sense of moral duty.

In a trance like state, I shakily forced myself over towards the curtained doorway and pulled back the heavy drapes. As soon as I entered the chapel the low murmurs from the pews came to an abrupt halt and silence fell throughout the congregation.

Out of the corner of my eye I could see my Aunt and Isaiah peering apprehensively in my direction, in fact all eyes were upon me, but not once did I return their gaze, I dare not, for to do so would certainly be my undoing; I would crumble to pieces and become unable to utter a word. So instead, I lowered my head and focused on the scattered rose petals on the floor.

My voice broke upon the stillness of the chapel. 'I regret to inform you all but the wedding has been cancelled. I apologise for your wasted journey.'

There, the deed was done, short and sweet with no messing about. To this day I'm not entirely sure what possessed me to walk up the aisle, instead of going back behind the curtained door; perhaps I deserved to suffer for denying everyone the pleasure of a joyous wedding, and my punishment was to take a walk of shame along the long, narrow aisle. How poignant I thought, not to be the beaming bride arm in arm with my new husband, no I was still Effie Farraday, and I was still alone.

In a daze I automatically made my way to the silent graveyard around the back of the building, for I had no wish to be standing there on exhibition whilst the guests filed out the chapel, ready to gawp at the poor, disorientated bride as they passed by.

And as I sat there on a bench, I crouched forward and stared at the ground, trying to comprehend what had just happened. I knew for certainty that this particular day would forever be imprinted in my memory and one that I would reflect upon with sorrow and embarrassment. Sometimes I imagined the presence of a tiny demon, crouched on my shoulder, whispering in my ear, cruelly reminding me of events in my life that hadn't gone entirely to plan, and causing me to needlessly agonise over what I could have done or said to rectify the situation; I was aware what a thankless and completely unnecessary process this was to undertake, after all we cannot turn back the clock of time and do not possess the ability to rewrite the past. And yet I'm unable to prevent myself from reliving these horrendous moments, like a burden of misery, and that tiny demon will never leave me alone.

I stood in the living room staring out the window.

'We'll pack your wedding gown up and store it away in the attic.' My Aunt said. 'Out of sight out of mind.'

Without turning I nodded. 'Yes, yes that sounds like a good idea Aunt.'

I felt her lingering behind me. 'What really happened at the chapel to make you change your mind? Please tell me Effie, I must know.'

Turning round to face her I was slightly taken aback by the look of pain in her eyes. Instinctively I gave her a light hug, burying my face into her shoulder. 'I'm not really sure Aunt.' I looked up into her face. 'But I'm so very sorry for putting you through all of this, you don't deserve it.'

She patted me on the shoulder and moved away slightly. 'Oh Effie, don't you fret about it. I'm made of sterner stuff than you give me credit for. I'm not angry with you dear, I just wanted to know why you couldn't go through with the ceremony.'

I turned away from her and stared out at the garden. 'Have you ever had anything happen in your life that you believed to be fate? What if the stranger was meant to burst through those doors, what if I was meant to faint, and what if I was meant to have that dream.'

She appeared speechless for a moment and just stood there staring at me.

'Well, they do say that everything happens for a reason. But surely the dream is inconsequential.'

'I don't believe it was merely a dream Aunt, I believe the man in my dreams was real...and I think my future may lie with him.'

My Aunt looked at me, completely bewildered. 'Oh, Effie really, listen to what you're saying.' Her voice was terse. 'I grant you it's possible to dream about someone who's real, but if this man really existed then why haven't you mentioned him before, and why have we never seen him, where is he?' She shook her head in disbelief. 'It just doesn't make any sense.'

We both turned and looked as Isaiah came bursting through the doors with a tray of drinks.

'Your Aunt is precisely right Effelia. How can you even consider using that preposterous dream as an excuse not to have married Duncan?' It's completely absurd.' He huffed, raising his eyes to the ceiling. 'How glad you must have been when that stranger entered the chapel and you fainted, because ultimately you wanted a way out. You never really wanted to be Duncan's wife did you, you never truly loved him.' He placed the tray down on the small table in the middle of the room. 'Why don't you just admit it Effelia.'

I drew in a deep breath and clenched my hands together. 'I did love him, but sometimes that's not always enough. And I came to realise today that we wouldn't have made one another happy.

'Well now we'll never know, will we.' He scoffed.

'It's done now Isaiah, there's not point dwelling on such matters.' Uttered my Aunt.

A gradual smile spread slowly across Isaiah's face. 'Yes Constance, you're absolutely right.' He approached the table. 'Let's look to the future and put the past behind us.' He gestured for us to come over. 'Come let us have a drink. I think we're all in need of one.'

With a sigh I went and joined my Aunt and Isaiah. 'I'd rather not thank you, as you know I'm really not partial to alcohol. I think I'll go and have a tea instead.'

Isaiah chuckled. 'Oh, there isn't any spirits in it Effelia, it's just a little homemade remedy I whipped up to calm us all after such a stressful day.' He handed a glass to my Aunt and I. 'Believe me, we'll all feel so much better afterwards.'

'Well that sounds completely satisfactory Isaiah.' Commented my Aunt. 'Come on Effie, it may bring a little colour to those pale cheeks of yours.'

Isaiah sniggered. 'Yes quite. 'Drink it up the two of you.' He watched as my Aunt drank hers then turned to me. 'Be quick Effie, I promise it will do you good.' He smiled ingratiatingly at me as I knocked back the drink. 'It's full of natural ingredients.'

I screwed up my face. 'It tastes completely foul.'

'Well what did you expect Effelia, strawberry flavour?'

I raised my eyebrows and forced a smile. 'I suppose not.' I glanced at his untouched glass on the tray. 'Why haven't you drunk yours Isaiah?'

'Oh, I shall have mine later.' He replied flippantly.

Without another word he took the tray and headed towards the door, whistling a little tune.

# Chapter 2

The season of summer is somewhat forgiving to the exterior of my old debilitated home and cleverly deceives the onlooker into only seeing the abundance of flowering wisteria, creeping generously over the decrepit building and the colourful display of summer plants that conceal the weeds so adequately; The south wall is now smothered with clematis and your eyes are drawn to the subtle colours of the warm scented roses surrounding the rear of the property, and all about the border paths are an array of pink and purple poppies. The exterior of Rawlings however could not be so easily concealed: the foundations of the old house creak and groan with age, pleading for someone to come along and make them better; damp has stained the ceilings in many of the rooms and cracks run down the inner walls in jaggedly lines, and carefully positioned buckets stand here and there to catch the dripping water when it rains. We did our best of course, to patch it up when necessary but it was always an amateur repair that never really lasted very long.

There was a timeless quality about those long, glorious summer days that stretched onwards like an ever-ending soothing song, and in the brightness of the day it was easy to while away my time contentedly; for nature had become my saviour that year and could evaporate all my woes in the quietness of the garden when all you could hear were the gentle chirping of the birds and the intermittent drone of the bees busily searching for nectar.

The wedding had now become little more than a distant blur of a memory. I likened the whole episode to the chapter in a book I'd been reading that had been rather horrid and unsettling, and although part of me wanted to read more I was fearful of what the unread pages would contain, and was wary of the ending. So, I'd buried it deep within the library of my mind where one day I would retrieve the book and read it in its entirety. For I could not face my past, as indistinct as it may now be, and was fearful of what awaited me further along the road of life, so I chose to hide myself away in the confines of Rawlings, just like one of my musty old books in the library, where nothing could hurt or harm me, and where I was safe.

I contemplated how long I could exist in this manner before I would have to venture outside of my secure existence and face the outside world. Feeling restless I would go and sit on the windowsill during the late evenings and stare out into the night, breathing in the balmy air, and the sweet perfume of the roses. And as I sat there in the still silence, I pondered over my life, and how I wanted to let go of my old habits and bring the past into the present; for it seemed to me that by creating one complete picture of memories, both old and new was the only way I could move on. But there was another reason for peering outside in the dead of night, I would wait to see if the shadowing figure that lurked in the garden was still visiting, watching me from afar; how I wished I could dismiss such an apparition as a mere figment of my imagination, and how I wished it would go away and not return.

It was during the latter part of the summer that I finally plucked up courage to go beyond my home, and take a trip into Abercrombie. Rather annoyingly Isaiah had insisted on being my chaperon. I'm not exactly clear on why, perhaps he thought I didn't have the capability to act rationally in a public place, and would fall to pieces if someone spoke to me. Perhaps he was right. He proposed we should luncheon in Hudson's café and then take a short stroll along the promenade, before returning to Rawlings. Apart from having to spend the afternoon with Isaiah, it all sounded perfectly acceptable, however, not wishing to upset him I reluctantly agreed.

Stepping into Hudson's café I immediately thought of Mace, sitting at our favourite table: I could picture him now with his scruffy hair and cheeky smile, devouring a large slice of cake, whilst trying to put the world to rights. How I would laugh at his dry sense of humour and patiently tolerate his barrage of sarcastic comments. An acute wave of sorrow flooded over me when I realised how much I missed him.

'How crowded it is for a weekday.' Commented Isaiah, rather gruffly. He gestured for me to go ahead of him. 'Lead the way.'

With a sigh I made my way across the busy cafe, automatically heading to the far-right corner of the room where our favourite table was situated. For a moment I half expected to see Mace sitting there grinning at me, and my heart sank when I saw an elderly couple occupying the space. Without thinking I stood there staring menacingly at them, like a person deranged, until Isaiah yanked my arm.

'There's an empty table over here Effelia.' He laughed nervously. 'Don't dawdle.'

'Very well then.' I replied glumly, slowly turning away from the couple.

'I think bringing you here was rather a good idea of mine, don't you Effelia? It's about time you had a change of scenery.'

I forced a smile but didn't reply. I'm not sure what possessed me to agree to his suggestion of visiting the café, as now we were here, I just wanted to leave. Somehow without Mace the place had lost its sparkle, and that homely quality that made the café so special had all but gone now, along with its memories. Perhaps it was the change of décor that made it feel so different; the room had been redecorated in rather gaudy, floral wallpaper along with matching curtains, and several additional tables had been added, making the whole area rather cramped.

Mechanically I slumped down in the vacant seat opposite Isaiah, staring over at the elderly couple who had taken our table; they looked back at me rather uneasily as they tentatively sipped their tea. I had a sudden urge to run over and confront them, demanding that they move seats. Of course, this silly whim of mine vanished as swiftly as it had appeared, for I had no desire to sit there, not without the company of my best friend.

'Oh, do cheer up Effelia.' Isaiah exclaimed as he picked up the menu. 'I thought you'd be pleased to be back here once more. You used to frequent Hudson's café all the time before…. Before -' Isaiah paused.

'You mean before Mace moved away. Isn't that what you're trying to say Isaiah?'

He threw me a steely look. 'Yes, I suppose so.'

'I was rather hoping to go and visit Mace. You've got his address, haven't you?'

'Somewhere, yes.' He murmured under his breath. 'But I do not think it prudent to go and see him.'

'Why ever not?' I exclaimed in surprise.

'He is settled now with his wife, and as I told you when you enquired about him the other day, they're now expecting a child.' He exclaimed, barely glancing at me. 'I feel such a visit would disrupt them and would deeply upset you. You're making excellent progress in rebuilding your life after the disastrous wedding and I don't want anything or anyone to hinder you.' He lowered his voice. 'Besides, do you not think he would have contacted you if he so wished.'

'Perhaps.' I slouched forward and sighed. 'I would just feel better if I saw him for myself.'

Isaiah grunted. 'Do you not think that's a little selfish Effelia? The boy is obviously contented with his life, please do not spoil it for him.' He leant forward towards me.

'It's time to put all of that behind you now. Leave the past to rest and focus on your future.' He mumbled. 'You have much to look forward to Effelia.'

Feeling pensive I turned to gaze dreamily out of the window. 'Someone once told me how our past is a piece of us that we cannot and must not detach ourselves from, despite how painful some memories may be they are unique to us and are paramount to our sanity.' I uttered in a faraway voice.

I snapped out of my daydream state and turned to face Isaiah.

He looked aghast. 'That's utter boloney, whatever ignoramus told you that drivel?'

I narrowed my eyes. 'I can't remember.' I replied wistfully. 'I imagine it was someone from my past.'

Isaiah glanced at me from over the top of his spectacles. 'Huh.' He studied the menu. 'Let's order, I'm famished.'

As I sat there staring vacantly at the menu, I contemplated Mace as a father, and tried to picture him caring for a baby. He was so irresponsible and foolhardy, scarcely able to look after himself let alone a child. I suddenly felt dreadful for being so critical of my friend; perhaps becoming a father would be the making of him. Whatever my feelings on the matter I should at least be happy for him and his wife. There was of course a small part of me that envied Mace's situation; there he was all settled and contented with promising times ahead whilst I had no idea where my life was heading. What a mess I'd made of everything; my wedding day had turned out to be rather a catastrophe and now I was alone again, with no thoughts of what to do next. However, the more I thought about it the more I came to realise that this wasn't really what was troubling me, there was something else skulking in the shadows which I was desperately trying to pretend didn't exist, as the truth was too hard to swallow.

A familiar voice drifted across the café and I turned to see Mrs Worthington heading straight our way.

'My oh my, how marvellous to see you again Effie, it's been so long.' She moved forward and gave me a light embrace. 'You must update me on what's been happening.' She directed her gaze to Isaiah and gently patted her hair into place. 'Good morning Isaiah, what a pleasure it is to see you.'

Isaiah reached out and took Mrs Worthington's hand and planted a kiss upon it.

'How delightful to see you my dear Clematis. 'As always, you look truly beautiful.'

A squeal of laughter erupted from Mrs Worthington making me jolt in my seat.

'Oh Isaiah, what a lovely thing to say.'

'I'm only stating what everyone else is thinking. I hope that husband of yours appreciates you my dear.' He looked at the menu. 'Now, please may we order tea for two and the lunch time special.'

Mrs Worthington stood there for a while gazing fondly at Isaiah. Then smoothing down her apron, she scribbled our order onto a tiny notepad. 'Certainly.' She smiled. 'I shall be back in a jiffy.'

Suddenly someone called Isaiah's name and I looked over to the left to see several of Aunt's committee member friends. They were beckoning him to join them.

'Oh, not now.' Isaiah murmured in a disgruntled sounding voice. 'I can't go anywhere without bumping into someone I know.'

What it is to be so popular, I thought. Not that the crowd of ladies didn't know me too, but I knew it was Isaiah they really wanted to engage in conversation; of course I knew if I went over they would exchange pleasantries with me and ask how I was keeping, commenting on the weather and some such thing, however, ever since the day of the wedding they seemed unclear as to what to say to me, embarrassed or fearful of mentioning the wrong thing just in case I shattered into a thousand pieces, like a fragile china doll.

'You should go over and say hello Isaiah. If you don't mind, I'll stay here.' I said, shuffling awkwardly in my seat.

He reluctantly rose from his seat. 'Yes, very well then, but don't go anywhere, I'll be back in a moment.'

I watched as he ambled over to them with his pronounced limp. 'Yes sir.' I uttered under my breath. Without him sitting next to me I relaxed a little and leant back in the chair. The elderly couple had left now, leaving *our* table free. I was half tempted to go and sit there but then decided it would be too painful. Besides, Mrs Worthington was now heading in my direction, with a tray.

'Here we are Effie.' She uttered, clanking the cups and saucers down on the table with a loud clatter. 'Your father told me he'd be joining you shortly, as he doesn't want you to be sitting here all on your lonesome.' She placed her hand upon my shoulder. 'I do hope you're feeling better now.' Not waiting for a reply, she carried on talking in a quiet voice. 'That chap of yours has been in here most days waiting for you to make an appearance. He sits there in the corner, staring out the window.'

I gave her a quizzical look. 'Sorry Mrs Worthington, what chap?'

Mrs Worthington glanced round to look at Isaiah then pulled up a chair beside me.

'I would hate for your father to think I was keeping a secret from him, he's such a good, decent gentleman, always thinking of others, especially you.' She said, pouring out the tea. 'But I really think we should keep this between ourselves, for the time being anyway.'

I raised my eyebrows at her. 'Very well then, yes.' I nodded my head in agreement. 'So, what's this chap's name?' I asked, totally perplexed.

Mrs Worthington swiftly glanced the perimeter of the room as if what she was about to say was of such great importance that it was crucial no one overheard.

'Well I don't know the man's name but he's desperate to see you. Evidently, he's been over to Rawlings many a time but your father always tells him to go away. So instead he waits for you here, in the hope of seeing you.'

'But who is he?' I asked in an impatient voice, eager to discover the identity of this man before Isaiah came back over.

She leant forward over the table and whispered.

'From what I can gather he's that chap who interrupted your wedding.' Tilting her head a little her eyes became filled with sympathy. 'Is he a passed love of yours who you never got over, and that's why you couldn't go through with the ceremony?'

I glared at her indignantly 'No, absolutely not. 'I've no knowledge of the man, whatsoever.' I bit my lip. 'But Isaiah was wrong to send him away from Rawlings. I would at least liked to have known what's going on.' I exclaimed, looking furiously over at Isaiah, who was deep in conversation with his admiring audience.

'Oh Effie, your father was only trying to protect you, don't you see? Isaiah confided in me, saying how much you'd been through over the past years and that any complications of a romantic nature could tip you over the edge. So, I feel a little bad for mentioning it to you, but this poor chap is desperate.' You do understand, don't you?'

'Yes Mrs Worthington. And anyway, I believe I'm over the worst and can deal with anything that life throws my way.' I said, smiling. 'And don't worry, I promise not to breath a word of this to Isaiah.'

She put her hand to her chest. 'Phew, that's a relief. I should hate to upset him.'

Mr Caruthers, the manager began calling Mrs Worthington.

'Oops looks like I should go and bring over your lunch.' She said, rising up from her seat.

'But Mrs Worthington, what else can you tell me about this man.'

'Very little apart from what I've already told you. I do have a feeling though, a feeling the poor chaps of limited means. Frequently I've sneaked him over a free meal, as quite frankly my sweet he looks like he could do with it, and please don't think I'm being disrespectful, but his appearance is that of a tramp.' She picked up the tray and began to move away, but just as she did so she gasped. 'Talk of the devil, here he comes now Effie.'

My eyes travelled over to the window where I saw a tall, scruffy looking man approaching the café. I was suddenly transported back to the day of my wedding where the strange figure had been standing in the chapel doorway, and I immediately realised they were one of the same. As I continued to gaze out the café window our eyes fleetingly met and we stared at one another, then abruptly the man turned away and fled back up the street. It seemed he wasn't that desperate to see me after all, I thought to myself. I however couldn't bear the suspense; I had to know who this mysterious man was.

Glancing over at Isaiah and seeing he was still deep in conversation with the ladies, I smiled at Mrs Worthington then quietly and discreetly made my way over to the entrance and ran outside after the stranger.

The early afternoon sun was unforgiving as I sprinted down the street and I could feel beads of perspiration forming on my face from the heat. Seeing the man rapidly disappearing along the avenue of trees of Cedar Street I quickened my run, worrying that I would soon lose him. Whoever he was, this person certainly could move, I thought, looking up the empty tree lined street.

'I've lost him.' I muttered to myself.

Feeling dejected I slackened my pace, trying to get my breath back, and began ambling slowly up the end of the street towards Montgomery park. I was just about to admit defeat when I spotted a lone figure of a man up ahead sitting on a park bench by the river; even from a distance something told me it was he. A wave of apprehension came over me as I slowly approached the bench, creeping along the pathway in silence just in case he fled. For a moment I stood there, waiting for him to look up but he was oblivious to my presence; deep in thought he was hunched forward, gazing out onto the river. Starting to feel a little foolish I cleared my throat and tentatively reached out to touch his arm.

Instinctively he looked up at me and gasped, his eyes wide with alarm.

Swiftly I clutched his arm. 'Please, please don't run again.' I uttered. 'I just need to talk to you.'

The man looked startled, staring unfalteringly at me without saying a word. I was rather perplexed and unnerved by his penetrating gaze, but was undeterred. My mission was suddenly clear: I had to know what this strange man wanted with me. I'd been deluding myself into believing that my wedding day had been banished from my thoughts, for the truth was that ever since the ceremony, the happy event that never came to fruition, there had been very little else occupying my mind other than to solve the mystery surrounding this man who'd stormed into the chapel on that fateful day. How could I have any hope of moving forward in my life without discovering his identity, to remain in the dark on such matters would surely bring on a gradual madness that would eat away at me like an evil presence inside my head.

Trying to ease the tense situation I smiled politely at him.

'This truly is a lovely spot isn't it?' Releasing his arm, I went and sat beside him on the bench. 'I often come here for some peace and quiet.'

My face began to flush. The truth was I hardly ever came to Montgomery park so I'm not really sure why I said it; I suppose I thought it might help him relax a little, as I really didn't want him to scurry off just yet, not until I'd discovered more about him. For a few moments we both sat in silence, gazing across at the ducks that had gathered around a group of young children feeding them bread.

'My name's Effie.' I said without looking at his face. 'But I do believe you already knew that.' I bit my lip. 'It was you wasn't it, at my wedding?'

He turned to look at me and for the first time I took in the features of his face. I found myself drawn to his large, almond shaped eyes; not only were they truly beautiful, but they also displayed a quality of earnestness about them. His complexion was rather pale and faint lines were visible around his broad mouth, his lips were slightly pressed together over a pair of seemingly faultless white teeth. And I couldn't help but wonder if his thick, dark hair was intentionally tied back from his face to disguise how unruly and matted it had become. Looking into his eyes suddenly evoked an odd sense of poignancy within me, a peculiar feeling of homesickness that one experiences for no apparent reason. But it was no good trying to recognise this man, he was completely unknown to me.

When he finally spoke, I noticed how deep and rich his voice was. 'Yes, yes it was me at your wedding. I'm so very sorry for my conduct. I do not know what possessed me to make such an announcement.' He furrowed his brow and shook his head. 'My only defence is that I've been unwell.'

'Oh.' I said in somewhat vague manner. I suddenly wondered if it was a physical complaint or a mental one. To ask him what was wrong seemed wholly inappropriate, as he was after all, a stranger. Perhaps he was one of those poor wretches from The Manor on the other side of Abercrombie who would often take it upon themselves to go for a stroll outside the grounds of the institution and become lost. This could explain his odd outburst at the chapel. 'Well I do hope you've recovered.'

His face became filled with anguish. 'I cannot fully recuperate until I find my home.'

I glanced at him with pity in my eyes. 'If you tell me where you live perhaps I can help you get back. We could catch the train there together.'

Deep laughter erupted from his mouth and he began to rock backwards and forwards on the bench.

I recoiled in shock. 'What's so funny?'

'My home's a long way away, and can't be reached by train.'

Even in the warmth of the sun I felt a sudden shiver run through me.

'Whatever do you mean?' I asked, beginning to think he really was an occupant of The Manor.

He looked me fully in the eyes. 'I don't belong here. For so long now I've been trying to reach my home but it seems I am forever trapped somewhere else.' He gulped. You see, I…I come from another world.'

'Another world' I exclaimed, slightly bemused. 'I see.' After thinking for a moment, I decided to ignore his ridiculous talk of other worlds. 'So, how long have you been here in Abercrombie?'

He became still. 'Not long.'

'Did you travel alone?'

'Yes. I was supposed to travel with a friend but she was delayed and had to remain in the other world for a while longer. She promised to meet me here as soon as possible, but so far has not arrived. So now I'm all alone in a strange place with only you for company.'

I eyed him suspiciously. 'But you hardly know me; we've only met properly today. What do you want with me? I asked rather confrontationally.

Rising from the bench he started to walk along the riverbank, and for a second, I thought he was leaving.

'Please, please don't go. I have to know what's going on.'

Slightly unsteady on his feet, the man ambled back to the bench and slumped down.

'Forgive me Effie. What I *meant* to say is you are my only companion because you are the one person to whom I seem to have a connection with since arriving in this place.' He paused and retrieved a tatty old notepad from his pocket and flicked through the pages. 'Referring to my notes helps my memory; every new snippet of information I collect is written down in here, and I refer to it daily.' He tapped a page with his finger. 'This page is about your mother. Seeing her in Abercrombie was the key, she led me to you.'

The mere mention of my mother caused my heart to pound.

'I don't understand, you're talking in riddles.' I uttered, feeling exasperated. 'What has my mother to do with all this, when did you see her?' I asked in an unsteady voice.

'Your mother was the one that persuaded me to cross over into this land, she is the friend that hasn't arrived yet.'

'But...but you just said you'd seen her here in Abercrombie?'

He hesitated for a moment and rubbed his eyes.

'It's difficult to explain.'

'Perhaps you should start from the beginning.' I suggested, giving him a sympathetic smile.

He smiled back at me with his large eyes. 'Yes, you are right. 'When I arrived here, I banged my head rather badly and had severe concussion, and had it not been for a rambler in the woods discovering me I'd probably be dead by now; he took me to one of your hospitals where I spent a long while with severe concussion. The doctors there believed me to have amnesia as I couldn't remember anything at all, but I'm not so sure.' He sighed. 'Travelling to other worlds is not meant to be, and therefore our brain somehow removes any trace of our previous memories from that place so we can start afresh in the new world.' He glanced at me. 'I know it sounds completely impossible but I can assure you it's not; I'm certain this is what's happened to me. My only hope of remembering anything is to have a reminder of that memory and to note it down before I forget it again.'

I nodded slowly, not believing for one minute his theory was credible. 'Do go on.'

'On leaving the hospital I found myself all alone, not knowing what to do or where to go; for many days I wandered like a vagabond from street to street, sleeping on park benches and searching for scraps of food, with no clue of what to do for the best.' He paused for a moment as a couple strolled passed, arm in arm. 'I had almost forsaken all hope when I caught a glimpse of something out the corner of my eye; there in a shop window was your mother staring out at me.'

A dull ached moved across my heart as I listened to what he was saying. My head was telling me this man was unstable but my heart was telling me otherwise. Dare I believe my mother had come home?

'You actually saw my mother in the shop?'

'Yes, the resemblance was so uncanny that I found myself entering the shop and enquiring about it.'

I looked puzzled. 'It?'

'Yes. The portrait. Seeing the picture jogged my memory and thoughts of your mother came back to me, along with the realisation I was trying to reach home. When I went inside the art gallery the proprietor was extremely helpful and told me all about you and your forthcoming nuptials; that is how I arrived at the chapel.'

My heart sank in disappointment. 'So how do you know my mother?'

'Your mother, Freya was my constant companion, when we were trapped in the other land, and together we went about finding a gateway that would lead us here to Abercrombie. I can't remember how we found it, but eventually we had success. Of course, we weren't entirely sure where we would end up but she was pinning her hopes on coming here to see you.'

I stared at him for a while trying to decide if he really was mad.

'I think you are mistaken.' I said, shifting a few inches away from him on the bench. 'My mother lives overseas, with her new family.' My voice sounded vague. 'You're clearly confused.'

He shook his head violently and began to look flustered. 'No, you have been misinformed. Your mother's only aim in life has been to reach you, so you can be reunited.' He looked deep into my eyes. 'Your mother loves you more than life itself.'

A brief wave of happiness swept over me, but then common sense took over. How could I believe anything this man was telling me when he claimed to have come from another world?

My face became sullen. 'No, no you have it all wrong.' I exclaimed, glaring at him with a pained expression on my face. 'Anyway, if what you say is true then where is my mother now? Is she still trapped in the other place?' I asked, deciding to go along with his charade.

'I'm not sure.' His expression became grave. 'Perhaps the gateway became unstable and your mother was unable to travel, or she was thrown off course during transportation.' He bowed his head. 'I feel so guilty Effie. I know how much your mother wished to see you. And yet it seems only I have managed to reach you.'

'Perhaps my mother simply had a change of heart and decided to remain in the other world, and delaying her journey was just an excuse.'

He stared at me in disbelief. 'Nothing in this world or any other world would have caused your mother to change her mind. I...I can't remember the reason for the delay, but it must have been a good one, and certainly wasn't an excuse not to go. Of course, I was adamant on remaining with your mother until we could travel together but she insisted that I should go on ahead.' He glanced at me. 'Your mother can be very persuasive when she wants to be.'

'Can she?' I uttered dryly. 'I wouldn't know. Her personality traits are totally unknown to me.'

There was an uncomfortable silence between us for a moment and we both stared out onto the river.

'Do you think she's safe?' I asked in a low voice.

'I sincerely hope so. She would do anything to see you, and of course to find the book.'

'The book?'

'Your mother spoke of a book that contains a complete record of ancient doors, magic gateways to other lands and beyond.' He looked grave. 'This book is my only hope of getting home.'

'Do you have any idea where this book is located?'

He looked at me seriously. 'Yes, at Rawlings. For some time now I've attempted to gain access to the house but have been prevented by Isaiah. Night after night I've carefully watched the house, waiting for an opportunity to enter.' He peered at me sheepishly. 'I apologise if I scared you, it was not my intention.'

I thought of him hiding in the shadows, like a thief in the night.

'I'm relieved to finally meet the mysterious stranger whose been spying on me all this time.' I sighed. 'And I'm sorry about Isaiah, he's very protective over Aunt and I. He doesn't really mean you any harm.'

'I see Isaiah has got to you as well as your Aunt.' He sniggered.

'What, what do you mean?'

He turned over the pages of his pad. 'Making notes keeps things fresh in my mind.' Nervously he cleared his throat. 'As soon as I spotted Isaiah at the chapel it all came flooding back. Not only did I remember Freya saying how evil and manipulative he can be, but I also recall his face from long ago, when I was a child.' He leaned towards me. 'When Isaiah hurried me out of the chapel on the day of your wedding, he told me how he was going to kill me if I ever came near you again.' He stared at me intently. 'And that's when I remembered he was a murderer.'

I looked at him in astonishment. 'Isaiah may be many things but he is not a murderer.'

'Do you not see -do you not realise how he's tampered with your mind. That's what he does with his homemade concoctions. He lulls people into a false sense of security and makes you forget.'

I laughed rather mockingly at him. 'I can assure you that's not the case.' I cast my mind back to the night of the wedding when Isaiah had given my Aunt and I a homemade remedy to calm our nerves. 'Surely he hasn't got the power to alter our way of thinking or to make us forget.'

He studied my face closely. 'I'm not sure to what extent he can dull your memory but I'm sure he is capable. Tell me Effie, what can you actually recall? What parts of your memory are missing?

I looked down at the ground, not wishing to acknowledge what he was saying.

'Just bits and pieces. I grant you my memory isn't brilliant but that doesn't necessarily mean Isaiah is responsible, it's a ludicrous notion.'

'Then what other explanation would there be?' He began to chuckle. 'It's not as if you've been...' He glared at me in astonishment.

I laughed nervously. 'It's not as if I've been where?'

He continued to stare at me then turned away. 'Oh, it's nothing of any consequence.'

We sat in silence for a while, deep in thought.

I looked at him pensively. 'So, are there any other pieces of information you can recall?'

He shrugged his shoulders. 'Only tiny little things.' He laughed ironically. 'It seems my journey here to Abercrombie has all but destroyed my mind.' Pain was etched across his face. 'It's such a horrible feeling, not knowing your past.' With a deep sigh he turned a little on the bench and faced me head on. 'I cannot even recall where I entered this land, it is a total mystery.' He closed the notepad and put it away in his pocket. 'Please tell me you can help me Effie, you are my only hope of finding my way home.'

I stared into his pitiful face and forced a smile. 'I'm not sure I can.' Although I was still trying to decide if he came from The Manor, it was hard not to be sympathetic towards his plight. And the things he'd told me this afternoon were impossible to ignore. I still thought him rather peculiar but there was something about him that intrigued me, and sparked my curiosity. 'Oh, very well, I shall be of assistance as best I can. I looked him up and down. 'Please don't think me rude but I really think you need to.... to freshen up somewhat.' I flushed with embarrassment. 'Living out on the streets cannot be easy. Come back to Rawlings with me and...well you can get cleaned up.' I gulped. 'Stay for dinner.'

'What about Isaiah?

'Oh, you don't need to worry about him, he always goes over to Miss Davenport's house on a Tuesday night to dine. He won't be back until late.'

He looked at me dubiously. 'Are you sure?'

'Yes, Isaiah is a creature of habit. Come round to Rawlings at five and I promise you he'll be gone for the night.' I watched as he considered my offer. 'We're having roast beef.'

With a sigh he rose from the bench and made his way to the edge of the riverbank.

'Well in that case I'm powerless to refuse.' He turned and glanced at me, trying to muster a smile. 'Five it is then.' He nodded and made his way slowly along the pathway.

As I sat there watching the summer sun glisten on the river, sending intermittent flickers of shimmering brightness across the water, it occurred to me how surreal this all seemed. I'd just had a conversation with the stranger who had put an end to my happy ever after wedding day, the stranger who'd been watching me, night after night like some madman, the stranger who claimed to know my mother, and the stranger that had escaped from another land to search for a book that would lead him home. And still after knowing all of this I'd gone and invited him to Rawlings for dinner, as if he was an old acquaintance. But oddly enough I felt confident in my decision; my conscious told me I was doing the right thing. Perhaps I was the one that belonged at The Manor.

'You didn't tell me your name.' I shouted after him, suddenly realising I had no idea what he was called.

Fleetingly he stopped and turned to face me. 'Noble, it's Noble.'

In a daze I stared after him as he gradually disappeared out of sight; I didn't take my eyes off him until he'd left the park and was entering Cedar Street. For an instant a dark cloud passed over the sun, causing me to feel a little sad. I shivered.

# Chapter 3

When I arrived back at Rawlings in the late afternoon a frantic Isaiah appeared at the doorway, demanding where I'd been. Evidently, he'd become most distressed on finding I'd left Hudson's café without him and had been searching for me all over Abercrombie, before giving up and returning home. I apologised for leaving him, explaining how I'd merely gone for a stroll whilst he was chatting with the ladies in the café. This was the truth, or part of it at least, I just failed to mention meeting with the stranger from my wedding. After peering at me rather suspiciously he stormed off into the garden and only emerged later when he had to get ready to go out. And then, with a fleeting farewell to my Aunt, he had driven away in his car, precisely at 4:30pm to dine with Miss Davenport. Only then did I creep into the kitchen, rather bashfully, to let my Aunt know we had a guest for dinner. She began complaining bitterly that I should have told her sooner and that there wouldn't be any leftovers for Isaiah's late-night supper. "Agnes Davenport never feeds him enough, Effie, you know that. The poor man won't be able to have a decent meal when he returns home, and will go to bed hungry." She moaned. Trying not to look too amused I suggested he could always have a roast beef sandwich, as there was bound to be a few scraps left. Looking rather perturbed she ordered me out of the kitchen.

Noble arrived on time, looking rather anxious. Before my Aunt had a chance to witness his tramp-like appearance, I hurried him through the door and up the stairs to the bathroom. I'd already put out a fresh towel and hung a set of clean clothes on the back of the door. The clothing had previously belonged to Isaiah, who one day had decided to discard them in paper bags in one of the spare rooms, no doubt expecting my Aunt and I to donate them to the church bazaar. I thought it wise not to mention to my new found friend that the clothes belonged to someone he believed to be a murderer, and just hoped he would be too polite to ask who their previous owner had been. After leaving him to take his bath I went back downstairs and waited, hovering nervously in the hallway, for what seemed like an eternity.

'Effie?'

Jumping slightly, I turned to see him slowly descending the staircase and found myself gasping in surprise at the transformation. How imposing he now appeared, with his thickly waved hair hanging loose about his shoulders, framing his clean-shaven face rather appealingly and emphasising his unusual looking eyes; they had an indefinable quality about them that reminded me of someone from my past, someone unknown. But what struck me most was the change in his countenance: gone was the downcast, tense face of this morning and instead his expression seemed warm and amicable.

Realising I was standing there staring at him open mouthed, I promptly placed my lips together and coyly lowered my eyes, until he'd reached the foot of the stairs, when I tentatively met his gaze and smiled at him.

'Feel better?' I uttered in an unsteady voice.

'Yes, thank you.'

I stood there waiting for him to elaborate, but all he did was look at me rather unnervingly.

'It's this way to the dining room.'

As he followed on behind, I had the distinct feeling he was staring at me, and I hastened my pace. My Aunt had already laid out the food on several serving platters, that usually only saw the light of day on special occasions, and had placed a pair of newly polished candlesticks on the table. I also noticed the fire was lit, something she would never normally do unless it was mid-winter.

'Do take a seat.' Seeing him hesitate I went forward and drew out a chair that was nearest to the fire. 'It's rather chilly for a summer's evening, isn't it?' I laughed nervously glancing in the direction of the window. 'There's dark clouds looming overhead so I imagine we may have a storm later.'

Taking a seat, he continued to watch me but didn't utter a word.

Exchanging pleasantries certainly wasn't a gift I had yet been able to master, in fact I often thought how unnecessary and meaningless such talk was, but in this particular instance I couldn't think of anything remotely interesting to say.

'Are you hungry?'

He nodded in silence.

The warmth from the fire was making the colour rise up in my cheeks and I suddenly felt flustered, wanting to run away and escape the uncomfortable situation. Not being able to think straight I began strolling towards the door to see where my Aunt had got to but then changed my mind and awkwardly took a seat beside him and began drumming my fingers on the table.

The door swung open and my Aunt appeared with a basket of rolls. 'Good evening.' She peered strangely at Noble, before placing the basket down on the table and taking a seat. 'I don't believe we've been introduced.'

I glanced at her apprehensively and when I spoke my voice was rather indistinct.

'Aunt this is Noble.'

He greeted her with a nervous smile and rose to his feet. 'Please to meet you madam.'

'Constance, it's Constance.' As she forced a smile, I sensed a slight aloofness about her. 'Effie told me we had company but failed to tell me anything about you.' She gestured for him to sit down. 'It's very rare we have a guest, especially a young man.'

Looking taken aback Noble glanced from me to my Aunt.

'Effie can tell me all about you whilst we eat.' She moved one of the platters closer to him. 'Please help yourself Noble.'

I watched as he spooned a large portion of beef onto his plate then reach for the roast potatoes.

'Aunt, I don't suppose you recognise Noble, but he was the stranger that interrupted the wedding.' I watched her face cautiously. 'He is a friend of mine who has fallen on hard times.' I briefly glanced at Noble who was heartily tucking into his food. 'He's recently been involved in an accident and has amnesia, and really needs our help.'

39

She was motionless for a moment and just sat there staring at me, her eyes looking rather steely.

'Aunt?

With a small sigh she began to spoon some food onto her plate then passed the platter to me. 'Isaiah did warn me that this man might make an appearance.' She looked steadily at Noble. 'And advised me to show him off the premises forthwith.'

Noble glowered at my Aunt, dropping his cutlery down onto his plate. 'And do you always listen to Isaiah?' He rose abruptly from his seat. 'I know when I'm not welcome.'

I reached out and touched his arm. 'You are welcome Noble, really you are.'

He turned away and looked into the fire

'Aunt please. Noble is alone and needs time to recuperate. Please show him some compassion.' I clenched my hands together tightly. I'm sure Isaiah means well and wants to protect us, but on this occasion he is wrong.'

Looking stunned she swung round and widened her eyes in alarm. 'Wrong? How can he be wrong when this man prevented you from marrying Duncan.' She sprung up and pointed at Noble. 'He completely ruined your special day and your rosy future and now you are…. you are.' She gulped, reluctant to finish her sentence. 'Now you have no one and will probably never marry.'

I felt the heat rise up in my face with anger and embarrassment. 'You cannot hold Noble responsible for what happened that day.' I lowered my face to the floor. 'And I didn't know you were so keen for me to be married off.'

She hunched forward in her seat. 'Effie, I don't mind so much if you never marry, I just want you to be happy.' With a deep sigh she stretched her arms out on the table and clasped her hands together. 'And if you don't feel any resentment to this man then neither shall I.'

I smiled coyly at Noble. 'None whatsoever.'

He stared intently at me for a moment, his eyes warm and smiling, before turning to my Aunt.

He cleared his throat. 'I totally understand Constance that you are angry with me. There is no excuse for what I did.' A cloud came over his eyes. 'I wasn't feeling well that day and stumbled in purely by accident. I just need some help to get back on my feet then I promise you will never have to see me again.' He looked directly at her, smiling charismatically. 'And I wouldn't worry about your niece, she will surely find another man to love when the time is right.' His eyes switched to me. 'After all she is truly beautiful.'

I swiftly shifted my gaze from him and stared across at the fire, hoping to lose myself within the flames.

My Aunt let out a high-pitched laugh. 'Oh, Noble now you have embarrassed Effie. It is very easy to make her feel uncomfortable. Her mother was exactly the same.'

With a nod he smiled but remained silent.

Forgetting my awkwardness, I turned to stare at her.

'You remember that about my mother?' I laughed in surprise. 'I thought you didn't have any memories of her.'

'Your expression must have reminded me, Effie.' A haunted look crossed over her face and she stared vacantly across the room.

'Aunt?'

She let out a drawn-out sigh, and then a light smile crossed over her face.

'Anyway. I suggest we all finish our food then adjourn to the living room and wait for Isaiah to return home.' She threw Noble a reassuring look. 'I'm sure he will understand your predicament when we've explained it to him.'

Placing down my fork I caught sight of Noble's concerned face and quickly spoke before he could comment.

'I'm sure he will Aunt, but I wonder if you wouldn't mind keeping this all a secret from Isaiah, just for a little while.' Nervously I stared down at the table. 'He has a lot on his mind and we don't want to add to his burden.'

As I continued to eat, I studied her face closely, eager for a response.

My Aunt nodded reluctantly. 'Oh, very well then, I shall not breath a word of this to your father.' Narrowing her eyes, she looked sternly at Noble. 'But we must tell him eventually. It's not in my nature to be deceitful.' Slowly she began clearing away the empty plates. 'The question is Noble, will you need a bed for the night, as I take it you haven't got anywhere to stay.'

'Usually I find a park bench. It isn't so bad as long as it doesn't rain.'

She gasped with shock. 'That certainly won't do Noble. I will not have you sleeping outside like some kind of tramp. And besides, you will catch your death.'

For a moment there was quietness in the room.

'Perhaps we could set up the camp bed in the shed at the back of the garden.' I said enthusiastically. 'I know it's rather a state in there what with all the various garden equipment and half-finished canvases and paints, but it's warm and dry, and most importantly Isaiah rarely ventures that far down the garden. It would be more than adequate for a temporary home for Noble.' I briefly glanced at him before turning to face my Aunt. 'What do you think?'

Of course in an ideal world none of this cloak and dagger business would be necessary: Noble would come and go as he pleased without having to worry about Isaiah in the slightest; at the end of the day Rawlings still remained the property of my Aunt and I, and supposedly we should have the overall decision on who could stay in our own home. Nevertheless, something told me that this arrangement of putting Noble up in the shed would suit everyone involved, with the least disruption or fuss, and would prevent a nasty confrontation with Isaiah.

My Aunt peered at me with an odd look in her eyes. 'It seems you have it all worked out Effie. Tell me, is this an idea you've had for a while or have you just thought of it on the spur of the moment?'

Finishing my mouthful of food, I wiped my mouth with the napkin. 'I've just this minute thought of it.' Staring at the table I let out a little laugh. 'Or there's always the attic.' I grinned at Noble. 'But the ghostly apparitions lurking up there may disturb your sleep.'

With a beaming smile he leaned towards me. 'Oh, I don't believe they would bother me. I may however disturb them from their ghostly activity, and therefore I believe the shed would be preferable.' Noble glanced at my Aunt apprehensively. 'If it is alright with you Constance.'

Her face softened a little as she placed some of the plates on the tray. 'Well I think that sounds a super idea.' Let me clear away the dishes then we shall go and organise your bed.'

He rose abruptly. 'Allow me to assist in the clearing up Constance.' He glanced at me. 'And I'm sure Effie and I can arrange the shed by ourselves whilst you go and put your feet up.' He looked at my Aunt with a charming smile. 'And may I just say how much I enjoyed the dinner. You are a superb cook.'

With a smile she nodded at him and went out the room.


When Isaiah returned from Miss Davenport's, Noble was already settled in his new temporary home. What a thrill it gave me to know we were hiding something from Isaiah, especially when the person in question was responsible for me passing out on my wedding day. Noble was so mysteriously odd I still couldn't decide if his story was genuine; did he really know my mother and was it true he'd travelled here to locate a book that would send him home. However outlandish it all sounded I found myself warming to this strange man, and had unconsciously already made up my mind to believe him.

I didn't sleep well that night, too excited by the day's events and too aware of the man sleeping in the garden shed. Despite already warming to Noble I still didn't really know if he was normal and safe, and in the darkness of the night when all our fears are magnified, I became fearful that he may be dangerously unstable. Moving over onto my side I hastily dismissed this notion and turned my attention to a matter rather more paramount, Isaiah. Initially I'd scoffed at Noble's ridiculous accusation of him being a murderer, thinking it preposterous, however the more I thought about it the more I believed it possible. There had been moments when I'd noticed a cold sinister look in his eye that was rather disturbing, but as everyone else seemed to think he was wonderful I believed it was merely my overzealous imagination playing tricks on me. He was so accomplished at making everyone love him, and there was no doubt his popularity amongst the residents of Abercrombie was extremely high. My Aunt in particular was mesmerised by him, it almost seemed he'd cast a spell upon her, which was so steadfast and powerful that it could never be broken.

A sudden rumble of thunder caused me to shudder.

Another great concern for me was my Aunt. Lately she had become increasingly forgetful and struggled to recall any events in the past. I kept visualising her doddering around the grounds of Rawlings, lost and bewildered, unable to recognise her own home, and powerless to prevent it my Aunt would be taken away and left to endure the drab environment of a care home or mental institution where the poor woman would be unable to recognise a soul and would spend her days repetitively moving to fro on a rocking chair. I would try and ignore these visions and tell myself that my Aunt had simply blanked out any painful memories, and her forgetfulness was simply down to her increasing years. Rawlings would continue to be her home for many years to come, until the cold hand of death led her away.

Although my Aunt's failing memory could be put down to old age, I could not blame this theory on my own forgetfulness, and however hard I tried to come up with a comforting solution to the sceptical thoughts crowding within my mind, I could no longer ignore their cries and pretend they didn't exist. I had buried my head in the sand for far too long and now the time had come to face the awful truth in its entirety: there was something seriously wrong with me. My new friend Noble seemed sure Isaiah was to blame, but how would he have the power to totally eradicate a large chunk of my memory, and why? Nevertheless, someone or something had stolen my memories, and I had to find a way to bring them back, before it was too late.

# Chapter 4

My initial doubts over Noble had all but gone now, and little by little he became part of our daily lives. I would take great care to ensure Isaiah was far away from Rawlings before Noble emerged from the shed, and so far, my plan had worked; the thought of them bumping into one another filled me with dread. Life was made easier with Isaiah's constant visits to Agnes Davenport's house; he would help her out around the house and do her shopping. Of course, there had to be an ulterior motive for all his good deeds, either that or I'd become so cynical that I couldn't see how he could possibly do anything out the goodness of his heart.

As it turned out Noble was very green fingered, and as soon as Isaiah left Rawlings each morning he would wander inside the house for a cooked breakfast from my Aunt, then head straight back outside, gather the wheelbarrow and various garden equipment and begin to tackle the weeds and nettles that crept rampantly over the garden walls. And there he would remain, relentlessly working away, hardly stopping a moment for lunch. Although I imagined his enthusiasm and determination to be genuine, I also think this daily ritual prevented him from dwelling on other matters, matters he was powerless to do anything about. For apart from a few scribbled notes, Noble had forgotten his past life and was trapped in a world where he didn't belong, without any idea of how to get home. We had half-heartedly searched for the book which Noble seemed to think was the key to him going home, but so far been unsuccessful. By teatime he would pack away, shower and settle back into his cosy little hideaway where he would wait for me to bring along a plate of food for his evening meal, and there we would sit on upturned crates and talk. Usually it would take me a while to feel comfortable in a new person's company and I would either wish to crawl away and hide, or I would ramble on about a totally inane subject just to prevent those awkward silences from occurring. However, even though our conversation was extremely limited, with Noble I felt quite comfortable. Of course, there were still times I had my silly moments where I wasn't thinking what I was saying, but that was just a particular trait of mine that I seemed to be stuck with.

The mystery of my past was never far from my thoughts, and I would often sit there cogitating over why I couldn't remember much and how I could resolve the problem. I could recall most of my earlier life and my school days and I recollected my friendship with Mace, but mostly after that it was rather hazy. Occasionally I pondered over whether or not to broach the subject with Isaiah, but surely, he would deny such an accusation. My mind also lingered on my mother, and how she wished to be reunited with me; some nights I would lie in bed and visualise our meeting, how emotional and overwhelmingly wonderful it would be to look upon her face.

It was during one of those summer evenings that I came up with the idea of visiting the art gallery where my mother's portrait was housed. If anything, I just needed to see it again for myself. And also, I would be intrigued to see if any other of my work was at the gallery, as I was sure several canvases had gone missing from the shed at Rawlings, and was certain Isaiah had taken the landscapes and sold them.

After our short train journey, we'd arrived in the market town where the art gallery was situated and were passing by the bustle of traders and shoppers.

'How much further Noble?' I asked, following alongside him.

'If I remember correctly it's just past the market.' He strode ahead. 'And set back from those cluster of trees up ahead.'

'Slow down a little, there's no rush.' I panted, half running to keep up with him.

He immediately lessened his pace and looked at me.

'Sorry, I'm not used to having company when I walk.' He grinned. 'It's not that I don't wish to walk with you, because I do.'

I caught his eye and smiled. 'Well that's alright then.'

The art gallery was in clear sight now and I immediately scanned the paintings in the window searching for the one of my mother, but I couldn't see the portrait or anything else I'd painted. A deep sense of loss came over me at the thought of my mother adorning someone else's home, and for one silly moment I thought of the picture as a real life being that possessed a soul, how hurt and betrayed it must feel at having been abandoned so cruelly, and how it longed to be returned to its rightful place of Rawlings, where it would truly be home.

Noble looked perplexed as we approached the gallery.

'That's most odd. The painting of your mother was definitely in the window.' He frowned. 'Perhaps it has been sold.'

'Let's go in and ask.'

As we entered the gallery my eyes focused on the back of a figure unwrapping some packages, and it wasn't until he swung round that I realised who it was. A brief sensation of relief swept over me as I suddenly realised I could recall something. The proprietor was Mr Lombard, the same gentleman who'd attempted to purchase my mother's portrait a few years ago at my exhibition.

He nodded at me in recognition. 'How lovely to see you Miss, I mean Mrs Bartholomew.' A laugh escaped his lips. 'I trust married life is suiting you?' He fleetingly glanced at Noble and a look of confusion swept over his face.

I looked into his genial, trustworthy face, which instantly put me at ease.

'I wouldn't know Mr Lombard, I...I called off the wedding.' An uncomfortable silence followed before I briskly changed the subject. 'I'm here to enquire about my paintings.' I muttered in a low voice. 'I was wondering if they've been sold.'

The expression on Mr Lombard's face quickly changed from a look of surprise to an agonised grimace. 'Oh Miss Farraday, I'm very much afraid they have all gone.'

'Oh?' I replied, rather taken aback.

'Yes, it's most odd.' He narrowed his eyes and peered at Noble suspiciously, then turned to look at me. 'Your paintings displayed in the gallery window have been destroyed.' He

47

shook his head in disbelief. 'Some vile individual slashed them all to pieces.'

A dazed feeling came over me. 'All of them?'

His face brightened. 'Apart from the painting of your mother, as luck would have it, I removed the portrait of her just after your gentlemen friend enquired about it.' He glanced at Noble, who threw him a stern look.

'I wouldn't have harmed it in any way or stolen it, if that's what you're implying.' Noble exclaimed indignantly.

Mr Lombard chuckled rather nervously and shook his head at Noble. 'No, no you misunderstand me. I'd previously been considering keeping it for myself. There's been much interest and offers for the painting but it seems I cannot part with it.' He stepped back from Noble, who still looked rather agitated. 'Your fascination in the painting that day, young fellow, was the deciding factor.' He turned his attention to me. 'Something told me that I must hang on to it as it's extremely unique and special; far too valuable to part with.'

I had the sudden urge to embrace him. 'Mr Lombard, I'm so pleased. So, the painting's intact?'

'Yes Miss Farraday. It's displayed above my fireplace in my living room, would you like to see it?'

'Oh yes.' I exclaimed.

'Perhaps your friend should remain here.' He uttered, throwing Noble a doubtful look.

'I shall wait outside.' Mumbled Noble. He eyed Mr Lombard angrily, and then looking rather dejected, headed for the door.

Mr Lombard waited until he was outside then turned to look at me curiously. 'Have you known that young man long Miss Farraday?'

I gave him a weak smile. 'No, he's just a recent acquaintance.'

'Hmmm.' He exclaimed.

For a second, I thought he was going to accuse Noble of destroying the paintings, but then thought better of it.

He paused. 'Please don't think I'm prying my dear but as I recollect at the art exhibition you were most resolute that the portrait of your mother should remain in your possession, so I

48

was rather surprised when your father contacted me saying you'd had a change of heart.'

I stood there for a moment, gaping at him. 'Isaiah...my father was mistaken, he should never have taken the portrait away from Rawlings' I gulped, feeling myself becoming distressed. 'I hadn't given him permission to sell any of my paintings.'

Mr Lombard threw me a peculiar look and raised his eyebrows. 'Oh dear.'

Looking rather embarrassed he led me through the back to a large, pleasant looking room with smart, antique looking furniture and a cast iron fireplace, which had the portrait directly above it, the portrait of my mother. I cast my gaze over the paintwork, taking in her bright, endearing eyes and her dark auburn hair that swept down over her pale blue dress. The strange familiar feeling of homesickness swept over me as I stared at the woman who I should have known so well, but in reality, was a mere stranger. I'd forgotten how lifelike I'd made her, and half expected the figure to climb out the frame and join us in the room. I was suddenly filled with indignation. What an injustice this was that Mr Lombard owned my painting, the painting didn't belong with Mr Lombard it belonged to me, and should be above my fireplace at Rawlings.

I took a deep breath.

'Mr Lombard, I appreciate you taking good care of the painting but I'd really like it back please.' I bit my lip. 'I shall of course reimburse you.'

He stood there contemplating my suggestion for some time before sighing. 'Yes Miss Farraday.' He gazed up at the picture. 'I shall be sorry to see it go but you are right to take it. It's just a shame the portrait of the young man was destroyed. Is it sentimental to your friend?

I gave him a blank look. 'You mean Noble?'

'Is that his name? His eyes grew wide. 'How unusual, I can't say I've heard such a name around these parts.'

I ignored his remark and got back to the conversation of the ruined painting. 'This other painting, was it completely destroyed. I would very much like to see it.'

'Sadly, that won't be possible. It was slashed to pieces so badly I had no choice but to get rid of it.' He looked sadly down at the floor. 'Such a striking, imposing portrait of a young man I've ever come across. Your friend, Noble seemed most perturbed when he saw it that day. Was it his brother I wonder? He stared into my face waiting for me to reply. 'They looked so alike I was sure they were related.'

I had no idea why Noble hadn't mentioned this before, but it seemed he was hiding it from me, or perhaps it was too painful to discuss.

'Well...' I hesitated, placing my hand up to my forehead in an attempt to lessen the pain that was throbbing through my temple. 'I really can't say Mr Lombard.' I slowly made my way to the door. 'I know nothing about Noble, or his family.'

'And Gideon?'

I froze at the doorway. When I spoke, my voice was but a murmur. What, what did you say?'

'Gideon, that was the name inscribed on the destroyed painting. I assumed you knew him as it was you who painted him in such brilliant brushstrokes.'

My body began to shake. 'Are you sure I was the artist?'

He stared at me rather strangely before letting out a little laugh. 'Yes, most certainly. You have a certain unique style to your paintings that makes your work very easy to recognise.' He chuckled 'And you signed your name in the bottom right-hand corner of the canvas.'

Feeling unsteady on my feet I leant against the doorframe.

'This may sound rather odd but I'm not sure, I....' My head was spinning and without warning I slid down onto the floor.

Mr Lombard came rushing over and knelt down beside me.

'My dear Miss Farraday, are you unwell?

'No, it's just the name Gideon, it...it sounds so familiar, but I'm not sure why.' I gulped. 'I'm so tired of not being able to remember anything.' I began to sob. 'Oh Mr Lombard, what's wrong with me.'

For a minute he just knelt there staring at me, then gently took my hand in his. 'Now listen Miss Farraday. There is nothing wrong with you, nothing that can't be fixed.

Forgetfulness can occur for a number of unexplained reasons. Forgive me my dear but perhaps the wedding is to blame, the stress of it all could well have had an adverse effect on your mind. But I'm sure it's only temporary; in time it shall be restored.'

I looked up at him and smiled. 'Do you really believe that Mr Lombard?'

'Yes, yes I do.' He patted my hand. 'In the meantime, I suggest scribbling down everything in a notepad, that way you can refer to it if you forget.' He stood up and reached for my hand, pulling me up. 'Now, how about a lovely cup of tea?'

I looked at him bashfully, suddenly feeling foolish for my little outburst.

'Thanks Mr Lombard but I really should be leaving. Noble will be wondering where I've got to, and besides I really need to get to the bank before it closes.'

He nodded. 'Very well.' His face looked sympathetic.' I'm sorry I can't return your mother's portrait for free my dear, but a token amount is all that is needed, not the full price.

As I stood there, I couldn't help but think what a lovely man Mr Lombard was, so kind and wise. A fleeting thought entered my head of how much easier life would be if he was my father: he would bring a steadfast, honest, influential and positive approach to life and play a significant role in my upbringing, he would advise me on difficult matters and always be there when I needed him. All the attributes one required in a father, none of which Isaiah possessed.

After a little persuading I'd finally managed to ascertain from Mr Lombard how much he had indeed paid for all my paintings, and was stunned to discover the amount. Isaiah had been wrong to charge such a high price, especially without my knowing. So, it was only right and just that Mr Lombard received the entire amount for my mother's portrait, and even then, it would leave him out of pocket for the paintings that had been destroyed, but I imagined he had insurance, he wasn't the type of man not to. After thanking Mr Lombard for his kindness and advice I left with Noble and we went to find the bank.

I turned to face Noble, who'd been rather quiet since leaving the art gallery. 'Why don't you wait outside, I shouldn't be long.'

'Mr Lombard thinks it was me who ruined your work doesn't he?' He exclaimed rather sombrely.

I brushed my hair away from my face. 'Probably yes, but I can't say I blame him.' Apparently, you acted rather strange when you saw...when you saw the portrait of Gideon.' My heart leapt in my chest as soon as I spoke his name. 'I turned and stared at him. 'Is Gideon your brother?'

Noble glared at me then stumbled backwards. 'Don't say that name, don't say it.' He screamed at me, covering his face with his hands. 'It confuses me.'

Passers-by began to stare at us, and I could feel my face begin to colour.

'It's alright Noble.' I said trying to placate him. 'I won't mention him again.' Carefully I guided him over to the wall by the bank. 'Stay here, I'll be back before you know it.' Going over to the entrance I paused and turned back to Noble, who was hunched forward as if in pain 'You won't run off, will you?'

Pulling back, he looked up and stared at me.

'Not if you don't wish me to.' A faint smile appeared on his face. 'Don't be long.'

I grinned nervously at him then entered the bank.

In an ordinary world, where daughters don't have crooks for fathers one would no doubt be rather taken aback at the shock of discovering their bank account had been completely cleared out by their loved one. I however was not surprised in the least to find that Mr Isaiah Penhaligon had been withdrawing funds on my behalf; it was exactly the kind of underhanded thing he'd do.

After leaving the bank in a trance like state I calmly rang Mr Lombard and informed him I had to delay buying back my mother's painting and would contact him shortly. Noble and I journeyed home in silence; every so often I glanced at his face, and watched him as he stared vacantly out at the green fields and passing cattle. He appeared completely lost in his very own world, a world far away and distant from reality. I suddenly realised how lonely he must feel at finding himself stranded in another world, where everything was unfamiliar and strange, where he didn't have his brother Gideon... Just saying his name in my head sent a surge of pain through my body. At least something good had come out of today; for I now knew that Gideon wasn't just a fictional character created in my dreams- he must be real. At some point in the past I had sat down at my easel and painted this man; and his ruined portrait was evidence of this, evidence that I knew him and loved him.... How curious I thought, that my memory should remember so little of this person and yet for some unknown reason fate kept intervening, sending me faint poignant reminders of his existence. With a deep sigh I closed my eyes and tried to picture his face, but all I saw was a blank canvas.


After popping into Fishers, the local corner shop to purchase a notebook, Noble and I made our way back to Rawlings. Striding along the winding pathway in the cool shade from the overhanging oaks, the gentle afternoon breeze softly rustled and stirred their leaves, causing the ground to come alive with an abundance of dancing shadows; evoking a sensation of restfulness that could cause one to drift off on a cloud of tranquillity.

'You'd better go Noble; I shall sneak you out some food later.' I uttered as we reached the shed. 'Are you feeling better now?' I asked, thinking of his peculiar behaviour outside the bank.

He gazed at me as if he didn't know what I was talking about.

'Yes, yes much better thanks.' Smiling slightly at me he turned and headed towards the shed. 'Don't forget to visit me later this evening, will you?'

I looked at the house. 'I won't.' I said, only half listening. My focus was now on Isaiah, and what I was about to say to him. 'Bye Noble.'

My stomach was churning, making me feel slightly nauseous, and then I realised I'd not eaten since breakfast, but that was a minor concern and one that could be remedied later, for now the only matter relevant was confronting Isaiah. With a look of determination, I strode inside the house then stormed into the dining room where Isaiah and my Aunt were having supper. She was chuckling with laughter at something he'd just remarked about. I thought how it was most likely some ridiculous comment, full of flattery that she had just lapped up.

I glared at the both of them.

'Having an enjoyable dinner are we Isaiah? Robbed any poor defenceless souls recently?'

My Aunt nearly dropped the wine glass she was holding.

'Effie. That's no way to speak to your father. Whatever has possessed you to say that to him?'

'I've just been to the bank to get the money to buy back the painting of my mother, the one Isaiah sold without my permission, but it seems I have no funds left Aunt: the entire contents have been removed by Isaiah. The bank has a statement, that apparently I signed, giving my consent to allow him to withdraw money on my behalf.' I folded my arms in defiance and screamed at him in fury. 'Do you deny stealing money from me, like a common robber?'

Isaiah started to laugh.

'Oh Effelia, you really have no idea, do you? I didn't steal that money, I borrowed it.'

Looking sceptical, my Aunt swung round and gawped at him.

'But Isaiah, that's really deceitful without informing Effie. I'm sure she would have lent you the money if you'd asked her.'

'Thank you, Aunt, for agreeing with me.' I said jubilantly. 'However, I would not have willingly given the money to Isaiah, he doesn't deserve it.'

I half expected my Aunt to scold me but to my surprise she remained silent.

Isaiah grimaced and walked towards the window. 'How much do you love living at Rawlings Constance?'

She laughed. 'Isaiah really, you know I couldn't live anywhere else.' She scoffed. 'This is my home -it always will be.'

He swung round and faced us. 'That is why I had to take the money: I had to plough it back into Rawlings. Unless you've both been walking around with your eyes closed you cannot have failed to notice that the house is gradually crumbling to the ground. That money went on re-pointing the brickwork at the rear of the house, and on mending the leaking roof in the study. There's still an endless stream of repairs that are urgently required.' He looked pleadingly at her. 'I was desperate Constance, desperate to help you and spare you the added burden of yet more worry; that is why I didn't tell you. You're a strong woman but you've been through so much recently, what with Effelia gallivanting off overseas for so long and then the upset of the wedding.' He took her hands in his and looked deep into her eyes. 'You know I would give you every penny I owned if I could, but I have very little.' He looked at me, his expression changing to a scowl. 'Effelia probably would have used her money on the house anyway, wouldn't you?'

'Yes, but it was my choice, not yours.'

'He raised his voice. 'You lost your choice when you decided not to marry Duncan. Have you any idea how rich he is?'

'Well yes but....' I glowered at him. Suddenly it all made sense, the reason Isaiah had been so eager for me to marry Duncan. 'So that's why. You wanted his money.'

'A little money for Rawlings, that is all.' He retorted.

My Aunt slammed her hand down onto the table, then stumbled over to the armchair, and collapsed into it.

'Aunt, Aunt are you unwell?' I uttered desperately, running over and kneeling down beside her.

'Both of you squabbling like children will not help.' She bent forward and covered her face with her hands. 'Nor will mending the brickwork, or a leaky roof.'

We both looked at her in a stunned silence.

'The horrible truth is too much to bear, but bear it I must. I cannot carry this burden any longer.' She muttered, in a sobbing voice. 'Rawlings is lost, I can no longer retrieve it.'

'What do you mean Aunt?'

She looked up into my face with tears in her eyes. 'It's not just the repairs it's the unpaid bills too: for a while now they've been piling up, and now we only have one option. We will have to sell Rawlings.'

Isaiah and I looked at one another in horror. It suddenly occurred to me that we actually had one thing in common – Rawlings. For once he was silent, and I watched him as he slunk down in one of the armchairs.

'Aunt no, surely it hasn't come to that.' I uttered in dismay. But she too didn't speak, deciding instead to stare forlornly out the window. An acute feeling of sorrow swept over me as I pictured us moving: we would have to sell most of the furniture to accommodate our new, smaller house, which would have a neat, postage stamp size garden, hardly large enough to fit in a small flowerbed for my Aunt to tend to; we would endeavour to put on a brave face but inside we'd be falling apart, until eventually it would completely break us.

Isaiah rose and clapped his hands together. 'It's just as well I have a plan, a failsafe that will keep Rawlings afloat for many years to come.'

I threw him a curious glance. 'Whatever are you talking about Isaiah, what plan?'

'Ah ha that would be telling.' He exclaimed jubilantly. 'But rest assured everything will be organised soon.' He went and rested his hand on my Aunt's shoulder. 'Do not despair Constance. Rawlings is your home and will continue to be so until the day you die.'

A sudden surge of fear came upon me, not so much by what Isaiah had just said but the sinisterly worrying way he had said it; it brought to mind Noble's stark warning that Isaiah was a murderer. Perhaps he had been right all along, which meant my Aunt really was in mortal danger.

She seemed oblivious to this and gave Isaiah a pensive smile. 'What would we do without you Isaiah. Thank you.'

'Oh, it's really nothing Constance.' He clapped his hands together. 'Now, how about a lovely cup of tea.' Throwing my Aunt a simpering smile he slowly limped out the door, humming happily away to himself.

# Chapter 5

Sleep didn't come easy that night, and for some time I found myself restless, mulling over the events of the day. Just like Noble and as Mr Lombard had suggested I began jotting down certain things in my new notebook; it was somewhat reassuring to scribble everything down in writing, and knowing I had my notes to refer to if the occasion arose made me feel rather much better. I'd written the name Gideon in large print on the very first page, and underneath was every detail I knew about him so far; he had become a puzzle I was determined to solve.

Unable to get comfortable I felt myself turning the pillow over and pummelling it with my fist in an attempt to make it softer, and it was only then I noticed a small lump within the pillow. Curious to know what it was, I removed the pillowcase and began making a small slit in the pillow with a pair of scissors from my bedside table. As I delved in with my hand, I pulled out a tiny white cotton bundle, tied together with yarn, and with trembling hands I opened the package. Almost immediately I was struck by the strong unpleasant potency, the exact sweet aromatic scent of rich camomile that was forever present within my room, the smell I had become so accustomed to, only now it was so overpowering that I began to feel sick and light headed. Rather baffled, I stared down at the bouquet of dried herbs and flowers lying in the opened bundle, trying to work out what was going on. And as I continued to look a strange rush of realisation came about me- this hadn't been placed here to provide the room with a pleasant fragrance, no, it had to be one of Isaiah's memory loss concoctions. How I hadn't discovered it before was beyond me. Taking the bouquet, I swiftly wrapped it back up in the cloth and tiptoed downstairs, where I disposed of it in the kitchen bin.

After returning to my room I flung the window open allowing the fresh, night air to flood my room, clearing my senses. I pondered how long my memory had been put at risk by the effect of the innocent looking bunch of herbs, and what lasting harm it may have done. I suppose only time would tell, and that is something I had in abundance. How it bothered and unsettled me that Isaiah would do such a thing to the both of us, for even though Noble had warned me of such a thing I still felt surprised. Now it was becoming increasingly clear that my Aunt too had been exposed to some type of memory loss potion, which I imagine Isaiah had been administering to her regularly over the years. I would no longer blame age or ill health on her condition; the culprit was Isaiah, her so-called friend.

In my dream there was a cinema, an old traditional looking room with thick velvet seats and the slight odour of damp. I was sitting in the darkness with popcorn and the place was completely full. As the whirl from the projector started up and the dust particles floated overhead, I rested back in my seat, ready to enjoy the film. Almost immediately it began and I looked upon a windswept desert, waiting for something to occur, but to my dismay everything remained the same. Curious to know what was happening I glanced around at the people on the seat beside me and saw how they were gazing at the screen, laughing and busily cramming sweets into their mouths; in fact, everyone seemed to be enjoying the film, everyone except me. I bent forward and narrowed my eyes, thinking that perhaps I was missing something, but no, there was nothing, nothing but sand. For a moment or two I sat there hunched forward in my seat, eyes glued to the screen, determined to spot something, and it seemed my patience was soon rewarded as just then a mound appeared in the sand, moving along at a rapid speed until it came to a sudden halt directly in front of the screen, where it quivered for a moment. Unable to tear my eyes away I watched in fascination as a spindly leg appeared from one side of the mound; at first, I believed it to be a giant spider, however as it emerged further from the mound of sand, I noticed the thing had a wooden head and body. Terror quickly swept through me as my dummy friend Gilbert gradually shuffled magically through the screen and into the cinema. It was at this moment I became aware of how silent everyone had become, and with a quick glimpse around I saw the seats were empty, I was completely alone.

My popcorn tumbled to the floor as I rose from the seat.

'Greetings Miss Farraday. What a joy to see you once more.' He snarled, moving towards my seat. 'Have you missed me?'

My voice was dry as I spoke. 'No, not in the least.' I exclaimed in a shaky voice, edging my way along the row.

My legs felt unexpectedly heavy and every movement was painfully strenuous, but somehow, I managed to reach the end of the row and began to head slowly towards the exit, my breath laboured with exertion and fright. However, I hadn't reached far before Gilbert blocked my way, grinning abnormally at me with his toothy grin.

'Going so soon.' He shrieked in a hoarse voice.

I recoiled, stumbling blindly backwards. 'Keep away from me Gilbert.' Instinctively I made my way to the back of the cinema. 'You're not real, you're just an old discarded dummy left to rot in the attic.'

His bulbous eyes glared at me in fury as he began to shriek out a poem.


'Don't be cruel you little fool.
Stop wasting time and listen to this rhythm.
You should seek me out not hide me away.
There's a clue in my head that needs to be read.
So quickly hop to it and get out of bed.
Now take my hand and I'll lead you to the sand.'


Before I could stop him, the dummy had grabbed my hand and I found myself almost flying across the cinema at a rapid speed. A scream escaped my lips as I passed through the screen and was transported to the desert in the film. In desperation I yelled out at the audience who had reappeared in the cinema, begging for their help, but they just sat there laughing along with Gilbert, who had pride of place in the middle aisle and was greedily stuffing popcorn into his mouth with one hand and waving at me with the other. An invisible force was pulling me down now, into the sand, dragging me into the dark depths of the desert grave.

With a start I shot up in bed, trying to compose myself.

For so long now I'd been free from such nightmares so it seemed rather odd that Gilbert should suddenly materialise once more. However horrifyingly awful my dummy friend was I couldn't deny that he was somehow linked to both myself and my mother, and quite possibly my grandmother, who had passed away before I was born. This sinister wooden toy had been lurking at Rawlings for many a year, ready to pounce on you in your dreams when you least expected it. At first, I thought it a mere coincidence, an unlucky fluke, but it was becoming increasingly evident that there was more to it- Gilbert had been trying to tell us something.


That morning Isaiah left the house early on a so-called business trip, where it was, I do not know; he'd always so secretive over such matters. One day I'll follow him and see what he'd got up to, but for the moment I had more pressing issues to attend to. Knowing my Aunt was busy downstairs meant now was the opportune moment to search her bedroom; creeping inside I firstly checked her pillow, hoping to find a bundle stitched up inside, but rather disappointingly there was nothing. Feeling perplexed I felt the cushions on her rocking chair, wondering if Isaiah had hidden something inside one of them instead, but yet again I didn't have any luck. With a long drawn out sigh I randomly rummaged through her dresser and wardrobe, and behind the pictures on the wall. However, it all seemed rather futile.

I heard a call from downstairs. 'Effie, are you going to come down and have some breakfast, or are you going to languish in bed all day?' She chuckled, 'Noble is waiting patiently in the kitchen.'

Mumbling under my breath I left my Aunt's room and made my way to the bathroom.

'Yes, I shall be down in a short while.

'Well do hurry along dear.'

'Yes Aunt.' I yelled.

I dressed and made my way downstairs.

As I entered the kitchen Noble gazed at me rather appraisingly and drew out a chair for me to sit down.

'Hello there stranger.' He said, smiling. 'Constance and I thought you'd got lost.'

'Sorry, I was rather pre-occupied.' I stared down at the table for a second then coyly looked at Noble. 'I thought perhaps we could spend the morning in the attic.'

My Aunt placed a cup of tea in front of me. 'Good gracious Effie, why on earth would you want to go up there for? It's by far the worst room in the house.' She turned to Noble and giggled. 'When Effie was a child the attic would fill her with dread, she got it into her head that ghostly apparitions really lived up there and would appear right before her very eyes.'

I gritted my teeth. 'Yes, thank you Aunt for telling Noble all my secrets.'

A broad smile appeared on Noble's face as he gazed at me, his eyes gleaming.

'Don't worry Effie, I think it's rather sweet.' His face became serious. 'Why do we need to go into the attic?'

'There's something in there I need to search for.' I took a sip of my tea. 'Well actually, two things.' I glanced at my Aunt. 'There's an old toy which I believe is hidden away up there, do you remember that old dummy Aunt?'

She stared at me for a moment without saying a word.

'Oh...oh yes. Isn't he named Gilbert? Such a strange looking thing as I recall.' Her face clouded over and a faraway look appeared in her eyes. 'I believe your mother used to be plagued with dreadful nightmares about him.'

Looking pleased that she remembered too I nodded my head eagerly. 'That's right Aunt.

She appeared bewildered. 'Whatever's possessed you to look for the toy?'

I shrugged my shoulders. 'I'm not too sure really, I'm just curious to see the dummy again.' I took a sideways glance at

Noble. 'And there's a book that needs to be found, a very important book, which I believe might be up there somewhere.'

Noble threw me a knowing look. 'Right, very well Effie. Make sure you eat some breakfast then we can go hunting.' He rose from his chair and took his empty plate to the sink. 'Allow me to do the washing up Constance, it's the least I can do after that delicious breakfast you cooked for me.'

'Well okay Noble, thank you. What an appreciative young man you are.' She chuckled. 'And so handsome, don't you think so Effie?'

I caught Noble's eye and smiled. 'Yes, a little perhaps.'


The attic always strikes me as a mysterious place, full of lost, unwanted items of yesteryear. As a child I was fearful of entering the room, as I believed the room was at the very centre of ghostly activity. I was especially afraid of the mannequin that stood in the far corner, dressed in the attire of an Edwardian lady: every time I ventured near, I would half expect the statue to come to life and grab me. And to make matters worse it stood opposite an ancient full-length mirror, and when I peeked into it, I would instantly see the reflection of the mannequin in all its finery; no matter how frequent this occurred it still caused me to jump in terror, making me believe a ghostly figure was lurking behind me.

'You were right you know, about Isaiah.'

He looked perturbed. 'What about him?'

'I found a bundle of dried herbs and flowers concealed within my pillow -I believe he hid it there.'

He pursed his lips. 'I see.'

'Well. Do you think such a thing could work?'

I watched as he stood there scratching his head. 'It seems unlikely.' Picking up a box of books he began searching through them. 'It could contribute to your forgotten past but it isn't strong enough to completely obliterate it.'

'Oh.' I exclaimed, feeling rather disappointed. 'I believed I was onto something.'

Stopping what he was doing he strolled over towards me.

'If the mixture was potent enough it could very well cloud your concept of the past, making it appear indistinct and distant.' He moved a little closer. 'And that combined with the remedy your father gave to you directly after the wedding could be enough to have the desired effect.' His hand reached up and moved my hair back from my shoulders. 'I'm afraid it's all guesswork and the only way to know for certain is to wait and see if your memories return. In the meantime, I would be on my guard, and regularly check your pillow.' He gave me a broad grin. 'So yes, I believe your discovery was fruitful.'

I moved a few steps back.

'I always wanted to be a detective, perhaps I wouldn't make a bad one after all.'

A puzzled expression crossed over this face. 'I don't know what a detective is but I've no doubt you'd make a good one.' Looking a little sad his eyes travelled across the attic. 'So, where did you put the toy?' He asked, stepping over some discarded items of clothing. 'You do realise we could be up here for ages, searching.'

I looked at him pensively. 'I know, sorry.' I said, apologetically. If you'd rather not stay too long, that's fine. I don't mind looking by myself.

He stared over at me with a smile on his face. 'No, I'm more than happy to stay here all day with you.'

For a moment we both looked at one another until my face began to turn crimson and I swiftly turned away, focusing on a random box to rummage through.

He laughed nervously. 'I apologise; I didn't mean to embarrass you. What I was trying to say is that I'd gladly spend all week up here if it meant finding that book.'

Still unable to look him in the eye I carried on searching through the boxes.

'Yes of course the famous book. I'd almost forgotten we were looking for that too.' I exclaimed quietly. 'We'd better get searching then.' I said with a girlish laugh that was rather out of character for me. 'Before Isaiah returns home.'

We spent the best part of the morning rifling through the masses of boxes and trunks until finally we struck gold. Tucked away in an ornate trunk, carved with eagles was the scary looking dummy Gilbert. He looked exactly like he always did with his protruding eyes and threadbare jumper.

I gave a gasp as I pulled him out the trunk.

'Here's Gilbert.'

Noble reached out and took him from me. 'How strange. I've seen this dummy before. Have you ever painted him Effie?'

'Never, to my knowledge.' I said looking at Gilbert's spidery like hair. 'You know, now I come to think of it, I knew the dummy was here all along.' I exclaimed.

Noble looked sullen. 'If that was an attempt to humour me, I really can't find the funny side.' He uttered rather gruffly. 'I haven't got time to waste on such things.'

I gaped at him, surprised at his unexpected change of mood. 'No really, it wasn't until I came across Gilbert that I remembered where I'd put him.' I grimaced. 'I know that sounds rather strange.'

Noble nodded silently, looking perplexed.

Without warning Mace suddenly came to mind and I thought how this would be the precise moment he'd throw an extremely sarcastic comment at me. All of a sudden something didn't ring true about him having a wife and a child on the way. And as a chill ran through me, I realised the picture of Mace playing happy families never existed, Isaiah had planted it in my mind. Mace was lost somewhere, somewhere not of this world, because my dear father had callously thrown him into the portal, the exact same portal I myself had travelled through.

'Effie, Effie can you hear me?' Noble was shouting

A sharp pain shot through my head. 'Pardon? I replied in a daze. Taking a gulp, I turned my attention to Noble, who still seemed rather confused.

'You appear to be in shock.' He gently took my arm. 'Come, let us leave this awful place and go back downstairs. I have a feeling we won't find the book in the attic.'

'No, neither do I.' I murmured, still pondering over Mace.

Noble cleared his throat.

I looked at him in alarm. 'Sorry.' There was little point explaining Mace to Noble, not yet anyway. I recovered my composure and grinned at him. 'I have a habit of drifting off into a world of my own. I'm afraid it's something you'll have to become used to.'

To my utter dismay Noble was gazing at me with the same intense look of earlier.

'I don't mind, it's rather endearing.' He said, laughing. I do believe your mother would do the exact same thing.' Moving a step nearer he brushed a curl away from my face. 'You two look so much alike, the same vibrant hair and large, emerald eyes.' 'It's uncanny.'

His penetrating stare caused me to lower my eyes and change the subject.

'What about the book, if it's not in the attic then where do you suppose it is?

Moving away from him I casually picked up some old paperwork that was laying on one of the boxes and pretended to read it.

He shrugged his shoulders. 'Rawlings is a large house it could be anywhere.

The muffled voice of my Aunt came into earshot.

'I think that was my Aunt saying lunch is ready.' I forced a smile. 'We should go down.' I placed the paperwork back on the box. 'She hates it if I'm late for lunch.'

'Yes, I've noticed how Constance loves punctuality.' He continued to gaze at me for a while longer as if he was reluctant to leave. 'Even though we didn't find the book I have enjoyed our morning in the attic Effie.' With a charming smile he turned and strolled over to the door with Gilbert firmly in his grasp.

'Where shall I put this little fellow?'

I stepped over the boxes and made my way to the entrance.

'Here, I'll go and put him in my bedroom for now.' Begrudgingly I took Gilbert from him and without looking at the dummy, I placed him under my arm. 'He could very well hold the key to finding the book.'

'Yes, then I could return home.' He hesitated. 'You should come with me you know. I don't remember much about it but I'm sure you would like it there.' His look was steadfast. 'Of course, it's entirely possible you've already been there and just forgotten about it, that would explain the huge gap in your memory and...and.' He swallowed hard. 'Well you know.'

'My association with your brother Gideon?'

With a faraway look in his eyes he turned from me. 'We should go back downstairs before Constance calls again.'

I watched him as he left the attic and paced along the hall. Quite unexpectedly I had a sudden vision of a wondrous place tucked away from the world in a timeless enchantment, and an unanticipated surge of emotion enveloped me.


On a whim I sneaked into Isaiah's bedroom and began to search through his belongings. Ever since discovering the bundle of herbs stuffed inside my pillow, I'd been curiously wondering what secrets lurked in his room, and if he possessed any items in there that would someway assist me in returning my Aunt to her former glory. After thoroughly checking through various pieces of furniture, I came across a large box in the very back of his wardrobe, filled with a large variety of sachets, bottles and dried herbs, all carefully labelled. I saw on the very top there were camomile, hop blossom and meadowsweet, and a bunch of sachets simply marked as sleeping draught. As I pulled the box out further, I saw an object wrapped in cloth, stuffed directly behind it. Carefully I removed the cloth, revealing a small handgun; how funny but staring down upon it I knew Isaiah had possessed the weapon all along, sometime, somewhere I had seen him with it, and he had almost killed someone.

Hearing the familiar sound of Isaiah's engine, I swiftly took one of the tiny sachets of sleeping draught, thinking it may come in handy, and hurriedly put everything else back where I'd found it.

Sadly, after close examination of Gilbert we weren't able to discover any clues to the whereabouts of the book. For some unknown reason I didn't have the heart to hide him away in the attic again, so instead I placed him upon a shelf in my wardrobe where I didn't have to look at him.

Noble and I took one more look in the attic for the book before searching every single room in Rawlings without success. It had now turned into one of those thankless tasks that were exceedingly mundane and aggravating to carry out, so much so that we found ourselves making up excuses: seldom had I been so eager to leave my home and venture out into Abercrombie, Noble and would stroll along the promenade and go down to the seashore, or spend time looking in the endless second hand bookstores or the various antique shops along by the harbour, and we always made a point of visiting Hudson's café or the ice cream parlour. It was a happy time, and gradually I began to become used to Noble's company. And when we were at home, I would help my Aunt with the house, and Noble would spend hours tending to the flowerbeds and tidying up the borders. There had been several narrow escapes with Isaiah but so far, we'd managed to keep Noble a secret.

Although certain recollections were returning my mind was still impaired in a fog of blurred memories that didn't make any sense; they were scattered to the wind in tiny fragments that desperately required retrieving and piecing back together. There was a large chunk missing from the period of time in between going and returning to the portal, where it seemed I was lost in a strange dream. It did however seem logical to assume that I had indeed travelled to this land where Noble and Gideon had come from. And, after that, I had returned to Abercrombie and convalesced at Isaiah's for a spell where I recall Mace and I being involved in a ruckus with Isaiah, who had then been injured. After returning to the circle of trees by the little waterfalls my dear father had blown up the portal immediately after throwing Mace into its depths. And thanks to Mr Lombard I now knew Gideon was real, and that he was the sibling of Noble. Oh, but how I longed to remember his face! But it was hidden like an oil painting that had been ruined by so many layers of colour that the subject had been obscured, and only by removing the layers would the real picture emerge.

# Chapter 6

As I wandered down a sloping bank I stumbled across a peaceful woodland, where the shadows are deep and the branches cluster tightly together overhead. An undeniable enchantment lingers in the air that's so familiar that I'm certain I have been here before, in another time and place. Venturing further into its heart I came upon bunches of bluebells, and scattered between the wet green moss were sweet smelling violets, their exquisite scent lingering in the moist heavy air, covering the ground in a purple carpet of splendour. As I breathed in the scent of the dank earth, I saw a shadowy shape flitting quickly past me, and without hesitation I swiftly began to sprint after it, curious to know who or what it was.

In a strained voice I cried out. 'Stop, please stop.'

But the shadowy figure kept on running up ahead through the trees.

'Please don't leave.' I cried out in desperation.

Unexpectedly discovering I could run at superhuman speed, I quickly reached the spot where the figure was standing motionless, facing a tree. I could clearly see that it was a man now, but who was it, did I know him? When I spoke, my voice sounded strange and weak. 'Gideon?' I uttered. 'Is that you? When nothing happened my trembling hand reached for his shoulder, gently pulling him round so he was facing me. But as I did so a high-pitched scream escaped my lips, for the face didn't just look blank, it was entirely featureless.

I awoke with a start, flinging myself out of bed. My entire body was trembling uncontrollably, and even though it dawned on me that it had only been a nightmare, my eyes still darted around my room in search of the chilling image I had just witnessed. Eventually, after reassuring myself that nothing was there, I crawled back into bed and tried to clear my mind. As I lay there, I began to think how odd it is that dreams can seem so vivid and real when in slumber but when we awake our brain has a way of purposely snatching them away and they become little more than disjointed fragments that make little sense, and how quickly they are forgotten. Suddenly I became intrigued to know if a person could possess the ability to physically step into their dreams and make them reality. And as I felt myself drifting off to sleep, I came to realise that this had indeed happened to me; I had grown up in a dream, and in my dreams I hadn't been alone.

A sudden crash made me cry out and as my eyes opened a sense of complete disorientation swept over me and a wretched cry of misery escaped my lips.

'What is it now?' I muttered sleepily. 'I just want to go to sleep.'

It was barely light and as I strained my eyes, I noticed the window was open and was banging against the wall outside. Feeling extremely irritable I rose and went over to close it but as I did so a strong gust of wind blew into the room causing the heavy curtains to upset the lamp on the dressing table; it toppled over onto Gilbert sending him hurtling to the floor with a soft thud where he lay in a heap on the rug. With a sigh I picked up the toy dummy and peered into his terrifying eyes.

'What are you trying to tell me Gilbert?' I said, smiling grimly at him. 'Please tell me I retrieved you from the attic for a good reason.'

I was just about to place him back on the dressing table when I noticed something off-white protruding from the side of his head. It appeared to be a tiny piece of paper. Parting his straggly hair, I grasped the paper with my fingertips and carefully pulled at it until it had completely come away from the dummy's head. To my utter amazement I realised it was a crumpled-up note. Hastily I closed the window and flung back the curtains, bringing light to the room. And with shaking hands, I opened the letter and stared intently at it. The inked writing had faded with age and was barely visible on the ancient looking letter.

***Dear Gilbert***

*Sometimes I imagine myself to be living in my very own dream of yesterday. I drift far away from my home, from Rawlings and live in a far-off land, which has such splendour that I never wish to be awoken; for it is everything I have ever hoped or wished for, and I truly believe it to be a precious glimpse of a place I travelled to as a young woman.*

*Alas, even if I had wished to once again return to this land, I fear my old age would hamper me, for my long life is drawing to its inevitable end. Therefore, I've resigned myself to living the remainder of my life at my beloved childhood home of Rawlings.*

*And so, Gilbert my dear old faithful friend, I trust in you and leave this note in your safekeeping. You are the only one left now who can protect the secret that remains hidden away, and therefore I shall leave this rather ingenious riddle within your capable hands! And, if one day some clever soul comes along and solves my riddle then I pray they take great care with what they discover -*

STEP INTO THE PAST AND SEEK OUT THE TRAVELLER, FOR HE HOLDS THE KEY IN HIS POCKET. FIND HIS HEART AND HE WILL BE YOURS FOREVER.

*Forever yours*
*Florentine x*

For a long while I crouched down by the bed, mesmerised by the note. How I wanted to rush outside to the garden shed and show Noble but I was too exhausted. Clambering back into bed I tried to get some rest before morning. The last thing I remember before dozing off was how Gilbert had come to be sitting on my dressing table when I knew for certain I had placed him in the wardrobe.

That morning I had meant to rise early but after the night's disruption I found myself oversleeping. Dragging myself out of bed I hurriedly got dressed and without looking in the mirror,

I grabbed the note from Florentine and rushed a little unsteadily down the stairs and stumbled into the kitchen. My Aunt was at the stove cooking and Noble was sat at the kitchen table looking pensive.

'Good morning to you both.' I mumbled. 'I apologise for my lateness but I had a rather interrupted night's sleep.' Feeling bleary eyed I sat down opposite Noble and placed the crumpled note on the table in front of him. 'It seems Gilbert has helped us after all. I found this note sticking out his head.'

Looking amused Noble ran his eyes over my hair before focusing on my face. 'Did Gilbert attack your hair as well as helping you?' he said with a twinkle in his eye.

My Aunt began to giggle. 'Oh Effie, you look like you've been dragged through a hedge backwards' she put her hand over her mouth to stifle her laughter. 'Sorry dear but really, look at you.'

Feeling myself blush I attempted to smooth down my hair with my hands. 'I shall go and comb it properly later.' I muttered, lowering my eyes to the table. 'The important thing is this note.'

Noble and I reached for the crumpled letter at the same time and his fingers accidentally brushed against mine. Our eyes locked for a moment before he picked up the note and began to carefully study it.

I sat there hunched in my seat, watching him.

He suddenly looked up and caught my eye. 'Find his heart and he will be yours forever.' Rather intently he continued to stare at me, and only turned his gaze away when my Aunt gave him his breakfast. 'Thank you, Constance.' He said smiling at her before returning to the note. 'Have we a time machine hidden away somewhere, that's the only way we can step into the past.'

My Aunt came over and rested her hand on Noble's shoulder. 'I think you'll find that it doesn't literally mean going back into the past. It's a hint to something old, like objects kept in a museum.'

I pulled myself up straight, suddenly feeling animated. 'There's the museum in Abercrombie, maybe we can find a clue there.'

'Well, why don't you two lovebirds go along and find out.'

I raised my eyes at her and frowned, not knowing what to say.

Noble winked at me as he finished his breakfast. 'I'm just going to water the bedding plants then I shall be ready.' He rose from the chair and took his plate over to the sink. 'Thank you, Constance, that was delicious.' I watched as he approached the door, turning to glance at me as he went out. 'See you in a moment Effie.'

When I was certain Noble couldn't hear I began speaking softly to my Aunt, trying to control my temper. 'Aunt, you do understand that Noble and I are just friends, don't you?'

Her face looked solemn. 'Sorry, slip of the tongue dear. Noble said how embarrassed you'd be if I discovered the two of you were courting.' She patted me on the hand. 'That's why I promised him I'd keep quiet.'

'But Aunt, Noble is merely an acquaintance, nothing more.'

'Oh dear, don't be bashful about it. Don't you think it was romantic of Noble, turning up at the chapel that day and demanding to stop the ceremony? I can see how the two of you must love one another.' She started to butter her toast. 'I really think we should tell Isaiah, I'm sure he'd be perfectly understanding about the whole thing.'

I rose from my chair in alarm. 'Please Aunt, no. Whatever you do, don't tell Isaiah.' I tried hard to smile at her. 'You know how distraught he was at the wedding, how angry and upset that I didn't marry Duncan. Well surely it would be unwise to upset him without good reason.' I took a deep breath and looked towards the window. 'If indeed there comes a time when... when Noble and I become more than friends then I promise you I will inform Isaiah.'

She looked amusingly at me. 'If you say so dear.'

Deciding to change the subject I went over to the sink and began washing up. 'So, Aunt, what are you going to do today?'

'Well, firstly I thought I'd make a list of guests to invite to our annual garden party.'

I widened my eyes in surprise. 'Are you sure you want to have one this year Aunt. It's a lot of work.'

'Absolutely. The weather should be pleasant, so everyone can remain in the garden.' She lowered her eyes. 'That way they won't notice the state of the rooms.' Her face brightened as she looked up and smiled. 'And after that I thought it was about time I ventured into the library to do a little dusting.'

'Oh Aunt, are you ready to face it again?' I asked, in a concerned voice.

Ever since the scary experience of seeing the apparition of my mother hovering in the library she'd avoided entering the musty old room, and had only gone in there with me that once, when we had to replace the books back on the shelves after they'd been thoughtlessly thrown on the floor by Isaiah. He'd put it down to his head injury, saying he didn't know what he was doing.

'If you like Aunt, I can dust in the library when I get back from the museum.'

'No, no I need to overcome my fear.' She started to clear the table. 'They only require a quick tidy and dust, many of them are so ancient that I fear they may crumble to nothing, if disturbed unduly. They're as old as time.'

'Hmm.' I replied, only half listening. It was only then that it came to me. 'Aunt, you clever thing.' I exclaimed going over and kissing her on the top of her head.

She threw me an odd look. 'Lord Effie, whatever have I done?'

I burst out laughing. 'Aunt, the comment you made about the books being old.' I took her by the shoulders. 'Don't you see what it means? Step into the past must mean the library, going in there is like going back in time, and...and The Traveller, must be the name of a book.' I excitedly grabbed her hands. 'I'm going there now.' A look of concern crossed over my face. 'Do join me Aunt, I know you can overcome your fear.' Eagerly I ran over to the door. 'Would you tell Noble where I am.'

I heard her squeal with delight as I left the room.

'Yes. Oh, how exciting Effie.'

The atmosphere in the library hadn't changed, the damp musty odour still lingered in the air, and the darkness of the wooden panelling made the room oppressively gloomy. Going over to the curtains I pulled back the heavy material, sending dust particles flying across the room. Even with the light coming in the room it still held a mysterious presence of times gone; I would often stand there breathing in the age of the books, becoming lost within their pages; taken away into the depths of their content.

The sudden sound of a voice behind me caused me jump.

'Constance says you've solved the riddle, Effie.'

I turned to face Noble, and for a second, I was speechless. Standing there in the shadows he looked so imposing with his thick, wavy hair and deep penetrating eyes that I momentarily felt transfixed by his gaze.

'Effie?'

'I...I ah. Yes, well it was my Aunt that gave me the clue. The library is the past and The Traveller is a book.' I said in a shaky voice. 'We...we need to start looking through the books - though I'm sure they're in rather a muddle, ever since Isaiah threw them all on the floor, we've never put them back in alphabetical order.' I laughed nervously. 'I realise now he must have been searching for the very same book, don't you think?'

He reached out and grabbed my arms.

'Slow down Effie, you're gabbling.' He lifted up my chin with his hand so my eyes were in line with his. 'Yes, Isaiah most probably wanted to get his hands on the book and destroy it, to stop his lovely daughter from escaping through another gateway.' Moving his face nearer to mine he looked down at my lips. 'If I were him, I would surely do the same.' He whispered softly, planting a delicate kiss on my mouth.

'Any luck dears?'

Hearing my Aunt's voice, I instantly stumbled away from Noble.

There was an awkward silence.

'Oh, am I interrupting? She exclaimed with a mischievous laugh. 'It's so dark in this room I can't see properly.'

My voice sounded strange as I spoke.

'No Aunt, nothing whatsoever.' Avoiding Noble's eye, I began rifling through the books, trying to compose myself. 'But we've only just started to search.'

My Aunt clapped her hands together with glee. 'Oh, how thrilling this all is. Allow me to help the both of you.' Swiftly and methodically she began searching through the books at the other end of the library. 'It reminds me of when I was a child and your mother and I....' She froze on the spot. 'Ah.'

Rushing over I placed my arm about her

'Aunt? What was it you were saying about you and mother?'

Her expression was vacant as she stared at me.

'Sorry dear, whatever it was I was trying to say it has gone now.' A haunted look came about her. 'It can't have been very relevant.'

'Did you and my mother search for a book when you were children, is that what you're trying to say? I eagerly waited for a response, searching her face for an answer. 'Was is some sort of game?'

I steadied her as she staggered back against the books.

'I don't know Effie, I can't remember.' She gripped my arms tightly, her face etched with worry, making her appear suddenly older. 'Why can't I remember Effie, what is wrong with me, am I going mad?'

'Aunt no of course not.' I pulled her forward so her head was resting on my shoulder. 'Being a little forgetful at times is nothing to be concerned about. It doesn't mean there's anything wrong with you, honestly it doesn't.'

She raised her head from my shoulder, a poignant smile upon her lips.

'Isaiah always tells me how we're meant to remember all the good things in life and forget all the bad. And I'll never forget anything about you Effie, or our lovely home. However, your mother deserted us a long while ago Effie, and I have no wish to waste my energy thinking about her. She's an old memory, a dead memory.'

My eyes widened with shock as I looked into her emotionless face, and an inescapable sorrow crossed over my heart, causing me to step back from her.

'No Aunt, she's not...'

'Oh, come on Effie, let's carry on our search for the book.' She retorted snappily.

I watched as she turned back to the shelves and continued to look at each book. As the blood rushed to my face I walked forward and confronted her.

'How can you say that about your own sister, you don't even know the reasons for her leaving, perhaps she had no choice, or was forced to leave. Please do not pass judgement until you have the full facts.' I stood there and faced her, waiting for a response. 'Aunt?'

She held a book by its cover and began to shake it.

'These books are awfully old and dusty, aren't they? Your father mentioned giving some away to a jumble sale, or one of the second-hand bookshops along the seafront. Maybe you and Noble could select a few and take them along tomorrow.' She began to chuckle. 'I know how much the two of you enjoy your little jaunts into town.'

I glowered at her.

'What? I retorted, disregarding her last sentence. 'Aunt none of these books should be removed.' My voice grew louder. 'Not one of them, and if Isaiah so much as touches them, he shall have me to answer to.'

I felt a tap on my shoulder. 'Calm down Effie, I'm sure Constance will not allow your father to remove any without your permission.'

With a sigh I turned away from my Aunt who was still nonchalantly searching the books. 'Yes, yes very well.' I retorted bluntly. 'We should carry on looking.' Dejectedly I crossed over to where I'd begun looking. 'Before Isaiah returns home.'

I'm not sure how long we spent there, silently pulling out book after book, and just when I began to think we were wasting our time, Aunt let out a triumphant cry.

'It's here. I've found it. The Traveller, by Harold B Jamieson.' She began giggling uncontrollably. 'Fancy me discovering it.'

Noble and I rushed over and gazed at the book in her hands. It was an ordinary looking hardback depicting a bearded man hiking across landscape with a walking stick.

Noble glanced at my Aunt. 'Is there anything in the pocket cover Constance?'

With trembling hands, she opened the book and we all peered curiously at the slight mound underneath the paper pocket on the inside cover.

She hesitated for a minute, glancing at me. 'Shall I see what's underneath?'

I nodded. 'Yes, please Aunt.' I uttered, feeling excited.

Gently she slipped her fingers underneath and pulled out a small package, wrapped in muslin. Without a word she passed the book to Noble and began to unwrap the bundle, revealing a tiny decorative key.

I beamed at Noble. 'We're getting closer,'

'Find his heart and he will be yours forever.' My Aunt said in a slow clear voice. 'Isn't that what the riddle states?' Clasping the key firmly in her hand, she returned to where she'd discovered The Traveller and began pulling out books either side, dropping them on the floor. 'There's something here.' Her hand moved up to the empty space at the back of the bookcase. 'Someone has carved a heart in the wood.' She exclaimed animatedly. 'I could be mistaken but I think the heart is a door with a tiny keyhole in the middle.' Shakily she slotted the key in the hole and turned it until it clicked lightly and she instinctively jumped back as the door popped open, revealing a small cupboard- like safe. With a look of elation, she turned to us with a beaming smile upon her face. 'This is it -this is where the book must be hidden- in the heart.' Confidently she placed her hand in the small recess and pulled out an ancient looking book encompassed in dull leather, the binding of which was falling apart. 'Here, you take it Effie.' She handed the book to me. 'It belongs to you. You should be the one to open it.'

I took the delicate looking book from her and cautiously opened it, carefully flicking through the pages. The entire contents were at least four hundred pages thick, and was completely filled with numbers and passages of illegible handwriting, scrawled very chaotically on every page. The book seemed to be someone's record, a ledger of some sorts that I knew immediately was going to be a nightmare to decipher.

Noble came and stood close beside me, curiously peering at the book. 'Thank you, Constance.' He said smiling at her. 'Effie and I are very appreciative of your help.'

'Oh, it's nothing, really.'

'Yes, we couldn't have found it without you Aunt, so thank you.' I ran my thumb over the rough leather cover. 'The last person to touch this book.' I paused. 'Or perhaps we should call it a ledger, must have been Florentine Heatherington. I wonder why she felt it should be hidden away.' I laughed. 'What harm can a ledger full of scribbled notes and numbers do?'

'That we shall never know.' Said my Aunt, slowly walking towards the door. 'Read it by all means but do take care Effie. Florentine hid the ledger for a reason, maybe she never wished it to be found.' Her face softened and she gave me a little smile, and then turned to glance at Noble. 'Why don't the two of you toddle off somewhere.' Isaiah will be home shortly.'

'You won't mention the ledger to Isaiah, will you Aunt.' I asked, as she was about to leave. 'It's probably best to keep it to ourselves.

'Oh Effie, you and your secrets. I can't imagine what harm it would do; your father would find the ledger most interesting.'

I raised my eyebrows. 'Indeed. But I'd much prefer we keep him in the dark about it. I believe the ledger holds the key to Noble returning home, so we need to study it as much as possible. You know what Isaiah's like when he finds something historic that interests him; he'll be looking at it for months. And it's not as if we can obtain a copy from the bookstore or the town library.'

'Oh Effie, you are a funny one. If it means that much to you, I promise not to tell your father. And if the ledger will help

Noble then all the more reason for the both of you to begin looking through it.'

Noble smiled warmly at her. 'Thank you, Constance, I know how uncomfortable it makes you keeping my presence here a secret from Isaiah, but it won't be for much longer.'

'I do hope so Noble. You're such a nice young man, and I should hate for you to go, but I cannot keep up this ridiculous pretence indefinitely. If you fail to resolve the issues with Isaiah then I fear your only other choice is to leave Rawlings.' She sighed. 'How Effie will miss your company, won't you Effie?'

I looked shyly towards Noble. 'Well yes I....'

My Aunt interrupted abruptly. 'If only the two of you will admit how you feel about each other. I'm sure Isaiah would understand.' She giggled. 'We could be arranging another wedding by the end of the year, and this time it would be a successful wedding.'

I watched as she left the library, happily humming to herself.

Gulping with embarrassment I stared down at the tatty old ledger. 'Don't worry about my Aunt, she has a tendency to ramble on at times, and jump to wild conclusions.'

'That may be the case, but I also think your Aunt is very astute. She can obviously sense that we love one another.' An amused smile appeared on his face. 'And therefore, should get married.'

As I felt the colour begin to flame into my face, I glanced at him and spoke in a slow rather shaky voice. 'Please can we stop this ridiculous conversation and focus on what's important.' I waved the ledger in front of his face. 'We need to begin searching through this.' Avoiding his eye, I went out the door and made my way to the stairs. 'I'm going to get my notebook so we can jot down any useful pieces of information we might come across in the ledger.' I briefly looked over the banisters to see him hovering in the hallway. 'Wait there, I shall be back in a moment.'

As I made my way to the bedroom, I had a sudden urge to hide away in there; the solitude would allow me to concentrate on looking through the ledger without anyone bothering me. I knew this would be unfair to Noble but I just wished he'd disappear for a while and let me be.

A noise outside made me go over to the window. It was Isaiah, and he had returned early. I watched him for a moment as he retrieved something from the boot, and it was only then that I remembered Noble was waiting for me in the hallway. With a gasp I flung the ledger down on my bed and raced downstairs. I thought of the commotion there'd be if the two of them bumped into one another and all the aggravation it would cause. Trying to catch my breath I came to a halt at the foot of the stairs and swiftly looked around for Noble, but he was nowhere to be seen.

Isaiah stepped through the front door, with a parcel in his arms. He turned to stare at me. 'Oh, hello there Effelia.' He seemed shifty and a little taken aback to see me. 'I thought you'd be out in the garden enjoying the sunshine.'

I smiled serenely at him. 'As a matter of fact, I was just about to.' Trying to act relaxed I slowly made my way pass him, glancing briefly at the parcel. 'Bought anything nice?'

He gaped at me rather strangely. 'No, nothing of any consequence.' With a nervous laugh he began climbing the stairs.

Whatever was in the parcel it seemed clear he wasn't going to show me; not that it mattered, I wasn't intrigued in the slightest. My only concern at this precise moment was finding Noble before he did.

I stood there watching him limp up the stairs until he was out of sight. Then with a deep sigh went to check if Noble was in the kitchen with my Aunt.

'Isaiah's home.' I said in a quiet voice to her, as she swept the floor. 'Have you seen Noble anywhere?'

Without looking up she carried on sweeping. 'Don't worry dear, he's safe.' She uttered in a rather stern tone. 'He went out the back door as soon as he heard your father's car.' She stopped for a moment and glanced at me. 'I said you'd join him shortly.'

'Oh, that's a relief.' I reached out and patted her arm. 'Thank you, Aunt for helping me keep Noble a secret.' I smiled endearingly at her. 'I know it's not easy for you.'

'No, no it's not Effie.' Her voice became emotional. 'Truth be told I'm finding the whole situation extremely distressing.'

I stared at her without saying a word, and with a heavy heart I left the room. Poor Aunt, I thought, feeling rather guilty all of a sudden for putting her through all of this, maybe it wasn't a good idea to keep Noble in the grounds of Rawlings; I should have hidden him someplace else, at a friend's house perhaps. If only Mace or Clarice were here. A lump came to my throat as I thought of them both. Rather swiftly I strode down the back of the garden and into the shed, expecting to see Noble sitting on an upturned crate, but the building was empty. I called out his name urgently, but there was no reply. Feeling more annoyed than anxious I stood there with my hands on my hips and frowned. It was then I saw the note pinned underneath a stone on the table.

*Effie*
*Let us leave the ledger for another day.*
*Meet me in town - I shall be waiting for you by the clock*
*tower.*
    *Noble*

Feeling the anger boiling up inside of me I screwed up the note and threw it across the shed. How extremely annoying of him, I thought, to disregard the ledger and expect me to follow him into town as if we had nothing better planned. Well he could jolly well wander around Abercrombie on his own for all I cared. Slamming the shed door, I had intended to go up to my room and study the ledger, but instead I found myself cycling towards the great oaks that lined the pathway leading away from Rawlings.

On reaching the clock tower I saw the figure of Noble leaning against the wall, his large compelling eyes stared at me as I approached, and as I looked into his smiling face my anger melted away, and against my better judgement I returned his smile. We casually strolled along the seafront with our bikes and bought an ice cream, then sat on a bench watching the waves repeatedly roll into shore then withdraw back into the sea; the timeless sound was soothing and would have been tranquil had it not been for the screeching gulls overhead. It was whilst we were there, we happened to bump into one of my old school friends, Cassandra who I'd not seen for a number of years. We had never been particularly close; she was a self-assured and gregarious type of person, so we were very dissimilar, and yet for some reason she liked me. However, as we all stood there together it soon became apparent she was more interested in Noble than catching up with me. I took a step back as she blatantly began chatting away to him as if they were old friends, eyeing him up and down appraisingly. Feeling an unexpected sensation of resentment, I grabbed Noble's hand and pulled him away, coldly informing my school friend we were in rather a rush and must be going.

Later on that evening, after my bath, I finally had the opportunity to examine the ledger in the quietness of my room: it was undeniably old with its worn leather cover and rather delicate looking pages which were browned with age. And as I turned to the very first page, I saw a short inscription stating that Monk St James had compiled the entire notes of the ledger from various sources and manuscripts, and underneath he had signed his name. Eagerly I began studying the pages, half expecting to find mention of a gateway that would take Noble home, and foolishly hoping the name of his land would spark a flame of recognition within my mind, but a I tried desperately to understand what each scribble note said I came to the conclusion that this would be no easy task; finding the solution in this ledger would be very time consuming, and it was entirely possible I would discover absolutely nothing. As I became more despondent, I skipped to the very back page, just to see if the writing was in the same style, which sadly it was. However, rather than random sentences and numbers there were two long paragraphs, neater looking than the other writing but still illegible. On closer scrutiny I managed to decipher the words god and sacrifices, and thought perhaps it was a type of declaration or prayer.

With a yawn I snapped the ledger shut, placing it on my bedside table, and lying back against my pillows I reflected on the day's events. Just before drifting off to sleep my thoughts turned to my school friend Cassandra; how strange it must have looked when I yanked Noble away from her like some jealous, adolescent schoolgirl. Whatever possessed me to behave in such a manner was baffling. Although my Aunt and Noble had made comments about our relationship I knew it was all just harmless banter, Noble and I weren't really a couple; he didn't love me and I didn't love him. He was just a friend who needed my help, and when he returned home, we would never see one another, ever again.

# Chapter 7

As I recall it was the day after finding Florentine
Heatherington's hidden ledger that Agnes Davenport came to
tea. My Aunt, Isaiah and I were sitting with her in the shade of
the yew tree, patiently listening to her stories of long ago. She
was a sweet old lady whose sorrow of losing her sister seemed
to have imbedded itself in the deep wrinkles of her face, setting
it in a perpetual state of grief. For a while she would stare at
you with her melancholy, crystal blue eyes and reminisce
about the past, when she and her sister were young; then her
eyes would glaze over and she would drift off into her own
little world. Try as I might I found myself struggling to keep
awake. Last night's happenings had created a tantalising
conundrum for me to solve, and I lay there in bed trying to
decipher the unreadable scribbles until sunlight spilled
through the gap in the curtains, bringing me the morning.
However, as my eyes flickered with fatigue, Miss Davenport's
conversation suddenly seemed to change course, causing my
tired eyes to widen with shock.

'Of course, I'm still certain Lydia's death was foul play.' She
uttered. 'My sister was most meticulous about her sleeping
draught.'

We all sat and stared at her in silence.

My Aunt put her hand over her mouth and coughed
nervously.

Isaiah clattered his cup loudly down onto the saucer.

'Oh Agnes, we have gone over this many a time. It's been
over two years since her passing, should we not allow your
dear sister to rest in peace?' His voice was slow and precise.
'Lydia had a temporary lapse of concentration and accidentally
took too much of the medicine. It is an easy mistake to make.'

'But Lydia always waited for me to fetch the bottle from her
bedside table, along with all her pills.'

'Perhaps she went and got them before you arrived home Miss Davenport.' I said, smiling sympathetically at her.

She turned and gaped at me her eyes wide with alarm.

'No Effie, no, don't you see?' She muttered in an agitated voice. 'Lydia and I had a set routine, and each of us had tasks that we religiously stuck to each and every day. I would always bring down her medicine in the evening.' Her voice became louder as she stipulated her point. 'Always. You see Lydia had trouble going up and down the stairs so would only use them if it were absolutely necessary. And therefore, I believe that, whilst I was out for the evening, someone else was in the house with Lydia, someone she knew.' Looking distressed she shakily placed her cup and saucer back on the table. 'That is my only explanation for her taking the sleeping draught early. This person fetched the bottle from her bedside and gave her too much.' Her voice began to break up as she spoke. 'They murdered dear Lydia.'

Isaiah became fidgety.

'Oh, Agnes what you're saying is pure conjecture, and dragging all this up would not be prudent. It will not bring Lydia back.'

'Avenging my sister's death will bring closure, allowing us both to rest in peace.' She moved forward in her seat and struggled to rise. 'Therefore, I should like to go home now, and in the morning, I *shall* be contacting Constable Ridley.'

Instinctively I rushed over and helped her up. 'I completely understand Miss Davenport, as distressing as it must be, you need to know the truth.' I glanced at my Aunt, who'd been sitting there quietly. 'Do you not agree Aunt?'

She gulped and looked over at Isaiah. 'Well yes, but the truth isn't always what we wish to hear, and won't necessary make for a happy ending.'

Miss Davenport swayed slightly and leant against my arm.

'Yes, you are right Constance.'

Isaiah smiled. 'I'm glad you think so Agnes.' He swiftly turned to my Aunt and took her hand. 'What a wise lady you are Constance, your great mind and beauty never ceases to amaze me.'

An acute feeling of revulsion crept over me as I watched him kiss her hand.

'Oh Isaiah, she said, suddenly oblivious to Miss Davenport. 'You really are incorrigible.' Laughing she playfully smacked his leg.

'Aunt?' I said tersely, feeling embarrassed for poor Miss Davenport. 'Are you not going to see your friend to the door?'

She looked startled for a minute before smoothing down her dress. 'Yes, yes of course.' Getting up from the chair she slowly came over to Miss Davenport and took her hand. 'So, Agnes dear, have you decided to put all this dreadful business behind you?

Miss Davenport stared glumly at my Aunt. 'The truth is all I have left, and any chance of a happy ending died with my sister.' She gripped her arm. 'You understand don't you Constance, you see why I have to know?'

My Aunt nodded. 'I shall fetch your coat.'

Isaiah came and stood in front of Miss Davenport, blocking her way.

'If you must go to the police Agnes, please ask for Chief Inspector Vale. The both of us go way back and he's extremely competent. In fact, if you wait until tomorrow afternoon, I shall take you along myself.'

Miss Davenport stood there contemplating Isaiah's suggestion. 'That's awfully decent of you Isaiah, but this is something I need to do on my own. And besides, Constable Ridley strikes me as being a little more approachable than that supercilious Chief Inspector Vale.'

Isaiah looked slyly at her. 'So be it.' Continuing to stare, his face slowly broke into a smug smile. 'What will be will be. I shall go and start the car.' Isaiah murmured with a cold detachment. 'You'll be safely home before you know it Agnes.'

A sudden fear crept over me, fear for Miss Davenport. 'Please, allow me to drive you home Miss Davenport.'

Isaiah groaned. 'Oh Effelia, you really are a terrible driver. I'm sure Agnes would like to return home in one piece.' He snapped at me. 'Therefore, I insist on giving her a lift myself.'

I stared at my father, trying to think of a swift response to his loathsome words, and to quickly come up with a way to prevent him from taking Miss Davenport home. However, feeling exasperated at not having the ability to fling back a witty answer or solution immediately, I just frowned at him and said nothing.

'Right you are Isaiah, thank you.' Uttered Miss Davenport. She patted me lightly on the arm. I appreciate the thought Effie, really I do, but Isaiah is used to seeing that everything is in order before he leaves to go home.' She smiled radiantly at him. 'You really do have an extraordinary man as a father Effie.'

Isaiah exploded in laughter. 'You're too kind Agnes. 'I'm only undertaking what's necessary.' He paused, throwing me a fleeting glance. 'I'm sure Effie appreciates my good deeds and will one day even praise me.'

Taking no notice of his remark I helped Miss Davenport to the back entrance of the house, trying to banish the voice in my head, warning me that I would never see this sweet, old lady again.

The remainder of the day was rather uneventful. As soon as Isaiah had left Rawlings to take Miss Davenport home, I collected some leftovers from tea and took them down to the shed, where Noble greeted me with a charming smile. And as he sat there and ate, I told him my concerns for Agnes Davenport's safety. I saw that he was quietly smiling at me, his eyes gleaming, and I began to wonder if he was really listening to what I was saying. After I'd been rambling on for quite some time, he continued to stare at me and exclaimed how well I was looking. Feeling my face turn crimson, I bid him goodnight and ambled back to the house, rather annoyed by his lack of interest in Agnes Davenport. Languidly I made my way to bed, sick with tiredness from lack of sleep the previous night; I curled up in my bed and drifted off to sleep. I'm not sure what time it was when I awoke to hear the familiar sound of Isaiah's car on the gravel outside the house, but it must have been late. And as I lay there, listening to him stomp up the stairs, my mind became saturated with dreadful thoughts of how he'd done away with Miss Davenport. For peace of mind it was clear now I should go and visit her first thing tomorrow morning. I just prayed it wasn't too late.


There was a distinct chill in the air that early summer's morning when I ventured out of the house, and a shiver went through me as I walked swiftly eastwards towards the park. My worry for Agnes Davenport had gnawed away at me relentlessly for the remainder of last night, and after a restless night's sleep I rose early, eager to go and visit her, knowing I couldn't rest until I knew she was safe.

The Davenport's property was situated in the secluded grounds of Montgomery Park, almost hidden from sight by the leafy trees that encircled it. I'd forgotten how imposing the great, rambling house was, and I could see by the large sash windows and freshly painted exterior, that it was regularly maintained to a high standard, as were the surrounding gardens which were tended to exceptionally well by the gardener.

Reaching the front entrance, I almost turned back, too cowardly to knock and apprehensive that no one would answer. Trying to convince myself that everything was all right, I gently tapped upon the door and stood there waiting for what seemed like an eternity, until I could wait no longer, and with added urgency I began knocking continually until my hand began to ache. Of course, it was entirely possible that Agnes Davenport had already left for the police station, that's if Isaiah hadn't dissuaded her otherwise, or prevented her in some way, in some awful way. With a deep sigh I focused my thoughts on more positive scenarios; perhaps she had gone shopping instead, or the library or was visiting friends. But despite my vain attempt at looking on the bright side it couldn't prevent the distinct sense of foreboding from gradually creeping over me; for as feasible as my optimistic assumptions were, I couldn't escape the fact it was too early in the morning for Miss Davenport to have gone out.

In a daze I ventured around the back of the property in the slight hope that Miss Davenport was in the back garden, perhaps she was tending to her plants, or hanging out the washing. However, to my dismay I found it empty. Unable to find an open window, I hastily grabbed a rock from the garden, and before I allowed myself to consider what I was doing, smashed it through one of the panes; like a common burglar, I crawled through and into the study. In retrospect my actions were a little rash, but I couldn't rest until I knew the truth, I couldn't stay at Rawlings, waiting for news, even if it was unwanted.

I crept through the silent study and into a large entrance hall where the only sound was the continual tick of the grandfather clock, and the pounding of my heart.

'Miss Davenport?' I yelled. 'It's only me, Effie.' My voice sounded strained and weak. 'Hello?'

Unexpectedly something sprung out from nowhere and brushed against my legs. I screamed in fright and looked down to see it was Miss Davenport's cat, Wilson.

'Oh, Wilson you startled me.' With a faint laugh I reached down and stroked her, and she began to meow persistently. 'What's wrong girl, are you hungry? Gathering her in my arms I made my way to the kitchen, searching for some food for the poor, hungry cat. It wasn't hard to discover the tins of tuna in the bottom cupboard, and tipping the contents of a can into a bowl, I laid it on the floor. 'Here we are Wilson.' I watched as she ravenously ate it.

I took a deep breath and exhaled, trying to stop the anxiety I felt from totally overwhelming me. So far there'd been no sign of Miss Davenport, and it was obvious that Wilson hadn't been fed. Agnes was usually very attentive towards the cat; in fact, both the sisters had always been great cat lovers, especially Lydia.

Fetching some water for Wilson and placing it next to the empty bowl of food, I tentatively stepped out of the kitchen and made my way across the other side of the entrance hall.

A high-pitched scream erupted from my throat.

Agnes Davenport was lying in a heap at the bottom of the stairs. I knew straight away she was dead, as her staring eyes were dull and lifeless.

Crying out I stumbled backwards and knocked a lamp off the table.

Unable to wrench my eyes from her still form, I gasped and placed my hand over my chest, trying to catch my breath. Time seemed to stand still as I gazed down at the body in strange, morbid fascination; I'd never seen a corpse before, nor had I wished to, but in my delirious state of shock I felt sure her stony cold hand would reach out and grasp my ankle the minute I ceased staring at those vacant eyes. I had fallen into a terrible nightmare, one from which I would never awaken.

'Oh, Miss Davenport, I'm so sorry.' Tears began to trickle down my face. 'Please forgive me. I...I should have come sooner.'

Trembling with shock I began to move away from Miss Davenport's body, gradually edging my way towards the entrance hall. A sudden panic came about me, and I had a frantic urge to be free of the house; I rushed along the entrance hall and shakily fumbled with the locks on the front door until I was able to open it, then swiftly ran outside. Never before had I been so relieved to feel the freshness of the air upon my face. And, in an unconscious motion of a sleepwalker, I blindly staggered through Montgomery Park, almost oblivious to the early morning dog walkers. I half sensed they were peering at me as they passed by: mystified by the deranged looking woman with the desolate eyes.

I'm wasn't really sure where I was heading, and didn't really care, I just had the urge to keep on going, to walk away from that house of death and to lose myself somewhere remote, to wallow in self-pity at not being able to save Agnes Davenport, and to give myself time to digest what had happened. And the only way to do this was to be alone, with only my thoughts for company. Unintentionally I found myself gravitating towards the seafront and in a strange type of daze I blundered over the uneven pebbles and sat down. Thankfully any beachgoers had not yet arrived and I found myself glad of the silence. I gazed out at the lapping waves, staring into the blue depths of the water, and for one surreal moment I wanted to surrender myself to the sea, to dive in and lose myself forever, for in doing so it would rid me of my heavy heart, my sorrow and heartache.

Approaching footsteps broke my train of thought and I turned to see Noble approaching me. 'Here you are Effie, I wondered where you'd disappeared to.'

I glared into his dark eyes. 'How did you find me?' I asked in a rather cantankerous sounding voice. 'I don't wish to be rude Noble but I'd rather like to be alone.'

He came and sat down beside me, staring directly ahead.

'Over the past few weeks, I've got to know you rather well Effie Farraday, and I had an inkling you'd come down to the sea.' Picking up a pebble he tossed it into the water. 'And please don't ask me to go.' Swinging round to face me he very lightly touched my hand. 'If you've something on your mind it's often wise to share it with another, it will lessen your burden.'

Wiping a stray tear from my cheek I slowly moved my gaze to his. 'Agnes Davenport is dead. I...I went to her house early this morning and discovered her.'

For a few moments we sat there in complete silence.

'You poor thing that must have been dreadful for you Effie.'

I sprung up from the pebbles. 'Do not be concerned for me.' I exclaimed harshly. 'It's Miss Davenport you should feel sorry for, she's the poor thing who had her life cut short last night.' I continued to glare at him. 'Do you not care about anyone but me?'

An agonised expression showed in his eyes and I could see that I'd hurt his feelings. With a sigh he rose up and stood beside me.

'It is true, yes. You are my main priority.' He lowered his head sullenly. 'But if you believe I do not care about what has happened to Agnes Davenport then you are sadly mistaken.' Rather cautiously he stepped nearer to me. 'Do you believe it to be an accident?'

'No.' A look of infuriation came into my eyes. 'As I explained to you last night, if you'd been listening, I had a terrible feeling that something awful was going to happen to her.' I swept the hair from my face. 'Miss Davenport was going to speak to the police before.... before the end.' Instinctively I shivered. 'She was going to tell them how she believed her sister Lydia was murdered, hoping they'd investigate.' I swung round to face Noble. 'Sadly, she never made it. I had a feeling Isaiah would somehow.' I paused. 'Prevent her.' A lump came to my throat and I turned away from him. 'I should have warned Miss Davenport of what was going to happen. I...I should have been there for her. Then perhaps she would still be alive.'

I felt him firmly grip my arms. 'Please do not blame yourself Effie. If what you say is true then Isaiah would have still found a way to...to dispose of her. It's something he's learnt to perfect over time. You cannot be held responsible for your father's acts, it was his doing, not yours.'

'Yes, yes you are right. But I can prevent him from harming anyone else.' I swung round to face him. 'You could take him with you Noble. This world would be free of him forever.' I looked beseechingly at him. 'What do you think?'

'And what of you, will you stay here and linger at Rawlings until you are an old spinster like your Aunt, with nothing else to fill your time but the garden and how you're going to find the funds to stop the house from crumbling to the ground.'

I slapped him hard across the face. 'You've no right to say such a thing. My Aunt chose the life she has because Rawlings means more to her than anything else, and if Isaiah hadn't appeared on the scene, I believe she would have been a whole lot happier.' I placed my hands on my hips in defiance. 'And for your information I would be quite content to while my life away tending to the garden and maintaining my ancestral home.'

His face took on a mixture of bemusement and concern. 'If that is what you wish then I shall take your father with me and leave you here.' With a drawn-out sigh he began moving the pebbles with his foot. 'So, have you discovered anything interesting in the ledger, such as a way for me to travel home?'

'No, not as yet. The notes are very complicated to decipher, but I shall take another look at it tonight. In the meantime, I should go and contact the police and hospital about Miss Davenport.'

'Is that advisable? I mean you found the body, which means the police will most certainly wish to question you. Your association with the crime could cause you to be a suspect.'

Noble's apparent concern for my welfare was rather irritating, I did however agree with what he said. I'm not sure I could face and interrogation by the police, and it would have to involve Aunt as well, and she would be distressed enough as it was. And even if I was to accuse Isaiah of Miss Davenport's murder, I'm sure they would not believe me, especially if Chief Inspector Vale had anything to do with it, being an acquaintance of my father. Isaiah would come out of the whole sorry mess unscathed, leaving him free to linger at Rawlings. And in punishment for my betrayal he would push poor Aunt down the staircase, just like her friend Agnes.

'I shall give the police an anonymous call from a phone box.' Reluctantly I began strolling up the beach. 'I should go and do it now.'

'You should inform them about your father. If we're lucky they might discover some evidence against him and find him guilty.'

'Noble you don't know Isaiah like I do, even if they were to suspect him or hold him for questioning, I very much doubt if they would be able to prove it. My father is an accomplished liar and very good at covering his tracks.' I sniggered. 'And ironically he is very good friends with the head of Abercrombie police station, Chief Inspector Vale.'

'Effie, surely it is worth taking a chance. For all you know the police may already have doubts about him. After all, Miss Davenport's sister also passed away rather suddenly did she not? And then there are the disappearances of your friends.'

'Yes, Lydia died a couple of years ago. She supposedly took too much sleeping draught.' My face was solemn. 'Ultimately going to the police about Isaiah is a huge gamble, one I'm not sure would be prudent to take. It could have implications for us all.'

He trailed behind me up the beach. 'Just promise me you'll consider it Effie. If Isaiah was put in prison it would mean I wouldn't have to leave.'

For an instant I stopped and glanced back at him. 'Very well Noble, I shall think about it.'

He ran ahead and stood in front of me. 'I'd like to apologise Effie -it was not my intention to offend you or be disrespectful about your Aunt.'

I smiled softly at him, trying not to blush by his intent gaze. 'Apology accepted.' I hesitated. 'And I'd like to say sorry for being so grumpy, and for slapping you. It's rather out of character for me.' My face became grave. 'It's not every day one stumbles across a body.'

Reaching up he gently caressed my cheek. 'Come on, let's make that phone call. Then you and I shall go and have breakfast in Hudson's café.' He put his arm around my shoulders. 'And I suggest we have a strong cup of tea.'

As we stepped upon the promenade, I felt the inevitable heat rising up in my face at the feel of his arm about me, and as we strolled across the road a fleeting vision entered my mind of him reaching forward and kissing me, just like that day in the library.

# Chapter 8

As the days slipped by, I was haunted constantly by the vision of poor Agnes Davenport's lifeless body sprawled out on the rug at the foot of the stairs, her dead eyes staring perpetually into nothingness; it had caused a cold shadow to creep over my heart, leaving me with a distinct sense of uneasiness and a sinister feeling that wouldn't go away.

To my utter astonishment there was not to be an inquest into her death, something of which I believe to be the doing of Chief Inspector Vale. Apparently, Agnes Davenport was unsteady on her feet, and being a frail old lady, she had accidentally tripped and fell to her death. Isaiah of course pretended to be completely grief stricken and racked with guilt. Evidently, on the night in question, he had only seen Agnes to her front door, as even though he was usually in the habit of seeing her safely inside it appears she ensured him it wouldn't be necessary on this occasion. But what astounded me most was how Isaiah had conveniently gone to visit Chief Inspector Vale and his wife, directly after seeing Agnes to her door, where they had all spent the evening playing backgammon. I can only ascertain that in the unlikely event Isaiah needed an alibi, he would have the perfect excuse, and even if the Chief Inspector had known Isaiah had dropped off Miss Davenport that fateful night, I'm sure he would dismiss it as a mere coincidence.

There was something indefinably odd about the Monk's ledger, and for some reason I had the urge to destroy it. Why this was I do not know, it was after all a harmless notebook, and disposing of it would not be in our best interests. Night after night I would carefully flick through its delicate pages looking for a clue of how to get Noble home, and to be rid of Isaiah. And eventually I found the answer I was searching for: it was scribbled in such tiny writing I didn't notice it at first, but it mentioned an abbey near the old mill at Wheatfield, a tiny village a few miles away which we could easily reach by train, or if necessary, car. I've a vague memory of visiting the ancient site when I was a child, and knew roughly where it was situated. The ledger stated that we must wait until dusk descended then a monk would lead us through the gateway. Unfortunately, I couldn't decipher what it said after that as it would just an illegible scribble, however it did mention the name Briarwood on the same page. On seeing the name, I instantly had a flashback of a tiny village I had once visited, nestled amongst magnificent countryside, and instantly I knew for certain that this was the place we were seeking. It was Noble's home. Call me insane but I took this as a good indication that this was the path we should take, and anyhow it was the only real clue we had to go on.

Eager to share my exciting discovery with Noble I rushed out into the garden and told him my news, but for some reason he didn't appear very happy about it; I got the impression he was suddenly reluctant to leave, and wondered if having to drag Isaiah along on the journey was putting him off the idea. But in my heart of hearts I knew the real reason, and it didn't have anything to do with my father, it was I….

How much he had hinted that I should also come along on the journey, and I strongly suspected that if I agreed he would take me by the hand and leave this very instant.

I looked on as he yanked the great, relentless thistles that had crept with so much vigour up against the walls, hiding cleverly amongst the lobelias, delphinine and hollyhocks. Humming gently away to himself he seemed to make quick work of the awful weeds.

'Did you do the garden in your old home Noble?' I asked, accidentally brushing into the gorse with its yellow flowers.

Wiping his brow, he momentarily stopped and turned to face me. 'I wouldn't know, would I.' He replied rather tersely. He threw a handful of weeds into one of the garden bags. 'If I did, I'm certain it wasn't as bad as this.' His face softened and he smiled. 'Would you like to employ me as a permanent gardener, I think you need one.'

I laughed 'I doubt if we could afford one.' I uttered, looking downcast. My eyes crept over the great expanse of tall grasses in the distance where we had allowed nature to take over; it was only the immediate garden, surrounding the house that we could manage to keep tame.'

'Well luckily for you I'm free.' He exclaimed, clambering over towards the next clump of thistles. 'I shall have to spend each and every day out here if you want the garden to be glorious for your party.'

'You've already done so much in the garden Noble.' I scanned the flowerbeds. 'There's really not that much more to do.'

He began to laugh. 'I beg to differ. Gardening is a full-time task. And besides I would never forgive myself if I didn't do it properly.

I smiled forlornly at him. 'What a shame you can't enjoy the remainder of the summer at Rawlings.' I replied with a long drawn out sigh. 'Especially now you've almost transformed the garden to its former glory.'

With a handful of thistles in his hand he stood and stared at me. 'Then perhaps I should stay longer.' A look of hopeful anticipation spread across his face. 'In fact, I was actually thinking how agreeable it would be to spend Christmas here. Constance has told me all about the festivities here at Rawlings and I would very much like to see them for myself.'

I pictured us sitting beside a Christmas tree, next to the blazing fire, handing one another presents. There would be just the three of us: my Aunt, Noble and myself; we would have the most marvellous of times, but then Isaiah would appear and everything would be spoilt.

I bit my lip. 'As lovely as that sounds, I really think we should concentrate on organising the trip' slowly I looked into his face, expecting him to answer me immediately, but there was silence. 'You do still want to go home don't you Noble?' I asked, studying his face carefully.

With a deep sigh he stopped what he was doing. 'Yes, and no.' He mumbled under his breath. 'I'm afraid that if we go to the abbey we may find nothing, nothing but a ruin.' He lowered his eyes. 'And, well I've become rather used to being here.' He looked up and caught my eye. 'With you.'

The familiar flush of colour began burning my cheeks, and for a moment I couldn't think straight.

'Well...well what about Agnes Davenport? With her recent death I really think it's imperative we remove Isaiah from Rawlings as soon as possible.' I stared pensively across the garden. 'And I'm sorry Noble, but I'm extremely reluctant to involve the police. So, the only other option is to return him to the home he originated from.'

Noble sneered. 'I can think of a more immediate way to be rid of your father, and it doesn't involve me leaving Rawlings.'

I raised my eyebrows. 'Even if we were to...to make Isaiah disappear forever, it doesn't change the fact you need to go home.' I gulped. 'I looked at him fleetingly then turned away, pretending to busy myself with the plants. 'Surely you must be wondering what's happened to your family, to...to Gideon.

I flinched as he brushed passed me and threw the trowel and rake into the wheelbarrow. 'Perhaps, yes, and that's why you need to come with me.' He swung round to face me. 'You too must be curious to solve the mystery of Gideon.' A peculiar look appeared in his eyes. 'I'm not a fool Effie; I know you've been to the place where I grew up and have met Gideon. He studied my face closely. 'And I believe the two of you loved one another. Am I not right?'

My face appeared puzzled. 'I I don't know.'

He continued to stare intently into my eyes and then shook his head. 'Never mind. I have no wish to learn what has passed between the both of you, nor do I wish to cause you pain by questioning you on a subject you clearly feel uncomfortable about.'

An intense ache began throbbing across my temple. Without commenting on his remark, I slowly made my way across the lawn to the house.

'Effie?'

I half turned to look at him. 'Yes?

I shall willingly go through the gateway, and take that loathsome father of yours with me.' He took a deep breath. 'Like I've explained to you before, it would gladden my heart if you would come with us. Promise me you'll consider it.'

I smiled coyly at him. 'I shall think about it Noble.' I uttered in a soft voice. 'Really I shall.'


That night I sneaked into the library and sat in the far corner overlooking the back of the garden. My Aunt and Isaiah we playing cards in the living room and I could hear the distant sound of their laughter. I was often perplexed at how well suited they were to one another, how they genuinely enjoyed each other's company, and it amazed me how accomplished he was at hiding his devious ways from her, and how well he lulled her into a false sense of security with his various memory tonics. Had my Aunt been aware of all the facts then the situation would be rather different; knowing how resolute she could be I'm sure Isaiah would be thrown out of Rawlings forthwith, with strict instructions never to return. How I longed for that day, and how I longed to sit my Aunt down and tell her the truth about the man she worshipped, but in doing so I feared my words would fall on death ears. The only way to wake her up from this spell of forgetfulness would be to prevent Isaiah from poisoning her mind with his various remedies and clever words, although I often pondered whether she would want to be; perhaps she was happy this way, perhaps to face the truth would be her undoing.

Over fatigue had made me chilly and I wrapped the rug around my legs then picked up my book. My conscience told me I should be searching for more clues in the Monk's ledger, but it was such heavy, difficult reading that I'm sure I would fall asleep, and besides I had all the information I required for now. However as I began to read my mystery novel I found my mind wandering off onto other thoughts; a vision of Mace and Clarice suddenly came to me, and I realised I'd not allowed myself to think about them properly up until now, I'd pushed them away hoping the pain of not seeing them would lessen with time, until eventually they would completely fade into a memory, almost like Gideon. What an enigma this Gideon person was, and how little I had mentioned him in my notebook, just tiny little things that seemed inconsequential and were not enough proof that I loved him, or he loved me.

I looked out onto the darkening night, pondering over what to do for the best:

Should I bury my head in the sand and turn my back on my friends, languish at Rawlings and allow my heart to become cold and hard. How bitter and angry I would become towards everyone, with no one to talk to who would understand my state of mind, and if I dared utter one word about travelling through a portal and going to another world, they would surely think I'd gone mad. Alternatively, I could take the plunge and go with Noble, for I knew he had to go, with or without me. But I feared this other world; in fact, everything about it scared me. What if we became lost whilst travelling there, would it be dangerous, what horrors might await me once we arrived, would I find my friends, would they be alive. And then there was Gideon...

I may even become stranded in this other land, never to return; and my Aunt would eventually die a sad and lonely old lady, believing I had abandoned her. Ultimately, as is often true of the dilemmas we must face in life, there was no easy solution. Nevertheless, as I sat there on that summer's evening contemplating my future, I suddenly realised what I must do.

The following day was spent strolling casually around the local art display at the village hall. It reminded me of the time I'd had my art exhibition, how shy and nervous I'd been, how convinced no one would purchase one single painting. And yet it had actually turned out rather well. Of course today wasn't completely different from the time before, I still had my Aunt's committee friends hovering in the background in quiet conversation with each other, and had it not been for their obvious glances in our direction I could have almost convinced myself that nothing was wrong, that they weren't intrigued to know my present state of mind and had no interest in knowing who my companion was.

'Perhaps we should leave.' I whispered at Noble as I spotted the group of old ladies gradually edging their way towards us. 'We're about to be interrogated by some of Aunt's friends.'

'Sounds like fun.' He linked his arm through mine. 'Come on then, let's go and speak to them.'

I pulled him back abruptly. 'No, we shouldn't. It's bound to get back to Isaiah as it is, we shouldn't make matters worse by providing them with more information. If they recognise you from the wedding or discover your name it could put you in real danger.' With our arms still linked I dragged him to the entrance.

He sighed as we went out the hall. 'There's something that really bothers me Effie. Why do you not paint anymore? You're so talented.'

I widened my eyes and laughed. 'I...I don't know.' Narrowing my eyes, I stared thoughtfully through the window of the hall. 'Ever since those painting of mine were destroyed at Mr Lombard's art gallery, I've been putting it off.'

He came and stood beside me. 'Would you consider painting me?'

I responded with a smile. 'If you like.' I slowly swung round and faced him.

'Although I'm not sure it's a good idea.'

A look of bewilderment crossed over his face. 'Why is that?'

'Your expression is constantly changing for one thing and...and.' I purposely turned away from him. 'And, well I shouldn't imagine they'll be enough time.'

He moved around to face me. 'What do you mean?'

'You'll be leaving Abercrombie soon.'

Not replying he stared glumly ahead.

'I shall of course accompany you and Isaiah to the abbey, that's the least I can do.' Intentionally pausing for a moment, I fleetingly glanced at him. 'I'm not entirely sure but I sense that my last journey was rather similar to being tossed into the heart of a tornado. Let's hope this time it's a little easier, and all three of us make it through safely.'

He swung round to face me. 'Does that mean you're journeying with us through the gateway?'

'If that's alright with you.'

His mouth broke into a large grin. 'Yes, yes that will be most acceptable.' On impulse he lifted me up and began to swing me around in a circle. 'Thank you, Effie, thank you.' Placing me back down he instinctively leant over and kissed me lightly on the lips and then hugged me. 'Oh, look we have an audience.'

I glanced at the elderly ladies peering out at us from the window of the hall.

'Let's give them something to really talk about.' He said in a laughing voice.

'Whatever do you mean?'

Before I could stop him, he held me in a tight embrace and was kissing me hard on the mouth.


The inevitable march of time is something we have no control over. Having the ability to control time, to pause it indefinitely must surely be a truly wondrous gift; we could stop it whenever we wished, at a moment we were most content and safe and not be burdened by the worries of tomorrow. How I wished to hold onto those warm summer days of blissful ease as they sped by in a blurred state of tranquillity, and never let them go, for I knew they would not endure for very much longer.

Noble and I had decided to wait until after the garden party to leave, and even then, it was unclear as to when we would go on our journey. As the forthcoming weeks passed by the garden party loomed forever nearer and my Aunt began to snap at the slightest thing; why this was I do not know, as everything was in hand. Noble had done wonders in the garden and it was looking truly glorious. Providing the weather was fine everyone would congregate in the garden and have no need to enter the house, apart from using the downstairs bathroom just off the kitchen. So, with any luck the guests would hardly notice the peeling wallpaper and cracked ceilings, or the threadbare sofas and armchairs, or the chipped furniture. Of course, in the event of rain, all our careful planning would be ruined.

'It looks like everyone's coming tomorrow.' I mumbled, swiftly flicking through the garden party replies. 'All except Mace's foster parents, Giles and Marigold.' I furrowed my brow in puzzlement. 'Strange for them not to get back to us, they're usually so prompt with such things.'

A look of dismay swept over my Aunt's face and she threw Isaiah a knowing look.

Isaiah cleared his throat. 'There er....there was an accident a while ago.' He said, avoiding my eyes. 'Mr & Mrs McIntosh perished in a gas explosion at their house.' He spoke the sentence quickly and quietly.

I looked aghast. 'What? I got up rapidly from the chair, knocking it backwards onto the floor. 'No, no that's not possible.' I felt choked up with emotion. 'You must have made a mistake, I...I would have heard about it.' I uttered shakily.

My Aunt's face was filled with anguish as she came and put her arm around me.

'Effie, I should have told you before, but it happened shortly after your ruined wedding day. You were in such a bad state that Isaiah and I felt it best to keep it from you, just for a while, just until you were back to your old self.'

'What?' I screamed, removing her arm from my shoulder. I could feel my heart pounding in my chest as a surge of acute rage enveloped me. 'Well it may have escaped your notice, but I've been back to my old self for a long while now Aunt.' I yelled extremely loudly at her. 'Be honest, you had no intention of telling me, did you? I banged my fist on the table. 'You were hoping it would just go away.'

'Well actually dear it slipped my mind.' My Aunt said in a weak voice. 'I'm so sorry Effie, I don't know what I was thinking.' She put her hand out to steady herself and tumbled forward slightly over the table.

Isaiah leapt to her rescue, helping her into a chair.

'See what you've done to your poor Aunt.' He crouched down beside her. 'Are you alright Constance?' He turned and scowled at me. 'This is why we kept it from you, your Aunt is of a very delicate disposition.' He lowered his eyes. 'What happened to The McIntosh's was indeed a tragic accident, and we are all very saddened by the event.' A faint smirk crossed over his lips. 'Sometimes these things just happen.'

I stared at him open mouthed. It was blindingly obvious that Isaiah was responsible for their deaths, those two lovely people who had never done anyone any harm in their life had become unfortunate victims of my vile father. Rubbing my eyes, I attempted to compose myself and tried to hide the look of disgust on my face. My urge to accuse him of their murders was overwhelmingly tempting, but that would be irresponsible and unwise at this stage; if I uttered a word of his crimes to my Aunt or the police, there could be dire consequences. I remembered the grim warning Isaiah gave me about my Aunt accidentally tumbling down the stairs, exactly like poor, dead Agnes Davenport.

Doing my best to act calm, I went over to my Aunt and lightly placed my hand on her shoulder. 'Forgive me Aunt, I didn't mean to yell at you.'

She covered my hand with hers and squeezed it. 'Oh, don't fret Effie all is forgiven. Why don't you go and see....' She stopped in mid-sentence. 'Why don't you go and see the garden.' She laughed nervously.

Isaiah looked puzzled.

'I need to check it's all neat and tidy for tomorrow, that's what you mean, don't you Aunt?

'That's right dear.'

As I headed for the door, I heard Isaiah's bellowing voice. 'Don't be long, I'm going to make us all a delicious cup of tea, a sugary sweet one for you I think Constance.'

I ran blindly down to the shed and stumbled in. 'Noble? Noble, where are you?' I whispered urgently. 'I really need to speak to you.'

His shadowy figure emerged from the far corner by the canvases.

'Whatever's the matter?'

Seeing him standing there I impulsively ran up and flung my arms around his neck.

'I can't do this anymore Noble, I just can't.' I began sobbing. 'We've got to do something before, before it's too late.'

Noble took my arms from round his neck and sat me down on an upturned crate. 'What's happened?'

I wiped my face with my sleeve and sniffed. 'He killed Mace's foster parents, as well as the Davenport's.' I clenched my hands together. 'And if I don't watch it Aunt will be next, I just know it.'

Kneeling down beside me he reached out and took my hands in his. 'Calm down Effie, if he was going to get rid of your Aunt, don't you think he'd had done it by now?'

I looked at him solemnly. 'Isaiah disposes of people that he thinks are a liability, and I fear that my Aunt is becoming a hindrance to him.'

'Do you really believe he would harm Constance, for to do so would totally destroy any chance he had of gaining your love and trust.' He tenderly stroked my hands with his thumbs. 'However rotten that man is, it cannot be denied how much you mean to him, and if he was to do away with your Aunt you would never forgive him, and he would therefore never forgive himself.'

Looking into the depths of Noble's eyes I felt a strange contentment stirring within me, and I became enveloped in an inexplicable homesickness, so much so that I felt myself swaying forward into him.

'Effie, are you alright?' He steadied me slightly. 'You look a little faint.'

I gulped hard. 'Yes…yes I'm fine.' Regaining my composure, I rose from the crate and walked over to the far side of the shed. 'Your words of wisdom have reassured me about Aunt's safety.' I laughed lightly before my face turned grim. 'But I can no longer sit back and do nothing, I can't allow Isaiah to literary get away with murder.'

Noble shrugged his shoulders. 'So, what do suggest we do?'

'I know we've not discussed it recently but perhaps it's time we took that trip to the abbey.' I glanced at his startled face. 'What do you think?'

'Effie, I know you're apprehensive about contacting the police, but I still believe it could be the answer to all our troubles.'

My eyes clouded over as I stared vacantly at one of my paintings Noble had hung on the shed wall. 'If only it were that easy.' I ran my index finger over the dust on the workbench. 'Without real evidence they will not take us seriously. And a police enquiry will infuriate my father.' I muttered glumly. 'As far as Chief Inspector Vale is concerned both the Davenport sisters lost their lives in tragic accidents, and the matter is closed. And as for Mace's foster parents that too will be put down to an unfortunate disaster. Trying to convince him that Isaiah is a cold-bloodied murderer will be an impossible task.'

Noble had become silent, and as I looked round, I saw how very despondent he looked. 'There is no justice in this world.'

'No, no there is not.' I glanced at my watch and sighed. 'As much as I'd like to continue this conversation, I promised my Aunt I'd help her with the baking for tomorrow.' I suddenly felt wretched. 'I'm sorry you can't join us but Isaiah...'

Abruptly he interrupted me. 'Yes, yes I know your father will be there.' His eyes grew dark. 'As he always is.' In a sudden fit of temper, he kicked over a stack of paint tins. 'You'd better go before he comes looking for you.'

I gaped at his brooding, resentful face, not really knowing what to say. 'Well, goodnight Noble.'

Nodding at him I swiftly crossed over to the shed door, and glancing briefly at him once more, I smiled coyly before creeping away, leaving him to spend another miserable night in the garden shed.

# Chapter 9

The day of the garden party had finally come and my Aunt was scurrying around with frantic urgency. All the guests had arrived and were busily inspecting the garden, which Noble had tendered to so lovingly. I felt a pang of guilt that he had to hide away when instead he should be amongst the guests, being praised for all his hard work. Isaiah was in his element, and as usual was monopolising much of the conversation. I flitted from guest to guest offering them homemade scones, cakes and endless cups of tea, smiling when I had to and trying to blend in as much as I could without saying something foolish or unnecessary.

Making my way across the lawn I found a hand tightly grasping my arm. It was Mrs Lapworth, Clarice's mother. She was staggering ever so slightly and waving her sherry glass carelessly in the air.

'Effie, how lovely to see you looking so well.' She hiccupped. 'How contented your Aunt must be having you back home.' She cautiously looked around before dragging me away from the guests. 'I know I've asked you before but if you know where Clarice is please tell me Effie. Please, I'm begging you.' She started to roughly shake my arm.

Looking at her agonised face I was almost tempted to tell her the truth. God only knew the poor lady had suffered enough, but wouldn't it be cruel to give her hope then snatch it away. I didn't know if Clarice was still alive, she could be lost forever.

'There is a slight chance I can find Clarice.' I said in a low voice.

'Promise me Effie, promise me you'll bring her back to me.'

'I took her hands in mine and squeezed them.

'I promise to do my best Mrs Lapworth, my very best.' I said sincerely.

She looked disappointed for a minute but then her face brightened.' I knew you would help me Effie, I just knew it.' Her voice became a whisper. 'There's rumours flying about that Rawlings is in financial trouble. If you return Clarice safe and sound then I will help with the repairs. It will only be a little mind, but it all helps doesn't it?'

I stared at her for a while without uttering a word, and when I eventually spoke my voice sounded strained. 'Yes, yes indeed Mrs Lapworth, that's very kind of you, however that really won't be necessary.' I looked at her empty glass. 'Let me take that from you and bring you a lovely cup of tea, or perhaps a strong coffee?' I took her arm and led her to one of the garden benches.

'Another sherry will suffice please Effie; I find it helps keep the demons at bay.'

I nodded and without saying another word took her glass. I would purposely make her a coffee and see that she drank it. Making my way towards the house I was stopped by Mr Marshall, who began chatting to me about his allotment. As I stood there, trying to grasp what he was talking about, I absentmindedly glanced over his shoulder and my eyes rested on Isaiah, who was standing directly behind us. He was hovering over Miss Weatherly, patting her arm, and although they were having a completely innocent conversation his words suddenly filled me with terror.

'We have more garden chairs in the shed. Do let me fetch you one Miss Weatherly.' His eyes travelled my way and he threw me a long, hard stare. 'You'd be utterly surprised at what's lurking in that tumbledown shack.'

An uneasy feeling crept over me as I came to realise Isaiah knew about my dark secret hiding in the shed.

Totally forgetting my conversation with Mr Marshall, I vacantly brushed passed him. 'Isaiah, allow me to get the chairs for you.' My heart was thudding frantically. 'You carry on speaking to Miss Weatherly.

He smirked at me. 'No no Effelia, there's no need to trouble yourself. I'm perfectly capable of retrieving them.' He sniggered and limped his way awkwardly towards the shed.

I opened my mouth to speak but no words came out. After all what could I say to stop or delay him; all I could do was stare after him like an imbecile. For some time, I waited with baited breath, praying that Isaiah would emerge alone, until my Aunt came over and took my arm, appearing rather flustered.

'Effie I really don't appreciate you standing there like a statue. I really need your help in the kitchen.'

I threw her an impatient glare.

'Yes, Aunt I shall be along as soon as I can.'

I felt her tugging my arm. 'No, I need your help this very minute.' Her voice was terse. It seems I didn't lay out enough cakes for our guests and they are running short on tea.' Appearing flustered she reached up and wiped her brow. 'These events are becoming far too strenuous and taxing for me, I'm considering making this my last one.'

'Oh, Aunt I'm sure you mentioned something similar last year.' I exclaimed with a smile as she led me nearer to the house. 'You don't mean it.'

She gave me a peculiar stare. 'How would you know; you haven't been present in the last couple of years.' Her face became concerned. 'Do you not remember Effie?'

As we went into the kitchen, I placed my hand across my forehead and sighed.

'Yes…. yes of course I replied, trying to hide the look of pain on my face. 'How silly of me.'

I stood there for a moment in a strange sort of daze. It was becoming clear that although my memory was returning, it was very inconsistent, which was rather annoying and also worrying.

'Really Effie, do pull yourself together.' She mumbled as she began to make the tea. 'Now is not the time for being idle.' Her face softened a little. 'Please be a dear and help me with the cakes.' She asked. 'Certain guests are extremely gluttonous.' Glancing at me she suddenly looked agitated. 'Oh, and have a word with Clarice's mother, I do believe she's a little inebriated, and I'm rather afraid she'll make a spectacle of herself.'

'What do you expect Aunt; her daughter's been missing for over two years. If that was me, you'd be frantic with worry.'

I reached for the coffee pot and began pouring the liquid into a large mug.

My Aunt slammed down the teapot on the table in fury.

'Effie, no one could have been more distraught than your father and I when you decided to go off on your little jaunt overseas. It was most irresponsible of you.'

'But Aunt I came back, Clarice is still out there somewhere, lost.'

She looked dazed and confused for a moment.

'Yes, I suppose so, but I do wish I'd not invited her mother. All along Isaiah has warned me that she'll be a nuisance but I thought it only right to invite her.'

Yes, how convenient it would be for Isaiah, I thought. Not to have to deal with the aggravation of Clarice's mother asking probing questions and spoiling our little gathering, reminding him of his dark deed. I'd like to think that perhaps somewhere deep inside him he felt a smidgen of guilt for tossing poor Clarice down into the abyss of the portal but I doubt it very much; he was far too heartless for that.

Taking the mug of coffee, I moved over towards the door.

'I've already spoken to Mrs Lapworth, and she's perfectly fine. In fact, she's just asked for a coffee.' I said in an agitated sounding voice. 'I shall be back shortly to help you bring out the tea and cakes.'

As I ventured back outside, I was shocked to find the majority of guests had congregated in a large group by the flowerbed on the south side of the garden, it seemed something or someone had attracted their attention. Swiftly giving Clarice's mother her coffee and insisting she drink it, I slowly stepped towards the group, curious as to what was so engrossing. And as I approached them, I was startled by an unexpected shrill voice near my ear. It was Mrs Higgins, one of the town librarians.

'Panic over, I've found Miss Farraday.' Turning to gaze at me she chuckled. 'Your fiancée's here, he was hiding in the shed, ready to surprise you.'

My heart leapt in my chest, as I stood there motionless.

'I'm sorry, I don't understand.' I muttered vaguely.

The guests had moved away slightly, allowing me to see into the middle of the crowd. Standing directly in the centre was Isaiah and Noble.

With a sly look in his eyes, Isaiah approached me, looking at me steadily.

'Evidently you've been engaged to this man for a while now, but haven't had the opportunity to share your good news with myself or your Aunt.' Isaiah's face was seething with anger as he spoke. 'Apparently your fiancée thought it would be pleasant to make the announcement today, with the guests being present.' He eyed Noble, looking him up and down.

Noble was looking sheepishly at me.

'Sorry Effie, it was silly of me I know but I thought it would be amusing to suddenly spring out from the shed and surprise you. He hesitated. 'You know how we talked about making our engagement public.' He strode forward and took my hand tightly in his. 'I want to share our love with the world.' He stared intently at me -his eyes gleaming.

I quickly snatched my hand away and glared at him. There was a deathly silence, as all eyes were upon me, eagerly awaiting a response. As much as I disliked being put on the spot, I felt I had little choice but to go along with the charade.

'Well yes, there's no time like the present to make our announcement.' I said in a quiet voice. I glanced down at the grass.

'So, it is true then?' Isaiah asked solemnly. 'You really are going to marry this... this individual.'

I caught Isaiah's eye for just a second then looked away.

'Yes, yes I am.'

An arm came round my shoulder and I saw it was my Aunt.

'Oh, how delightful.' She exclaimed, clapping her hands together in glee. 'I knew the two of you were in love. When and where is the wedding to be?'

'Soon, very soon.' Noble declared, smiling at me adoringly.

Taking Noble's hand, I purposely dug my nails into his palm, and felt him flinch.

'No, no we talked about this, didn't we Noble and decided on a long engagement.' I peered at him unsteadily. 'We haven't even thought about a ring yet.' I said trying to sound like the whole thing was rather casual.

'Well you must have a ring Effie,' uttered my Aunt. 'That really won't do.' She looked thoughtful for a moment then impulsively grabbed Noble's arm. 'Come with me Noble, I think I can help you.'

I began to panic as my Aunt dragged Noble by the arm, pulling him towards the house, for I didn't feel prepared to face everyone on my own, especially under the circumstances. Having to cope with a barrage of questions from the guests was daunting enough, but knowing I would be deceiving them too made me feel lousy. My face grew red with embarrassment and anger as I thought of how Noble had placed me in this awful predicament, and as the crowd gathered around me, I drew in a deep breath.

It amazed me how well I was suddenly capable of fibbing so easily; perhaps I would soon become an accomplished liar like my dear father, but despite my newly founded gift, I wasn't comfortable being so deceitful. I'm sure in time such things all have a nasty way of unravelling, falling apart before your eyes until everyone will come to realise what a fraud you are. Sooner or later I would slip up, sooner or later I would come a cropper, and then people would revert back to their original way of thinking, but not only would they think I was a timid, unstable wreck of a person who fainted on her wedding day then called the whole thing off, in addition to that I would also be known as someone that was untrustworthy, a trait that seemed worse than anything else.

Just as I thought this afternoon couldn't become anymore fraught, my Aunt and Noble came bounding back into the garden and presented me with an antique ring. Aunt had so kindly allowed Noble to pick a ring from her jewellery box, many of which had been passed down through generations. It was an exquisite ring, with a deep, illuminating emerald stone, which oddly enough fitted perfectly on my wedding finger, as if it was made purely for me. How swift I was to dismiss it, to cast it aside, but as I stared at it on my finger, I became mesmerised by its beauty.

Out of the corner of my eye I spotted Noble being accosted by a couple of elderly ladies, they seemed to be hanging on his every word; as they chatted, I saw him glance over and stare at me lovingly. On reflection, it was at this point that realisation came flooding over me. I think I'd known for a while but hadn't wanted to face it, but now there was no escaping it – Noble actually loved me.

As the last of the guests said their goodbyes my Aunt, Noble and I began the tireless job of tidying up. Isaiah had done a sudden vanishing act, and I imagined he was sulking somewhere after the bizarre event of the afternoon. But he would emerge sooner or later, of that I was sure. As Noble took the last of the glasses into house I pulled the tablecloths from the tables, carrying them in my arms, and headed indoors. My Aunt and Noble were busy in the kitchen, putting everything neatly away.

'Is that everything from outside dear?'

'Yes, I believe so Aunt. I shall just go and check.' As I glanced at Noble, I detected a faint expression of uneasiness in his eyes. 'You might as well stay in one of the spare bedrooms tonight Noble.' I gave my Aunt a fleeting glimpse. 'Do you not think Aunt?'

Her face was full of uncertainty. 'Well...perhaps, yes.' She looked passed me, peering out the window. 'Has anyone seen Isaiah? I do hope he hasn't gone for a walk. It looks like we're in for a heavy downpour.'

'Oh, I'm sure he's fine.' I replied casually. 'A little rain never did anyone any harm.' Laughing I opened the back door. 'But I shall have a hunt around for him all the same.'

Aunt beamed at me. 'Oh, thank you Effelia. I would hate for him to develop a chill.'

'Perish the thought.' I mumbled under my breath.

The humid weather had caused low, grey clouds to linger across the late afternoon sky, cooling the air quite considerably. Picking up a stray napkin I spotted a lone, shadowy figure seated in the wicker chair beneath the cedar tree. It was Isaiah, and he was carefully watching me.

My heart sank as I realised he'd noticed I'd seen him.

'Effelia. May I have a word with you?'

Drawing a deep breath, I reluctantly strolled over and stood beside him.

'Yes?'

Isaiah studied my face closely.

'What are you playing at Effelia? Do you really think I believe that utter piffle about your engagement?'

I stared into his red face, beaded in perspiration. 'It doesn't matter you would never accept Noble anyway. He's not rich enough is he? He couldn't contribute to the upkeep of Rawlings.'

He forced a smile. 'That is true. Which is why he's rather surplus to requirements.'

Folding my arms, I glared at him. 'What a dreadful comment to make.'

'I'm only speaking the truth.' He hunched forward in his seat, his eyes cold and unfeeling. 'I want the boy gone by midday tomorrow or I shall take a torch and burn that shed to the ground.' He snarled at me. 'After I've put a bullet in his head.'

A chill ran through me and I started to tremble a little. However, my voice was surprisingly calm when I spoke. 'How dare you say such a thing, how dare you make such a despicable threat.' I stepped closer, looking furious. 'And it may have escaped your notice but this is my property, mine and my Aunt's, and who we have to visit is really none of your concern. My Aunt is very fond of Noble and it's time he moved into Rawlings, rather than live in that decrepit old shed like a tramp.' I turned my back on him and began marching towards the house. 'I shall make arrangements immediately. And if you don't like my plans then please feel free to move out our house.' I mumbled under my breath, not meaning for him to hear. 'You've outstayed your welcome, anyway.'

His voice came bellowing across the garden. 'In case it's slipped your mind young lady, I am your father, which therefore makes Rawlings my home too. Your poor Aunt would be horrified to see me go, and she would be furious with you for treating me in such a shabbily manner. And as for that confounded boy Noble, how he has the audacity to claim to be your fiancée after ruining your wedding to Duncan, is beyond me.' He rose to his feet. 'I completely refuse to allow him to stay in the house, and I shall be discussing the matter with your Aunt Constance this very minute.'

Shaking my head in sheer frustration I hurried back into the house, closely followed by Isaiah, who was frantically limping after me. All of a sudden, I made it my mission to get to my Aunt before him, to persuade her to see sense and let Noble sleep in a proper bed. I marched through the empty kitchen and into the living room where I saw her curled up on our rather large, ostentatious velvet chez lounge, a recent purchase from Isaiah.

'Aunt. Aunt?' I called out softly, crouching over her.

I felt a light touch on my arm and looked up to see Noble.

'Do not disturb your Aunt, Effie. She is having a nap.' He carefully covered her with a blanket. 'It's been a busy day for her.'

A momentarily annoyance swept over me as I briefly glanced at Noble then back to my Aunt, and I couldn't stop myself from thinking how very inconvenient it was of her to have a snooze this very second. I was almost tempted to rouse her, but seeing sense I held back; what kind of niece would wake her worn-out elderly Aunt from a well-deserved slumber,

Feeling remorseful I looked sheepishly at Noble. 'Yes, you are right.' Slowly I tiptoed to the door, peering out into the hallway. 'Watch out for Isaiah, he isn't particularly happy.'

'I wonder why?' replied Noble in an amused voice.

Tugging his arm, I lead him into one of the unused rooms off the hallway.

'We had words in the garden.' I frowned. 'He's adamant that you do not sleep in the house. I was hoping to convince my Aunt otherwise.' I looked up into his eyes. 'She's very fond of you, and I'm certain she will allow it if…if it wasn't for Isaiah.'

He smiled radiantly at me, his large, soft eyes staring intently into mine. 'And I would very much like to stay in this grand house too. But I know it will cause problems with that father of yours.' A flicker of coldness appeared in his gaze. 'Men such as Isaiah should be kept away from decent folks such as yourselves, he should be cast out and left to rot in a prison.' His faced brightened. 'Anyway, what I was trying to say was, I will be perfectly content to remain in the garden shed' A broad grin spread across his face. 'That is until we are wed.'

I could feel the blood rushing up to my face.

'Please Noble.... do not joke.' My voice sounded flustered.

Unexpectedly the door violently swung open and Isaiah entered. 'So, this is where the two of you are skulking. 'He looked solemnly at Noble. 'I order you to leave this very instant, your presence is not welcome in this house.'

With a short laugh I paced forward and stood in front of Isaiah. 'Noble is staying inside the house, and that's the end of it.' With a look of defiance, I brushed passed him and went out the room. 'Come on Noble, I shall show you to your room.'

As Noble followed me out into the hallway, Isaiah suddenly pounced on him, pushing him up against the wall. It was only then I noticed the gun pointing at Noble's head.

'Let us end this now boy.'

Without warning Noble swiftly seized the gun from Isaiah, then violently shoved him to the floor. 'Yes, let us end this now you evil man.' He aimed the gun at his temple. 'Allow me to kill you.'

As Isaiah began to whimper, I heard a loud screech from up the hallway.

It was my Aunt. 'No, for heaven's sake no.'

'Help me Constance. Save me from this deranged man.'

Slightly unsteadily she rushed forward. 'Noble, what are you doing?' She reached her hand up to her mouth. 'Please do not harm Isaiah.'

Noble seemed oblivious to her plea and continued to hold the gun to Isaiah's head.

Aunt stood there shaking. 'Effie? 'Do something, tell Noble to leave him alone.'

'But Aunt, Isaiah was going to shoot Noble, did you not see?'

She gasped. 'That's a dreadful thing to accuse your father of Effie. I'm quite ashamed.' Leaning towards me she whispered into my ear. 'Noble is clearly not himself.'

Realising it was pointless arguing with her I tentatively reached out and lightly placed my hand on Noble's shoulder. 'You need to leave Isaiah alone Noble. Remove the gun from his head.' My tone was soft and controlled, as if trying to placate him. 'Please listen to me.'

With a long drawn out sigh, Noble dropped the gun and moved away.

Isaiah let out a loud sob as he shakily rose from the floor, discreetly picking up the gun and placing it in his back pocket. 'Oh Constance.' Snivelling, he feebly went over to her and put his arms about her. 'I thought I was going to die.' He began to bawl.

'There, there, you're safe now.' She patted him on the back. 'I won't let any harm come to you again.' Her expression became grave as she glanced at Noble. 'I don't know what's going on Noble, and quite frankly after what I've just witnessed, I cannot see how we can repair our friendship.'

Noble's face was full of pain. 'I can see any attempt to vindicate myself would be in vain. Would you like me to leave Constance?'

Isaiah, who seemed to have composed himself, swung round and glowered at Noble.

'Is the sky blue? Well of course we want you to go.'

Furiously I stepped forward. 'Please Aunt. All is not as it seems. Surely there is no harm in Noble remaining in the shed. Let us discuss this tomorrow when we've all had time to calm down.' My voice became stern. 'And it is your decision to make, not Isaiah's.'

She narrowed her eyes, deep in thought. 'Very well then Effie, Noble can stay for tonight.' She hesitated. 'But I'm not sure about any longer.' Nodding her head, she reluctantly turned her gaze to Noble. 'Leave us now please and do not enter the house until I give you permission. Do you understand Noble?'

'Yes Constance.' He edged his way slowly away and headed down the hallway to the front door. 'Thank you for allowing me to stay, I'm extremely sorry to have caused you such grief.' Looking sorrowful he glanced from me to my Aunt. 'I bid you goodnight.'

I watched forlornly as he left.

'Good riddance, that's what I say.' Mumbled Isaiah. 'Completely unstable.' He took my Aunt's arm. 'Go and take a seat in the living room Constance, I shall make us both a strong tea.' He chuckled. 'I think we're in need of one.' He took a sideways glance at me. 'You look tired Effelia. Perhaps you should get an early night.'

'Your father is right Effie; you do look rather weary.' She approached me and gently kissed me on the cheek. 'Go upstairs and get a good night's rest, everything will seem clearer in the morning.'

I watched as she wobbled slightly towards the living room and went through the door. Isaiah was lurking behind me.

'Well dear daughter, what an eventful day we have all had.' He sniggered. 'Would you like your Aunt to bring you a delicious sugary sweet cup of tea, once I've made it?'

'No thank you.' I replied bluntly as I headed for the stairs. 'Oh, and Isaiah. If you even think of harming Noble in his sleep tonight, I promise you most emphatically that your life will no longer be worth living.'

With a deep sigh I ascended the stairs.

It wasn't until I heard Isaiah's ponderous footsteps coming up the stairs that I sneaked quietly back down. Wrapping my dressing gown tightly around me I went and huddled in the armchair by the fireplace. I'm not sure how long I remained there, staring into the coldness of the unlit grate; without thinking I picked up the poker and moved it around in the coals, as if I were putting out the dying embers. Despondently I moved over to the bay window, staring out at the grey mass of storm clouds looming threateningly close by, and as I watched the lightening play across the sky, my thoughts turned to Isaiah and how it was becoming crystal clear he was responsible for everything that had gone wrong in my life. My anger had culminated to such a degree that I now detested him with every fibre of my body. Gilbert was no longer the root of all evil this title now belonged to Isaiah. There was no more time left to linger, no more time to waste on idle chatter, mulling over what to do for the best; the time had come to take action, for there was no going back now from what had happened today, matters had finally come to a head.

I didn't hear him at first; he crept so quietly across the floor, like a hovering ghost skulking in the shadows.

'What is it Isaiah?' I asked curtly. Not bothering to look at him.

'Oh Effelia, you did give me a start.' He exclaimed in a panicked voice. 'I thought we had a burglar in the house.' His voice became more controlled. 'Can you not sleep?'

'No, the storm is keeping me awake.' I replied nonchalantly.

'Yes, it is rather frightful.' He laughed apprehensively. 'It's been quite an eventful day hasn't it, what with one thing and another.'

Not wishing to respond I continued to gaze out the window, watching the rain beat down on the pane.

He cleared his throat. 'I...I take back my preposterous statement of this afternoon. Of course I won't kill Noble, or burn down the shed.' He was laughing as he spoke. 'And I can assure you I wasn't seriously going to shoot him. However, you know he doesn't belong here. He's lost and desperate, so much so that he'll cling onto anything to ease his pain.' He laid his hand on my shoulder, and when he spoke his tone was cold and unfeeling. 'Now your Aunt is aware of the absolute truth she understands what must be done.'

I swung round to face him. 'The absolute truth?'

'I warned Constance about Noble's severe mental problems, how he has a tendency to erupt into anger and lash out violently.' He chuckled. 'As she witnessed first-hand earlier on this evening.'

I flinched, moving forward to escape his hand, which was still firmly pressed on my shoulder. 'Yes, but my Aunt doesn't realise that Noble was acting in self-defence, and he doesn't have any mental problems, as you well know.'

120

'Forgive me Effelia but what do you really know of this man? He appeared from nowhere and invaded your life when you were at your most vulnerable, and now he lurks around you like a leech. It's just not normal.' He sighed and bowed his head as if in torment. 'I therefore had no choice but to call The Manor.'

Just hearing that name filled me with dread. 'What?' My eyes widened in astonishment. 'You...you want Noble to go to The Manor?'

'Well yes, I've warned my good friend Dr Stirling to expect a new patient tomorrow morning; they have a bed available. Noble only needs to spend a little while there, just until he's stabilised.' He looked beseechingly into my eyes. 'The Manor is the greatest mental intuition in the county. Your Aunt and I believe it's the best solution for everyone.' A simpering smile spread across his face. 'And when he's fully recovered, the both of you can be together.'

His face was remarkably composed considering he was lying through his back teeth. I knew only too well that in the event of Noble becoming an occupant of The Manor that Isaiah would see to it that my friend was institutionalised for many years to come, and he had no intention of the two of us being together.

He searched my face for a response. 'Well. What is your opinion Effelia?

I pretended to be deep in thought, deliberating over his diabolical suggestion. 'Mmm. So, the only other alternative would be for Noble to leave Rawlings first thing tomorrow morning, never to return?'

'That's certainly an option. But you must understand that if this is to be so, he must not contact you ever again, he must sever all ties with you Effelia.' He began to pace the room looking agitated. 'Your Aunt and I have agreed that either way he must be off our property by noon tomorrow.' He leant in close to me, his expression full of pity. 'We're doing it to protect you Effelia, to prevent you from becoming harmed in any way shape or form. Surely that is a good enough reason.'

I bit down hard on my bottom lip. 'Yes, yes you are right Isaiah.' Trying to remain calm I rose and crossed the room, heading for the door, oblivious to the loud clap of thunder reverberating overhead. 'Please allow me to sleep on it, and I shall give you my decision first thing tomorrow.' Without looking at him I opened the door and casually strolled out, knowing he was watching me like a hawk.

How much I relish those quiet moments of peaceful contemplation when you're lying in bed in the silence of the night; it's the easiest thing in the world to close your eyes and cast your thoughts to nothing; to allow yourself to drift without restraint or care to a pleasant, if somewhat imaginary world. However, on this particular night my mind wasn't allowed the luxury of dreaming; for it had become apparent, after my talk with Isaiah a moment ago, that I needed to finalise my plan by tomorrow morning; even though Isaiah's suggestion of placing Noble in a mental asylum was completely farcical, it was nevertheless a stark warning of the present situation, and yet another reminder that the time had come to go on our journey. As sadly the only way to keep Noble at Rawlings would be for Isaiah to conveniently disappear from our lives this very night, something I knew would never happen, not if my Aunt had anything to do with it; Isaiah had his claws in her so deep that she would never listen to me, and even in the unlikely event that I managed to talk her into allowing Noble to stay in our home, with Isaiah lurking about it was only a matter of time before something terrible happened to Noble: it would be a tragic accident that was unforeseen, such as losing his footing and plummeting over a cliff, or falling into the path of a train or bus, or perhaps he would fall asleep one night then mysteriously never wake up. But it didn't matter what method was used as the result would still be the same-Noble would be dead. Of course, there was always the option to dispose of Isaiah, but as tempting as that seemed I wouldn't allow myself, or Noble to resort to murder, even if my father did deserve it. Knowing that Noble had nearly

122

succeeded in killing him this evening made me shudder, for he wasn't a murderer, he was too good for that.

Over the past few weeks, I now know I had been delaying the inevitable, pushing it away like an unwanted thought, and I hadn't been the only one guilty of this, Noble too had hardly mentioned leaving Rawlings, he seemed happy and settled. But however right everything felt, I knew the both of us could never truly be happy until we had found what we were looking for, and that could only be achieved by going back to the land where Noble came from, to where his brother Gideon lived. And only then could we finally find an answer to where our future lay, and who with....

Feeling restless I clambered out of bed and went over and sat on the windowsill, gazing out at the lightening ricocheting across the night sky. Sighing, I thought of how there'd be no more idle days of ease with Noble, pottering around the garden, or pleasant strolls along the promenade, or searching for bargains in antiques shops, or having tea and scones in Hudson's café. However, the biggest wrench of all would be leaving Aunt. I had already left her in the lurch once before, and now I was going to do it again to the poor woman. And yet however heart-breaking it would be I knew deep in my soul that it was something I had to do.

Oddly enough, gazing out at the thunderstorm seemed to help me focus, giving me a strange clarity, and almost instantaneously a solution popped up in my head. The plan I'd devised to take Isaiah with us was simple and straightforward and involved very little effort; of course, in reality it may not run as smoothly as I was hoping for, but I could only pray that it did.

After tiptoeing out to the back garden, I briefly relayed my plan to Noble, who appeared completely unfazed by my decision. After the happenings of today he must have been prepared for what was about to happen, he knew we had to leave.

I returned to my room and lay back against my pillows, listening to the constant lull of falling rain and the gentle rumbling of distant thunder from the summer storm. Just before I drifted off, I reflected on the afternoon's garden party, of the fake engagement, and as I turned the ring round and round on my finger a tingle of excitement ran through me.

# Chapter 10

Last night's storm had blown over and the morning sun was bright with promise. I took it as a good omen for the day ahead. My Aunt had left Rawlings early to help set up the bazaar at the church hall, and she would be gone most of the day. I made a point of rising early so as not to miss her, giving her a warm embrace. She seemed concerned about my welfare, about me spending time with Noble, and urged me to go along with Isaiah's suggestion of having him committed; I of course, not wanting to upset her, pretended to accept this absurd idea, for I didn't wish to leave on a bad note. Tearfully I watched her amble up the gravel path with her basket, and continued staring at her until she was out of sight amongst the trees up ahead. I didn't want to do this to her again, leave without a word or explanation, but I had little choice. Of course, if we couldn't find the portal at the abbey then I would return and she would be none the wiser, but if we were successful then I could be absent for some time. I decided to leave a letter with Clarice's mother, with instructions to pass it onto my Aunt in the event of me failing to show up in the next few days. It wasn't much of a note and failed to the go into great detail, but it was from the heart....

*Dearest Aunt*
*    I am so dreadfully sorry but I've had to go away again on a trip that is essential. Noble and I found something of great importance in the ledger that we believe can lead us to his true home. Please don't be angry that I have accompanied him, it was my choice. I have to find out for myself what awaits me in this other land.*

*Isaiah is also travelling with us; he is dangerous Aunt and had to be removed from Rawlings before something dreadful happened.*

*How long I will be absent I cannot say, but I WILL return as soon as I am able. Promise me you will carry on with your normal life and don't worry about me, I shall be safe and well.*

*Love always,*
*Effie xxxx*


One of Isaiah's daily routines was having tea and toast for breakfast whilst reading the newspaper. Slipping the sleeping draught into his drink was so easy, the taste would be disguised with the vast amount of sugar he always added, and just like myself when I'd been held prisoner in that awful room at his house, he would be oblivious. My only concern was how much of the draught to use, I wasn't exactly an expert on these matters. So, after much deliberation, I poured in half the sachet, and with bated breath took a seat opposite him, patiently waiting for the draught to take effect.

'I trust you've seen sense and informed Noble that he must leave the premises.' He said, peering at me from underneath his spectacles. 'Otherwise I shall inform The Manor immediately.'

'Yes, Noble is packing this very minute.' I answered in a clear voice. 'So, when did you discover he was staying in the shed?' I muttered, watching him sip his tea.

Isaiah frowned. 'Just before the garden party, I noticed him sneaking about in there.' He snorted. 'So, I decided it would be amusing to pretend to discover him when all the guests had arrived.' His face darkened. 'A decision I now regret, considering what happened.'

For one breathtakingly tense moment I watched as he tapped the side of his cup with his fingers and carefully scrutinized my face, but then thankfully he gulped back the rest of his tea. 'You are acting too complacent, what are you up to? He mumbled. 'Your face always gives you away Effelia, and right this minute it's a lovely shade of crimson.' He chuckled. 'Don't tell me you really love this boy?'

I was just trying to think of a feasible reply when I saw him stumble and fall forward against the table, knocking over the teapot and cups.

'I... I'm feeling rather unwell.' His speech sounded slurred. 'What have you done to me?

'It's just a sleeping tonic Isaiah.' I said in a reticent voice.' Rather like the one you gave me.'

Somehow, he managed to sit back down. 'Where, where did you get it from?' He asked in a slow voice.'

Calmly I began tidying the table. 'I took it from you Isaiah, from your wardrobe.'

His head lulled forward. 'There was poison there too, what... what if you got the wrong one?'

'I knelt forward and whispered in his ear. 'Well I suppose we shall soon find out, won't we Isaiah.' I patted him on the head. 'Now why don't you rest, why I prepare for our journey.'

He groaned. 'Effelia...what are you doing?'

'I'm taking you away Isaiah, far, far away from Rawlings, where you can't interfere and destroy people's lives. You see dear father I know all about your evil scheming.' I sat down next to him. 'I'm very much afraid that the sweet, potent bouquet that you so lovingly placed in my pillow to make me forget all the despicable acts you've committed is no longer having its desired effect. I remember pretty much everything now. How you drugged me and held me captive, how you sold my paintings without my permission, how you made me believe Mace had moved away and married, when in fact you disposed of both him and Clarice, and now they are trapped in another time and place. You then, in your infinite wisdom, decided to destroy the portal, thus preventing anyone returning home, including my mother, whose life you have already ruined. Then of course there is the worst possible crime of all – murder. The Davenport sisters didn't stand a chance did they, not with you as their friend. You callously extinguished their lives. And Mace's foster parents, I know you were responsible for their deaths too.' I glanced at him. 'Would you like me to continue?'

He was completely comatose now, gently snoring with his head on the table. I stood over him for a while, contemplating if I should go and get the gun from his room and shoot him. By doing so I would be ridding this world and other worlds of this odious man; Abercrombie would become a safer place to live, and in time my Aunt and her friends would acclimatise to life without their saviour. His demise would cause the enchantment that he held over my Aunt to be severed. It would be beneficial to everyone.

A loud bang caused me to jump, bringing me to my senses. Noble was standing in the doorframe, staring at me. 'You did it then.' He said with a grin. 'I'm impressed fiancée.'

My face reddened. 'Please Noble do not call me that.' I twiddled the ring on my finger. 'And yes, after the announcement you made yesterday at the garden party and the fact you almost killed Isaiah, and that it was witnessed by my Aunt was quite sufficient enough to force me into coming up with a speedy idea.'

He looked gruffly at me 'Yes, well if I'd not acted quickly and snatched the gun from him, he would surely have murdered me. And as for the garden party, when Isaiah discovered me in the shed, he would have shot me had it not been for me yelling at the top of my voice that I was your fiancée, the guests wouldn't have heard and he wouldn't have been forced to go and introduce me.' His expression was bleak. 'Instead you'd be arranging my funeral.'

'Oh, don't say that Noble. Besides, he wouldn't have been foolish enough to shoot you in the shed, the sound of gunshot would make an awful racket.'

'Your father would have muffled it with a cushion or something, and even if the guests were to hear a gunshot you must know how well practised he is at getting himself out of sticky situations.'

Staring down onto the sleeping Isaiah, I pictured him shooting Noble then telling everyone it was self-defence; he would pretend to be devastated and feebly explain to the guests how he'd discovered an intruder in the shed; how convincingly he would justify his actions and make out there had been a scuffle between the two of them and without warning the gun had accidentally gone off.

I avoided his eyes and began to clear away the breakfast dishes, carefully rinsing Isaiah's cup. 'Yes, I suppose so. Either way he would have disposed of you sooner or later.' I sighed.

Noble roughly pulled back Isaiah's arms and bound his hands together tightly with the rope. 'Of that I have no doubt.' His voice lowered. 'You've got his gun, haven't you?'

'I'm going to get it from his room.' I said. 'I know where he keeps it. I've got everything else we need in my rucksack, including the ledger.' I hesitated. 'You grab his arms and I'll take his legs.' I suddenly envisaged my Aunt returning early and seeing what we'd done. 'Actually no, let me drive the car around to the front first, that way we won't have to carry him too far, and it will be quicker.'

Without waiting for a reply, I rushed out to the garage, and clambered into the car I had driven home that time, the car left at Browning's Wood, as I could see the keys conveniently lying there on the dashboard. The keys to my own car were somewhere in my room and I didn't have time to find them. With shaking hands, I put them in the ignition, but in my haste, they dropped to the floor. Mumbling under my breath I reached down and begun searching under the seat until my hand grabbed something, but it wasn't the keys, it was a pendant with an ornately carved figure of a bird, similar to an eagle. So mesmerising was the necklace that I imagined I was stepping into a dream, a dream of Gideon and the darkness of the forest. He was looking at me with his large, bewitching sable eyes, staring into my very soul. I gasped and remembered with sorrow and joy how he'd given me the pendant before I'd left him. Somehow when I'd arrived home it must have become loose in the car, where it lay forgotten, under the seat. Pressing it close to my chest I sighed, and feeling wistful I allowed my thoughts to momentarily linger upon this precious memory that had lain dormant in the deepest, darkest corner of my mind for so long. Then, shaking my head I carefully placed the pendant around my neck, retrieved the keys and started the engine. I began to regret my decision of not taking the train, but how we'd manage to board a train with an unconscious man would be risky. I suppose we could tell the ticket inspector he was drunk, although I rather suspect this would get us removed from the train. There were a few other likely options swimming about in my mind but it was too late now to try, for we were already to leave, and I had a fear of Isaiah waking up and causing trouble.

After we'd bundled Isaiah into the back of the car I rushed upstairs and got the gun from his room. Quite by accident I came across the parcel he had been so careful to keep a secret, swiftly I tore the package open, and under several layers of tissue I discovered a toy train set. I sat there on the floor for a few moments trying to think why he would have purchased such a thing. With an exasperated sigh I stuffed the parcel back in the wardrobe.

As we left Rawlings I drove rather wobbly up the gravel drive, instantly reminding me of how very much I detested driving, it was one of those tasks in life that I found extremely unpleasant; it was such an ordeal for me to fully focus my concentration on the road, rather than gazing out the window at the scenery thinking of other things, and invariably I would find myself taking the wrong turn; Noble had no knowledge of how to drive and Mace wasn't here to take the steering wheel. I also had the added worry of the sleeping Isaiah on the back seat, an unnecessary distraction I could do without, for although I tried to convince myself I was doing the right thing, part of me felt guilty for putting him to sleep, and the entire situation made me jittery, especially when I glanced in the mirror and noticed how Noble sat rigidly on the back seat next to my father, glaring menacingly towards him with the gun clutched in his hand.

On the way out of Abercrombie I dropped in to see Clarice's mother and gave her the note for my Aunt, asking her only to deliver it if I failed to return within a few days. And peering into her sleep deprived eyes I did my best to reassure her that I would try and find her daughter, Clarice.

The abbey was as remote as I'd remembered, and although falling into ruin, the brown stoned building still held a sturdy romantic elegance about it, and as is often the way with historic buildings, the ruin emanated a certain mysterious aura, with its silent towering walls, shadowy corners and ghostly stillness; one only had to close their eyes to be taken back over time and imagine the secrets that were concealed within the crumbling walls, forgotten secrets of a long, lost age ago.

'According to the ledger the monk should appear when dusk descends and when the sweet smell of perfume materializes in the air.' Noble said, peering closely at the ledger. 'It also mentions the occurrence of bees.' He snapped the ledger shut and passed it to me. 'You should take this Effie; it belongs in your safe keeping.'

We both turned to stare at Isaiah as he let out a long, drawn out yawn. He had awoken soon after our arrival and Noble had reluctantly helped him to a nearby bench.

'If you ask me that ledger is nothing but a curse on humanity, the sooner it's destroyed the better.' Isaiah exclaimed with a yawn, manoeuvring himself to get comfortable on the bench.

'Well no one is asking you Isaiah, are they?' Noble responded gruffly. He turned towards me. 'If I have to spend any more time in this man's company then I shall be the one committing a crime.'

Isaiah smirked at him. 'The feeling is entirely mutual, why don't you go and crawl away into some hole.'

'Ignore him Noble, he's just trying to antagonise you on purpose.'

Isaiah chuckled.

As Noble started to march over to Isaiah, with a furious look on his face, I swiftly intervened by grabbing his arm. 'Come on Noble, go and wait over there on the grass and rest for a while. I'll call you as soon as something happens.'

His face softened a little and he sighed. 'Here, you should take the gun.' Holding it carefully, he passed it towards me. 'Use it on him at the first sign of trouble.'

Isaiah huffed.

An expression of shock crossed over my face. 'I'm sure that won't be necessary, especially with his hands bound. But I shall take it all the same.' My face broke into a smile. 'Now off with you.'

Taking my hand in his he began to swing it from side to side. 'Don't run off anywhere without me, will you?' He grinned then slowly made his way over to the grassed area surrounding the abbey.

Feeling myself blush I placed the ledger in my rucksack and went to join Isaiah, ensuring I was sitting on the furthest edge away from him. Fleetingly, I glanced over at Noble, who was now lying back on the grassy bank, with his arms folded behind his head, his eyes closed. Seeing him there one could almost believe he didn't have a care in the world, he was happily visiting the sites and enjoying the remains of the sun before returning to his normal home and normal life.

I was hastily brought back to reality by the sound of Isaiah.

'That boy is besotted with you. It makes me nauseous just to watch him.'

With a short, nervous laugh I turned to him in surprise. 'I hardly think so Isaiah, you must be imagining it.'

He grunted. 'I don't think so. 'That engagement stunt wasn't a complete sham, was it? That uncouth ignoramus really does want to marry you.' He sneered.

'Look I don't want to discuss Noble.' I exclaimed sharply. 'There are matters I need clearing up before...' I hesitated. 'Before we leave, I may not have another chance.'

'What is it Effelia that seems to be puzzling you so much?' he exclaimed sardonically. How can I enlighten you.'

'Agnes Davenport's mysterious fall down her staircase, you pushed her, didn't you?'

Isaiah glared at me indignantly. 'How can you be so callous Effelia, I merely gave her a helping hand to the top of the stairs and quite by accident she must have tripped over my foot and toppled all the way to the bottom.' He paused, looking thoughtful. 'I actually did her a favour, old age is such a curse, and in the case of dear Agnes she was glad to leave this world and join her sister.' He chuckled. 'A smidgen sooner than I'd anticipated but after the shattering news that we may lose Rawlings I was forced to take matters into my own hands.'

I gawped at him. 'What are you saying Isaiah?'

'I'm saying that Agnes Davenport, is inadvertently responsible for saving Rawlings.' He gazed ahead dreamily. 'That sweet, wise old lady had the foresight to change her will some months ago; instead of leaving her entire estate and savings to some random cats charity she decided to bestow her riches on a poor, humble man such as I.'

To startled to say a word, all I could do was stare at him with my mouth ajar.

'Of course, Agnes had absolutely no idea that Rawlings was in financial difficulty, it didn't seem fitting to share our money troubles with an outsider. No, she merely felt it justifiable to entrust her inheritance in the safe keeping of her loyal friend.'

I must have sat there for a few minutes, unable to speak or move. It mystified me how he had the power to charm his way so ingratiatingly into people's lives, and steal away their money as well as their lives.

Dazed I got up and stood in front of him, with my back turned. 'And so, you would allow my Aunt to unwittingly use the money on the house.' My hand reached into my back pocket to check the gun was still safe. 'Because if my Aunt knew the truth, she would never permit it, she would be disgusted and appalled at using blood money to save Rawlings.'

He sniggered. 'That is why you and I will never tell her. Thanks to me your precious Aunt Constance can remain in her childhood home, rather than some grotty, rented accommodation that she undoubtedly would've had to eventually reside in. You surely wouldn't wish to inflict that misery upon your Aunt, would you Effelia?'

Furiously I swung around to face him. 'Of course not.' I retorted, bluntly. 'But I can't live in a house that's been tainted with evil.'

'I have a simple, very effective remedy for that.' He wiggled on the bench, trying to move his hands. 'Please unbind me

Effelia, let me go and all will be forgiven. We can go home and put all this unpleasantness behind us.'

'Huh.' I exclaimed with a laugh. 'So, you can administer another one of your memory potions and I can spend the foreseeable future in a perpetual cloud of forgetfulness.' I tilted my head to the side. 'What a lovely notion.'

'Please don't be sarcastic Effelia, it really doesn't become you.' He flinched as a bee suddenly flew past his head. 'You may not agree with my methods, but everything I've done has been necessary to protect you from this hazardous world. Ever since you were a child and that puerile boy harassed you at school, I've been taking care of you.' I removed the problem then, just like I can remove the problem now.' He inclined his head over to Noble, who appeared to be asleep. 'If it wasn't for his arrival in Abercrombie you'd be happily married to Duncan, and all this nonsense of going to another world would be long behind us.' He sighed deeply. 'We'd all be residing at Rawlings as one big, happy family.'

I bowed my head and let my mind drift for a moment.

'Duncan still loves you, I'm sure of it.' Isaiah said in a soothing voice. 'It's not too late for the two of you.' He whispered. 'Untie me and give me the gun Effelia.'

For a split second I was almost tempted to do as he said, but then I came to my senses.

'Please stop trying to trick me Isaiah, it won't work.' I gulped and stood there, puzzling over something he'd just said. 'The boy from school- did you mean Mace?'

'Sadly no, that idiotic friend of yours Mace was a whole lot harder to dispose of. That boy just wouldn't give in an admit defeat.' Isaiah began to mumble under his breath. 'Stubborn like his mother.'

'Then who?' I uttered, completely perplexed.

He pursed his lips. 'That ghastly child who kept tugging your hair and calling you names, do you not remember?'

A stark, cold blanket of realisation crept slowly over my heart. I began to tremble. 'There, there was a boy.' I narrowed my eyes. 'His name was Abel Hannigon, and yes he used to yank my hair and call me Faraway Farraday.' I gulped. 'He also used to pinch me really hard.' My eyes began to mist over. 'One day he went missing, and as I recall there was a search party out every week for months, but he was never found.' Shaking I turned to face Isaiah. 'You can't mean him, can you?' my voice was unsteady. 'Please tell me you weren't responsible.

There was a long pause.

'You used to come home in floods of tears.' He looked beseechingly at me. 'Can't you see I had to do something?'

'What, what did you do?' I whimpered. 'Did you kill him?'

'No.' bellowed Isaiah, glaring at me in the face then slowly lowering his eyes, he looked at the ground as if in shame. 'I sent him through the gateway.' His voice was quiet and without emotion. 'So, you see there's a chance he's still alive, just like the boy and Clarice.'

'I know what a thoroughly despicable man you are, but even I didn't think you capable of such a crime.' I screamed at him. 'Abel Hannigon was just a child, not a very nice one I grant you but he didn't deserve to be taken to another dimension and left to rot. And, and what about his poor parents, how they must have suffered all these years, not knowing the fate of their son.' I reached in my back pocket and pulled out the gun and pointed it unsteadily at Isaiah's head. 'There's only one punishment for you Isaiah, and that is death. This is the only way to rid all worlds of such a foul monster.' I declared.

Isaiah started to whimper. 'Please Effelia, think what you are doing.' He fell forward onto his knees and then began to laugh nervously. 'I know you're just trying to scare me; you wouldn't really shoot me.'

'For what you have done, yes I would.' I screamed at him.

Without warning a rapid swarm of insects suddenly caused me to flinch and drop the gun, and it was only then I realised they were bees. They flew simultaneously around my head then drifted off towards the abbey. I gazed at them in astonishment as they dipped and circled throughout the ruin in perfect unison then disappeared up into the darkening sky. An unexplained aroma of roses began to fill the air; I closed my eyes and allowed myself to be momentarily taken away on a fragrant wave of ghostly intrigue.

'Effie, it's time.' Yelled Noble, running over towards us. His eyes grew wide for a second as he saw Isaiah cowering on the ground. 'We must leave now Isaiah, get up.'

'No, I'm not going, you can't force me.' Isaiah cried. 'You and Effelia go, but leave me, I'm a weak old man who's too sickly to travel.' He began to cough violently.

Coming to my senses, I hastily picked up my rucksack and retrieved the gun from the grass, only to have Noble immediately snatch it from me.

I glared at him in annoyance, but said nothing.

Noble grabbed Isaiah by the jumper, forcing him up.

'Nice try, old man, but your complaining is just an act.' He shoved him roughly forward and pressed the gun up against the back of his head. 'Move.'

I didn't see it very clearly at first, only an indistinct cloud of vapour appearing from the crumbling stone, but then gradually the mist began to mass in one particular spot, forming the shape of an object, a cloaked like figure. It was the monk, just as the ledger had predicted. I watched in strange fascination, as he remained stationary for a moment, hovering ahead, waiting for us. I tried to catch a glimpse of his face but it was shrouded in the billowing cloth of the hooded cloak; I told myself it was hidden from sight for a reason, and if I looked upon the features of his face it would haunt my thoughts forever.

'Come on, he's waiting for us to follow.' Whispered Noble.

'No, no please don't take me with you. I shall not survive the journey.' Isaiah muttered in a shaky voice. 'It shall be my undoing.'

Ignoring him, Noble pushed him forward.

The monk turned and gradually drifted up a flight of steep, narrow steps that appeared so hazardous that I wondered if they would fall apart as soon as we stood upon them.

Noble felt for my hand and gave it a squeeze. 'Don't worry, those steps have been there for many years, they'll not collapse.

I gave him a little smile, contemplating if he could read my mind. I quickly however, came to the conclusion that it was my startled expression giving me away. Aunt would always tease me about it, saying how my face was readable as an open book.

'You expect me to climb up there without the use of my hands?' Isaiah complained, bitterly.

'Perhaps we should untie him.' I uttered. 'For now.'

'Very well, Noble said reluctantly, beginning to untie Isaiah's bound hands. 'But any trouble and I shall tie you back up immediately.'

'Huh.' Exclaimed Isaiah.

Carefully we began moving up the narrow steps, supporting ourselves by clinging to the ancient brickwork, praying it didn't subside, and before long we'd managed to reach the top. The ghostly monk floated onwards through a doorway and across a floorless room to a large, open brick fireplace, where it drifted through and disappeared from sight.

Isaiah began muttering under his breath. 'We can't, we can't reach over there.' His voice became louder. 'The entire floor has gone. Surely we must abandon this ludicrous journey.'

'Hush, old man.' Noble hissed at him. 'We shall simply go round.' He pointed at the few bricks that remained, forming a narrow ledge along the outer wall.

'There's just enough space to walk.'

'Are you mad as well as stupid boy?' Exclaimed Isaiah. 'We shall surely plunge to our deaths.'

Noble's face became red with rage. 'That's why you're going to test it first.'

'Perhaps Isaiah is right Noble. It does look rather unsafe.' I gripped his arm. 'Is there another way?'

'Effie, this is the only way, He looked at me unwaveringly. 'The only way home.'

Isaiah threw Noble a look of disgust. 'So, you would risk the life of your beloved just to attempt to get to another world that most likely will be impossible to locate.' He sniggered at him. 'And even if you do, it won't guarantee your happiness.' He looked intently at him. 'Better to stay in a land where you are safe, where you can find peace with my daughter.'

My face became flushed. 'Please Isaiah stop referring to Noble and I in those terms.' I lowered my eyes to the ground, not wishing to meet Noble's gaze.

A deathly silence followed.

'The gateway isn't going to stay open for long.' Noble exclaimed, stepping forward and handing me the gun. 'This is our one chance.' He looked solemnly down at the ground, and then gazed at me intently. 'I wish for you to travel with me more than anything Effie, but...but I'll understand if you feel you must remain here.' Continuing to stare he reached out his hand. 'Are you coming with me?'

My unexpected hesitance was extremely exasperating, for I had certainly considered the dangers of this journey, and up until now had felt prepared for it, or so it would seem. But now a sensation of sheer panic had materialised from nowhere, engulfing me in a chilly blanket of fear.

Trembling, I began to shake my head. 'Noble, I don't know...I'm just not sure.'

His expression was filled with agony, and then a flicker of tenderness appeared within his eyes. 'If you stay then so shall I. My place is by your side.'

I was becoming frustrated. 'But what about Isaiah?' I exclaimed loudly. 'We can't take him back to Abercrombie.'

Isaiah groaned and rolled his eyes.

Noble's face looked stern. 'We don't have to take him back. All this can be ended now.'

I swallowed hard and gazed down at the gun in my hand. 'You...you mean here at the abbey.'

Noble reply was short and direct. 'Yes.'

Isaiah began to laugh nervously. 'What on earth are you both muttering about? If you're thinking about doing away with me then I strongly suggest you banish such a fatuous notion from your thoughts. If I disappear, you'll have the Chief Inspector onto you immediately.' He sneered at Noble. 'I've already informed him of how you attempted to shoot me last night, and how Constance was a witness. And I've also told him how I believe you've been plotting my murder for a while now, and will no doubt try again.'

Noble glowered at him. 'I really don't care.'

A sudden cold chill spilled out from the empty fire and spread across the ruin, and as I glanced over, I was stunned to see the faded outline of the monk, hovering in the fireplace. Perhaps he had returned to see why we hadn't followed him, perhaps it was a sign to indicate we needed to go. Either way his sudden re-appearance had woken me up, and shaken me to my senses. I would put a halt to this foolish behaviour of mine, and stick to the original plan.

I watched disconcertedly as Noble whispered in my ear. 'I promise it will be quick. Just a little push, is all that is needed.'

'Wait.' I screamed in rather a hysterical sounding voice. 'We should go through the gateway.' For an instant I glanced back at Isaiah. 'It's the right thing to do.'

A hot, sweaty hand touched mine, attempting to snatch the gun. 'Please Effelia you are allowing your emotions to cloud your judgement. Can't you see he's using you? Go with him now and you will bitterly regret it.'

'No, no I won't.' Swiftly I pulled my hand away before he could reach for the weapon. 'The only thing I would truly regret would be allowing you to remain at Rawlings and having to endure your poisonous ways. Now I'm leaving, and you are coming with us.' I shakily held the gun and pointed it at his chest. 'Otherwise I shall have no option but to shoot you.'

Isaiah began to laugh hysterically. 'You haven't got the guts.'

Despite his amusement I sensed an air of nervousness in his voice.

'Wouldn't I? I uttered. 'Perhaps I shall shoot you in the foot for starters, just so you know I'm serious.' I pointed the gun down towards his feet. 'I imagine it would be rather painful.'

Isaiah's spoke rapidly and rather high-pitched. 'Very well, I shall do as you say.'

Noble was standing close to me now, his face etched with concern. 'Are you sure about this Effie?

I nodded decisively at him.

He smiled tenderly at me. 'I'm so glad.'

'Well I'm not. This is suicide.' Moaned Isaiah.

139

'Come on old man, you go first.' Noble got hold of him and began dragging him forward in front of me, onto the ledge.

Isaiah grunted. 'This is utterly absurd.' He mumbled something inaudible under his breath as Noble began pushing him along. 'Alright, alright, I'm going.' He exclaimed in an impatient voice. 'Surely there must be an easier route than this one.'

As I watched Isaiah slowly shuffle his way along the ledge, I placed the gun in my rucksack and began following on behind Noble.

'Here, take my hand Effie.' Said Noble, as he kept a close eye on Isaiah. 'Watch your step.'

It wasn't an easy path to take with the ledge being so narrow and crumbling with decay, and several times I nearly lost my footing. However, we managed to cross along it without any harm, and before very long found ourselves standing before the fireplace. The monk had all but vanished now apart from the folds of his billowing robes that lingered inexplicably in the gateway. I pondered what would happen if I reached out and touched them.

'Ready?' Noble asked in a serene voice, still clutching my hand.

I gulped. 'Yes, I said in an unsteady voice. 'Should we allow Isaiah to go first?'

Noble glanced at Isaiah. 'Yes, age before beauty.'

Isaiah looked stunned. 'Well I...'

With lightning speed Noble shoved him forward and I heard a muffled scream escape Isaiah's lips as he disappeared from sight within the fireplace.

'Let's go through together.'

I suppose I should have been petrified but with Noble by my side all my anxieties seemed to wash away, and confidently we both moved forward, through the gateway and into another world.

# Chapter 11

Going through a portal is such a strange sensation that it's difficult to explain what you are feeling. The time before had been turbulent and violent, and I had to endure it all alone. However, this experience was vastly different. I wasn't caught up in a whirlpool, being tossed through the air like a rag doll. It was exactly like strolling into another room, and this time I had company, I had Noble.

I gasped in surprise as we walked forward, happy to feel the ground beneath my feet. My joy was however short lived as I took in my surroundings. In a dream like state I glanced around, hoping to see magnificent landscape that would take my breath away, but to my horror I felt blinded, hampered by the impenetrable fog that engulfed us. The grove came to mind, the spellbinding power of its atmosphere that had caused me to become shrouded in a peculiar, dense mist and had very nearly claimed my life when I sank into a deadly bog. Gideon had pulled me out that night and I remember how he'd told me the tale of the pixies and how travellers crossing their lands angered them. But this wasn't the same as the grove, there was no entrancement, and no familiar voices of loved ones calling out. An overwhelming feeling of loneliness and despair flooded through my mind as I breathed in the clammy air, I choked on it as it rushed down my throat, finding it hard to breathe.

'See what you've done, see where you've stranded us.' Isaiah shrieked in complete panic. He collapsed to the ground.

'Where are we?' I asked in a hoarse voice. 'Where has the monk gone?'

'It appears he has deserted us.' Noble gulped. 'And I'm not entirely sure where we are but it seems we've arrived in an interface between two worlds.' He replied in a distant voice.

'What does that mean exactly?' I asked perplexed.

'It's a link between this world and another world.' He paused. 'We need to find the end of the link.

'How? I shouted. This fog is everywhere.' I hunched down onto the damp ground and wrapped my arms about my body.

'You've brought us to hell.' Exclaimed Isaiah rather loudly.

'Sshh, keep your voice down. They will hear you.' Noble said in an emotionless voice.

'They, who are they?' I asked in alarm.

'They are the lost souls of dead travellers who are marooned here. They will want us to join them.' Mumbled Isaiah in a monotone voice. He nudged my arm. 'Look, they are coming.'

I gasped in pure fright. Not wanting to look but unable to prevent myself I glanced ahead through the thick mist. At first, I saw nothing but then the faint outline of gathering figures emerging from nowhere. They looked no more than fragile apparitions; their faces caught in a permanent frown of despair. The fog had cleared a little now and I could just make out a trailing pathway that the travellers seemed to be gliding along, a pathway that came right by us.

'We are doomed.' Cried Isaiah, burying his face in his hands.

'Shut up old man, your comments are not helping.' Noble knelt down beside me and put his arm around my shoulders. 'Keep your head bowed, don't stare at them directly or catch their eye.' I could feel his breath on my face. 'We will be alright Effie, trust me.'

A cold, creeping shadow was sweeping over my heart. 'What are we going to do?'

'Once they have passed by, we must follow the travellers alongside the path, and at the point at where they vanish must be where the path and the link between worlds ends. Once we reach this spot, we should be able to cross over into another realm.

'Are you sure this will lead us to a way out?'

Noble spoke in an unsteady voice. 'No, but we haven't got a choice. Remaining here longer than we need will' He faltered for a second. 'Well, it would not be advisable.'

'Why can't we meet their gaze, will we become like them?'

His face looked grim. 'Yes, to look upon them will cause a strange presence to invade our thoughts and we will be stranded here; even after death takes over, our spirits will linger on, left to wander along the path for all eternity, hopelessly searching for a way out but never finding it.'

'But what happens when they vanish, do they not find a way to escape?'

'It's too late for them, don't you see? As soon as they reach the interface and vanish, they will once more reappear in this awful place, destined to repeat the same journey until the end of time.'

I stared dauntingly at Noble, and then bent my head forward, into the crook of my arm. I tried to envisage remaining in such a place forever, where all that had existed in my old world, and all that had been familiar would have long since passed away in the midst of time; no one would be alive to remember me anymore, no one would care. I had simply disappeared one day and never returned. But I would still be trapped here, left to endlessly roam this prison between worlds like a tormented soul.

I shuddered. 'Let's get out of this place Noble. Noticing how silent Isaiah had become I peered over to where he sat. He was crouching forward, with his hands covering his eyes, muttering away to himself, as if madness had taken him over. 'Before we all become insane.'

Trying not to sob I buried my face into Noble's arm, and waited. For one horrible moment I had the distinct sensation of someone brushing pass me, and the urge to look up was overwhelming, but I feared that by doing so I would look upon death itself.

It seemed ages before Noble tapped me on the shoulder. 'It should be safe to follow them now, they are away ahead.'

'Are you sure?' I asked, too scared to open my eyes.

'Yes, come on.' He whispered, pulling me up. 'Get up Isaiah, unless you wish to remain here of course. Effie and I won't mind if you do.'

Isaiah's face was grey and full of terror. 'Help me, help me Effelia.' His shaking hands reached up for me. 'Please do not desert me in this evil place.

Although Isaiah more than likely deserved to be left here to rot I couldn't bring myself to leave him to such a fate.

'It's okay Isaiah.' I took his hand and yanked him up. 'I'm not going to leave you here.'

He clenched my hands tightly, not letting go. 'Thank you, my dear daughter, thank you.

Noble narrowed his eyes and glared at Isaiah. 'We must hurry, come on.' He said, urgently. 'Time's running out. It won't be long before they return.'

All three of us crept along the pathway, mindful of becoming into close proximity of the lost souls. The fog was swirling around our feet making it difficult to keep to the path, but somehow we managed to follow it. It carried on for some way until each traveller simply vanished at the same part up ahead, until they had all gone.

'Run, it's now or never.' Shouted Noble, no longer worrying about lowering his voice. 'We mustn't lose the location of the link to the other world.

Frantically we all ran towards where the last of the traveller's had passed across. It was only then I noticed how well Isaiah was keeping up, and then I realised his limp appeared to have miraculously healed. Strange how rapidly things could alter once one arrived in another dimension, including one's mind; I thought of my notebook with page after page of treasured memories of home, and knowing it was safely tucked away in my rucksack brought me great comfort.

As we approached the interface there was no time to stop and think what we were doing and where we would end up, no world could be worse than this one. Without hesitation we crossed over.

Seldom had I been so petrified, it crept over me so completely that I began to shake uncontrollably. When it appeared that we had got through, and had escaped the clutches of the evil, haunting place, I felt myself surrounded by the aura of trees, and could sense their ancient wisdom, I was aware of the rustling sounds within their branches, and felt the moisture from their bark upon my face, refreshing my soul.

The soft murmur of voices came from nowhere, but I couldn't understand what they were saying. Everything seemed out of focus, and in my dreamlike state I stumbled forward, my arms outstretched, until I collapsed into someone.

'Effie, Effie we are safe.'

As my vision became clear I realised I'd fallen into the arms of Noble.

'You seem a little disorientated, which is to be expected after our strange journey.'

I leant up against him, trying to regain my senses. 'We made it? Smiling gently at him I let out a sigh of relief. 'I'm so glad.'

'As am I.' He replied in a calm voice.

Glancing around, I saw that we were in a meadow filled with wild flowers, and near to where we stood were two large elm trees.

'Did we enter between the trees?'

'Yes, although it is invisible to the naked eye, there is a gateway.' He frowned. 'We were lucky to get through, as I believe it only opens on occasions.'

'How do you know?'

'Noble's face was etched with confusion. 'I really have no idea. It must be one of those old fables that tend to linger in your mind. Apparently secret entrances between ancient trees is one of the preferred methods of travel by faeries, and on occasions it has been known for humans to discover it by mistake.'

A wave of sadness engulfed me as I thought of those poor, forgotten souls trapped in the other world we had just left.

'So, if we or any other creature was to go back between the trees would we all end up back at that awful place we've just fled?'

'It doesn't work that way. Faeries supposedly sense what paths to take that will lead them to their desired destination, humans however, could find themselves anywhere.'

'Maybe fairyland.' Piped up Isaiah, looking amused. 'Or perhaps we shall see faeries within this meadow.' He cackled. 'You really do speak a load of gobbledegook Noble.'

'Looking infuriated, Noble strode across to Isaiah and hauled him up from the grass. 'There's only one place you'll be going old man, and it certainly won't be as joyous as fairyland.' He swiftly re-bound his hands, pulling the rope extra tight.

'We should carry on moving.' I remarked. 'Before it becomes dark.'

At first, I didn't recognize where we were, however as we emerged from the meadow and I gazed upon the rolling hills, my heart skipped a beat. I don't know how, but to my joy I realised we had arrived in Briarwood, the sleepy village lost in the midst of time, preserved in a blanket of everlastings protectiveness, a place where one could swiftly lose their woes and become immersed in the magical enchantment that lingered all around like an invisible presence. With renewed vigour we travelled southwards through several fields where farmers were tending sheep and then came upon the golden splendour of cornfields. Then I spotted the quaint little church, sheltered amongst the towering yews, and knew that home was nearly in sight.

Noble began to lessen his pace as we approached the path to the cottage, and I detected a faint sign of uneasiness upon his face; I suppose it was to be expected, after being absent for so long, he more than likely wasn't sure what reception he'd receive, although undoubtedly it would be more favourable than mine or Isaiah's.

'What is it Noble?'

'You go ahead with Isaiah, Effie. I...I need to pluck up the courage to...to' His words faltered. 'You know.'

I lightly touched his arm. 'Of course, Noble, your reaction is perfectly natural in the circumstances.' Giving him a reassuring smile, I gently squeezed his hand. 'Come along to the cottage when you feel ready.'

Turning from him, Isaiah and I headed further down the path.

Now the moment of reckoning had finally arrived it seemed unreal, I felt like I had stepped into one of my dreams, and briefly I wished it had been exactly that and no more. As we approached the red-bricked cottage two figures happened to emerge, shaking hands. I immediately recognised one of them as being Caleb, but the other was unfamiliar. They were laughing over something; something I imagine was trivial, village business or some such thing.

I had a sudden impulse to run, mindful of Caleb's reaction at seeing us, and frightened at what awaited me. I was panicking at the reality of finally seeing Gideon again, and wasn't sure if I was ready to face him, of course there was a real possibility he wasn't at Briarwood, and I had lost him forever. Either way, I would soon discover the truth.

'It may be best if I wait here.' Exclaimed Isaiah in a low voice. 'Don't worry I won't scurry off and leave you in the lurch.'

I glared at him. 'No, you shall not.'

Raised voices came from beside the cottage and I turned to see Caleb and his companion heading towards us at an alarming rate.

'Effie, Effie is that really you?' asked Caleb, strolling right up to me and studying my face intently. 'You have returned.' He glanced behind me at Isaiah and his face darkened. 'You…how dare you return to Briarwood.'

I gazed at them in shock. 'You…you know one another?'

'Why of course, we are old friends Effelia.' Isaiah said sarcastically.

'You're not my friend.' Retorted Caleb.

Isaiah stepped back a little. 'Perhaps not, but anyway I thought it would be rather pleasant to travel down memory lane. To once again look upon the cosy little village where I once resided.' He glanced around. 'And it hasn't changed whatsoever.' He let out an ironic laugh. 'How disappointing.'

Caleb glared at me. 'Why on earth did you bring this despicable creature with you Effie?' He went across to Isaiah and placed his face near his. 'He is the vilest of men.'

'Well my daughter thought it wise to bring me along.' He sniggered at Caleb. 'My daughter Effelia.'

Caleb looked stunned. 'No, surely that cannot be.' He swung round to stare at me. 'Effie?'

I gulped. 'I'm afraid it's true Caleb.'

Isaiah began to chuckle at him. 'Shocked, are we?'

I bit my lip as I saw the look of utter disbelief on Caleb's face. 'You see Isaiah couldn't stay in my world, for I feared he was a danger to society, and if he remained there something dreadful would happen to my Aunt.'

Caleb grimaced. 'Well he cannot stay in Briarwood. A long while ago it was decided he would be banished from our village forever, a sentence I thought too lenient for such a man.' Without warning he spat in his face. 'We should have hung him when we had the chance.'

'Isaiah seemed undeterred by Caleb's actions and just grinned at him. 'There was no real evidence against me, no proof that I was a murderer.' He shrugged his shoulders. 'Innocent until proven guilty, isn't that the phrase?'

'Who did Isaiah supposedly murder in Briarwood?' I asked curiously.

Caleb began to laugh 'Oh many people, including his wife Violet, who was found bludgeoned to death.' He put his face close to Isaiah's. 'The two of you never did get on, did you?'

'Just because Violet and I had a few minor disagreements doesn't mean I killed her. I... loved her.' Isaiah uttered in a strained voice. 'She bore my children.'

Caleb grabbed Isaiah by the scrap of the neck and snarled at him. 'I don't wish to hear your pathetic drivel, I just want you gone from my sight, and if you think you're staying in my home you're sadly mistaken.'

'I have no desire to enter that tumbledown shack you call a home.' He sneered at Caleb. 'Especially when that dear wife of yours is no longer present.' An amused look spread across his face. 'Any news from your spouse?'

Before anyone could stop him, Caleb punched Isaiah straight in the face, sending him sprawling over onto his back. 'You mention her again and I'll strangle you, do you hear?' His face was like thunder.

Trying to regain his composure Isaiah sat up. 'I do believe I've struck a nerve.

'Be quiet Isaiah. The only suitable place for you is the crypt underneath the old church.' He turned to the man, who'd been waiting silently by the gate of the cottage. 'Go over to the church Sidney and inform the parson of what's happened, tell him we have a prisoner to accommodate in the crypt. I shall keep an eye on him until you return.'

Sidney nodded at him then began to run down the path.

Caleb sniggered as he stared at Isaiah. 'What a sorry sight you are.' He fleetingly looked at me. 'How awful for Effie having a father such as you.'

'Oh, it's not so bad, is it Effelia?'

Disregarding his question, I stepped forward. 'Why didn't you tell me you'd been married before Isaiah, and lived in Briarwood?'

An ingratiating smile spread across his face. 'My dear Effelia that was my past life, an old life I have no wish to dwell on.' He looked affectionately at me. 'I was forced to move to Hartland after the villagers here in Briarwood wrongly accused me of murder and that's when I began dreaming about your mother. But my true life started when I came to live at...' He paused. 'What's the name of the house?' He uttered in a panicked voice. 'This cursed place is already ruining my memory,' Struggling forward a little he collapsed onto his knees. 'Please, please Effelia, untie my hands and allow me to write down my treasured thoughts of home, before they desert me completely.'

Smiling serenely at him I produced my notebook and began flicking through the pages until I found the right one. 'The name of the house is Rawlings, the grand old house that you adored so much.' I snapped the notebook shut. 'And the answer is no, you may not be set free.' I crouched down beside him 'What kind of daughter would I be reminding you of such a memory, a memory that will bring you nothing but torment.' Rising to my feet I glared down at him. 'It's best to put it all behind you and concentrate on being here, because you'll never be returning to Rawlings.'

Consumed with wretchedness he began to sob. 'No, no please Effelia don't say that. I cannot bear it.'

Sidney had returned now, accompanied by another man. 'The parson has been told and says we should bring Isaiah over to the church, where he can be locked in the crypt.'

Caleb looked pleased. 'Excellent Sidney, will you and Joseph take him across there now.' He glanced at me. 'I would offer my help but I'm a little preoccupied at the moment.'

'As you wish Caleb. Replied Sidney, grabbing Isaiah's arm and pulling him up.

'Come on you.'

Making a miraculous recovery, Isaiah erupted into hysterical laughter as the two men led him away. 'Trust me when I tell you, the crypt is but a temporary home, and when I've spoken to the parson he will come to his senses. And I shall be set free.'

Caleb stared after him, shaking his head. 'That man is mentally disturbed. He belongs in the crypt with all those who are dead, and if I had my….' Stopping in mid-sentence he gazed over my shoulder, his eyes widening in astonishment. 'It…it cannot be.' His eyes welled up with tears. 'Noble?'

Swinging round, I saw the figure of Noble tentatively approaching. In the chaos I'd temporarily forgotten about him.

Rushing forward, Caleb went up to Noble and cupped his face in his hands, studying him closely. 'My son, my son has returned.' Flinging his arms about him he began to sob.

Feeling my eyes beginning to water at their touching reunion I decided to leave them alone together and let them come reacquainted. I would sneak round to the back garden, rather than entering the cottage; somehow it didn't seem appropriate to just wander in. As I came nearer to the cottage, I smelt the unmistakable scent of woodbine, its very distinct scent filled my senses with an inexplicable memory of long ago, causing me to feel a little sad. As I made my way down the side of the cottage, I became apprehensive, and the sensation grew as I spotted a figure sitting on the garden bench. Although I could only see his back, I could make out it was a man, with thick curly hair.

As I hesitantly stepped nearer, my heart started to hammer in my chest and I felt myself trembling.

I cleared my throat. 'Gideon? Gideon is that you?' My voice sounded strange and vague.

The figure in the chair stirred then stretched out his arms. I watched in complete fascination and nerves as he stood up and turned around to face me. The lanky figure with the unruly mop of hair and scruffy clothes was unmistakeable.

'Mace.'

We both stared at one another for a long while until I could wait no longer. I bounded over to him and flung my arms around him. 'Mace, oh Mace, it's so wonderful to see you.' I looked up into his blank face.

He narrowed his eyes in puzzlement. 'Do I know you young lady?'

'Mace it's me, your friend Effie.'

He gaped at me. 'I have no recollection of you.' He screwed up his face. I'm very sorry.' He gave me a look of pity then walked by and back into the cottage.

For a moment I collapsed on the grass and gazed out onto the brook and at the cornfields beyond. Tears came to my eyes as I thought about Gideon, not only did it appear he was absent, but my best friend Mace didn't seem to know me anymore. I wasn't sure if I felt so emotional due to the journey here or if I was just depressed and disappointed at the unsatisfactory reception. It was only then I came to my senses, and realised that this was just another silly game Mace was playing, something he was renowned for. My suspicions were confirmed when I heard the sound of stifled laughter behind me, and turning my head I saw Mace crouching down behind the chair.

'Fooled you.' He came striding across the lawn, hugging me tightly. 'What took you so long to come and rescue me?'

I raised my eyebrows. 'Well, it's a long story, one that I'll explain later.' I beamed at him. 'I can't tell you how glad I am you're here.' I smacked him playfully on the arm. 'And that you're still as annoying as ever. You had me worried there for a while, I thought you'd forgotten who I was.'

He pulled a face. 'Well that would be easy I suppose.' He giggled. 'Only teasing. It's all a question of controlling one's mind rather than it controlling you.' He produced a small notebook and bashed it against his knee. 'This helps too. It keeps the old memory ticking over.'

I nodded. 'I've been keeping notes too.'

'Really? That's very industrious for you E.' He glanced down at his notebook. 'But have you more information than me about Abercrombie?' He seemed pleased with himself. 'Anything you need to know; I possess the answer.' Suddenly he turned to a page he'd folded over, and studied it for a second. 'By the way E, how are Giles and Marigold?'

My face dropped.

'Effie?' What's wrong?'

I looked dumbstruck. Unfortunately, the vision of Mace's foster parents was as clear in my mind as the day I'd discovered their fate. I wanted to scold my brain for remembering the one thing I'd rather forget.

I stared into his waiting face. 'Well...they.' I gulped.

He immediately became distressed. 'What? What is it Effie.' He gripped my hand. 'Are...are they alright?'

'Mace I'm so sorry...but I can't remember.' I lowered my eyes. 'And unfortunately, I didn't write anything about them in my notebook,'

Despite it being such a credible excuse and conveniently easy to say, I still felt rather guilty for not explaining what really happened; although I wasn't in the habit of hiding the truth, I didn't wish to be the bearer of such devastating news on our first day together, it had been such a long while since I'd seen my best friend that I wanted our meeting to be a happy one, not filled with sorrow. Of course, I would tell him, eventually.

'Oh.' He exclaimed, looking bewildered. 'I thought by your face that something dreadful had happened to them.' Pensively he stared over at the cottage, deep in thought.'

Trying to hide my distress I changed the subject. 'Anyway, are you going to tell me how you came to be in Briarwood?'

'What?' Oh yeah.' He mumbled. 'Well after that delightful father of yours chucked me into that swirling pool of doom, I found myself in the creepiest of forests, the kind you'll find in a nightmare.' He stopped for a minute and scratched his nose. 'Any ordinary person would have been half frightened to death; I however am made of stronger stuff. Casually I strode towards the edge of the forest and came to a meadow.' He leant back down onto the grass and closed his eyes.

'And?' I uttered.

'It just so happens Caleb was in the meadow. He took pity on me, even though I was perfectly alright, and offered to give me a lift on his rather large eagle called Cross.'

'Croft, his name is Croft.' I said with an amused look on my face. 'Was...was Caleb with anyone else.

'No, he was all on his lonesome.' He plucked a blade of grass and caressed his cheek with it. 'I think he'd been searching for Gideon.' He gave me a fleeting glance. 'Anyway, he suggested I stay for a while in Briarwood, said he'd put me up in his cottage, until I got back on my feet.' He stared dreamily up at the sky for a few moments then leapt up and joyously threw his arms about me. 'I knew you'd come Effie; I knew you'd find me.'

'So, Gideon is missing then?'

Mace stared sheepishly into my eyes. 'I think you know the answer to that Effie.' He held his arms tightly around me. 'Caleb rarely speaks of him; I think he finds it too distressing.'

I pulled back and looked into his eyes. 'And Clarice?'

Mace solemnly shook his head. 'No one knows where either of them are.' He planted a kiss on my forehead. 'Don't fret Effie we will find them.' The tone of his voice rose considerably. 'But hey, don't become dejected. Your best friend Mace is here to cheer you up, to add a little drama and intrigue to your life.'

I smiled up into his face. 'I've missed you so much Mace.

He looked tenderly into my eyes. 'Well of course you have. How dull it must have been without me by your side.'

We both stood there, laughing together.

Hearing the slam of a door, I turned to see Noble lingering outside the cottage with a stern look on his face. 'Supper is ready' He said.

'Great.' Declared Mace. 'Funnily enough I famished.' He began to stride towards the cottage, pausing when he reached Noble. 'Pleased to meet you by the way, I'm Mace. Effie's most likely told you all about me.'

Noble gave him an unfriendly glare, but said nothing.

With a nervous laugh, Mace brushed passed him and entered the cottage.

'Noble? Is everything all right?' I asked, concerned at the disgruntled look on his face.

'I didn't realise Mace was such a good friend of yours. You both seem close.'

'Well yes, we've known one another since we were school children.' I said, impressed that I could remember such a thing. 'We've been through a lot together.'

'Yes, I can imagine.' He said coldly, marching away and leaving me standing there, staring after him in disbelief.

I rolled my eyes. 'Men.' I mumbled to myself.

Breathing in the early evening air, I followed him inside.

Supper was a strange affair, filled with uncomfortable silences. Caleb was naturally extremely attentive towards Noble, saying how well he looked and praising him at every opportunity, whilst Noble appeared overwhelmed by all the, seemingly, unwanted attention by his father. However, at not one point was Gideon mentioned, which was both strange and alarming. In the end I decided the only answer was to broach the topic myself, even if it was a touchy subject.'

I cleared my throat and peered at Caleb. 'Is there any news on Gideon?'

It was quiet for a moment, before Mace accidentally dropped his fork on the floor, causing a loud clatter.

Caleb expression was dispassionate as he spoke. 'Now is not the right time to discuss such matters, and I therefore ask you not to mention his name during my reunion supper with Noble.'

'But Gideon is just as important.'

'Effie, Gideon is surely no longer your concern, you left him and went home.' He paused. 'Therefore, finding Gideon is my business, not yours.'

I stared in confusion at Caleb, shocked by his cold heartedness. How I wished to scream at him, to strike him for being so cruel, but I decided to remain calm.

Serenely I rose from the chair and crossed over to the door. 'I'm sorry you feel that way Caleb, because you're wrong about me. As you well know I had to go, and I still care about Gideon, I always will.'

Without another word I left the room.

Trying to hold back the anger I ran blindly up the stairs and flung open the door to my room.

'Effie, Effie wait.'

Noble stood behind me, looking sympathetic.

'Father had no right to speak to you in such a manner, please accept my apologies on his behalf.'

I gently placed my hand on his shoulder. 'It's all right Noble your father is full of frustration and anger at Gideon's disappearance. It is to be expected. Seeing me again is more than likely a painful reminder that his son is missing.'

'That still doesn't mean he can behave so callously towards you.' He placed his hand over mine and gazed tenderly into my eyes. 'I will not allow him to upset you of all people.' Slowly he leant forward and gently kissed me on the cheek, his lips lingered there then gradually moved towards my lips.

Before he had a chance to touch my mouth, I swiftly moved away. 'Good night Noble.' I muttered in a hoarse voice. Without looking at him again I went into my room and shut the door.

# Chapter 12

I awoke early the next morning, eager to take a stroll and be alone. My first dilemma of the day was what I should wear. Now that I was back in this land it didn't seem appropriate to wear my usual attire, as even though I would have liked to put on my own clothes they just weren't in keeping with the way of life here. Rather reluctantly I peeked inside the wardrobe and saw that it still only contained the lilac gown that had once belonged to Florentine Heatherington and the crimson dress from the festival. With a poignant smile I turned my attention to the lilac one and pulled it out the wardrobe. Once I had dressed and combed my hair I happened to glance in the tall mirror in the corner of the room. Staring at my reflection I reached forward and touched the glass, half expecting that I could magically change my image into Florentine, and by doing so her spirit would come through the glass and embrace me, and we would stand, side by side like identical twins. I felt a sudden unexpected coldness come into the room, engulfing me in an icy chill. I thought this rather odd as all the windows were shut; and for one irrational moment I really thought it was my ancestor, Florentine come to join me. A rather strange laugh erupted from my mouth as I realised how ridiculous I was being. Hurriedly I stepped back from the mirror and reached for the shawl on the chair, and draping it over my shoulders, I headed for the door.

Mindful of causing a disturbance, I carefully crept down the stairs in my socks and only put my boots on when I was in the back garden. And as I strolled along the little path that led down to the stream a deep contented sigh escaped my lips. Without a care in the world I followed the course of the river as it wound its way through the golden cornfields and beyond to the green fields covered in early morning dew, and as I headed towards the tranquillity of the nearby meadow, I imagined that this peaceful world belonged to me, and to me alone, no one else existed. On reaching the meadow I rested for a while and must have drifted off to sleep. I dreamt of faeries and they were dancing in a circle to the sweetest music imaginable; unable to help myself I joined in their merriment, whereupon I became lost forever within their realm.

On awaking I panicked for a minute, trying to work out where I was, and then I remembered. A strange sense of melancholy swept over me, as I thought how Gideon was lost somewhere and I was here in Briarwood without him, acting like nothing was wrong. Of course, finding my dear friend Mace had taken my mind off his absence, and then there was Noble... My sorrow was replaced with a mixture of guilt and confusion. I shut my eyes and sighed in an attempt to clear my mind, then rose from the grass and made my way back to the cottage.

As I entered the kitchen, Caleb was sitting at the table mixing herbs together in a pestle and mortar, and barely glanced up as I entered the room.

'What are you making?'

He didn't answer straight away, and just carried on grinding the herbs together.

'It is a remedy to induce a restful sleep.'

'For one of the villagers?' I enquired.

Without looking up he stopped and began spooning some of the mixture into a cup. 'No, for me.' He answered, looking subdued. 'Ever since Gideon went away, I've had trouble getting a good's night sleep. It's helped a little with the return of Noble, but....'

He paused.

'But what?'

With a drawn-out sigh he moved the mixture away and focused on my face.

'It's you Effie, your arrival here has shaken me.' He cupped his hands underneath his chin and glared at me. 'I commend you for returning Noble, but now you should return home, and be with your family. No good can come of you being here.'

I look bewildered. 'I have returned for Gideon.'

'Forget Gideon and return home, before it's too late.' He narrowed his eyes. 'You live in a splendid house, do you not?

A dull ache appeared in my chest. 'Yes, yes I believe I do.' I mumbled, not able to recall the name of my beloved home. 'I just need to refer to my notes.' Reaching into the pocket of my dress I produced my notebook. 'I don't know what I would do without this.' I let out at nervous laugh, as I began flicking through the pages. 'Yes, here it is, it's called Rawlings.' I hesitated for a moment. 'I live there with my Aunt Constance, she is...she's.' An acute ache shot through my heart and I hunched forward across the table. 'I'm sorry I feel a little strange.'

He shook his head in despair. 'People such as yourselves never learn. And you obviously didn't pay any heed to what I warned about on your previous visit. You cannot go skipping from world to world without consequences, why do you think our brain deliberately erases memories from the world we have just left, it is to protect us.'

As the ache subsided, I peered into his grim looking face. 'Protect us from what?'

'From damaging our mind, from preventing us from going mad.' He glanced at my notebook. 'And if you really think that referring to your notes every day will help, then you're sadly mistaken. It's better to be totally oblivious of your old life than be reminded every day of what it was like.'

'But I don't wish to forget.'

He drew in a deep breath. 'Then you run the risk of permanent impairment. Look what happened last time when Verity jolted your memory, you experienced an overwhelming urge to go home.'

'I believed my Aunt to be seriously ill, I had no choice.'

'But you still wished to return as soon as you remembered, and that is how it should be.' He stood up and rested his hands on the table, leaning towards me. 'You don't belong here Effie, you never will. Take your friend Mace and return to where you came from.' An agitated look appeared in his face. 'And never again return to these lands.'

Why are you so against me Caleb, is it solely because of Gideon?'

158

'Well yes, your presence here reminds me of his absence. If it weren't for you, he'd be safe and sound at home. But what is done cannot be undone.' A glazed look appeared in his eyes. 'We must not dwell on matters that have passed. Time passes by regardless and is the healer of all things.'

I shook my head in frustration. 'You talk as if Gideon is dead, as if he is lost beyond hope. He is your son, you should never give up looking for him, ever.'

He banged his fist on the table and raised his voice. 'Do you not think I'm aware of that, do you not think I've been searching for him? Do you not think I've laid in my bed night after night thinking about him, and wondering if he's alive.' His demeanour relaxed a little and he took a step back. 'If Gideon wished to return, he would have done so by now. If the forest or the wilderness hasn't taken him then he's most certainly at Hartland, which means he is already gone.'

'Well I'm rather surprised you've not already searched for him in Hartland, at least then his whereabouts would be known to you.'

Without warning he rocked with laughter, then began shaking his head in amusement, mumbling something indistinct under his breath.

I looked bewildered. 'What's so amusing?'

'Why risk losing myself to that evil place, as well as my son. He bowed his head. 'I would be foolish to do such a thing, especially now that Noble has returned.'

'Do you not think that's a rather selfish attitude?' I snapped at him.

He gawped at me for a moment without saying a word, then laughed. 'Please do not lecture me on my behaviour, you really have no idea.' He went across to the little window, staring out onto the garden. 'Gideon is a man not a boy and I cannot dictate where he goes and whom he loves. I always imagined Gideon would end up marrying Verity, and even though she is a little melodramatic at times I do believe they would have made a good union.'

My eyes widened in surprise and horror. Briefly I attempted to visualise the madwoman and Gideon living their lives

159

together, but all I could foresee was misery, not just for me but for them too, and it was entirely feasible she would end up destroying Gideon in every way possible. Caleb clearly couldn't see the true monster that lurked beneath the surface of Verity's cool exterior, he was oblivious to her madness, and more importantly had no idea she had almost killed Gideon, inadvertently as it may be, he had still nearly perished. I thought of telling him the truth, warning him of her true character, but now wasn't the right moment; I would save that juicy tale for another time.

'I can see by the look of astonishment on your face Effie, that you find that concept entirely preposterous.' He sniggered. 'And perhaps you are right, however Gideon wouldn't have gone gallivanting off to face the dangers of the wilds if he and Verity had wed.' Caleb took in a deep breath then exhaled, and made his way back over to the table. 'He would be here now, in his true home of Briarwood.' Gazing at me he began to laugh softly. 'Noble seems so happy to be back, do you not think.' He sighed deeply. 'And having him back has eased my suffering. At least one of my sons is with me.'

I look puzzled. 'Perhaps you should try and be more optimistic, and open your mind to the possibility of Gideon returning.'

'Folks who leave this village rarely come back. My absent wife is proof of that.'

I titled my head slightly, looking at him enquiringly. 'Forgive me for asking but why did your wife leave, did it have something to do with Isaiah?'

Caleb folded his arms, and stared off into space.

'You may be surprised to learn that Isaiah and I grew up together, we were the best of friends, and we did everything together. Then a girl called Sabina came to our village and everything changed.' His eyes became wide. 'She was the most radiant thing we had ever set eyes on, and we both fell hopelessly in love with her, but it was me she wanted. From that day hence Isaiah hated me, he began going out his way to cause trouble; at first it was just small happenings, such as the destruction of the honeysuckle covering the front of the cottage, or the incident with the brick through the window, but then I found my hens slaughtered and my poor faithful dog, Fabian....' He began stumbling over his words. 'I...I found him hanging from the front porch. Then the vicious rumours started spreading through the village, blackening my family in every way imaginable. I thought that when he wed his wife Violet that the situation would improve, but sadly it did not. It was only later when the murders started that I was finally able to be rid of Isaiah.' Caleb gave a little laugh. 'Truth be told he's never forgiven me for marrying Sabina; in his twisted mind he believes I stole her from him.'

'And did you?'

'No.' he exclaimed indignantly. 'From the minute we laid eyes on one another we knew we were meant to be together. For much of the time our life was full of happiness.' Sorrowfully he shook his head. 'Then one day she simply left. And as much as I'd like to blame Isaiah for her departure, sadly I cannot, for he had already been banished from Briarwood following his wife Violet's death. Although I cannot help but think he is responsible in some way shape or form.'

I nodded.

Something was bothering me, something to do with Sabina. For it seemed I'd heard somebody speaking her name before; at first, I thought it to be Gideon or Noble, but I couldn't recall them even mentioning her.

'Sabina is such an unusual name.' I remarked. 'What was she like?'

He walked forward and placed his hands over the back of the chair. 'Sabina was a mystery to us all; I never did really know what she was thinking. She was one of the rare, lucky ones that succeeded in fleeing her homeland of Hartland, and after settling in Briarwood at first it appeared she would remain here. But not everything was as it should be, she never quite fitted in, never quite found herself at home in our village. I knew she loved me, of that I'm sure, but she was a restless soul, and often talked of wanting to travel, of exploring new lands.' He laughed ironically. 'I guess my boys have inherited her sense of adventure.' Sadness flooded his face. 'I shall never forget the day she left. At first, I believed she'd risen early and gone to the meadow to pick some berries, or some such thing, however as night fell, I began to become concerned, wondering if she'd fallen and injured herself.' His face clouded over. 'Then I found the note.' He gulped. 'It was such a short note for a goodbye, so blunt.' A deep frown crossed over his face. 'But the content was clear and straight to the point. It seemed Sabina's need for adventure had overtaken her devotion to her family and she therefore had but one choice – to leave.'

I studied his face. 'Did she not say she would return?'

'Not that I remember, no.' Caleb threw me a sorrowful look, his eyes tearful. 'The worst part of this whole situation is that I do believe my wife was expecting another child when she left.' His voice was faint and a faraway look appeared in his eyes. 'I often wonder if that was the case if that baby survived. I'd like to think that this child is out there somewhere, happy and contented.' He sniffed.'

I nodded my head in acknowledgment, not really knowing what to say. 'Oh well, at least you can draw comfort from the fact that it is indeed possible to escape Hartland. If Sabina did it, then so can Gideon, if he's there. And you forget, Isaiah and my mother, they left Hartland too.'

His face grew stern. 'I wouldn't know. I've never asked Isaiah and I've never met your mother.'

I stared at him for a while, contemplating what to ask next when the kitchen door was flung open so violently that it crashed into the small table beside the dresser, sending a vase crashing to the floor.

Mace stood in the frame of the door, looking bashful. 'Whoops, sorry.'

Caleb and I glared at him in disbelief.

'Accidents happen, don't they?' He exclaimed with a nervous laugh, looking from me to Caleb. 'Have I missed anything interesting?'

'What a clumsy boy you are Mace.' Exclaimed Caleb crossly, moving forward to pick up the broken crockery. 'Go and get the brush from the cupboard and help me clear this mess up.'

I stifled a laugh.

'Yes sir, right away.' Mace stumbled over the crockery. 'I hope it wasn't anything valuable Caleb?'

'Lucky for you, no, however it's becoming crystal clear that you are extremely accident-prone. Is it a family trait?'

Mace stood there for an instant, gaping at Caleb. 'No sir, not that I'm aware of.'

Peering at Mace I noticed a peculiar look in his eyes that troubled me. I couldn't shake off the feeling that I was missing something, something vital. And that evening I would discover what was staring me right in the face.

Secretly I was glad when supper was nearly over. For although it was somewhat comforting to hear Mace rambling on relentlessly, it also reminded me of how completely aggravating he could be. Nevertheless, it was rather amusing to witness Caleb and Noble politely tolerating his over-embellished story of how he'd escaped from monstrous trees that had attempted to drag him off by the hair; apparently, he'd administered his lethal karate chop on their branches and they'd cried out in pain, whimpering back to the forest.

Mace guzzled back the rest of his wine, slamming his empty glass down on the table and wiping his mouth. 'Then there was the troll, I must tell you about that ugly brute.'

Caleb cut in abruptly. 'Let's save that story for another occasion, shall we?' He said, rising up from his chair and clearing the plates.

'Oh, okay.' Exclaimed Mace, looking a little put out. 'I'm rather a chatterer, aren't I? 'Effie's the reserved one of us; I think that's why we get on so well. They say opposites attract, don't they?' Hiccupping, he smiled endearingly at me.

I grinned back at him. 'Over the years Mace I've come to the conclusion that it's easier to remain silent and let you enjoy the sound of your own voice.'

He chuckled and waved his finger in my face. 'Cheeky.'

Noble suddenly appeared irritated, shifting constantly in his seat. 'Tell me Mace, how long have you known Effie?'

Mace scratched his head. 'Since we were children.' He flung his arm around my shoulders. 'We've been through everything together haven't we E?'

'If you say so, yes.' I mumbled, watching him reach for the bottle of wine.

'I really think you've had enough to drink Mace.'

Nervously I glanced across at Noble, and observed how he was eyeing Mace rather threateningly. Caleb, on the other hand, seemed oblivious and was humming quietly to himself whilst clearing away the dishes.

'Nonsense. 'I've only had a couple of glasses. 'As I was saying, Effie and I are inseparable, and Effie's home, Rawlings is like a second home to me.'

Noble gave him a sceptical look. 'What about your family, are you close to them?'

Mace glanced down at his wine glass and a strange melancholy look appeared in his eyes. 'I er, yes after my mother passed away, I was brought up by my foster parents.' He took a slug of wine. 'They're such good, decent people, the salt of the earth.'

I gave Noble a fleeting glance.

Caleb came across the room and gently placed his hand on Mace's shoulder. 'It must have been an unsettling time for you, when you lost your real mother.' His voice was soft as he spoke. 'And what of your real father, did you not know him at all?

Mace started to cough and splutter on his wine, and I reached out and smacked him a few times on the back.

'Are you alright Mace?'

'Yes, went down the wrong way.' He coughed again, looking rather red in the face.

Mace hunched forward and put his arms on the table, pushing himself up from the chair. 'Well I think I'll call it a night folks, busy day tomorrow.'

'You didn't answer the question about your father.' Noble asked, rather tersely.

Caleb stepped forward in front of Noble. 'Oh, leave him be Noble, he obviously doesn't wish to discuss it.'

Noble looked sullen. 'I was only asking.'

Mace stopped at the door, wobbling slightly. He hesitated for a second, and then briefly turned to stare at Caleb before glumly lowering his eyes to the floor. 'Sadly, my real father is little more than a stranger. But one day I hope he will acknowledge me as his son.'

We all stared after him as he stumbled out the door.

'Poor lad.' Uttered Caleb. 'How dreadful he must feel.' He peered at me sympathetically. 'At least he has you to lean on Effie.'

With a screech, Noble pushed back his chair and got up. 'Huh.'

I cleared my throat. 'Excuse me.' I said a quiet voice. 'I better check Mace doesn't fall down the stairs.' I laughed awkwardly. 'I fear he's drunk far too much.'

In a rush I flew out the door and up the stairs. Mace was at the top of the landing, slumped up against the wall. Grabbing his arm, I flung it about my shoulders, then tried to walk as we staggered from side to side.

'Come on Mace, let me help you to your room.' Guiding him slowly forward, I whispered in his ear. 'Why didn't you tell me, why didn't you say that Caleb is your real father.'

He was silent for a moment before chuckling at me. 'Very impressive Effie.' He swayed a little and we both fell against the wall. 'Although it took you a while to catch on, didn't it, unlike myself who worked it out ages ago.'

'When?'

He hiccupped. 'Oh, I don't know, when I first arrived in Briarwood, I think. Caleb happened to mention the name Sabina one day, and after referring to my notes I put the two and two together.'

'I see.'

Reaching out he tapped my head with his index finger.

'Do you E, because I'm really not sure if your brain is functioning properly.' A large grin appeared on his face. 'Travelling to other realms messes with your head. Do you know the other day I couldn't remember the name of that chap you used to dream about; it literally went from my memory.' He burped. 'Caleb rarely mentions him and I didn't bother to jot it down in my notes. Then you turn up and suddenly Gideon's name pops back into my mind –the brother I've never

165

met.' He burst out laughing. 'And then I get to meet Noble, my other long, lost brother. Hic.' Without warning he slumped forward onto me. 'Sorry about being drunk, this family reunion business is a tad stressful.'

Yes, Mace you're completely inebriated.' I exclaimed, attempting to steady him.

A sharp voice called out to us. 'What's going on?'

We both turned to see Noble striding up the stairs, looking decidedly angry.

'Effie and I were having a moment.' His voice got louder. Can't she do anything without you lurking suspiciously in the shadows?'

Blanking Mace he looked directly at me. 'Do you need assistance Effie?'

With a shove I managed to move Mace forward a little, holding onto him just in case he fell over.

'Thank you Noble but no, I'm just seeing Mace to his room.'

Mace waved his arm at Noble. 'That's right, so toddle off and annoy someone else.

'Stop it Mace, you've had far too much to drink.'

With his face close to mine, he whispered in my ear. Don't tell him E, please don't tell him who I am.'

'No, I won't say anything.' I whispered in a rather annoyed voice. 'Will you at least try and stand up straight.'

'I shall leave the two of you to your secrets then.' Noble barked. 'Goodnight.'

Without uttering another word, he turned abruptly and stomped down the stairs.

My voice was vague as I spoke. 'Goodnight Noble.'

Mace slurred his words. 'Night, night Noble, sweet dreams.'

Placing his arm about my shoulder I hauled him down the narrow passageway to his room.

'Don't antagonise him Mace.' I said sternly, throwing him down on the bed. 'Noble has been a good friend to me over the past few weeks and if he's really your brother then I think you should make more of an effort to be pleasant to him.' I took off his boots and threw them on the floor. 'How long have you known about all of this?'

There was silence. 'Mace?' I looked down at his open mouth and closed eyes.

He was fast asleep. Brushing his unruly hair away from his eyes I reached for a blanket and draped it over him. 'Goodnight Mace.'


The day was full of promise as Noble and I strode down the shady footpath and meandered down towards the village, and as the sparrows chattered amongst the rose scented hedgerow, I wondered how the villagers would greet me, if at all, or would they simply turn and stare. Had I been on my own I would have made some excuse not to enter the village and happily gone for a stroll in the countryside. I would have been content in my own company, with no need for conversation, or deep meaningful discussions, for lately it seemed I was constantly with another, which was all very nice but I was the type of person who every now and again relished being on their own.

Emerging out into the village green my gaze was instantly drawn to the peculiar looking tree in the centre. If it hadn't been for the unusual way in which its gnarled branches reached distortedly up towards the sky, I would have thought it to be a blossom tree, for it was swaddled in exquisite pink blooms.

'What type of tree is that Noble?

'I believe it is a cedar, however no one really knows. It's the oldest tree within Briarwood, and is thought to be planted by monks, who stayed at Briarwood a very long time ago.' He held my gaze intently. 'Some say it is a magical tree, with healing powers. Others believe it can call on your one true love, and has the power to bind them to you for all eternity.'

'I'm not sure if that's a wonderful or frightening notion.' I lowered my eyes and smiled bashfully. 'Such a happening sounds extremely intense.'

'Oh, I consider it to be rather romantic.' He reached across and lifted my chin so I was staring up into his eyes. 'As long as they both love one another.'

A strange sounding laugh came out of my mouth, a nervous, unsteady laugh of someone who felt uncomfortable, and I was relieved to see several villagers pass by, throwing their usual odd stares. I noticed how they also gaped at Noble and wondered if they didn't recall who he was. I greeted them with a smile, although it was not returned, then glanced back at Noble.

'Perhaps we should run those errands for your father now.'

He laughed and grabbed my hand. 'Come on then, I know you're not particularly fond of the villagers. Allow them to become accustomed to seeing you here, and with time they'll come around.' He paused a little before continuing. 'This is your home now Effie, this is where you belong.'

My face became serious, as we made our way towards the village green.

Once we had visited Mr Greenacre's and Miss Broom's, and exchanged the medicine for a joint of lamb and several jars of damson jam, we returned to the cottage and laid the food out in the pantry. Noble suggested we go for a walk before his father asked us to do another chore, so as Mace and Caleb were busy mixing various medicines in the other room, we sneaked out the back door and crossed over into the cornfield that shone like pure gold in the midmorning sun.

Noble ran his hand through the corn. 'The men will be harvesting here soon.' He stared across to the sloping fields in the distance. 'It's something I always used to help with, when I was a young boy.' He turned to look at me. 'You and I could help the farmers bring this harvest in Effie, what do you say?

'Yes, I would like that.'

We both smiled at one another, and as he held my gaze, I could see how he was mulling something over.

'I've never asked you Effie, but are you ticklish?'

My eyes widened. 'A little I suppose.' I replied, tucking my hair behind my ears. 'Why?'

Without warning he began to tickle me relentlessly, causing me to laugh hysterically, and I automatically reached out and tickled his stomach. He grabbed my arms and pulled me back down onto the corn, and for a while we both lay there laughing, then his face became serious and he slowly leant forward and kissed me firmly on the lips. I should have pulled away immediately but I was lost in the moment, and unable to stop myself responding. Returning his kiss, my hand reached up and moved through his hair. But then a sudden vision of Gideon came from nowhere, and I pushed him back.

'No, no, this is all wrong.' I muttered in a weak voice.' I rose and brushed the corn from my dress, feeling myself flushing profusely. 'Very wrong.'

'No, this is all completely right.' He yelled. 'You and I are meant to be together.' He got up and took my hand. 'That day in the chapel, the day I called out for the ceremony to stop. The instant I set eyes on you I knew my fate was to be with you.'

He looked down at my ring. 'That day at the garden party I purposely created our engagement in the hope that it would become a reality. If you had doubts then why do you still wear this ring?' He asked, touching the sparkling stone with the tip of his finger.

I stared down at the ring, my thoughts turning to home, my other home I couldn't remember, despite reading my notebook the previous night. Obviously Noble hadn't been so idle, he must have checked his notes recently and thus was able to keep a hold on reality.

I gulped. 'Because it is so tight, I cannot remove it.' I retorted, trying to sound angry but failing miserably. 'And it's such a beautiful ring, it seems a shame not to show it off.'

He shook his head. 'Then why did you allow me to kiss you just then.' He asked. 'It's not as if it's the first time. We kissed many times at your home.'

I gazed at him wild-eyed. 'Did we? I...I don't recall you kissing me before, apart from when you tried the other night.'

With a sigh he moved slightly away, staring across at the woodland in the distance.

'You surprise me. You shouldn't be in need of your notebook to remember such a thing.' He swung round; his dark eyes filled with pain. 'Your memory should recall everything that has passed between us before we came to Briarwood.'

I swallowed. 'I don't know why Noble. The mind is a strange thing, perhaps it caused me to forget because our kisses at….at my home should never have happened.'

A sudden vision of Rawlings popped into my head and the familiar ache returned. Just thinking about it was becoming more painful with every passing second, especially when it came to my Aunt.

For a while there was a deep, uncomfortable silence, whilst the both of us glared at one another. Noble's face looked ambiguous and I wondered what he was thinking.

Unexpectedly he came near and knelt down before me. 'Effie Farraday, will you do me the honour of becoming my wife?

For a moment I became unsteady on my feet and stumbled backwards slightly.

He rose from his feet and clutched my hands in his. 'Effie?'

His face became little more than a blur as I drifted off into a world of my own. I imagined what it would be like to become his wife, loving him and bearing his children. I could not deny that the thought was appealing, greatly appealing; how happy we would be together, living our life to the full in this blissful place, watching our grandchildren grow up. However, as I stood there fantasizing of how my life could be, I realised it was just a dream, a dream that wasn't meant to be. There was somebody holding me back, preventing me from embracing this rosy existence.

When I spoke, my voice was hoarse. 'I cannot Noble.' I am sorry.'

'It's him isn't it, that brother of mine.'

My voice was but a whisper. 'Yes.'

'As father has probably told you, Gideon is gone Effie. If he didn't survive the wilderness then he's undoubtedly at Hartland's. Either way he won't be coming home.'

'That's precisely what Caleb said.' I huffed. 'And I told him how Isaiah used to live at Hartland and managed to leave without any bother.'

A little voice warned me not to mention my mother or Sabina; somehow, I didn't feel it necessary to bring them into it too.

Noble laughed. 'That man is a freak of nature. Even if he were to be imprisoned in hell, he'd still find a way to escape its clutches.'

My face became resolute. 'I cannot rest until I have at least attempted to find Gideon.' I stared into his almond shaped eyes. 'You understand, don't you Noble.'

He lifted my head, staring unwaveringly into my eyes.

'Please don't waste your life searching for Gideon; you will end up lonely and tired. I am here now, we could have a good life together, bringing up our children, watching them grow into adulthood.' He cupped my cheek. 'You do love me Effie don't you, just a little?

My face began to colour. 'Please don't ask me such things Noble.' I lowered my gaze. 'Since returning to Briarwood I've realised that my heart has always belonged to Gideon. So, you must understand my need to go and search for him.' I moved away. 'It's something I have to do.'

'And if you can't find him, what then?'

I shrugged my shoulders. 'I cannot say.' With a bleak expression I went across and tentatively held his hand within in mine. 'I don't expect you to wait that would be wholly selfish of me.' My voice started to break up. 'If... if you found someone to love in the village, I will completely understand.' Unintentionally I began digging my nails into the palm of my other hand. 'I'm sure there are many who would jump at the chance of becoming your wife.'

He sniggered, and spoke in a stony voice. 'Yes, I'm sure there is.'

I felt him snatch his hand away, and as his disgruntled face turned from me, he strode off across the cornfield, without uttering another word.


On entering the cottage, I had wished to go straight to my room and flick through my notebook, I needed a reminder of my life before Briarwood, however painful it may be.

My heart sank as I came upon Caleb in the kitchen.

'Effie, I was wondering where you'd got to.' he glanced over my shoulder. 'Where is Noble?'

'He…he is in the cornfield behind the cottage.'

Caleb face became concerned. 'Oh, I do hope he is all right.' Wiping his hands, he studied my face closely. 'Have the two of you been together the whole of this time?'

'Well, yes. It's such a lovely day we thought we'd take a stroll.'

I squirmed slightly as he continued to stare, never once removing his eyes from mine.

'I sincerely hope you still love Gideon.' His face became suspicious and a little stern. 'He would be utterly devastated to learn otherwise.'

Swallowing nervously, I turned my face away from his gaze. 'Yes, of course I do.'

Feeling somewhat unsteady I leant up against the table.

His voice continued to be cold. 'Imagine if he was to escape from Hartland only to discover the woman he loved has betrayed him.'

I huffed with annoyance. 'I'm not going to betray him Caleb.' I exclaimed, trying to sound convincing. 'And unlike you I'm not scared of going to Hartland. If Gideon doesn't come to me then I shall go to him.'

He turned and glared at me with anger in his eyes, then his face calmed a little.

'There's something you need to know.' With a sigh he drew out a seat and gestured for me to sit down. 'You see I've not been completely honest with you; I have been to Hartland before. When Sabina left her home of Briarwood, she didn't go alone.' He paused for a moment before continuing.' She took Gideon with her.'

I peered at him in puzzlement. 'She did?'

'Yes. I didn't mention it before as I thought it unnecessary, and I didn't wish to distress Noble, it's something he doesn't like discussing.' Frowning, he sat down opposite me. 'You see, Sabina always favoured Gideon over Noble.' He shook his head, looking solemn. 'Do not ask me why, for I do not know, maybe it has something to do with him being our first born.' He began drumming his fingers on the table. 'Waking up to find my wife had left me was bad enough, but to discover she'd taken one of my boys as well, was too much for me to bear.' A faraway look appeared in his eyes. 'I went after them; I went to Hartland to bring back my son.' He shook his head violently. 'I didn't care about her, but Gideon wasn't going to live a pitiful existence, locked away in the confines of that vile monastery at Hartland. Oh, Sabina pleaded her case well enough, begged me not to take him back, but as it turned out Gideon was deemed too young to remain there by the leader of the council, and allowed me to take him home.'

'What was it like there?'

A cloud of melancholy covered his face. 'It is hard to put into words, but it's the kind of place that no human should ever set foot in, the evil presence is everywhere, it is all powerful and fierce, and will corrupt your mind and destroy your soul, until there is little left of the person who once was.' He sighed. 'My poor son was in a terrible state when we left, and even when we were safely back in Briarwood, he would suffer the most traumatic nightmares imaginable.' With a look of sincerity, he gazed deep into my eyes. 'Then a young girl named Effie came to him in his dreams and from that day forth his nightmares ceased to exist.'

I smiled poignantly.

Caleb sighed heavily, and passed his tongue over his lips. 'Sabina's preferential treatment to her son Gideon is something that's always haunted Noble, and even as young boys, before she took Gideon, it caused animosity between the two of them.' He looked sullen. 'I will never forgive Sabina for that, and hold her responsible for Noble's departure.'

'Why did Noble really leave, did he wish to find his mother?'

'Yes. On the eve of Noble's leaving, he and Gideon had a terrible fight. Noble was desperate to find his mother, to win her love, and was adamant that he should try and find her without the aid of Gideon. Sadly, I knew nothing of this, had I'd been aware I would have done everything in my power to stop him from going. He was still so young, and vulnerable. Gideon searched everywhere for him, then I went looking, even to the gates of Hartland, only to be told Noble had never arrived.'

'Did you speak to Sabina?'

'No, I was informed that she was no longer there. I'm not sure how true that was, but I had no way of proving it, not unless I entered Hartland and faced the consequences.'

'The consequences?'

'On my previous visit when I went to fetch Gideon, I was told never to return, because if I did, they would assume I wanted to make Hartland my home, and I would be taken into their fold.' He hung his head in shame. 'Ever since then I wondered if I had made the right decision, and have tortured myself over whether or not Noble *really* was there, until finally I had to accept, he was lost to me.'

'Not anymore Caleb, he's found his way back home.'

'Yes, yes you are right.' He stared across at me. 'Do you know what I wish for most Effie?'

I shook my head.

'To once again have both my sons here at Briarwood, for us *all* to be together.'

My voice was but a whisper when I spoke. 'Then I hope your wish comes true Caleb, truly I do.'

There was a knowing silence between us, as we both became lost in our own thoughts.

# Chapter 13

How strange it seems, how one loses track of the days in this land, how swiftly one is entranced by the bewitching beauty of the fields, the meadows and the woodlands; I had an inexplicable sense of belonging, I belonged to them and they in turn belonged to me, filling my soul with an overwhelming sense of restfulness and peace.

I can't recall how many days past between my quarrel with Noble amongst the corn and Isaiah's trial, but the day of my father's hearing came sooner than anticipated, and much quicker than I had wished. I imagined it must be very much like a Sunday, for there was to be church service. And following on afterwards the trial would be heard within the church where most of the congregation would be present. It seemed a most unusual venue for such a thing, but Briarwood didn't possess a village hall or courtroom, the villagers although a little odd weren't in the habit of going around committing despicable crimes.

Caleb and Noble had gone along early to speak to the parson, leaving me with Mace.

'Are you sure you won't join us Mace? I asked, lacing up my boots.

'I'm not really a church goer, as you well know, E.'

'So, what will you do instead?'

'Oh, I might go for a run, or do some tidying up, or even do a jig'

I laughed as he started dancing around the kitchen, looking silly. Unexpectedly he slipped on the floor, and unable to do anything I watched on helplessly as he fell back into the dresser, sending most of the crockery crashing to the stone floor.

'Oh Mace.' I said, placing my hand over my mouth.

We were both speechless.

'What are we going to do?' I uttered, surveying the mess. 'All of Caleb's best china.' I exclaimed, picking up random pieces of crockery and putting them to one side. 'This is going to make me late for church.'

Mace stood there, rubbing his back. 'Sorry E.'

'Are you in pain?'

He doubled over and clutched his stomach. 'Agony, where's the nearest hospital?'

I gave him a scowl. 'This isn't the time for jokes Mace. If you're that bad then I'm sure there's someone in the village who can help you.'

'No, I'm fine. Although I may need a doctor when Caleb finds out what's happened.' He looked depressed. 'It's going to take forever to clear up this mess, and we can't hide the fact that half the crockery is missing from the dresser.'

'Well we can't do anything about that, but at least we can clear the china from the floor.' I grabbed the basket on the side and began throwing the broken crockery into it. 'I suppose it doesn't matter if I'm a little late for the service.'

He stood there watching me. 'Thanks E.'

'That means you help too Mace.'

'Of course.' He chuckled. 'You didn't think I'd get you to do it all, did you?'

I forced a smile. 'Come on, let's make a start.'

After Mace promised to clear up the remainder of the china, I left the cottage and darted through the cornfield, and begrudgingly entered the church, well aware of how late I was and how the place of worship would be full of curious villagers, ready to gawp at me. And I wasn't disappointed. I tried to ignore their lingering stares as I hurriedly went and sat down next to Noble, who'd been saving a seat for me.

He gave me a gentle smile. 'We thought you weren't going to make it.'

'Neither did I.'

He placed his hand over mine. 'It doesn't matter, you're here now.'

The man in front turned round, and I saw it was Caleb.

'Being late for church is extremely disrespectful.' He whispered surly. 'We're already half way through the service.'

I mouthed a sorry at him then turned my attentions to the parson, who appeared to be in the middle of a sermon, about how there are few men who have lived long enough in this world, and how we hath opened the heavenly door to them.

Unexpectedly I sneezed extremely loud, causing many of the congregation to turn and look at me, gaping in their usual odd way. My face began burning with embarrassment. If I'd been braver, and had the guts to confront them I would have leapt from my pew, and marched over to the parson, pulling him out the way, then taking his place on the pulpit I would have clearly declared. "I am not Florentine Heatherington. I am not a ghost. So, please do me the goodness of not gawping at me as if I was an exhibit in a zoo. I am plain old Effie Farraday, no more and no less." But my shy and retiring nature caused me to remain seated, restrained and incapable of making a spectacle of myself. Anyhow, I wouldn't be doing myself any favours by such a proclamation; it would make me look foolish and deranged.

My thoughts turned to the madwoman, and I began to search the aisles looking for her. It didn't take me long to spot the back of her raven hair, hanging limp down over her back. Gilbert, her simple brother, was sitting beside her; I recalled how he'd been half scared to death in the lane that day, the horror on his face when he saw me standing before him in the ghostly mist, looking exactly like Florentine's spirit. I had to look twice at the man sitting the other side of the madwoman, and I couldn't fathom why he was there.

I gripped Noble's arm. 'Is that Isaiah?'

'What?

Isaiah is sitting a couple of pews ahead of us, why is he at the service?'

'The parson allowed him to sit with his family during the service.' He whispered.

'Family?' I uttered rather loudly. 'What family?'

I stared in disbelief, unable to drag my eyes away from them all sitting there; it was so ambiguous and odd that I laughed to myself, for although it seemed unbelievable it also made perfect sense.

As everything became a blur, I only half listened as the parson made an announcement about the trial beginning, and hardly noticed as several of the congregation began filing out the church, stealing a look at me as they went.

'Effie. Effie?' Noble said urgently. 'What's wrong?'

'Nothing.' I murmured, barely able to find my voice as an overwhelming revulsion enveloped me, creeping over me like a sickening realisation.

'It's time for Isaiah's trial.' He gave a short laugh. 'It shouldn't take long.' He took my hand and guided me forward, to the small gathering of remaining villagers, who were standing with a disgruntled looking Caleb and the parson by the altar. 'Excuse me for a moment Effie, you wait here whilst I go and talk to father.' His face looked concerned. 'Will you be all right?

My voice was hoarse. 'Yes.'

Sudden footsteps came up behind me.

I felt a cold touch on my arm. 'Well, how perfectly lovely to see you again dear sister. Sorry I haven't bumped into you before now, but I've been away travelling and have only recently returned.' She glanced across at Isaiah who was deep in conversation with someone. 'Father wished to be the one to inform you that we're sisters, but I'm sure he won't mind me telling you.'

I glared into the piercing eyes of the madwoman. 'No, it's not true.' I muttered in a desperate voice. 'It...it can't be.'

'Sorry to disappoint you, but I'm very much afraid it is. Our father is Isaiah, so therefore we are siblings.' She dragged Gilbert forward roughly. 'Aren't you going to give your sister a hug Gilbert?'

'No, no, ca...can't.' He stammered.

'Oh Gilbert, you really are hopeless.' The madwoman reached forward and poked me hard in the shoulder. 'She's flesh and bone, not a ghost.'

I flinched. 'Don't touch me.'

With her thin lips twisted unnaturally into a smile and her hair swept severely from her face, I'd forgotten how frightening the madwoman looked. To discover we shared the same father filled my heart with an overwhelming coldness, it was an abominable, mortifying discovery.

Looking perplexed, Gilbert peered at me with his small beady eyes.

'How...how come you look like her in the painting?

He looked decidedly odd with his greasy hair, clinging strangely to his bony face and his peculiar attire of an overgrown overcoat and trousers that didn't quite meet his ankles. Learning he was my brother, although somewhat of a shock, wasn't so much of a devastating blow; however, it would take some getting used to, on both our parts.

I looked candidly at him. 'Well I...'

My madwoman interrupted, cackling loudly. 'They only look similar because they are related you dimwit.' She clouted him round the head. 'Can't your simple mind understand that?'

Isaiah came over and intervened. 'Don't taunt the boy Verity, it's cruel.' He exclaimed, looking tenderly at me. 'Verity has told you then. I realise this must be a shock Effelia, to suddenly discover you have a sister and a brother, but there really wasn't any need to tell you before, as all the time we were at home the two of you weren't likely to ever meet. Verity was the one that informed me that you'd been in Briarwood with Gideon for the past two years, when you were absent from.... from home.' He scrunched his eyes closed in frustration. 'Oh, what was the name of that house you used to live in?'

'Rawlings.' I said mechanically. 'But how did Verity contact you?'

'That's unimportant.'

'Oh father, don't be so dismissive to my little sister.' She clasped my arm tightly. 'I used the same method when I visited you that time, don't you remember Effelia, when you were cowering in your kitchen, begging me to have mercy on you.'

I laughed. 'That's not true. However, you *were* trying to kill me at the time.'

'Oh really. You do have a vivid imagination Effelia.' She glanced at Isaiah then back to me. 'I was merely making your acquaintance dear sister.'

'Is that so?'

With a false laugh she linked my arm with hers. 'Well of course, no come; let us part as friends, before you return home.'

Instinctively I tore away from her. 'I'm not going home, not until I've found Gideon.'

As Isaiah was pulled to one side by the parson, the madwoman's expression darkened. She brought her face close to mine, her eyes blazing with hatred.

'Please don't tell me you still want Gideon, not after deserting him so callously and leaving him with a broken heart. You don't deserve him, you never will.'

'Well I think I deserve him a whole lot more than you, especially after you almost killed him.'

She practically spat out her words. 'You know only too well that arrow was meant for you Effelia, Gideon was foolish to protect you.'

Isaiah came back over to join us.

'Daughters please, whatever are the two of you bickering about? This is neither the time nor the place for an argument, especially as we have finally been united as one family.

As I peered into his tired looking eyes it occurred to me how much he was enjoying our strange little family meeting, having all of his children together must be somewhat of a delight to him. I however just felt physically sick.

He smiled endearingly at us all. 'When this horrid business is all over, we shall have the opportunity to get together and bond properly, as a family. After all, blood is thicker than water.' A pained expression swept across his face as he glanced at the parson. 'Oh dear, I fear our fleeting reunion is exactly that.'

The parson ushered Isaiah forward. 'It's time for your trial Isaiah. Please step behind the pulpit.' He looked over at the rest of the congregation. 'All those who wish to remain, please take a seat and remain silent.'

The madwoman scowled at me before turning away and taking a seat. Gilbert mumbled something as he plonked himself down beside her, and she hissed at him to be silent.

An anxious looking Noble came bounding over towards me. 'Come Effie, sit with us.' He smiled. 'Sorry about leaving you, father was contemplating not being present at the trial.'

'Why ever not?' I asked.

'He feared he would lose his temper and lash out at Isaiah.' He grinned. 'But he assures me he will try and control himself, and I will restrain him if need be.' His voice became grim. 'As long as the verdict ends in Isaiah's death.'

I stared into his eyes. 'Your father wishes that more than anything, doesn't he?'

His gaze was steady. 'Yes.' Murmured Noble. 'Just as I wish to marry you more than anything.'

I immediately lowered my eyes in embarrassment.

We went and sat beside Caleb; whose gaze was fixed upon Isaiah. I saw the parson chatting to someone in the front pew, and then looking rather apprehensive he went and stood directly beneath the pulpit and faced the villagers.

'I would like to make this trial as short as possible, without interruptions or disruptive behaviour.' He fleetingly glanced at Caleb and the other villagers before looking up at Isaiah. 'The prisoner, Isaiah Penhaligon stands accused of numerous misdemeanours that were supposedly committed long ago, when he was part of our village community. Now I....'

Caleb stood up. 'Pardon me parson, for interrupting but would it be permissible for me to make a small statement?'

The parson raised his eyebrows. 'Oh, very well Caleb, as long as you remain silent for the rest of the proceedings?'

'Certainly parson.'

Caleb went and stood next to the parson, glaring up at Isaiah.

'There comes a time in our lives when we must account for our misgivings, confront our demons, and be punished for our sins. Isaiah Penhaligon gave the impression of being a solid, family man, a respectable member of our little community, and a charming and amicable fellow, but behind this façade lurked a man of pure evil, who deceived and harmed everyone unfortunate enough to know him. Over time, he left a trail of unexplained deaths, amongst them his wife, Violet, Mr Brown of Bishops Farm and Miss Gorman who lived above the bakery.' Caleb paused. 'These crimes are a few amongst many.' His voice rose. 'Everyone knows this man is guilty, so let's take this opportunity to make him finally pay for what he's done.'

Isaiah looked calmly towards Caleb, smiling silently, but saying nothing.

'Well Isaiah?' asked the parson. 'What would you like to say in your defence?'

'These accusations are mere speculation, as well you know parson. I can honestly say, with my hand on my heart that I didn't murder my wife. She was a good woman who I loved dearly, and when she was taken from me in such tragic circumstances, I truly believed I would never find happiness again, but then I met Effelia's mother, and I realised that god had granted me a second chance.

'And Mr Brown and Miss Gorman? Do you also claim not to have anything to do with their passing?

With a simpering smile Isaiah peered over the pulpit. 'My dear parson, both of these poor people were dear friends of mine, and their sad departure from this life was a very traumatic time for me. Their deaths were not by my own hand; they somehow misunderstood my instructions for the sleeping tonic I prescribed, and accidentally took the wrong dose.'

The parson frowned at him. 'As I recall from last time, I cannot prove or disprove your guilt. I therefore have no option but to disregard these accusations of murder.'

There was a cry of objection from Caleb.

'But...but parson, you *know* he's responsible.' He gulped. 'And what of Sabina, I'm sure this vile man had a hand in her disappearance.'

'I know you blame me for Sabina vanishing, but my dear fellow, I left Briarwood long before your dear wife disappeared, so where she went, I do not know.' His face was full of pity, as he looked at Caleb. 'Perhaps she found a better home, away from you Caleb. You must move on with your life, and accept she no longer wanted you.'

Caleb suddenly roared with anger. 'You...you despicable man, I will hang you myself.' He began clambering up to the pulpit towards an amused looking Isaiah, but just as he did so the man that the parson had been chatting to in the front pew swiftly grabbed him and pulled him down.

The parson looked perturbed. 'I suggest you go and stand outside Caleb, and let your temper cool a little.'

'But parson...'

Noble squeezed my hand then swiftly rose and went over to Caleb.

'Come on father. Let us take some fresh air.'

I watched as they went towards the church door.

'Thank you, parson.' Uttered Isaiah, smiling gratefully. 'That man certainly has a temper.'

'The parson let out a sigh. 'Perhaps he has good reason.'

'Huh. Poppycock.'

'Anyway Isaiah, what cannot be disputed is that you're back in Briarwood after your banishment.'

Isaiah leant forward over the pulpit and glanced into my face. 'Only because I was forced to.' His eyes slowly left mine and focused on the parson. 'Nevertheless, now that I am here would it be possible for me to spend some time with my family. I've missed them so parson. And I've forgotten what a delightful little village this is.'

'I do not think that would be wise Isaiah.'

There was silence.

One of the men in the pews suddenly rose.

'Let's hang him and be done with it. My little brother used to play with his daughter Verity in their cottage when they were children, then one day the poor mite didn't come home, and we never saw him ever again.' He pointed viciously at Isaiah. 'That man there is responsible. I just know it.'

Verity gasped at the villager.

'If I were you Merrick Hind, I'd watch my tongue.'

'Or what Verity, you don't scare me.'

She glowered at him but said nothing. The man returned her stare for a moment before suddenly lowering his head as if no longer capable of meeting her eye.

'Interrupting the trial isn't helping.' Commented the parson, looking slightly perturbed. I ask for you all to remain silent whilst I contemplate my decision.'

The villagers began whispering between themselves, ever so often taking a fleeting glance at Isaiah then swiftly turning away before he caught them looking. It almost seemed they were afraid of him.

The parson cleared his throat.

'There will be no hanging. The prisoner will go free.'

Isaiah gave him a simpering smile.

'Thank you, parson.'

'However, Isaiah, I cannot allow you to remain in Briarwood. So, unless you or anyone else comes forward with evidence that will vindicate you, I have no choice but to once again banish you from the village.' He looked suddenly grave. 'I've given you a second chance Isaiah, so if you ever return to our village you will *certainly* be hanged.'

The madwoman groaned.

Everyone's eyes were on Isaiah as if waiting for him to react but instead he remained relatively composed. His voice however seemed strangely weak when he spoke.

'So be it.'

Several of the congregation began to applaud loudly, including Merrick Hind. But as Isaiah glowered at them the clapping petered out.

'May I make a suggestion parson?'

'Yes Isaiah, what is it?'

'As you're most likely aware, Caleb's son Gideon has gone missing and we believe him to be in the vicinity of Hartland. I request that you allow me to journey with my dear daughter Effelia, and show her the way, and we shall endeavour to locate Gideon and return him to his rightful home. I will of course see them both safely back and then be on my way.'

'If you wish to go to Hartland that is entirely your choice Isaiah.' His eyes turned to me. 'Miss Farraday, are you in agreement?'

I looked stunned.

'I.... I'm not sure.'

The parson looked puzzled. 'You *do* wish to find Gideon, do you not Effelia?'

'I... yes, yes of course.' I mumbled.

'And do you wish for Isaiah to be your guide?'

There was a hint of hesitation in my voice. 'Yes...yes parson.' I heard raised voices.

The parson's voice came bellowing across the church. 'Silence.' He stepped forward, towards the villagers. 'Please remember that this is a place of worship, not a cattle market.'

There was a hush.

'Very well Miss Farraday, I will allow you to leave with your father. However, please be aware that the residents of our village do not take kindly to the comings and goings of visitors. Therefore, I suggest you do not return to our village community unless you mean to remain here for good.'

I stared into his face. 'I understand.'

'The trial is therefore concluded. I give thanks to all you good people for your time.' He stood there smiling as they slowly made their way to the church door, albeit one man, who was lingering beside Isaiah, and the madwoman. 'Mr Mason, please will you escort Isaiah back down to the crypts, where he shall remain until tomorrow.'

'Wait.' The madwoman demanded. 'I need to speak with my father.'

She approached Isaiah as he stepped down from the pulpit and pulled him to the corner of the church, whispering something in his ear. Isaiah's expression became infuriated as she carried on talking, and I saw them both stare across at me.

'Enough Verity.' Exclaimed Isaiah.

I watched curiously as he moved away from her, and Mr Mason led him away.

Realising the madwoman was heading towards me I hurriedly made for the door and practically collided with the parson.

'In a hurry to leave Miss Farraday?'

I smiled bashfully.

Verity came barging between us. 'Please parson, I beg of you. My father has been treated poorly whilst kept in the crypts, and he's become frail, and malnourished. Surely it would be wise to delay the journey, just until he regains his strength.

'My word is final. 'Your father and Miss Farraday shall both leave first thing tomorrow morning.'

She glared solemnly at the parson and gave him a little nod. Turning to me she grasped my arm and whispered menacingly in my ear. 'You haven't heard the last of this sister.'

I stared after her as she marched out the church.

The parson placed his hand gently on my arm. 'I bid you goodbye, Miss Farraday. I wish you well on your journey.'

'Thank you, parson.'

Oh yes, I thought solemnly to myself. Another journey...how foolish I felt for agreeing to go with Isaiah, but Gideon was supposedly at Hartland, and it seemed I had little choice but to go, whether I wished to or not.

With a heavy heart I ambled towards the tranquil seclusion of the graveyard, away from the prying eyes of the villagers. Such peace and quiet, where my only company were those who had passed on from this earthly world, seemed apt at this moment. Blindly wandering amongst the gravestones, I came to rest on a stone bench, tucked away out of sight, amongst the wild poppies. And there I slumped forward, looking decidedly melancholy. How heart wrenching, how completely unacceptable that I should have to leave Briarwood so soon; for although I'd only been here for a short period of time, I'd already fallen for the mysterious charm that covered this land. To remain here would be so easy, so right. And then there was Noble...

I let out a drawn-out sigh.

Never before had my mind felt so clouded in a fog of indecision and confusion:

The greatest dilemma facing me now was Gideon; since returning to these lands my recollection of him had greatly been restored, but I feared he no longer stood paramount within my mind, and if I didn't see him soon the memory of him would irreversibly fade altogether. It was true to say that I had lamented somewhat over his absence, however it hadn't been unbearable without him. Nevertheless, I was tortured with guilt for doubting my feelings for him, the man I was supposed to be in love with. And then there was Clarice, how cruel and inconsiderate of me not to take her into account, my dear friend from back home; she too was somewhere in this land, somewhere, I prayed, where I could reach her.

I blinked away the tears that were falling uncontrollably down my face, angry and frustrated with myself for acting so selfish. No, there was only one solution, I *would* go to Hartland and bring back Gideon and Clarice. My conscience would prevail.

'Effie?'

I jolted and glanced round to see Mace. 'Yes.' I uttered in a weak voice. I turned away from him and wiped the tears away with the cuff of my dress.'

Munching an apple, he took a seat beside me. 'What a superb spot to hide away from the world.' He murmured. 'No one to answer you back, and if they did it might be a smidgen scary.' He cackled. 'Of course, knowing you so well it was easy to track you down.'

'Are you sure you just didn't guess, knowing I'd just left the church?' I said, trying not to snivel.

'Perhaps that was a bit of a giveaway.' He mumbled with a mouthful of apple. 'I've just had a word with old Mr Stokes, and he informed me all about the ghastly outcome of the trial.' Angrily, he tossed the apple core across the graveyard. 'It's a horrendous thought, having to leave tomorrow, especially with that pig of a man.' He spat out a bit of apple. Of course, I'm coming with you to Hartland.' His voice sounded resolute. 'And that is my final word.'

I stared at him for a while without saying a word.

'Mace, as much as I'd like you to come with me to Hartland, I really think you should stay here. Tell Caleb the truth, and spend some time with your family.'

He hunched his shoulders, and lowered his head. 'What if Caleb doesn't want to hear that I'm his son, after all this time, perhaps it would be best not to let him know.' He glanced at me, dejectedly. 'What if he thinks I'm a disappointment?'

I let out a laugh, shaking my head. 'How could you even think such a thing, Caleb will be overjoyed to hear the news that he has another son.' I threw him a sideways glance. 'I think he will overlook how clumsy you can be, and how boastful.' I nudged into him with my arm. 'As long as you don't break anymore of his crockery.'

I expected Mace to laugh but his face remained sullen. 'Caleb may accept me, but not Noble.'

'Mace you've not given Noble a chance, once he knows who you are...well everything will be different.'

He snorted. 'Maybe.' Pulling himself straight he grabbed my hands and squeezed them. 'I'm just not ready to tell them yet, if they learn I'm the long-lost son of Sabina they'll start questioning me about her...and ask me what's became of her.' His face looked mournful for a moment then lightened a little. 'Let's just concentrate on our trip to find your dearest Gideon.'

'Mace, I'm still not sure....'

'Now Effie, I don't want any pointless arguments. You're my best friend and I am coming with you tomorrow, whether you like it or not.' He flung his arm round my shoulder. 'Besides who else is going to protect you from that scheming father of yours.'

I smiled sweetly at him. 'Thank you, Mace, I'll be glad of your company.' I looked pensive. 'Just promise me you'll tell Caleb your true identity when we return to Briarwood.'

'I promise E. That's if we don't become prisoners of Hartland, doomed to stay there until we are old and grey.' His face softened. 'That would be rather a calamity wouldn't it?'

We laughed together as we slowly made our way out the graveyard.


I was somewhat perturbed as I entered the cottage, to find Caleb on his hands and knees, picking up fragments of china from beside the dresser. After the events of the church I'd completely forgotten about Mace's little mishap, and I could clearly see from the state of the floor that he'd not finished clearing up properly. How convenient of him to go for a stroll.

'It was an accident Caleb; Mace didn't mean to break so much.' I gulped. 'He lost his footing and fell back onto the dresser.'

He glared at me with his dark eyes. 'Mace again eh. Had he been drinking?

'No. Not at all, Mace hardly ever drinks.' I replied indignantly. 'I think you'll find we gathered most of the.... broken bits.' I pointed across to the basket on the workbench. 'With a little luck I believe many of them can be fixed.'

'Huh. And what about the fine porcelain crockery, how in God's name are we going to mend that.' His face became solemn. 'Some of it has been in my family for generations.' Narrowing his eyes, he carried on collecting the tiny fragments of china from the floor. 'Since being here I've lost count of the numerous items Mace has destroyed. He should take greater care and not blunder about so.' He began sweeping up fragments with a dustpan and brush. 'If he were my son, I think I'd give him lessons on how to respect other people's property.'

I widened my eyes in astonishment.

Caleb rose from his knees and eyed me suspiciously. 'So where is the perpetrator?'

'He...he went for a walk.'

'Avoiding me, is he?

I nodded at him and gave him a weak smile.

Tucking my hair behind my ears, I went across to the tiny window, momentarily lost in the yellow splendour of the cornfields in the distance.

'If you're wondering where Noble is, he's gone to the village to fetch some groceries.' He let out a sigh. 'I can't tell you how ecstatic it makes me to have him home. I only wish Gideon was here to make our family complete.'

'My heart sank. 'Talking of families, I had a rather unpleasant shock today.' I swung round and stared at him. 'Verity and Gilbert are apparently my siblings.'

His expression was staid. 'Oh. You found out then.'

'Why didn't you tell me, warn me of who they were?'

'It wasn't my place. It's not my fault your father is dishonest and treacherous.' He slammed his fist down onto the table. 'How is it that the man who is responsible for so much misery gets away so lightly? My only hope is he'll rot away at Hartland in the deepest, darkest dungeon.'

'You heard about the outcome then?'

'One of the villagers informed me on their way home.' He looked pensive. 'So, you and your father will leave tomorrow.' Avoiding my eye, he sat down at the table. 'And once you arrive at Hartland, you're supposed to seek out my son and return him to his rightful home. Since you are wholly responsible for his absence, I find this rather fitting.' He rose abruptly and headed for the door. 'I shall call for Croft, however I cannot guarantee he will come. And how far he will take you. Since Gideon's disappearance the sorrowful beast has become unpredictable. He is faithful to his master and pines for him.'

'Does he not sense Gideon's at Hartland.'

'The cloud of desolation that hangs over that place prevents Croft from realising Gideon is there, and even if the great bird was to enter the domain of Hartland, the likelihood of survival would be slim.' He paused. 'For any man or beast.'

'Please don't be despondent Caleb. We will find Gideon.' I touched his arm. 'Just like you sought him out when he was a boy, and returned him to Briarwood.'

'Your optimism is wasted on me Effie.' He turned and glared at me steadily. 'When Gideon was a boy, he was only there a short while.' He let out a short laugh. 'I can only assume young children cannot cope with the severity of life there.' A deep frown appeared across his face. 'But Gideon is a man now, ready to be moulded into a servant of Hartland. Like I explained to you before, I have already resigned myself to the possibility of never seeing him again. Go there and discover for yourself what horrors await you. But do not rely on hope to save you, it is a foolish emotion of a young woman, who as of yet hasn't had to endure the pain and suffering of loss.'

Once Caleb had left the kitchen I stormed into the garden, and ran down to the riverbank, where I sat with my face buried in my hands. Although I was becoming used to his disgruntled manner, and found disregarding it the favourable option, I found it difficult to curb my infuriation for the blatant way in which he blamed me for Gideon's disappearance; then there was Noble, who'd gone travelling as a boy, never to return to Briarwood until he was a man. I'd like to think that I had a hand in his reunion with his father, and yet there was no word of thanks from Caleb, no smile of appreciation. And unbeknown to him he had another son, the clumsy one who had no respect for his belongings, and the one who was departing with Isaiah and me the very next day. The irony of it all was rather amusing, and I found myself glad that Mace hadn't declared his true identity to father, for I imagine there would be turmoil when it came to light that his newly found son was departing. Caleb would be fuming with utter rage.

Hearing someone behind me I turned to see Noble. 'I've been searching for you everywhere.'

I smiled sadly as he came and sat down on the bank beside me. 'I needed to clear my head.'

'It's been a rather eventful day, hasn't it? He shifted closer to me. 'Father informed me you're leaving tomorrow. Please tell me it's not so.'

With a sigh I took his hand. 'Yes Noble, I am. I have to.'

He began laughing. 'But we've only just arrived in Briarwood, at least stay a little longer.'

'Isaiah has to be gone from the village by tomorrow; he can show me the way to Hartland.' I stared glumly ahead. 'I've already discussed the matter with your father and he's in total agreement.'

'Effie, don't pay heed to what father says, you are not responsible for Gideon's disappearance, you are not beholden to him.' He looked frustrated 'Like I said before, your chances of finding him are extremely thin.'

Frowning, I got up and began to stroll along the riverbank, listening to the tranquil sound of the water. Noble followed alongside me, moving so close that I could feel the warmth of his skin against mine.

'Please Effie, I do wish you'd reconsider my proposal; we could be happy here, together.'

I moved a little away from him. 'I don't think you've been listening to me Noble.'

He came near once more. 'My love for you takes precedence over all other matters, so you can't blame me for my endeavours.' His voice became solemn. 'If you're adamant about going on this journey then I shall go with you, I belong near your side.' I felt his lips caress the corner of my mouth. 'I know you wish me to journey with you.' Without waiting for a reply, he planted his lips firmly over mine, then moving his mouth he murmured into my hair. 'I will go and prepare for our trip.'

Feeling restless and a little agitated, I half-heartedly began arranging my belongings on the bed, ready to put in my rucksack, but I found myself staring into space. With a deep sigh I crossed over to the window, deliberating over what Noble had said: his apparent wish to travel with me was so appealing I almost convinced myself that it was the right decision; my heart was heavy with sorrow at the notion of being parted from him, and if we stayed together that feeling would disappear. Shaking my head, I returned to the bed and tried to concentrate on packing. The gun, notebook and calling whistle were obviously essential, as were toiletries and clothing, but my instincts told me to leave the Monk's ledger at Briarwood, as I couldn't imagine needing it at Hartland; I would never forgive myself if I happened to lose it, or it ended up in the wrong hands, that would be dreadful. Also, despite its underlying quality of evil, the ledger was precious to me, and having been in the safe keeping of Florentine all this time, I felt it was my responsibility to take care of it.

Out of the blue, I had an inspirational idea- how fitting it would be to conceal the ledger behind the portrait in the church here at Briarwood, where my great ancestor, Florentine and her peculiar looking dummy friend, Gilbert, would protect it until my return. Wasting no time, I left the cottage with the ledger and hastily ran over to the church, cautiously making sure that the building was empty. With trembling hands, I ever so slightly lifted the painting and slotted the ledger behind it, so it was resting on the wooden framework. Then, standing back, I fleetingly gazed at the young woman in the portrait, still astounded at how unnervingly similar we both were. I pondered over whether Florentine would have approved of my life so far, would she have handled things differently. I swiftly dismissed such thoughts and ran out the church.

On returning to my room I finished packing then rested on the bed and made a few additional jottings in my notebook. Supper had been rather awkward that evening, with everyone looking rather glum. Not a word was uttered about the forthcoming trip, as if in doing so would cause unwanted conflict at the dinner table. Every so often Noble would glance over to where I was sitting, smiling softly at me in his usual way, and although he didn't intend to make me uncomfortable, I felt it all the same. It was rather a relief when Caleb began clearing the dishes away, and told us to go and relax in the garden whilst he made a pot of tea.

How calming it was to lay back on the lawn and watch the fireflies flit around, illuminating the garden in their gentle glow; the grasshoppers were busy keeping up their constant chirping, a sound so characteristic of a warm summer's evening, and the sky was so clear that the stars glistened in a way that was so mesmerising that one could remain there the entire night, just gazing up in wonder. For a long while we all lay in utter silence. The temporary lull was a necessary requirement for us all, a time to gather our thoughts.

Mace got up, stretching his arms out. 'Well folks as much as I'd like to stay here all night, Mr Sandman is calling.' He yawned. 'You and I Effie have a long journey tomorrow, so I really need to get some sleep.'

Noble sprung up from the grass. 'What? What do you mean?'

Pretending to ignore Noble's question, I looked up at Mace.

'Oh not yet Mace.' I grumbled. 'Surely stay for a cup of tea. Caleb should be bringing it out soon.' I uttered, wondering if I should go into the kitchen and help him.

Noble appeared enraged. 'I'm sorry Mace but I think there's been a misunderstanding; I'm going to Hartland with Effie. What is the point of you coming too?'

Mace stood there with a smug smile across his face. 'Oh, I'm sorry, would I get in the way, because you're in love with Effie.'

'Well yes.' He hesitated. 'And also because...well, don't take this the wrong way but I'm more familiar with the area than you, and...and better equipped if anything awful should happen.'

'You mean you're stronger, and more likely to fend off an attack.'

'If you want me to be frank, then yes.' Retorted Noble.

Reluctantly, I got up from the grass. 'Look I really don't...'

'Just a minute Effie, this is between Noble and I.'

I groaned with annoyance.

Looking determined, Mace strode up to Noble and folded his arms in defiance.

'I may be punier and more handsome than you, but that doesn't mean I'm not capable of delivering a punch or two.' He moved his face close to his. 'And you're forgetting that I've known Effie longer than you and she's my best friend.'

Noble's face became contorted with anger. With one swift movement he grabbed Mace by the collar of his shirt and pulled him towards him. 'I've seen the way you stare at her.' He snarled. 'Why don't you just admit you love her, and want her all to yourself.'

I widened my eyes in astonishment. Perhaps I should have been embarrassed at the awkwardness of the situation, but as my face began to colour, I realised how extremely amusing Noble's absurd comment was. In truth, the both of them were behaving like a couple of petulant schoolboys, squabbling over nothing.

Mace was silent for a second before exploding into laughter. 'You're not very astute are you Noble. Yes, I love her but not in the way you imagine, I love her like a sister.' He turned to glance at me. 'The sister I never had.' He gulped nervously. 'Now let go of me.'

Relaxing a little, Noble released his hold on Mace. 'I'm still travelling to Hartland with Effie. You're welcome to tag along if you like.'

'Well thank you Noble, that's extremely obliging of you. Would you like me to carry all the luggage and make the meals?'

'Excuse me.' I cried out. 'If you two are going to argue the whole journey I suggest you stay in Briarwood. I'm sure Isaiah and I can cope on our own.'

They both turned to stare at me.

Caleb approached with a tray. 'Apologies for my delay.' He gave a swift look back at the cottage. 'We have company.' Laying the tray on the table he began to pour out the tea. 'Verity is in the kitchen.' He lowered his voice. 'She's a little distraught.'

'Distraught?' I asked.

'Yes, what with everything that's happened today. Apparently, she had no idea of how much I detested Isaiah, and was worried it would affect our relationship, I assured her that despite her father, the both of us would always be friends.' He shook his head and frowned. 'The poor girl just needs a moment to compose herself before joining us in the garden.' He passed me some tea. 'She's terribly upset about her father leaving.'

My eyes widened in amazement. 'Really?'

'Since her mother's death, Isaiah has been absent. I think Verity was hoping they could spend some time together before he left again.' Caleb glanced tenderly at Noble. 'I know only too well what it's like being parted from a loved one. But you might have been absent for a long time son, but you're back to stay now.'

Mace began to cough then cleared his throat.

Noble stepped forward. 'Father.... father I have something to tell you.' He gulped. 'I'm so sorry but I'm going to Hartland with Effie.'

A peculiar expression crossed over Caleb's face. 'No, no you can't.' He dropped the teapot on the grass. 'Noble please, I've only just got you back. I beseech you, do not desert me once more.' He glanced at me in an unnerving manner. 'Effie goes because she has to, because she loves Gideon and wants to bring him home. Isn't that right Effie?'

I swallowed hard. 'Well, yes. I believe so.'

Every word he spoke was true; I did love Gideon, but what about Noble? I'd grown very fond of him. To have him join me on the journey to Hartland would be wonderful, but in many respects, it would make me seem extremely selfish, especially as Caleb had been without Noble for some time now, and when he'd finally got him back, here I was taking him away again. I already felt responsible for Gideon's absence, and Caleb had made it blatantly clear that he blamed me. This was my chance to redeem myself, to bring back his lost son, to reunite his family.

Noble began to laugh. 'Effie doesn't know what she wants.' He took my hand, gazing into my eyes. 'But I do.'

I snatched my hand away from his. 'You're absolutely wrong Noble, I *do* know what I want, I want Gideon.' My voice was stern. 'So please allow me to seek him out. You belong here with your father.

Noble looked enraged. 'You don't mean that Effie.'

'Yes, yes I do.' I could feel my voice breaking up. 'I only wish Mace to accompany me.'

The pained expression on Noble's face was heart-breaking. 'If that is your wish, who am I to stand in your way. I shall say my goodbyes now, for I very much doubt if I shall ever see you again. You shall be doomed the very moment you enter Hartland.'

Looking incensed he marched swiftly towards the cottage, without glancing back.

A sudden cold chill went through me, right through to my bones.

My voice sounded feeble as I called after him. 'Noble?'

As I made my way after him, Caleb took my arm. 'Leave Noble be Effie. He will come to realise that remaining here is the right decision.'

'That's right E, he'll get over it.'

Caleb stared at Mace.

'Do you wish to go with Effie, lad?'

Mace looked sheepish. 'Yes sir.'

A flicker of regret crossed over Caleb's face. 'Then so be it.' He sighed heavily. 'I will miss you. It's been just like having another son in the cottage.'

Torment and guilt became obvious in Mace's expression. 'I shall miss you too Caleb.' His eyes were filled with anguish. 'I thank you for your hospitality.' He scratched his head. 'And.... sorry for all the breakages.'

Laughter erupted from Caleb's throat. 'I forgive you Mace. Come back anytime, your presence is more than welcome.'

A cool breeze blew across the garden.

Caleb turned towards the cottage and reached out his arm. 'Verity, do join us.'

I watched as the madwoman crept across the garden in her sombre dress, like a ghostly figure emerging from the spirit world. Her attempt at smiling was pitiful and only intensified her sinister nature.

'How terribly rude of me Caleb.' She uttered. 'For keeping you waiting so long.' She dabbed her eyes with a handkerchief. 'May I come and join you all?'

Mace came up behind me, whispering in my ear. 'Wow, you weren't joking when you said how scary looking Verity is.' He gulped. 'I'm going back inside; I've had enough drama for one night.' He sniggered. 'Enjoy your time with your dearly beloved sister.'

'You know?'

'Caleb told me last night.' Kissing me on the forehead, he smiled. 'See you bright and early tomorrow morning.'

'Mace.' I whispered urgently.

'I bid you all goodnight.' He yelled, cautiously eyeing the madwoman as he passed by.

'Leaving so soon.' She exclaimed loudly. 'I don't believe we've been introduced.'

Mace glanced at her. 'No, I don't believe we have.' He nodded at her. 'Goodnight.'

He turned and marched towards the cottage.

The madwoman stared after him, looking rather perplexed.

'That was Mace, you'll have to forgive his erratic behaviour.' Exclaimed Caleb. 'He's a strange young man in many ways, but exceedingly likeable.' His face glazed over for a second, deep in thought. 'He leaves tomorrow with your father and Effie...your sister.'

My heart sank.

She gave me a sly look. 'Ah yes, my little sister.'

Not wishing to stay a moment longer I started towards the cottage.

'I'm suddenly overcome with tiredness.' I said. 'See you in the morning Caleb.' I gave the madwoman a glare as I went passed. 'Goodnight, and goodbye.'

She started to rock with hysterical laughter. 'Could you imagine us journeying together, what laughs we'd have.' Her eyes darkened. 'I was going to join you on your little adventure across the wilderness. You me and father, on a family adventure.' She sniggered. 'Gilbert would stay of course; he has no stamina for such things.' She let out a rather dramatic sob. 'So, you can imagine how devastated I was when our father insisted I remain in Briarwood to take care of our simple brother.' Wiping her eyes with the hanky she rested her head against Caleb's shoulder. 'I was so hoping to become reacquainted with the father I hardly know, to spend time in his company.' Another sob escaped her lips.

'There, there.' Said Caleb, patting her on the shoulder. 'As I've told you, you're very welcome to come over to our home, whenever you wish.'

'I appreciate your kindness Caleb.' She lifted her head and stared directly into my eyes. 'How I shall enjoy renewing my friendship with Noble, I've not seen him for such a long while, I envisage we'll have endless fun together.' She giggled. 'What a handsome man he has grown into.'

I felt the anger rising within me, but my heart was too heavy to think straight.

'If you'll excuse me, I have packing to do.'

Without another word I turned and fled into the cottage. Running up the stairs, I blindly made my way to my room and flung myself on the bed, desperately trying to hold back the tears.

# Chapter 14

Morning seemed to come early that fateful day, the day I had to leave Briarwood.

To my utter dismay I was unable to say goodbye to Noble; I searched the cottage and garden but he was nowhere to be seen. I visualised him trudging the fields in torment, his face contorted in pain and sorrow. But then Verity would appear, with her cold eyes and black heart. And there she would entice him into her web of evil, and when he was under her spell, she would devour him.

We met in the cornfield beyond the garden. Isaiah had already arrived and was elated to see me, but frowned at Mace and completely disregarded Caleb. It saddened me that Noble was nowhere in sight and I kept glancing back towards the cottage, expecting and hoping that he would charge up the field at any moment, his eyes gleaming. As soon as the great bird Croft approached, Caleb said his farewells to Mace and I, wishing us luck on our journey, and before going back to the cottage, he glanced at Isaiah, warning him to stay away for good, otherwise he'd personally put him to death. Not waiting for a reply, he began walking down the cornfield in big confidant strides, away from us and back to his cosy home, back to his beloved son, the son I had forsaken.

As we headed southwards, I had the worrying thought that one of us might fall, for although Croft appeared extremely powerful, I mulled over whether he was capable of maintaining the weight of all three of us, and the additional burden of our rucksacks, for a long period of time. I also was becoming agitated at the way Mace clung to me like a small child, rather than grasping onto the generous fur of Croft; my fear of leaning too far one way was paramount in my mind, and I had visions of us both plunging to our doom, leaving Isaiah staring down at us in despair.

'Whatever is wrong with this daft bird?' uttered Isaiah. 'Why is he slowing down?'

'Perhaps Croft needs a rest, it can't be easy flying so far without becoming weary.' I replied, steadying myself. 'Mace please don't hold me so tight. There's adequate fur to grab.'

'Isaiah roared with laughter. 'What do you expect Effelia, the boy's cowardly nature makes him incapable of looking after himself.'

'And your vile nature makes everyone incapable of liking you, let alone loving you. Even Verity treats you with contempt.'

The following events were undeniably frightening. With one swift movement Isaiah lurched backwards, flaying his arms about in an attempt to strike Mace. Whether he'd temporarily forgotten that we were high up in the sky, or he just didn't care, I couldn't say. Nevertheless, Isaiah's impulsive movements caused me to loosen my grip on Croft, and with a short scream I began to fall.

'Effie, NO.' cried Mace, desperately attempting to reach me as I toppled downwards.

In vain, I tried to grab hold of Mace, but it was too late. As I found myself dropping, something gripped my wrist, and to my utter astonishment I realised Croft had hold of me, dragging me along by one of his talons, as if I was his captured prey.

'Hold on Effelia. Try and clamber back up.'

'I can't.' Came my feeble voice.' My left arm felt like it was coming away from the socket as the bird clutched me firmly by my wrist. 'I'm too low down.' I screamed, feeling myself swinging wildly backwards and forwards.

Croft let out a screech and began swooping low.

'We're landing.' Shouted Mace. 'Good boy, good Cross.'

Despite my predicament I let out a laugh when I heard Mace misnaming Croft. And to my joy I found myself being lowered gently to the ground; delicately he released his hold on my wrist, and with a squawk he abruptly sprung his back up, causing Mace and Isaiah to tumble backwards onto the grass, with a scream.

'Thank you, Croft, I owe you my life.' I said affectionately, stroking his thick fur. 'You're so cleaver, just like your master.'

The bird let out another screech and nuzzled his face into my neck.

'Effie, are you alright?' Asked Mace, brushing himself down. 'I...I tried to reach you but...'

'You're a liar boy.' Screamed Isaiah. 'The only one brave enough to reach down and grab Effelia would have been my good self.' He glowered at Croft. 'But this beast had other ideas.' He glanced at the surroundings.' 'Why do you suppose he put us down here, I don't recognise this place.'

'Perhaps Croft was thinking of Effie, you stupid man.'

Isaiah made a beeline for Mace. 'Why you...'

'That's enough of that you two. Surely the important thing is that we're all safe and sound.' I grimaced. 'It could have been a whole lot worse.'

Croft shifted and began to flap his wings.

I bounded over towards him. 'You're not leaving are you Croft?'

Peering at me it almost appeared he was nodding.

With a sigh I patted his great head. 'You've been fantastic Croft. We appreciate you carrying us this far.'

Isaiah grunted.

He nuzzled up to me one last time then launched himself back up into the sky.

'It appears we've got to make the remainder of the journey by foot. Unless you can locate a portal from that ledger of yours, E.'

Lowering my eyes, I removed some fur from my dress. 'I er. I didn't bring the ledger.'

Isaiah looked flabbergasted. 'I grant you it wouldn't have helped us now, but Effelia you really should have.' He re-positioned his spectacles. 'It could be useful.' Studying my face closely his expression became suspicious. 'So where did you leave it then, in your snug little bedroom at Briarwood?'

'Perhaps.'

He shook his head in despair. 'Oh Effelia.'

'It just didn't seem right to bring it. There's something about that ledger that sends shivers down my spine, and my instincts told me to hide it, keep it safe, and out of harm's way.'

'It's too late now anyway.' He scoffed. 'I suggest we go through the woods up ahead, they do look vaguely familiar, and I do believe it will quicker to go through rather than bypassing them.

Mace slapped him on the back. 'There we go Isaiah. Your failing memory hasn't completely deserted you.'

'Be silent, cretin.'

'Excuse me you two, but do I have to endure this antagonistic behaviour the entire journey? Can you at least attempt to be civil to one another?

They both stood there glaring at me, without uttering a word.

'I will take your silence as a yes.' I said rather sharply.

Before entering the woods, we sat for a while on the grass and ate the sandwiches Caleb had provided. Mace grumbled about how there weren't enough of them to curb his hunger, and Isaiah scolded him for being so greedy.

As I stared in a daze across to the woods, I reflected on last night's events, wanting to blot out the look of rejection on Noble's face, but unable to succeed; he'd looked so furious, and so unwanted that I felt overcome with guilt and heartache. And then there had been this morning, not having the opportunity to say goodbye, to give him a farewell hug, to feel his arms about me.

I felt my heart leap in my chest and I began to blush.

But there had been another matter playing on my mind, something rather odd. After the madwoman's cheery warning about how she would be spending time with Noble, and after I had fled to my room and wiped away my tears, I'd noticed that the drawers of the dressing table were slightly ajar, and the contents of my rucksack were not in the order I had put them. There wasn't anything missing, of that I was sure, however somebody had been in my room, searching for something....

Isaiah's voice came bellowing across the field. 'Come on, we should continue our journey.'

I gave a big sigh as we headed towards the ominous looking woods.

'Have you ever stopped to wonder why Briarwood is the way it is, doesn't it bother you how the grass is forever green, how the trees are perpetually laden with fruit. There is always an abundance of good farmland and the crops are always healthy and the cattle are always fat.' Questioned Mace, as we trampled through the woods.

'Rather that than hunger and famine.' I replied, looking up at the strange looking trees, tightly bunched together.

It struck me odd how Mace had somehow managed to retain his hold on reality: his presence in the village had not clouded his judgement, and he hadn't been swept away by the captivating charm of Briarwood, enticed into its unique way of life, unlike my good self, who had been lost the very moment I'd arrived.

'But it's wrong, it's not natural.'

'Mace, you are questioning all this for no reason. The whole village are all good, hardworking people. Why do you think the farmers toil in the field's day after day? Because they have to, the crops do not miraculously harvest themselves.' I peered at him curiously. 'You should accept this way of life, and embrace its unique, simplicity.'

He raised his left eyebrow. 'I'm not as easily deceived as you E, I'm not ready to be smothered in a blanket of oblivion.'

'What an obstinate and witless boy you are. Your flippant nature shows your lack of morals, proving you're sadly lacking in any integrity, whatsoever.'

Mace gawped at Isaiah blankly. 'What?'

Isaiah looked pleased with himself. 'I rest my case.'

'No, you pathetic man, I understand what you're saying; I'm not a dunce. What I'm questioning is- who do you think you are to even begin to know my true character.' His face became darker. 'I may act the fool, occasionally.' He gave me a sideways glance. 'But I'm decent and honourable, and kind, and....'

'Mace.' I yelled, beginning to get a headache. 'I completely agree with you, but do you mind if we continue our journey in peace, for a while?' I gave Isaiah a stony look. 'Both of you.'

'Isaiah smiled ingratiatingly at me. 'Yes Effelia.'

For a while my plea for silence worked, however Mace had the infuriating knack of not being able to keep his mouth shut for very long.

'And no one lives in the wilderness or in the forests. Not one soul.'

'That's simply because there's nothing for them in the wilderness.' Exclaimed Isaiah, shaking his head with amusement. 'Honestly boy, did you leave your brains back at Briarwood.' He slapped his forehead with the back of his hand. 'Ops, how silly of me, you never had them to begin with.'

Mace decided to ignore his comment. 'Why is it called Hartland?'

Isaiah threw him a sullen look. 'Because of the Hart animals that roam the land.' He sneered at Mace. 'To put it in a simpler language – deer.' He chuckled at him.

Mace glared at him angrily, but said nothing.

As we fought our way through the nettles and bracken, I couldn't help but think how the woods seemed to possess a distinct sinister feel, with the oddly shaped trees and haunting stillness, I feared becoming lost and never finding my way out. And although it was rather a relief reaching the edge and emerging onto open land, it failed to lift my spirits; and instead a dreadful feeling of unease crept over me, which grew as I looked down upon the desolate stretch of land before me: all I could see was a wild moor, smothered in a dank mist, giving a decidedly eerie, bleakness to the landscape. I thought what a sharp contrast it was from Briarwood, the cosy little village nestled amidst some of the most spectacular scenery imaginable.

My heart began to ache, along with my feet.

'How far now Isaiah?' I asked, wondering if we should stop for a rest.

'Not long, not long at all.' He mumbled in a distant voice, looking pensive. 'I'm a little confused. If I made Hartland my home why did I leave it, where have I been all this time?'

Mace and I caught each other's eye.

What Isaiah could and couldn't remember was certainly puzzling. I could only assume he had unconsciously blocked out unwanted thoughts about Hartland, such as being sentenced to death. My prime concern was how he'd react when this horrifying fact came back to him.

'It's a long story Isaiah.' I replied. 'You're back now, isn't that what matters?'

'I suppose so, but, but something's missing.' He reached up and rubbed his forehead. 'Something vitally important.'

Before I knew it, Mace had stepped forward and put his face close to Isaiah's. 'I could tell you if you like Isaiah, put you out your misery.'

'Mace, no.' I screamed at him. 'Now is not the time to go down memory lane.'

'Oh, but the sheer delight of tormenting this odious man would be completely satisfying.'

Isaiah glared at him.

'Look, both of you. I'm tired and hungry and would like to reach Hartland before nightfall.' I paced forward in front of them. 'So come on, let's get a move on.'

'Perhaps you should have eaten more than one sandwich, E.' Commented Mace. 'I'd offer you another but they've all gone.'

'That's because you scoffed them all boy.'

I groaned.

As we wearily made our way down, I noticed how the air became bitterly cold and how a light dusting of snow was now covering the ground.

'Your wait is nearly over Effelia.' Exclaimed Isaiah in a joyous voice, pacing ahead. 'The passage of yews before you are in the realms of Hartland. We must pass under them to gain access.'

I stared ominously at the strange, medieval looking tunnel of arched yew trees; the unbroken arch of bent branches filled me with an eerie, inexplicable sadness and reminded me of old twisted hands, tightly clasped together in a perpetual lock.

'Can we not go around them?'

Isaiah glared at me as if I was insane. 'No, no that certainly won't do Effelia.' He exclaimed in a rather anxious voice. 'Legend has it that traveller's passing this way who have failed to enter the tunnel have become lost in the wilderness.' He gave me a long, steady look. 'Eventually the yews take the travellers for their own and their spirits are said to linger forever in these mangled trees.'

I heard a cackle behind me. 'What a load of gobbledegook.' Said Mace.

Isaiah's face became contorted in anger, as he swung round to look at him. 'Mock me if you wish boy, but you'll see.' A strange laugh escaped his lips. 'But please do go round, it will fill me with exultation not to look upon your idiotic face, ever again.'

Mace stepped forward, ready to strike out at Isaiah.

I swiftly moved in-between them. 'Please, stop it, both of you. 'We shall all go through.' I said in a steadfast voice.

And so we went forth, into the claustrophobic confines of the tunnel: I for one was secretly glad when we'd emerged out the other side, Mace was marching speedily ahead as if scared he may become trapped by the ancient yews, and heaved a sigh of relief when we had passed underneath it, and Isaiah casually strolled along the tunnel as if he was taking a stroll on a Sunday afternoon. After our short, uneventful journey through the yews, we headed northwards and came upon a long avenue, scattered with leafless beech trees, long past their prime, then gradually the way sloped downwards into a desolate looking valley surrounded by marshland.

'Can't we rest for a while? My feet are killing me.' Grumbled Mace.

Isaiah looked amused. 'The problem with some people is they have absolutely no stamina.'

'Huh.' Retorted Mace. 'And some people just don't know when to put a stopper in it.' He lowered himself to the ground and took off his boots. 'The only way to get some peace would be to gag you.'

'Likewise.'

Paying no attention to their petty squabbling, I sat down and stared glumly at the forlorn wilderness before me.

'Bleak, isn't it?

I turned to glance at Isaiah. 'Yes, extremely.'

An instinctive desire to turn back, to rid myself of the ever-growing feeling that nothing good would come of our journey, was at the forefront of my mind; spurred on by the uninviting nature of the landscape.

'Don't become low-spirited Effelia. I promise you your mood will soon lift.'

I stared into his face. 'I do hope so.'

'Come on, the sooner we move the sooner we shall be there.' He glanced at Mace. 'Take your time boy, stay out here until dark if you wish.' He sniggered. 'No one will miss you if you stray off the right path and become stranded in the wilderness. I for one will...'

'Hush Isaiah.' I said, swiftly interrupting him.

'Yeah, we've had enough of you droning on.' Mace retorted, carefully putting his boots back on.'

'Hurry Mace.' My voice became grim. 'Darkness will fall soon, and I have no wish to spend the night out in the open.'

Reluctantly, he got up and strode on up ahead of us.

The marshlands seemed to stretch on for miles and was rather treacherous in parts; we had to watch our footing just in case we sunk into the mire, but eventually we arrived at the end, relieved to have our feet on solid ground once more. The fog was extremely dense now and putrid, and I could hardly see the view before us, however, as we carried on it cleared a little and I saw that we were surrounded by frost-covered fields with herds of grazing deer.

'Are they the Hart deer?'

'Yes, magnificent creatures aren't they.' Isaiah said in a soft tone. 'These specific species are used to foraging for their food in icy conditions; over the centuries they've adapted to the weather and have become extremely hardy.'

A harsh wind blew into my face and I noticed how the temperature had dropped. I drew my coat tightly around me. 'Why is the weather so bad in this region?'

'You may have noticed how the trees outside the vicinity of Hartland have all but perished. Many believe they've been drained of all their goodness by the great trees planted by the monks.' Isaiah paused and did up his coat. 'They named them

The Elder trees and believed them to be the most powerful trees in all of existence, but as the years passed by these trees grew greedy and snatched away the beautiful landscape that once covered these lands, so it would no longer flourish.' He suddenly appeared melancholy. 'It is said that the earth mourns the passing of such wonder and yearns for its return by causing howling, icy winds to perpetually whistle and moan across the bleak, stark landscape.'

I felt woeful. 'How very sad.' I said looking at Isaiah's crestfallen expression. 'I can't imagine why anyone would wish to reside in such a place, it's enough to make the happiest person depressed.'

Mace grunted. 'And yet we are heading there all the same.' He sighed.

Unexpectedly I tripped.

'Watch the tree roots, they are everywhere near Hartland monastery.'

'Is the monastery the only building around these parts?' I questioned him, perplexed.

'Yes, all the inhabitants of Hartland reside at the monastery. There is nowhere else in the vicinity where they could possibly survive.' Shouted Isaiah in an aggravated voice.

'Oh, I said, feeling foolish for not knowing. I'd been so preoccupied in heading for Hartland I'd not considered the number of dwellings on the land. Of course, I had to face the fact that Gideon or Clarice might not be here at all, either one of them could have lost their footing and sunk into the mire, somewhere in the wilderness, or been snatched by one of those abnormal trees. It was hard, but I had to resign myself to the possibility that I would never see them, ever again.

'Of course, the monastery has other names that are thought by some to be considerably more appropriate for such a place, such as The Harshlands or The Silent Monastery.'

'Silent?'

Without glancing at me he frowned. 'Because it is silent as a graveyard.'

'Well, that certainly warms the cockles of your heart.' Exclaimed Mace. 'I can't wait.'

I rolled my eyes.

As I looked ahead I saw what appeared to be a towering fence like structure that seemed to reach up to the sky; it was only when we stepped nearer that I realised it wasn't a fence at all but trees, weaved abnormally tightly together in a solid mass like wall which ran along the entire perimeter of the area. In the centre of the great fence I observed a pair of colossal iron gates, covered in intertwined branches, and the left gate was very slightly ajar, as if awaiting our arrival. I watched in astonishment as Isaiah confidently grabbed the left side of the gate and pulled it further open, causing a long drawn out whine to escape from the seemingly, un-oiled hinges.

'Come on both of you, hurry through.'

It amazed me how eager Isaiah was to enter the monastery, so self-assured. I wondered when realisation would hit home, when he would eventually grasp the truth. I felt a little guilty for not warning him of his forthcoming peril, but mostly I had a sense of gratification that he would finally answer for his string of misdemeanours, both in this world and others. I'd jotted down all the crimes I knew about in my trusted notebook, along with a certain statement he'd made, the words of which were now ringing in my ears.

**"Isaiah informed me how he could never return to Hartland, because he would be put to death".**

Following on behind him, Mace and I gradually made our way inside, and both jumped as the heavy gates crashed shut behind us, causing an almighty racket.

I winced, screwing my face up.

Mace made a remark to Isaiah about keeping the noise down.

Amusingly, I thought of how the monastery didn't have a chance of remaining silent, not with Mace and Isaiah bickering with one another, and with Mace blundering about in his usual manner, it would be impossible to maintain a peaceful environment within the monastery.

An unexpected sound of moaning reverberated around us, causing me to shudder: it appeared the trees were creaking and groaning at our raucous arrival

'What was that? Asked Mace.'

'Nothing, it was nothing.' Isaiah said dismissively, striding ahead. He turned and saw that Mace and I were a way behind him, dragging our heels. 'Well come on then, you didn't come all this way just to stand at the gates, did you?' His voice suddenly became urgent. 'Quickly now Effelia, move away.' He uttered abruptly, grabbing my arm and pulling me forward.

As I turned back, I noticed how the sturdy branches moved slowly across the gate entrance, binding it tightly together in an almighty lock. Initially I thought my eyes were deceiving me, but then I remembered how the trees in this land were different, they were alive. I gasped, trying to catch my breath. An overwhelming feeling of panic came about me, and I wanted to run back out the gates, but it was too late, we were trapped.

'Here, take my arm E.' Mace whispered. 'I won't let anything unnatural happen to you.' He sniggered, tightly linking arms with me.

I sensed nervousness in his voice that was not usual for him, and realised he was just as scared.

'Well, that's reassuring Mace.' I said in a rather unsteady voice.

As a cold, mist enveloped us a sinister feeling crept over my body, intensifying with every step; I imagined I'd drifted into a ghost story where the hairs on the back of your neck seem to stand up in pure fright.

I swayed slightly against Mace. 'I…. I can't see anything, the mist, it's everywhere.'

Blindly I waved my free arm out in front of me, fearful of knocking into something, such as an evil spirit. My anguish was exacerbated when neither Mace nor Isaiah answered me, and I started to tremble uncontrollably.

'You should see it very soon now.' murmured Isaiah. 'Once this confounded mist has cleared.'

My distress was lessened somewhat by the sound of Isaiah's voice. And the realisation that Mace was shaking too, in fact he was leaning heavily against my side, clinging to my arm, and making it painful.

'Mace, are you alright?' I asked, gently removing my arm from his grip. 'You're abnormally quiet.'

'You bet E.' he replied in a faint voice. 'You know me, cool, calm and collective at all times.

'Huh.' Remarked Isaiah. 'Your voice reeks of fear boy.'

I waited for Mace's reaction but to my surprise he remained silent, a welcome change from the constant quarrelling that had been going on between the two of them.

Peering ahead I spotted the dim outline of a great structure, gradually emerging from the endless cloud of fog.

'Welcome to Hartland Monastery Effelia.' exclaimed Isaiah, as if he were the proud owner of such a place.

# Chapter 15

The monastery was remote as any building could be. It was so large and magnificently imposing, that it loomed over its beholder as if boasting a distinct feeling of aloof superiority in the very essence of its sturdy structure. I observed the ancient stone gargoyles, which were darkened with age, leering down upon us in their evil silence, watching and waiting as we approached their home. I suddenly visualised sweeping, majestic lawns, flourishing plants and exquisite flowers; in the middle would stand an opulent looking fountain with water flowing from the mouth of a regal looking statue. Of course, my picture of splendour was all in my mind; whatever joy may have existed in this place had long since passed.

Isaiah appeared elated. 'Unless my mind has forsaken me, I believe we pass through the narrow passage at the centre of the monastery, this will bring us out into the courtyard and to the entranceway' His voice rose in excitement. 'What a delight to be back where I belong; there will be no casting aspersions on my character here, they will welcome me with open arms.'

Mace and I glanced at one another and raised our eyebrows.

'That's right Isaiah, I'm sure the people here will be ecstatic to see you.' Mace said, sniggering. 'I'm sure they've been totally lost without you.'

Isaiah threw him a scathing look, but did not reply.

We came upon the courtyard, as Isaiah had said. A large expanse of granite paving covered the entire ground, which was cast in shadows from the surrounding walls of the towering monastery: directly ahead was a long arched, dimly lit entranceway, where we found ourselves ascending a wide granite staircase, leading up to two great wooden doors.

'Isn't it odd we've not seen anyone yet' I asked, turning to Isaiah. 'Was it like this when you used to live here?'

'From my understanding the occupants tend to keep to the confines of the monastery and the greenhouses around the side, where they tend to the vegetables.'

'Yes, really E, did you expect a welcome party?' Mace mocked. 'This isn't an historic monastery with a cosy little tea room like….' He faltered. 'Like the café at home.' He scrunched his face up, as if in deep concentration 'Oh what is it called.' In frustration he started to bang his fist across his forehead.

'Stop it Mace.' I shouted at him. 'You'll hurt yourself.'

'The boy's mind is already severely impaired.' Isaiah said, spitefully. 'It might help knock some sense into him.'

'Huh, that's rich coming from the man whose unstable behaviour has wrecked countless lives.' Mace retorted.

Isaiah glared at him, his face red with anger and confusion. 'Whatever do you mean, what…what have I done?'

'Please, stop it you two, this is hardly the time or place.'

'What haven't you done?' Mace mumbled under his breath. 'The list is endless.'

'Mace.' I screamed at him.

'He started it.' Mace answered, sullenly.

'Stop acting like an irritable child.' I said, placing my hand gently on his arm. 'Rise above it Mace.'

Without warning the doors swung open and a middle-aged, robed woman stood there, her hands on her hips. 'Yes, what is it?' she asked in a hurried voice. She was rather plump with cropped grey, brittle looking hair and a pallid complexion, but what really struck me were her small, mean looking eyes that looked down upon us in such a harsh manner. 'Well?' she snapped.

Isaiah stepped forward. 'Proctor?' He laughed. 'Do you not remember me, it's Isaiah Penhaligon.' Pausing for a minute, he grabbed my hand and pulled me forward, his face beaming. 'And this is my daughter, Effelia.'

Mace piped up. 'And I'm Effie's companion.'

Isaiah threw him a look of disdain then turned to the woman. 'We've come for a visit - I do hope I'm still welcome in my old home.'

The woman, who it seemed, was known as Proctor, glared at him for a few moments and narrowed her eyes, 'Follow me.' She snorted and turned, retreating inside. 'Wipe your feet on entry.'

'Somehow I don't think tea and scones are on the menu.' Mace said, laughing.'

I gave him a smile and couldn't help but giggle as he tripped over the step leading into the monastery. As I went inside and wiped my feet, my attention was instantly drawn to the interior of the building.

'Don't stand there gaping, we haven't all day.' Proctor exclaimed crossly as she led us across the spacious hall.

As we followed along behind her I gazed up in awe at the endless number of arches that ran in graceful curves across the high ceiling, casting long, dark shadows in the corners of the vast entrance hall. Leading off from this was an eerie, stark little room, which Proctor impatiently ushered us into.

'You are to wait here.'

'Yes, your highness.' Mace muttered under his breath.

Proctor threw Mace a stern look. 'Insolence will not be tolerated at our establishment; you should do well to remember that.'

Before Mace had a chance to answer she was gone, leaving the three of us in the tiny room. Standing on tiptoe I could just about see out of the small window, but the swirling fog obscured the view.

I sighed. 'I wonder what happens now.'

'That old dragon has gone to get her superior. There's no way she'd be in charge, everyone would be out of here like a shot.' Mace took a sideways glance at Isaiah. 'Isn't that right Isaiah?' He exclaimed in a mocking tone.

There was no answer.

Looking over I noticed how Isaiah's face had turned a deathly pale. 'Isaiah, what is it? I asked, stepping towards him. 'What's wrong?'

His expression was full of anguish. 'I...I'm not sure.' Closing his eyes, he rubbed his hand across his brow. 'I suddenly feel a little ill.' Without warning, he swiftly paced over to the door. 'I need to leave; I need to go now.' Frantically, he began violently turning the doorknob. 'That blasted Proctor had locked us in.' He banged his fist against the door. 'Open up.'

'Have you remembered something about this place?' I asked, something bad?'

He swung round to face me. 'You knew, you knew the whole time, didn't you? The sweat was pouring from his face. 'Had it written in that tatty old notebook of yours.'

'What? Mace enquired, pretending to be puzzled.

Isaiah went and crouched in the corner. 'I don't understand why it took me so long to recollect.' He hesitated. 'It wasn't until I entered the monastery that I remembered why I should never return.' Bending his head forward he began to sob. 'They're going to execute me.' He covered his face with his hands. 'My life will shortly come to an end.'

Instinctively I went over and placed my hand on his shoulder. 'You don't know that Isaiah, they may show you some clemency.' I jumped as he convulsed into hysterical laughter. 'What's so funny?' I asked, giving him a startled look.

'Do you really believe that? Perhaps if you put in a good word for me that will make all the difference in the world.' A look of hatred appeared on his face. 'But you won't will you Effelia, because this is what you wanted all along, to get rid of me.' He inclined his head towards Mace. 'You and that cretin.'

'I may be a cretin, but at least I'm not going to hell like your good self.' Said Mace with an air of smugness. 'He laughed. 'Poetic justice.'

Isaiah shot up and grabbed hold of Mace, pinning him up against the wall. 'Oh, don't worry boy, if I go I'm dragging you along too.' He snarled at him.

With a sigh I went to intervene, but froze as I heard the door being opened. Proctor was standing there with a burly looking man with ginger hair.

We all turned round and gaped at them both.

Focusing her morose stare upon Isaiah, Proctor ushered the burly man into the room. 'This is Abel; he will escort you to your accommodation.' She nudged the man forward. 'Go ahead Abel, our guest Isaiah will need a helping hand.'

Isaiah swiftly released Mace and sunk to his knees. 'Please, there has been a misunderstanding: I was brought here under false pretences.'

Ignoring his plea Proctor barked an order at Abel. 'Take him away.'

With one, swift movement Abel pulled Isaiah up from his knees, and began to drag him out the door.

Mace stood there, pretending to be tearful. 'Bye, bye Isaiah, I will miss you.'

A terrified Isaiah turned back and peered at me. 'Please help me Effelia.' His voice was pitiful.

I gulped and bit my lip.

A wave of remorse swept across my heart. Perhaps I had been a touch hard on him: despite our differences, I was his daughter; a daughter who'd willingly led him to his forthcoming death. I found myself on the verge of calling after him, to reassure him that I would do all I could to keep him safe, but I couldn't bring myself to do it; instead I stood there watching as Abel hauled him roughly along by his arm, disappearing up the corridor.

'Where, where are you taking him?' I asked feebly.

Proctor smirked. 'That is no longer your concern.' She snapped her fingers together. 'You two follow me.' Her billowing robes swished around as she abruptly paced out the room. 'The food will soon be ready in the great hall.'

'Tea and scones, or bread and gruel?' Mace whispered softly in my ear, as we walked down the stairway.

I chuckled. 'The way things are looking I would definitely say bread and gruel.'

We trailed behind Proctor, following her along a wide passageway. My eyes took in the ancient looking, granite covered walls and the vast, stone columns that were visible along the entire stretch.

'Do keep up.' Proctor uttered, stomping across the stone floor. From out of nowhere came the dull chime of a bell. She stopped for a moment and fleetingly glanced at a pocket watch that was on a chain around her neck. 'That bell has sounded late.' She huffed. 'I shall have to have a word with the bell ringer.'

'I didn't think anyone took any notice of the time.' I muttered, remembering the grandfather clock that stood silent and still at the cottage in Briarwood.

Turning to glare at me I saw that she was rather taken aback. 'What a ridiculous thing to say.' She exclaimed, looking astounded. 'Civilised society cannot possibly function without it.' Shaking her head in despair she carried on walking. 'Whatever land you come from must surely be primitive.'

Mace nudged me. 'Yes E, it's about time you emerged from the dark ages and invested in a watch.' He said, bringing his wristwatch up to my face.

I narrowed my eyes and grinned at him. 'A watch is only worth wearing if it's beneficial to its user; in your case it's pretty pointless as you'll still manage to be late for absolutely everything.'

He winked at me. 'But you wouldn't want me any other way.'

'Your constant chattering is unwanted and unnecessary.' Shouted Proctor. 'Pray be silent.'

Mace cursed underneath his breath.

'Pardon.' she yelled at him, her face like thunder. For a moment I thought she was going to strike him, but then thought better of it. 'What did you say?'

'I er...I just said how right you are.' He replied sheepishly. 'I shall bow down to the superior and mature nature of such a noble, larger than life lady as yourself.'

She glared at him in complete confusion, contemplating if his declaration was meant as a compliment or a rather insulting gibe. 'Huh. You certainly are very strange. I think spending time in Hartland Monastery will do wonders for your personality.' She commented with a cruel smile.

We both turned to one another, and although we were both smiling there was fear behind our eyes.

We'd reached the far side of the passageway now and Proctor led us through some heavy looking doors. 'This is the great hall.' She said, curtly, gesturing for us to enter the capacious dimly lit room. It was furnished with little more than long, wooden tables, with narrow benches, and upon the tables were jugs and goblets. 'Sit and wait.' She ordered, pointing to a particular table, on the far right of the hall. 'Newcomers are segregated from the others until they are ready.'

'Ready for what?' I asked.

Proctor scowled at me. 'I do not take kindly to being asked questions. Inquisitiveness is one of the many traits that we stamp out here at Hartland.'

I flung my rucksack down on the floor and took off my coat.

'Abel or one of the other residents will be in shortly to take all your belongings up to your rooms.' She said, grabbing my things. 'Tomorrow morning you will find appropriate clothing outside your doors.' With a disapproving look she ran her eyes over my muddy clothes. 'Now you are at Hartland everyone must wear the same attire.'

'But why?' said Mace with a laugh. 'That sounds completely daft.'

Proctor drew in a deep breath then exhaled. 'I can clearly see you're going to be trouble.' We both jumped as she suddenly raised her voice. 'Now sit.' She demanded, expecting us to obey her like an obedient dog.

Reluctantly we sat down on the bench.

Two figures emerged through the doors: it was Abel and another sturdy looking man with cropped blond hair.

'Ah, Abel, Mundy take our new arrival's bags up to their rooms.' She ordered, clicking her fingers at them. 'I do believe we have a couple of bedrooms vacant, don't we Abel?'

'Yes Madam, mumbled Abel 'As a matter of fact one became empty only today.'

'I stared at Abel. 'Did someone leave?'

Abel gawped at me with his mouth open then directed his eyes at Proctor.

'In a matter of speaking, yes.' Said Proctor in an indistinct voice, lowering her eyes. 'Put it this way, they certainly won't be requiring their room again.'

There was a momentarily stillness in the hall, as we all stood there looking at one another.

Proctor gave a sigh. 'Well, I certainly haven't got time to stand here all day. I have work to do.' She scowled at Abel and Mundy. 'Do get a move on you two, the residents will be arriving any moment.' She glared at Mace and I. 'The both of you will remain seated until you hear otherwise.'

'Well she's a jolly soul, isn't she? Mace exclaimed gruffly, as she shuffled across the hall, closing the heavy doors behind her with a deafening crash.

As Abel and Mundy began to pick up our belongings, I quickly grabbed my rucksack and looked up at the two hefty men.

'Really, there's no need. Mace and I can take it all when we go to our rooms.' I exclaimed becoming fearful they might search through our things.

'Proctor's orders.' Said Mundy in a mechanical sounding voice. With one swift movement he'd wrenched the rucksack from my grasp. 'It ain't going anywhere but your room.' He came close and looked at me with a steady gaze. 'Welcome to Hartland, Miss.' Quietly smiling he turned and headed for the door, his friend Abel close behind, who seemed to be acting rather shifty: for a fleeting moment he turned to glance at me, his face full of bewilderment, then he lumbered out the door.

I widened my eyes in confusion: I had no idea why the ginger haired Abel had given me such a strange look, and at that precise point in time didn't care, I had more serious matters to think of, such as the contents of my rucksack being searched. Instinctively, I felt for the notebook in my back pocket, just to reassure me. Then I remembered the gun.

I turned to Mace with an alarmed look on my face. 'The gun, it's still in my rucksack.'

'Those big oafs probably won't even spot it.' He said, drumming his fingers on the table. 'They don't look like they have a brain cell between them.' Casually he brushed a stray curl from his eye. 'I bet their bullies though.'

In ordinary circumstances I would have scolded Mace for being so cruel, but my mind was suddenly too preoccupied trying to work something out, something specific about Abel that was decidedly odd.

'Mace, did you notice the peculiar expression on Abel's face when he looked at me?'

'Huh. E, everyone I've met so far since entering the monastery have been uncannily peculiar.' He furrowed his brow. 'What do you suppose that Proctor woman meant about "being ready?"'

'I envisage we have to take some type of concoction before we're allowed to join their merry little community.' I uttered quietly, staring into space. 'We have to become one of them.'

Mace gave me an odd look, then screwed up his face. 'Well I'm not being turned into a dimwit like Abel and Mundy.' He grimaced. 'The sooner we find Clarice and Gideon the better.'

'And what then, will you return to Briarwood and declare to Caleb that you are his son? Or will you run back, back to....' I faltered, realising I'd already forgotten the name of my home. I'd checked my notebook earlier this morning, but clearly this wasn't frequent enough.

I gulped and covered my face with my hands. 'Oh Mace.'

'To the world in which we came from.' Mace said in a croaky voice. He reached over and pulled my hand away from my face, clenching it tightly. 'I need to refer to my notepad too E.' His large eyes were full of compassion. 'Don't become downhearted, we need to keep our spirits up in this place.'

We both smiled poignantly at one another.

'Here, have a drink.' Said Mace, pouring some liquid into a goblet. 'It appears to be water, he said, taking a sip then passing it to me. 'It's safe to drink Effie.' He sighed heavily, emptying some more into another goblet. 'Shame it's not wine, I could do with a drink.' He raised his goblet. 'Let's make a toast to Mace and Effie - the conquering heroes who brave the wilds of another world, slay the dragon, rescue the damsel's in distress and return home victorious.' We clinked our goblets together and drank our water.

'Dragons?' I said with a smile.

'Use your imagination E, who knows what lurks within this monastery, Proctor's a dragon, isn't she?'

I chuckled. 'Well, yes, I would have to agree with you on that one.'

A loud bang caused me to abruptly turn and look over my shoulder. The great doors of the hall had been flung, wide open and a steady stream of people dressed in dark, drab robes were tramping into the room, carefully watched by Proctor and the burly looking Mundy.

'Form an orderly queue.' Proctor barked at them.

My heart began to thud loudly in my chest at the anticipation of seeing Gideon. My eyes briefly examined each face as they made their way to the long tables around us. Perhaps he wasn't at Harland, I thought pensively, perhaps he had never made it, and instead been lured into the mire by angry pixies. Pain crossed over my heart as I recalled how he'd pulled me from the bog that night. It all seemed such a long time ago now, so distant, and yet the memory was an essential part of us, our love.

'Oh, there's that clot head Abel.' Commented Mace.

I observed Abel striding into the hall, he went and stood by Proctor and Mundy; once again I felt his eyes upon me, watching.

Trying not to let him bother me, I turned my attentions back to the remaining people entering the hall, shocked at how abnormally similar they all appeared with their glum, stony faces, devoid of emotion. It filled me with a distinct feeling of melancholy, so powerful that I wanted to weep.

Mace nudged me. 'It's like the living dead in here.' He whispered. 'Maybe the poor mites will brighten up a little if I go over and strike up a conversation with them.'

I smiled. 'There's no need to torment them further Mace.'

'You can be quite callous at times E.' he mumbled gruffly. 'How can you be so nasty to your loyal friend of old?

I stopped scanning the faces for a second and glanced at his downcast expression; even though I was sure it was all an act I was too preoccupied with looking for Gideon to retaliate.

'Sorry Mace, I was only teasing you. 'You're bound to rouse them from their lethargy with your magnetic personality.'

He winked at me. 'How right you are.'

It seemed to me that time had suddenly halted, for as I sat there, smiling, I saw a face amongst the crowd, the face of Gideon. Just like everyone else he was waiting, stoically in the long queue, staring straight ahead. An overwhelming surge of relief raced through my heart like a galloping horse, and suddenly it didn't matter that I was in this dreadful place, the only thing that mattered was Gideon, and that I had finally found him. Seeing him again, after all this time, I was not prepared for the tremendous impact of emotion that enveloped me. Everything in the background seemed to fade into obscurity as I looked upon his face, that exquisite face that I knew so well. His large, almond shaped eyes were just as dark and penetrating as I had remembered: their expression evoked a unique air of wisdom and mystery that was so intense that it caused me to drift away on an entangled cloud of entrancement. My heart wanted to call out to him so he was aware of my presence, but my head was saying no. I envisaged the scene I would create by uttering just one word, the whole hall would turn and stare at me with their blank, unanimated faces. Somehow this made me want to speak out more, as in their inhuman state I doubt if they would even acknowledge me. I suddenly felt guilty for my time spent with Noble, for allowing him to kiss me; how could I ever have doubted my feelings for Gideon, how could I ever imagine being with anyone else.

Mace started to shove me. 'Effie, Effie wake up?'

Gasping with shock I looked at Mace out of the corner of my eye, not wishing to take my eyes away from Gideon, just in case I lost sight of him.

'Gideon, it's Gideon.' I exclaimed in a strange voice.

'Is he the one with curly dark locks and brooding eyes?' Uttered Mace. 'I don't mean to be rude Effie, but his expression is rather menacing.'

Feeling aggravated with Mace I decided to ignore him.

I observed how Gideon joined a tall, frail looking man at the head table, along with Proctor, Abel, Mundy, and several other people I had not yet met. Patiently I focused my gaze upon him, believing it was only a matter of time before he saw me. And when he did, I visualised him bounding over towards me, and taking me in his arms. Of course, this wasn't really going to happen; I wasn't foolish enough to think that it would. Just an acknowledgment, a sign would suffice, but to my dismay he failed to even look up.

'You should stop staring Effie otherwise Proctor will come over and scold you.' Mace said in a low voice.

Trying to regain my composure I nodded and dragged my gaze away.

The frail looking man next to Gideon had risen and made a short speech about how we should all be grateful for the food we were about to eat. He had strange, peculiar looking eyes that seemed to possess a hint of madness within them; I saw how his hands shook as we all had to bow our heads why he said a short prayer.

The great doors opened once more and a number of people entered with long trolleys laden with numerous bowls, plates, baskets of bread and large dishes with ladles.

'This must be the food.' Exclaimed Mace, rubbing his hands together. 'Let's just hope it's decent.'

'I wouldn't get your hopes up Mace.' I said drolly as the bowls of food were passed out.

I stared at the young woman who passed us our food, and smiled, but she failed to even look me in the eye. 'Thank you.' I said, softly, nodding at her.

'Yes, thank you for the bowl of gruel.' Mace muttered as the woman walked away. He gazed despondently at the unappetising, soup like substance in his bowl.

'Actually, it's not gruel, but soup.' I exclaimed, taking a spoonful.

'Whatever you want to call it Effie, it's still disgustingly awful.' He moaned. 'I wouldn't even feed it to my dog, if I had one.' Pausing for a moment he groaned. 'My memories are in such a shambles that I don't even recall having a pet.'

I widened my eyes in amusement. 'Well don't look at me; my brain is just as muddled as yours. My notebook may hold the answer; perhaps it will mention a dog, a dog called Rover.'

Mace spluttered on his soup. 'Rover. Let's hope I can come up with a more original name than that.' He exclaimed rather loudly.

'Keep your voice down Mace.' I uttered nervously. 'We need to keep a low profile.'

He thought for a moment before answering. 'Yes E, you're right.' Glumly he looked at his empty bowl.

'So, the food wasn't too bad then?' I asked. 'You've managed to clear your bowl.'

Slowly he leant forward over the table and stared fixedly at me. 'That is because I was starving.' He moved back and inclined his head to the next table. 'How come they've got bread and we haven't, are we on rations?'

'Maybe they just forgot to put bread on our table.' I replied, as Mace leapt up from the bench. 'What are you doing? I said in an urgent whisper.

'Back in a minute.'

I watched in horror as he went over to the next table and politely asked for the breadbasket, snatching it away before they had a chance to answer.

'Thank you, you're all so kind.' Several of the people gaped at him, but said nothing. 'I bet they're all full anyway.' Said Mace with a grin, as he sat back down opposite me and began to stuff the bread in his mouth. 'Mm?' He mumbled, offering me the basket.

As I ate my bread, I took a look over at the head table. Gideon was staring blankly ahead, into thin air, as if in some kind of trance. Part of me felt frustrated with him and wanted to go over and shake him awake, but the other, cautious side wished to stay hidden, frightened of his reaction at seeing me. However, I noticed the tall man beside him was peering curiously over towards our table.

Unexpectedly Mace gripped my arm. 'Would you believe it, look Effie' His hold tightened. 'It's her, its Clarice, see?' He pointed over to the left of the hall.

As I sat there, hunched forward on the cold bench my eyes were drawn to a young woman of slender build, perched at the end of one of the tables. Barely recognisable, her flaxen hair was scraped back, tightly from her pallid face. Because my judgement was severely impaired by my inability to remember very much about her, I was very tempted to take a peak in my notebook, but after pondering for a moment I decided it wouldn't be a good idea; if one of them saw me they could easily confiscate my precious book, leaving me forever lost in the strange fog of forgetfulness of being in this land. However, it was then that I had a tiny, flickering vision from nowhere, materialising in my head: I was linking arms with a young woman, her face full of excitement and wonder, with all her hopes and dreams stretching out before her like a treasure trove of expectations.

I swayed slightly on my seat.

'Effie, do you recognise her?'

I refused to believe it, couldn't comprehend how this pathetic creature could be the bright, vivacious friend I once knew. As I stared long and hard at the woman she suddenly looked up and briefly caught my eye and I knew then for certain that it was Clarice. But her face didn't lighten up, her blue eyes didn't sparkle, they were dull and unchanging, just like all the rest of the diners.

I sharp pain shot across my temple. 'Clarice?' My voice was full of disbelief. 'What have they done to her Mace?' I said, tears welling up in my eyes.

I'm going over to speak to her.' He said, rising from the bench, with a rigid look of determination. 'She'll come back to the land of the living when she sees a friendly face.'

'Mace, Mace no.' I screamed, pulling him back. 'Now's not the right time.' I watched in alarm as the man sitting next to Gideon turned to glare at us. 'You're drawing attention to us.'

'Let go of me Effie.' He shouted, pulling himself roughly away from my grasp.

His arm flew forward, knocking several bowls and goblets from the table, they landed on the stone floor with a loud clatter.

'Oops.' Said Mace sheepishly. 'That was your fault Effie.'

I glared at him then looked across the hall. All eyes were on us, and I remember thinking that whatever strange power they were under it hadn't impaired their hearing.

A feeling of acute embarrassment swept over me and I wanted to crawl under the table, to escape their stare: my discomfort of being observed in such a way was an old habit I would never be able to shake off, it was part of me. I gulped as Proctor and Abel started towards us, and the unknown man sitting next to Gideon had got up from his seat.

Proctor stopped in front of our table and frowned. 'Newcomers, how disrespectful they all are.' She said sharply. 'Always causing a commotion of some kind.' The hard look on her face lessened as she called over to the head table. 'My sincere apologies Septimius, I shall deal with these two.' Her voice became harsh. 'Abel, give me a hand.'

The hefty Abel came up behind us and grabbed Mace by the arm whilst Proctor dragged me up from the bench. The plan had been to keep a low profile but it seemed we were failing miserably, however something told me not to struggle, I had to play it cautious for a while, until I knew how things worked here, and how and when all four of us could leave with the least fuss, sneaking out undetected.

Let go of me you big lump.' Mace exclaimed furiously, attempting to escape the clutches of the ginger haired Abel. He kicked him hard in the kneecap but the man hardly seemed to notice, instead he casually dragged Mace across the hall with one arm. Proctor, holding me with a firm grip, marched me along behind them.

A voice from the head table came bellowing across to us 'Wait.' It was the unknown man who I now realised was named Septimius; he began to walk over, leaving Gideon sitting there with his vacant expression. 'Allow me to speak with them first Proctor.' He eyed me curiously. 'What is the meaning of this disruption, who are you, what is your name?'

My voice was dry and faint as I spoke. 'Effie Farraday, sir.'

'She's one of our new residents who arrived with Mr Penhaligon.' Said Proctor, her arms tightly folded. 'I believe she is his daughter.'

I grimaced.

Septimus's eyes widened in surprise. 'Really, well, well, well.' He laughed. 'How extraordinary.' He continued to stare at me in a rather unnerving manner. 'Do tell me Miss Farraday, can you paint portraits?'

Taken aback by his odd question I began to mumble. 'Well yes...I can.'

'Effie's a talented artist back home in.... in.' Mace looked confused. 'Where we come from.'

I threw him an infuriated glare.

Septimus turned his attention to Mace. 'Really.'

Proctor stepped forward and whispered something in Septimius's ear. He nodded in agreement then looked back at me. 'And who is your blundering, troublemaking companion?'

'Mace.' I uttered apprehensively, glancing over at the pained expression on my friend's face. 'Please pay no heed to his behaviour, it is rare indeed for him to be disruptive.' I threw a swift glance at Mace hoping he'd catch on to what I was trying to do. 'He's usually so placid, aren't you Mace?'

Mace raised his eyebrows at me then smirked.

'Indeed, I am, I'm usually as silent and as impassive as the good people of this hall.'

Septimus peered at him suspiciously for a second, narrowing his eyes, he then reached out and touched Mace's unruly hair. 'You remind me of someone, have you a brother?'

Mace gulped. 'No sir, I am an only child.'

'And your parents?'

'They live far away sir' He lowered his eyes.

'Hmm.' Septimus carried on studying him. 'Well, from what Proctor has told me you certainly meet the criteria to join us here at Hartland.'

A look of terror appeared on Mace's face. 'Well...well I shall have to see about that.'

'Nonsense, I can already see that you shall greatly benefit from our special tonic.

Mace looked terrified. 'But sir, we arrived here by accident, we shall only be staying a short while.'

'The ways by which you entered Hartland are irrelevant, you are here now and here you shall stay. We are your family now.' He snapped his fingers at Abel. 'Take Mace to the infirmary.'

An agonised feeling ran through me. 'Septimus please, Mace and I would like to stay together. Surely there's no need to rush into anything.'

Septimus turned and growled at me. 'It is sir, do you understand, only old acquaintants are permitted to call me by my name.' He turned to Proctor. 'You can release her.' He gestured for me to go back to my seat. 'I shall talk with you later Miss Farraday.' Reaching forward he rested his hand on my shoulder, causing me to recoil. 'And please don't fret, your friend will be fine.' Clapping his hands, he bellowed across the room. 'Now, let us all continue with our supper.' And with that he slowly ambled back to his table.

I watched in utter torment as Abel continued to drag Mace out of the hall.

'No, let me be.' Whimpered Mace, his voice choked with emotion. 'Effie, help me Effie.' Automatically I began to move towards him, but immediately found a large, clammy hand pressing down onto my shoulder. 'It would not be wise to move.' Said Proctor, her face close to mine.

'It will be alright Mace, trust me.' I shouted after him, attempting to placate him but not really thinking or believing what I was saying. 'I won't let any harm come to you.'

In desperation he clung onto the doors. 'Effie?' But Abel, with his great strength, easily wrenched his hands from the wooden frame. 'What shall I do?' Cried Mace.

I jumped as the heavy doors crashed shut.

I'm not really sure how long I stood there, fixed to the spot, with my heart pounding in my chest and my head feeling dizzy.

'Mace.' I murmured in a low, weak voice.

With a sigh I reluctantly made my way over to my seat, not caring that people were looking, I was passed caring. My friend had been taken away from me, the glue that was holding me together. In my despair I hardly even noticed the way in which Gideon was staring curiously across at me.

After the unappetising supper, I was escorted by Abel up a steep flight of stone steps, through a series of complex hallways and then along a winding, dimly lit passageway with a high arched ceiling. The shadowy maze of creepy corridors seemed to stretch on forever, snaking off in every direction; there were a series of doors along the route, and I wondered which one would be mine.

Abel stopped unexpectedly. 'This be your room Miss Farraday.'

I shivered as a blast of cold air drifted passed me. 'Oh.' I exclaimed in an unanimated voice. 'Is... is it near my friend, Mace's room?'

'No idea.' He mumbled casually. 'I don't ask questions.' Passing me the lantern he ushered me into the room. 'When you hear the chimes of the bell in the morning come down to the great hall for breakfast.'

I nodded silently. 'And the bathroom?'

He signalled down the hall. 'Go to the end and turn left.'

'Thank you, Abel.' My voice drifted off as I realised he'd already left and was stomping down the passageway in his heavy boots.

The windowless room was narrow and dark with lots of shadowy recesses, and with only the lantern for a source of light the space looked gloomy. It was simply furnished with just a wooden bed and a stool; not surprisingly there were no pictures or ornaments to make it seem homely, just the bare minimum to get by, and to exist in such an environment of bleakness.

'Home sweet home.' I chuckled, in a vain attempt to keep my spirits up.

As I stood there shivering I felt an uncanny sense of unease rippling throughout the walls and ceiling, as if I was being watched. However, it was somewhat comforting to spot my rucksack in the corner; at least they'd not taken that from me. I rummaged through it for my toiletries, and thankfully all my belongings seemed to be there, except the gun, which wasn't really a surprise.

I laughed to myself.

Hartland wasn't the type of establishment to allow weapons, but that didn't mean it was a safe place to reside. From what I'd observed so far, the monastery was full of secrets, with danger lurking nearby, and I had an inkling I would soon discover what was concealed within these walls.

Retrieving my notebook from my back pocket I stuffed it underneath the mattress, for safekeeping, then taking a deep breath I picked up the lantern and went outside to find the bathroom, which thankfully I came across fairly easily. There were several of them situated at the end of the corridor on the left, just like Abel had said, and to my astonishment they had showers, rather archaic looking but they worked just fine; it was comforting to feel the piping hot water wash over me. After dressing in my pyjamas and cleaning my teeth, I crept back to my room, without seeing a soul. Shakily, I placed the lantern down upon the stool, and lowered myself onto the hard bed and clambered in, pulling the coarse blanket up over me. It was hardly enough to keep me warm, but it would have to do. Despite my dire situation and the discomfort of the bed, I knew that I would sleep soundly that night, too weary to even move I sleepily lay there, desperately trying to ignore the eerie sound above me; not wishing to believe what I was thinking. For in the darkness, I imagined there were creaking branches above my head, moving across the ceiling.

# Chapter 16

That time of total oblivion when you first awaken is soothing to both body and mind, and in that precious moment of total abandonment I was safely in my cosy bed, surrounded by an array of exquisite flowers, gently blowing in the warm summer breeze; it was a haven of wonderment. What a shame it always comes to an end.

A continuous hammering sound stirred me from my sleep and I blearily opened my eyes. Anguish and terror overcame me as I realised where I was.

'You've overslept Miss Farraday. Get thy self ready, now.'

Coming to my senses I realised it was Abel. I rubbed my eyes and peered around at the darkness surrounding me. Surely it couldn't already be morning.

'I... I will be out in just a moment.' I uttered in a shaky voice. Pain shot through my back as I slowly rose and staggered unsteadily out of the bed.

'Your robes are outside your door, make sure you put them on.' He bellowed. Then come straight down to the great hall.'

'Yes, alright, I shall see you down there.' I said quietly, standing by the door. I waited there for a second then called out his name, just in case he was still standing there. I didn't know why but there was something about him that unsettled me, something in his nature. Satisfied that Abel had left I opened the door and picked up the neatly folded bundle of clothing outside on the floor. After dressing I combed my hair and tied it back as best I could. With only a small hand mirror I couldn't really see what I looked like in my robes, but suspected I would appear rather ridiculous. The drab, grey cloth hung loosely about me, similar to an oversized overcoat, which had been sewn up at the opening, with a gaping hood, hanging halfway down my back. I envisaged Mace would have a laugh when he saw me, if he saw me. I felt a sudden dull ache in my heart as I thought of him, hoping that he wasn't suffering, and praying that he was still normal, as normal as he could be.

Taking a long, deep breath I made my way to the great hall. My sense of direction had never been good, so not surprisingly I found myself taking several wrong turns. In the end I decided just to tag along behind the people up ahead, as I imagined we were all heading to the same destination. As I followed them through some heavy doors, I was relieved to find myself in the roomy hall. My face coloured when I saw how crowded it was.

Biting down on my lip I stood there, looking lost.

A sudden tap on my shoulder caused me to swing round. It was Abel. 'Blimey Miss Farraday, look at you in your robes.' He exclaimed loudly. 'You'll be joining the others this morning.' Placing his hand on my back he guided me over to a table on the far right. 'Take a seat here Miss.'

Nervously I nodded at him.

As I sat down, I felt his eyes boring into the back of me. It struck me then how Abel seemed a little more human than most of the others: he had life behind his eyes, and despite the peculiar way he kept glancing at me, I found myself warming to him.

I'm not sure which is worse: having to endure sitting all alone, squirming with awkwardness, hoping no one looked at me, or sitting amongst strangers and having to make conversation. In ordinary life both of them would be a struggle for me, but here at Hartland I found myself sitting there with relative ease: the people at my table were content to remain in their docile state, barely looking up. Maybe life in the monastery wouldn't be as bad as I thought.

Whilst eating my breakfast, which was a substantial bowl of stodgy oatmeal, I scanned the hall for familiar faces: both Gideon and Mace were absent, however I spotted Clarice on the table in front, her flaxen hair gave her away. Yet again she seemed subdued and forlorn, not at all like my friend from home.

After eating, the unfriendly Proctor informed me that Septimus wanted to speak to me in his study. Like a dutiful sheep I followed her out of the hall, without uttering a single word. I'd already decided, that in order to make my stay here trouble free and uncomplicated, it would be wise not to ask too many questions, as I'd already figured out that being inquisitive was frowned upon. My theory was that in doing this it would make it easier to sneak away, when the time was right.

As we made our way along the wide passageway, I glimpsed a large library, and without thinking I stopped and took a few paces back, so I could have a closer look.

'Do keep up.' Said Proctor curtly, glaring at me with her spiteful eyes. 'Septimus is a busy man and does not take kindly to being kept waiting.'

'Sorry,' I exclaimed, running to try and keep up with her. 'But I couldn't help but notice you seem to have a library here at Hartland.'

'Yes, of course we do.' She replied, marching ahead. 'The library has an enormous range of books, some dating back to when the monastery was first built. Septimus spends a considerable amount of time in the grand room.' For a brief moment she turned and looked in the direction of the library, and a faint smile came upon her lips. 'He is an avid reader.'

My eyes lit up. 'How wonderful.' I commented. 'Perhaps I can go there later, I love reading too.'

She stared at me. 'Excuse me?

'I...I just said, that it would be pleasant to visit the library.'

'The library is entirely out of bounds to residents, especially when they happen to be newcomers.' A look of disapproval was spread across her face. 'You were rude to even ask.'

I look startled. 'So only Septimus is permitted to use the room?'

'Once upon a time the other council members of Hartland were allowed, but now....' She faltered. 'But now they have all gone, leaving only Septimius.'

'I see.' I answered, looking puzzled. 'Did they leave Hartland?'

Her face became infuriated. 'Enough of this, you're extremely nosey, just like that friend of yours.'

I became concerned. My strategy of not asking questions had already failed me, and by the looks of it, Proctor was becoming increasingly infuriated with me. I wondered if she'd grumble to Septimus that I was being bothersome, and that I too should be made to have the tonic, just like Mace.

We arrived at a rather ornate looking door, and Proctor rapped firmly upon it.

I heard a man's voice calling for us to enter.

Proctor stood at the doorway and pushed me lightly forward. 'Miss Faraday is here Septimius.'

Turning round I glared at her indignantly.

Without another word she turned and stomped up the passageway, disappearing into the gloom, leaving me hovering nervously in the doorway. I jumped and recoiled slightly as I came face to face with Abel, who must have been lurking nearby.

He stood there gawping at me. 'Excuse me Miss Farraday.' He uttered in a surly voice. 'Let me pass.'

I nodded and edged my way further into the dark room, and away from Abel, making sure to avoid his gaze. Peering forward I spotted Septimus seated behind a large desk.

He smiled when he saw me. 'Do come in Miss Farraday. And don't be scared of Abel, he is a simple soul, and completely harmless.'

Apprehensively, I moved forward and stood in front of Septimius.

'Has Abel been at Hartland very long?'

Septimus thought for a moment. 'Yes, he was brought here as a child; someone had found him wandering in the marshlands, lost and disorientated, and near death.'

I looked vacantly at him. 'What, what about his parents?'

Septimus shrugged his shoulders. 'I've no idea. Abel had no knowledge of them.' He sniggered. 'In fact, the poor boy had no knowledge of anything.' He rose from the desk and slowly shuffled round to the front, holding on for support. 'My theory is he arrived in these parts from another world.'

I stepped back from him, my face becoming serious. 'Oh.'

Septimus eyed me closely. 'Just like you and your friend Mace.' He shook his head. 'And your father Isaiah.' He covered his mouth with his hand and coughed violently.

'Are you alright?' I asked.

He seemed agitated, and took a while to compose himself. 'Yes, yes of course.' He snapped. 'Why wouldn't I be?' Not waiting for an answer, he continued to speak. 'So, Miss Farraday do enlighten me as to why you have all come to Hartland, what do you want?'

Lowering my eyes, I focused on the mound of books scattered on the desk.

'After becoming lost on our travels, we stumbled across this place by accident.' I laughed. 'It was only when we'd entered the monastery that Isaiah began to remember.' I gulped. 'He remembered that this used to be his home.' I glanced up and met his gaze. 'Mace and I would be very grateful if we could stay in your home for a short while, and then we will be on our way.'

'And your father, would you be happy to leave him here?'

'Isaiah and I do not really see eye to eye.' I answered. 'And besides, now he's back home, I would hate to see him leave.'

Septimus stared at me without saying a word, then exploded into laughter. 'My dear Miss Farraday, what a pleasant way of saying you dislike him. And yes, I too would not like to see him go; as a matter of fact, I insist he remains, all safe and cosy in his lodgings underneath the monastery.'

'What is to become of him?'

'Let us not dwell on Isaiah right this minute.'

My head started to ache. 'What about Mace, I don't believe it's wise or necessary to give him the tonic, especially as we have no plans to reside at the monastery.'

He gave me a curt look. 'Nonsense. Mace shall flourish at the monastery, and I'm sure he'll be happy to remain indefinitely in our glorious home. Besides, it's too late; he has already been given some tonic and is responding well to the first course of treatment. Presently, he is convalescing in the infirmary.'

My heart sank. It was as I suspected; Mace had already been given this mysterious concoction that seemingly turned normal people into a shadow of their former selves.

'Has it made him unwell?' I asked in a worried voice.

'No, of course not.' He paused. 'Keeping Mace in the infirmary is just a precaution; the initial stage of the tonic occasionally causes an adverse effect on its recipient.'

'What kind of adverse effect?'

He turned and stared at me for a while then began to gather some books from the desk.

'Questions Miss Farraday, so many questions.' A faint look of frustration appeared in his eyes. 'They shall be your undoing.'

I tried to smile at him. 'I don't mean to ask so much, it's just that I'm concerned about Mace.'

His face grew stern. 'Yes, I can see that you are, but your friend is in good hands.' Reaching forward over the desk he gathered several books together in his arms and headed towards the door. 'Now, not another word on the subject, it is becoming rather tiresome.' He called out through the door, which was slightly ajar. 'Abel, where are you?'

I swiftly ran over towards Septimius. 'Here, allow me to hold the door for you.'

'Thank you, Miss Farraday, but that won't be necessary. I'm quite alright.'

Heavy steps sounded close by and Abel appeared, poking his head around the door.

'Sorry sir.' He uttered rather red in the face. 'What needs doing?'

'Return these to the library.' Septimus carefully passed him the books then mumbled something in Abel's ear that I couldn't quite catch.

'Yes sir, right away sir.'

Abel threw me a strange look then staggered out the door, carrying the books rather haphazardly in his bulky arms.

Looking worried, Septimus called after him. 'Be mindful of the books, some of them are extremely fragile.' As Abel blundered down the passageway, Septimus shook his head in despair. 'That lad is very capable but rather prone to having accidents.'

'Oh.' I replied, thinking of Mace, and how clumsy he could be. 'The tonic doesn't completely alter one's habits then?'

237

'No. Not entirely. As you'll soon discover.'

A sinister coldness swept over me and I began to tremble. So Septimus did intend to begin me on the treatment, I thought. Soon I would become just like all the rest, doomed to remain here until the end of my days, living this miserable existence. On the bright side, I would be with all my friends. This however brought me little comfort, for it was becoming apparent that they were like strangers, with no intention or desire to become reacquainted. Mace would be next to go, and then myself...

Feeling slightly faint I stumbled backwards, banging my arm on the side of a cabinet.

Septimus came striding over towards me. 'Miss Farraday? He steadied me, taking my arm. 'Are you unwell?'

I gulped. 'No, I'm just not ready.'

He peered at me in confusion. 'I'm sorry, you've lost me.'

'The tonic.' I blurted out. 'I'm not ready to take it.'

To my astonishment he began to laugh. 'I've not intention of giving you the tonic, it's not the most suitable concoction to take for an artist.'

'What?' I uttered hoarsely.

'You're going to paint for me Miss Farraday.'

I looked flabbergasted. 'I don't understand.' I said becoming flustered. 'Why would you want me to paint for you?'

He shook his head in amusement. 'All that will become clear shortly, but first I would like you to be reassured that no one at the monastery is forced to take the elixir, all the residents are willing participants, and as long as they conduct themselves in a suitable manner, they are free to leave at any given time. The monastery is a place of faith and belonging, not a callous prison.'

'So why was Mace made to take the tonic?' I uttered in an adamant voice.

A look of annoyance crossed over his face. 'Some of our more challenging newcomers require a little helping hand, to lead them on the right path. It's for their own well-being.'

'But I like Mace the way he is, it won't be him anymore if you change him.'

'Oh Miss Farraday, you're acting far too melodramatic. Your friend will still be the same, only calmer and less boisterous.' He looked deep into my eyes. 'I promise you will prefer the new and improved Mace; it will still be him, minus the bad behaviour.'

I eyed him suspiciously, not believing a word he was saying. I could think of many qualities that Mace possessed that were somewhat exasperating: he was impetuous, high-spirited, conceited, and sarcastic to name but a few. However, to remove any of these characteristics would do him an injustice, and would take away the friend I knew and loved.

For a moment I pushed Mace out of my mind.

'So, because you'd like me to paint, I'm being spared.'

'I would hardly use the word spared, think of it as a period of time that will allow you to mull over the idea, and when you have completed your work you will be ready to join us.'

'Why is it not suited to an artist, what will happen?'

'Although the tonic is completely beneficial to our well-being it can occasionally cause any talents, an individual may possess, to be greatly diminished.'

'Yes, I said drolly. 'I can imagine one would be too sleepy and unenthusiastic to even pick up a paint brush.'

He furrowed his brows and stood there glaring at me. 'Your wit isn't very amusing Miss Farraday, and I will ask you do not to mock our unique way of living.' Without waiting for me to reply he began walking through a tiny arched entranceway at the rear of the study. 'Follow me.'

I found myself in a shadowy, wood panelled room where the only light was from the lanterns. If it had been night, the soft glow would have made the space cosy and homely, but it was morning and I had the overwhelming urge to fling back the heavy looking wooden shutters, covering the windows and flood the room with natural light. However, dim the room appeared I couldn't fail to notice the numerous portraits displayed about the walls, and my eyes were immediately drawn to the imposing painting of Septimius.

He stood beside me, and we both gazed up, admiring the painting. 'Magnificent isn't it. Recognise the style?'

I was curiously mesmerised by the portrait. And, for an instant believed I personally had worked on the painting, for the manner in which it had been completed seemed so familiar to me, the technique used so fitting to my style of work. But of course, it was impossible.

Then I realised.

An agonising feeling of emotion flooded through my heart as I realised who I'd inherited my gift of painting from.

'My mother.' I uttered in a low, sad tone.

Septimus nodded. 'Yes, Freya spent some time in this room, painting away.' He ran his fingertips gently over the picture. 'How well she captured my likeness, do you not think?'

I smiled poignantly, looking around at the other portraits, none of whom I recognised. I noticed one of the paintings was obscured with a large, velvet cloth draped over the canvas. For a moment I was tempted to lift it up to see why it was hidden, but then decided it perhaps wouldn't be wise. It was covered for a reason.

Quickly, I turned my attention to the other pictures. 'She painted these too I see.'

'Yes, your mother was very talented, and very charming.' His face darkened. 'But she let me down, like so many others.'

'How?'

Suddenly he looked very downcast. 'She fled from this place, never to return.' He peered at me. 'When did you last see your mother Effie?'

I...I've never seen her. We were parted after she gave birth to me.'

'And you do not know where she is now?'

'No, not at all.' I uttered despondently. 'I believe she was trying to return to me, but couldn't quite find her way home. It's my understanding Isaiah is responsible for her long absence.' I began to shake with anger. 'He prevented her from coming home to me.'

'And where is home Effie? You seem to possess a remarkable memory for someone who's travelled so far, across other worlds.'

I averted my eyes from his gaze and laughed nervously. 'My memory is very sketchy, I can't even recall the name of the house where I grew up, or even the town.' I rubbed my forehead; trying to think of the last time I read my notebook. 'I truly can't recollect any more than what I've just told you.'

Septimus appeared engrossed in what I was saying. 'Hmm. Interesting.' He moved slowly across the room and leant against the table. 'So, you don't know if Isaiah ever found the Monk's book?'

I looked bewildered. 'What book?'

'Many years ago, when monks still resided at Hartland monastery, a book was written, a very special book that contained information that could change the course of history. Having searched for many years without success, I was intrigued to hear that your father had knowledge of this book and knew where to find it.'

Without warning a flash of pain shot through my temple as I vaguely remembered Isaiah searching for a book, a book of great importance, somewhere in a library. Was it connected to the ledger I'd hidden behind the portrait of Florentine Heatherington and Gilbert in the old church at Briarwood? It still amazed me how events in this land were crystal clear yet my past life, in the other world had all but vanished from recognition. The question I asked myself, was this book and ledger one of the same.

'I could feel my cheeks burning. 'Do go on.' I said in a shaky voice.

As I waited for him to continue, I observed the beads of sweat on his forehead and how pallid his complexion had become. It was becoming increasingly obvious he was unwell.

He stumbled round the table and took a seat. 'I foolishly allowed your father to leave Hartland on the understanding that he would soon return with the book in his possession.' He wiped his brow with the sleeve of his robe. 'Not only did he deceive me with the power of his words, fooling me into believing he knew the location of the book, but he also robbed me of precious gems that have been at the monastery since time memorial. I also have reason to believe Isaiah was responsible for the deaths of several council members, who perished shortly before he left.' A look of anguish appeared across his face. 'And…. and someone who was very close to me, they disappeared.' His voice trailed off and he became lost in his thoughts.

There was an uncomfortable silence.

A loud tapping on the study door brought Septimus back to reality. 'He is here at last.' There was a distinct change in his mood, as his eyes became animated. 'Enter.' He bellowed out, clapping his hands together at the sound of the approaching footsteps. Gleefully, he turned to look at me.' Your arrival, Miss Farraday, was extremely unforeseen and immensely convenient for the task I have in mind.'

I turned to look at the figure standing underneath the archway, and my eyes widened with shock.

'I would like to introduce you to my grandson…Gideon.'

Without thinking I retreated into a corner, almost falling into a table. It was only then I noticed the various jars of paintbrushes and wide range of paints and palettes, arranged in neat little piles upon the table; tucked away behind it stood an easel and several blank canvases. It struck me how tidy it all seemed, so compact; not at all resembling the messy workplace of an eccentric artist.

Quite unexpectedly I found myself visualising an old, dilapidated shed.

Searing pain surged through my head, and I bent forward, placing my hands over my forehead.

'Is something wrong Miss Farraday, you seem a little taken aback?'

A soft moan escaped my lips.

Gideon remained where he was, oblivious to my discomfort.

Thankfully, the pain began to subside and I attempted to compose myself. I opened my mouth to speak but nothing came out. So instead I shook my head, gaping at them both in utter astonishment.

Proudly looking at Gideon, Septimus spoke in a soft voice.' To have my grandson immortalised in paint is such a splendid idea, do you not think Miss Farraday. I'm sure you will do justice to his imposing face.'

I stared fixedly at Gideon, still unable to find my voice.

Deep in thought, I momentarily tore my eyes away from him and looked at the floor. Of course, they were related, why had my brain been so slow to work it out; that is why they were sitting together in the great hall.

I cleared my throat. 'I... I've not painted for a while; it may take some considerable time.' I uttered, stumbling over my words.

Septimus rose from his seat and slowly walked to where I was standing. He rested his hand on my shoulder. 'I have every faith in you Miss Farraday.' He ruffled Gideon's hair. 'And I know you, Gideon will be an excellent model and remain precisely in the pose Miss Farraday requests.'

'Yes grandfather.'

Smiling confidently, Septimus made his way over towards the study door. 'Call if you need assistance.' He turned and gazed straight at me. 'And when I return later, I will expect to see you've started on the painting, Miss Farraday.'

Not answering, I turned away and tried to catch my breath.

'I'm ready to start immediately, Miss Farraday.'

I gaped dumbly at Gideon, trying to absorb what was happening.

Creating a work of art took time and patience, and that was under ordinary circumstances; in my present state of disarray I would find it near impossible to even begin the portrait: I was so nervous that my hands were shaking uncontrollably and hardly capable of holding a paint brush. However, what I really found disconcerting was how Septimus apparently believed his grandson and I to be strangers; had Gideon not even mentioned me? Pondering for a moment, I came to the conclusion that I shouldn't remain too perturbed; I would blame it on this medieval building, where normal people with human emotions were turned into strange, unthinking beings.

'Where would you like me to sit?'

With a jolt I came back to reality. Gideon had moved directly in front of me, with his face close to mine, and standing in such

243

close proximity to him caused me to become light-headed. The profound affect he had on me had not diminished, and I found myself wishing to kiss him. Automatically, my hand reached up to his face, but to my dismay he instantly moved away.

I was bewildered.

For now, I decided to ignore his standoffish behaviour, putting it down to the effects of the tonic. My long absence must also be an additional factor; perhaps he didn't think I would return to him. I was confident the situation would soon resolve itself, now that I'd returned to him. And before long we could go back home, together. I didn't stop to ponder over my somewhat self-assured theory; I didn't wish to consider the alternative -my fragile heart couldn't take it.

I smiled sweetly at him.

'I think perhaps in front of the windows? That way I can capture the light on your face.' Moving over to the window I began to pull back the heavy shutters, which made the room so dark and gloomy. 'I just need to make the room a little brighter.'

Immediately I found his hand firmly gripping mine, pulling it away from the shutters.

My heart skipped a beat, at the feel of his touch.

'No, you mustn't.' He mumbled. 'It will attract attention from outside.'

Momentarily I believed him to be just teasing, but then I remembered that any humour had been snatched away from him.

Feeling subdued I looked upon his serious face. 'Whatever do you mean Gideon, is there a dangerous creature lurking out there, waiting to attack the moment I open the shutters?'

He gave me a blank stare. 'No, grandfather always prefers them to be closed, he believes it is safer this way.'

'Safer for whom?'

Realising he was still grasping my hand with his, he abruptly snatched it away.

'Although they are far enough away from the monastery, with the windows exposed the trees can still notice movement from within.' He said, with a straight face. 'There is more chance of an incident.'

'What? I asked, screwing up my face. 'Are you saying that the trees could possibly smash through the windows and drag us away to our impending doom?'

He looked nonchalantly at me. 'Well, yes, especially if they notice the glow from the lanterns.' I watched as he began moving around the room, distinguishing the lanterns. 'I shall remove the light from the lanterns and then we may.... then I shall carefully open the shutters.' Pausing, he glanced across at me. 'But please do not try anything foolish, such as standing by the window and...'

I interrupted his sentence. 'Frantically waving my arms above my head.' I remarked, smiling gently at him. 'Or doing a dance.'

Nodding dispassionately, he turned and carried on putting out the lanterns, until we were standing in complete and utter darkness.

I felt his breath on the back of my neck. 'Move away from the windows, whilst I open the shutters.' He uttered, edging his way slowly around the room. Very cautiously he released the latch and slowly opened it. 'Would you like to see them?'

Feeling quite relaxed I stepped towards the window. 'Yes, yes I would.'

Being familiar with this land I wasn't disturbed or shocked by the unnatural behaviour of some of the trees, and their ability to make off with their victim with one snatch. I pictured the madwoman being taken by a gnarled, branch like claw. Perhaps I should remind Gideon of how he had saved her life, my dear sister, Verity, who had only earlier pierced his shoulder with an arrow, a fatal wound had it not been for the healing power of the flowers. How alike Verity was to her father, Isaiah, how corrupt and vile they both were. Then there was my half-brother, Gilbert, the namesake of my nightmarish dummy, who was a touch simple minded and believed I was the ghost of Florentine Heatherington. And finally, there was good old me, the complex Effie, whose shyness had hampered and frustrated her through much of her life, and was under the

245

illusion that she could win back the man she loved, even though he didn't recognise her anymore. What a strange family we made.

'Imposing aren't they.' Declared Gideon.

As I looked out upon the bleak landscape, it seemed nothing could have prepared me, no amount of reassurance would prevent the shudder of fear from creeping its way, coldly over my entire body, and nothing could stop the jaw dropping reaction from my face.

'They are The Elder trees, the oldest and most righteous beings in the entire expanse of Hartland and beyond. Their powerful wisdom is believed to be greater than any other living being in the universe.'

Even though I thought Gideon's comments to be absolutely ludicrous, I wasn't able to force my eyes away from the window. There was little doubt, that the trees were magnificent, but not in a good way. The five gargantuan monstrosities were completely out of proportion from any tree I had ever seen, their trunks extended higher than the monastery, towering off towards the sky, and their abnormally long branches were moving, spreading wide like a diseased freak of nature, almost like they had been touched by an evil force of sorcery.

'No one is permitted to enter the grounds near The Elder tress, except when we hold the ceremonies, and retrieve the berries for the tonic.' Gideon muttered, as he carefully moved back from the window and went over to fetch the easel.

'Ceremonies?' I asked, finally dragging my gaze away from the window.'

He remained silent for a moment whilst he placed one of the blank canvases onto the easel. 'Yes, we hold regular ceremonies in the grounds, in honour of the trees.'

'What happens at these ceremonies?' I asked apprehensively.

'Oh, nothing grave.' He answered.

I sighed with frustration at the lack of information he was providing.

Once again, I peered out at the trees, pressing my forehead up against the windowpane.

'Miss Farraday, I'd feel happier if you would move away from the window.'

'So, you do care if I was suddenly taken by one of the trees.'

He gaped at me before moving the table full of paints further to the centre of the room. 'Well, yes. Grandfather would be mortified if you failed to complete my portrait.'

Abruptly I swung round to see if he was smiling. However, my heart sank when I saw he still possessed the same subdued expression. 'Well, that would be too bad.' I replied, feeling despondent. 'At this precise moment I'm not even sure if I can paint you, not the way you are now.' My gaze returned to the trees.

'When do you think you will be ready to proceed?'

I turned away from the window. 'I...I don't know, and I don't care.' I strode forward and took his hands in mine. 'Gideon, do you not know me? Do you not remember?'

He instantly recoiled from my touch, nearly crashing into the easel. Quickly, he moved his hand to steady the canvas, and without looking me in the eye he spoke in a quiet and controlled tone. 'Yes, you are Miss Farraday, you arrived here recently with your father and a friend.'

'Gideon, we are....' I hesitated. I wanted to say how we loved one another, how we were going to be married, but under the circumstances I decided to remain cautious in what I declared. 'You are my friend; we've been friends for a very long time.'

A look of confusion crossed over his face, followed by agitation. 'I'm not interested in discussing such matters. 'You are here solely to paint me Miss Farraday, and paint me you will.' He stepped forward. 'If you continue to question me in such a manner, I shall assume you'd rather go to the infirmary to start on your treatment.'

'But Gideon, can't you see what they've done to you.'

He abruptly turned away and walked towards the door. 'I shall call for Abel to come and take you away, it's probably for the best.'

247

Panic took over and I rushed towards him, grabbing his arm. 'No, no please don't.' Witnessing his previous reaction to my touch, I swiftly released my grip. 'I'm ready to paint you now.' I uttered, biting my lip. 'Would you like to take a seat in front of the window?' Gulping, I dragged the sturdy chair in the right position. 'I promise not to move around too much, just in case the trees notice.' I felt foolish for uttering such a ridiculous sentence, but somehow it seemed appropriate in the circumstances, normality didn't exist within these walls. I could see how one could easily become unbalanced in this deranged monastery.

After a moment of hesitation, Gideon strolled over and sat down on the wooden chair. 'If you refrain from opening your mouth yet again, maybe we can actually begin.'

I sighed, feeling dispirited. 'If that's what you wish.'

Needless to say, our first sitting was spent in silence. Gideon, it seemed, was happy to stare blankly towards me, without a thought or care in the world, and for the time being I had little choice but to hold my tongue and be content to work. My hands had steadied themselves now and I found myself able to sketch a pencilled outline of his face; it was far from brilliant, but at least it was a start. I tried to comfort myself with positive thoughts: Although Gideon was not himself, at least we were together; the painting would take ages; I would drag it out as long as I could. And, as the days passed by, we would grow closer, until finally he would see me properly, and fall in love with me all over again. A rather optimistic notion of mine, but nevertheless an essential one.

Despite the awkwardness between us, the day passed swiftly and before long Septimus had returned, closely scrutinizing my work. His remarks were promising, although I did observe how he persisted in furrowing his brow. I suspected he wished for a speedier progress, but as of yet I couldn't fathom out why. Gideon walked off and out the study without as much as a second glance. It was very disheartening to say the least, but I suppose, for now, I would have to get used to his unpleasant manner, until he was better.

At supper everyone marched into the hall just like the previous night, with Gideon sitting at the head table with his grandfather. Proctor, Abel and Mundy were there, closely watching the residents as they sat down. I thought it odd that they hovered over them so intensely, almost as if they expected one of the poor mites to cause trouble, to perhaps attempt an escape. From what I'd observed the likelihood of this happening was extremely unlikely, not that I would blame them for trying.

To my surprise a young girl brushed passed and gave me a smile.

'Hello.' She whispered, hardly moving her mouth.

Too shocked to reply, my eyes followed her as she went and sat down on a nearby table. She must have been about twelve, with brown, curly hair and delicate features. I deliberated whether or not to go and sit beside her, and strike up a conversation, but then I spotted Clarice in the crowd. Discreetly I sneaked across the hall and sat down beside her.

'Hello Clarice.'

She looked at me vacantly.

Looking at her pale face I tried again to engage in conversation with her by commenting on the food and how unappetising it was, but she took no notice, choosing instead to stare glumly at her bowl.

I scanned the room, searching for Mace. What with everything going through my mind, the obvious had only just occurred to me. Mace not only had a brother here at the monastery, but also a grandfather. If Septimus became aware of Mace's identity it was bound to change his opinion of him. Septimus would treat him kinder, and give him the respect he seemed to show Gideon. How happy he would be with two grandsons to indulge.

'I can't see him anywhere Clarice.' I moaned in a low voice.

Somehow it cheered me to talk to her, even though I didn't expect a reply.

'I do hope he's not had a bad reaction to the tonic.' I imagined him lying in the infirmary, at death's door. 'I'm worried about him Clarice.'

Yet again her expression was impassive.

During the meal, Septimus rose from his seat and spoke of the ceremony that Gideon had mentioned. He explained how it was nearly time for the customary event, where two blessed residents would have the opportunity to volunteer by following the usual procedure of placing their name in the bowl, which was on the altar in the chapel. And on the day of the ceremony, Septimus would select the lucky names.

I fidgeted uncomfortably in my seat.

Whatever this was it couldn't be good, I thought with a distinct sense of foreboding. I knew the ceremony involved the trees, the unnatural trees that shouldn't be.

Septimius's face took on a pitiful expression as he went on to explain how The Elder's had snatched another resident whilst they were picking the berries for the tonic. He tried to defend the trees by proclaiming that they were the all wise and supreme species ever created and must have known what they were doing. We then had a short prayer for the unfortunate resident, and Septimus said how grateful we were to him for providing The Elders with the nourishment they so rightly required, and how we gave our thanks to the trees for taking the resident within their fold.

I looked stunned for a minute before glancing across to the head table, where I met Gideon's eye. Briefly we held each other's gaze, before he turned away, and began staring into space.

The sudden voice of Proctor bellowed throughout the hall. 'Supper has ended. Vacate your seats and return to your rooms.'

I trudged out of the hall with the others, trying to keep near Clarice, even though she was oblivious to my very existence, but somehow, we became parted. Looking lost, I stood like a statue in the cold hallway, watching as the residents marched off in various directions, until I was all on my own. I contemplated whether to head left or right.

Proctor came over, her eyes looking menacing. 'Why are you lurking in the corner, Miss Farraday?' she exclaimed harshly.

'I seem to have forgotten the way back to my room. Could you point me in the right direction?'

She huffed. 'Go directly up the steps and then along the passage until you reach the very end, your room is situated, second to last on the right. You should find your initials chalked onto the door.'

'Right, thank you.' I uttered in a half -hearted tone as I saw her turn and march away from me. Maybe I was imagining it but I'm sure she mumbled something under her breath, something about confounded newcomers.

Stumbling over the uneven cobblestones, I was acutely aware of an oppressive coldness that hung in the air. And, as I made my way up the cold, stone steps, then along the twisting passage, an unexpected drop in temperature made me shiver. The delicate aroma of sweet roses filled my nostrils, causing me to feel a little giddy. For a moment I stopped and looked behind me, as I had the overwhelming sensation I was being followed, but the corridor was empty. It was a relief when I finally found my room, and was just about to enter when I heard the faint sound of approaching footsteps.

'Hello, is there someone there?' I whispered in an unsteady voice.

I thought that it surely couldn't be one of the guards, as their step would be somewhat heavier, in fact whoever it was would have had to be remarkably light on their feet.

Standing there quivering, I held up my lantern and took a glance down the shadowy hall, but it appeared no one was there. This rather alarmed me, as the noise seemed to be coming closer. Not waiting to find out who or what it was, I frantically began turning the doorknob, trying desperately to open the heavy door.

'Open, why won't you open.' I whimpered, frightened that something abnormal was about to reach out and grab me. 'Come on, 'I cried, leaning my bodyweight against the door.

I froze. The footsteps had ceased, but an unexpected breath of bitter air blew across my neck and face causing me to feebly cry out. Shivering uncontrollably, I gave the door an almighty shove and it flew open, sending me careering into the darkened room. My initial reaction was to curl up in a ball and hide, but I had to be strong; I had to keep that thing away. Feeling my heart pounding in my chest, I seized the wooden stool and wedged it up against the door. Whatever unknown being that was lurking out there, I felt wholly unequipped to deal with it. I was used to nightmares; I could deal with those. This however was altogether different. I had no doubt that an evil presence lurked within this building, and it was entirely real.

# Chapter 17

As I sat there, perched on the edge of my chair, I gazed over the top of the canvas to where Gideon was sitting patiently, his demeanour was so calm and controlled I wondered if he'd jump if I flung a paint brush at him, or flinch if I suddenly reached out and stroked his tousled, shiny hair.

'I'm ready when you are, Miss Farraday.'

Not hearing him speak, I continued to sit and stare at him. Apart from his sallow complexion, the tonic hadn't altered his appearance, and didn't detract from his magnificent eyes, which were truly intoxicatingly evocative that they caused a spine-tingling surge of emotion to ripple through me. I wanted to slap myself for being so ridiculous, for acting like some giddy, scatter-brained schoolgirl, who was flighty and unpredictable. Still unable to look away from his steadfast gaze, I cast my mind back to when our paths had met within our dreams; how our worlds had collided so inexplicably.

I smiled serenely, looking deep into his eyes, convincing myself that I was the one to wake him from his mysterious spell of stagnation.

Gideon cleared his throat. 'It's tiresome you staring at me.' He shuffled in the chair. 'Are you not going to start painting?'

'Oh yes, I'd almost forgotten about that.' I chuckled, mixing some paints. 'What would you like to talk about?' I asked, hoping we didn't have to sit in complete silence.

His expression was reticent. 'We have nothing to discuss. I suggest you concentrate on your work, which will be considerably easier if you remain quiet.'

My heart sank, and suddenly I felt extremely foolish.

'Yes Gideon, of course.'

Lowering my face in embarrassment I carried on mixing the colours in the palette.

It became apparent that Gideon wasn't in the mood for talking, and so therefore I envisaged the morning being filled with an uncomfortable silence.

'I'm starting now, so do try and keep still.' I said in a laughing voice.

He grimaced at me.

So much for trying to be humorous, I thought. Not only had he become like a stranger, but also, he didn't seem concerned about making conversation. I was starting to have severe misgivings about the man I had known nearly all my life, the man who had been there for me when I drifted off on the road to dreams. Maybe it wasn't the potion doing this to Gideon; perhaps he had simply changed his mind about me, and didn't feel the same way anymore. Should I forsake him to his new home and flee with Mace and Clarice whilst we had the chance. Or should I bide my time, and wait for him, praying he will still want me when he wakes up from his dreamlike state.

The study door unexpectedly swung open and Septimus ambled into the room. 'How is my favourite artist progressing with my grandson?'

I let out a small, nervous giggle. 'I...we've both been exceedingly quiet.' I said, wiping some paint off my hand with a cloth. Throwing Gideon a swift glance I saw that he looked somewhat perplexed. 'I'm sure conversation will improve over time.'

Gideon gave me a strange glare. 'I think you've misunderstood; my grandfather was asking how the portrait's coming along, not how our friendship is developing.'

The colour rushed to my cheeks and I lowered my eyes. 'Yes, yes of course he was, how very silly of me.'

Septimus roared with laughter. 'And would you like to become better acquainted with my grandson, Miss Farraday?' He asked, still shaking with laughter. 'After all he's exceedingly fine looking, isn't he?'

'Grandfather, please stop it.' Uttered Gideon, squirming in his seat.

'My apologies Gideon.' Septimus said in a curt tone. 'Miss Farraday has not yet grasped that there is no place for romance in a place such as Hartland.' A distant look appeared in his eyes. 'Love is the ruination of us all.'

I looked at him quizzically. 'But what of my mother and Isaiah, they lived here together as husband and wife.' My voice trailed off. 'Didn't they?

Slowly, Septimus lowered himself into a seat. 'That was when your father was a valued friend of mine. I allowed their union for that very reason.' He flung his arms out in despair. 'And their marriage failed miserably.'

'Well, there must have been others at the monastery who've fallen in love? I declared, looking at Gideon. 'Take your grandson, I'm sure at one point there was someone special in his life.' Feeling brave I carried on. 'Surely there was a girl you were once in love with Gideon.' I began to stammer. 'That...that you dreamt about being with.'

He looked impassive. 'No. Not that I can recall.

'What about the woman who saved you and brought you here to the monastery.' Septimus said, deep in thought? 'Oh, what was her name?' He peered at me. 'Such a striking looking woman.'

'Verity.' Uttered Gideon, in a monotone voice.

Septimus gave me a sickly, sweet smile. 'Yes of course, the lovely Verity.'

The paintbrush dropped from my hand and clattered to the floor. 'Verity?' I said in a whisper.

My eyes glazed over.

'I owe Verity my life.' Gideon muttered. 'She discovered me in the land beyond Hartland; I was semi unconscious and bleeding from a wound to the back of the head, which she tended to then helped me to the safety of the monastery.' An expression of gratitude swept over his face. 'She is a remarkable woman.'

I had a sudden urge to go across and shake some sense into him.

I should have guessed the madwoman was responsible for Gideon's downfall; I visualised her smashing his head with a rock, from behind, then pretending to know nothing about it. How attentive and caring she would have acted towards him, how eager to steal him away from Briarwood, from me, and from himself.

255

'Indeed.' Exclaimed Septimius. 'I do believe Verity grew very fond of Gideon, and I think he felt the same.' He peered at Gideon. 'Didn't you Gideon?'

Gideon became slightly agitated. 'I...I imagine so, but I was convalescing and my mind was somewhat confused.' He got up from the chair and paced over to the window, being mindful of getting too close. He turned to face me. 'The blow to the head resulted in total amnesia, Miss Farraday, and to this day I cannot recall anything, prior to Verity bringing me here.'

I stared at him in shock. 'Oh.' I uttered in a weak voice. 'How perfectly dreadful for you.' 'So, nothing has recently happened to help jog your memory?' I enquired.

'Nothing.' He mumbled glumly. 'I have a vague recollection of carving figures from wood.' Very slowly he edged away from the window. 'A meaningless pursuit that I have no wish to regain.' He sighed, deeply. 'I'm quite content with my life now, and have no urge to gain back my lost memories; I imagine they were all insignificant and futile.'

So, just to clarify, there wasn't ever anyone you one day wished to marry?'

Gideon glared at me, looking deep within my eyes. 'Like I have just told you Miss Farraday, there is no one I love.'

An intense feeling of grief and disappointment ran through me like a cruel, hurtful wave. I'd already ascertained that Gideon didn't remember me, or chose not to, but to have him declare it so bluntly was more than I could bear.

Sadly, I lowered my eyes and gave a sigh.

Septimius got up and came and stood beside me.

He patted me on the shoulder. 'There, there Miss Farraday, please don't be downhearted. Being here at Hartland monastery has been the making of my grandson.' He gave me an odd look. 'He does not need a partner to keep him happy.'

I looked up at him coldly. 'And Verity?'

'Unfortunately Verity had to leave. The constant attention she showered upon Gideon was not conducive to his recovery. He was not well and I feared she was seducing him into falling in love with her. In fact, I do believe she half succeeded.' He shook his head and chuckled. 'How eager and presumptuous she was to lay claim to my grandson; if I hadn't intervened, she would surely have married him at his bedside, with his head still bandaged from his injury.'

My voice sounded far off when I spoke. 'Yes, that would have been wholly inappropriate and wrong.' I uttered, lost in my own thoughts. 'What an awful woman.' I mumbled. 'Completely mad.' My eyes drifted over towards the window, where they were both now standing, gawping at me. 'I er...imagine you were glad to see the back of her.'

Gideon stepped forward. 'Well, yes, and no. 'Whatever Verity's intentions were I cannot dispute that she saved my life, and for that I shall forever be in her debt.'

I tried to stifle my laughter.

How ironically farcical, that Gideon should believe such an act of kindness could come from such a treacherous, calculating woman; somehow, she had managed to give the illusion that she was his saviour, rather than a cold, and callous individual who had almost murdered him with an arrow, the arrow that had been meant for me. And, when I was safely out the way, in another world, she had once again attacked him, knocking him unconscious, and then pretending to be his rescuer. In her infinite wisdom the madwoman had seen this as the solution to finally getting her hands on Gideon, the man she adored, by taking him away from his home and putting him in the tight clutches of Hartland. How desperately she must have clung to him when they arrived, how convincing her story would have been. But, much to her horror, the cunning plan began to unravel and fall apart; her desperate need to possess Gideon had been her undoing.

I smiled.

Septimus began to cough. 'Well I shall take my leave.' He croaked. 'Pray continue the painting Miss Farraday.' Unsteadily he began to stumble across the room, and losing his balance he fell against the table.

'Gideon leapt forward. 'Grandfather. He swiftly took his arm and guided him towards the door. 'Let me escort you out.'

I watched as Gideon took his grandfather out the door. It was clear that something was wrong with Septimius, something rather serious; his failing health rather contradicted his assumption that the tonic was beneficial to all. I began to ponder whether Septimus had taken it at all, for he did appear more normal than the other occupants.

The rest of the day was rather uneventful, with Gideon returning to the sullen mood of earlier. He seemed content to remain in his seat without stirring; I was becoming used to his gloomy temperament, and was wary of firing too many questions at him all at once, just in case he became enraged. For now, I would be content to lose myself in my painting.

At supper that evening I was yet again able to take a seat near the silent Clarice.

'How's your day been? I whispered across to her. 'Oh, that's good. It's rather stuffy being cooped up in the monastery, isn't it? I think the both of us need to have a breath of fresh air, get some colour in our cheeks.' I took a fleeting glance at her stony face, still no response. With a deep sigh I leant forward and placed my elbows on the table, resting my hands underneath my chin. 'Has our friend Mace made an appearance yet?'

I ran my eyes over the blank faces and they came to rest on one particular figure, who was stretching along the table for some bread. Although an unruly mane of hair obscured his face, his tall, lanky frame seemed completely familiar. My suspicions were validated when he suddenly tripped and almost fell forward, knocking over a tankard of water on the table.

I stifled a laugh, placing my hand over my mouth.

'That has to be him, doesn't it Clarice?'

I continued to watch as he hastily picked up the tankard and began wiping the table with the sleeve of his robe. For a moment he caught my eye and I half expected him to wink, or at least make some gesture to reassure me he was still in the land of the living, but to my dismay he just turned away and looked glumly at the bowl in front of him.

'You may all begin to eat.' Said Proctor, her hard, steady eyes peering at the mass of people before her as if they were a herd of obedient sheep.

Reluctantly, I picked up my wooden spoon and started to swirl it round in the soup, as if by doing so would add more flavour. For I knew just by looking at the murky, brown bowl of unappetising liquid that it would taste completely foul. Perhaps that's why everyone looked so sickly, it was the soup. Hastily I grabbed two slices of granary bread before they all went and placed them beside the bowl; at least that would be palatable, if a little bland.

I gave Clarice a little smile as I tentatively spooned a small amount of the soup into my mouth, trying not to grimace.

'It's not exactly pleasant is it?' I said drolly, forgetting where I was for a minute. 'I think I shall just eat the bread.' Biting into it I noticed how it was a little stale. 'Even the bread is awful.'

'We should be thankful for the bread, and the farmers who provide us with the wheat for us to make it.'

'Ah, yes I wondered about the bread, there aren't any wheat fields nearby are there? So where do these farmers come from?'

'They come from the land beyond Hartland. Every so often they leave a supply of wheat outside the front gates, and in return we pay them for their good deed.'

I pictured a group of desperate farmers rushing up to the front gates to drop off sacks of wheat, taking their payment as quickly as possible, and then swiftly charging away before they were forced to enter the monastery.

'I see.' I replied, pushing the half-finished bowl of soup away with the stale bread. 'Well, that's awfully decent of them, but I really can't take another mouthful.'

The people opposite me gawped at me in bewilderment, including Clarice who stared at me with her large, unblinking eyes.

'We must eat everything put in front of us. Food is essential for our well-being.' Uttered Clarice in a monotone voice.

I looked disgruntled. 'The only essential thing for our well-being is to leave this place as soon as possible.' I whispered.

259

'It's purgatory.' I mumbled, glancing over towards Mace and trying to catch his eye.

Unexpectedly I felt a kick from underneath the table and abruptly looked at Clarice, not believing for a minute that it had been her. At first, I couldn't see any signs of life from the perpetrator, they all appeared to be eating their supper in the same mundane manner, but then I noticed the young girl who had spoken to me the previous night, sitting on the right side of Clarice. I couldn't believe I'd not seen her until now.

I gave her a little wave. 'Oh, hello again.'

She placed her finger to her lips, signalling for me to be silent.

I found myself staring at her in complete fascination, as if she was the strange one and all the others were normal.

Discreetly, she slid a note across the table, until it reached my hand, and acting swiftly I grabbed it and hid it in the pocket of my robe, nodding at her in acknowledgement. It was too risky to look at it now; I would read it later when I was back in my room.

With supper finished, Proctor ordered everyone to leave the hall.

'Night Clarice.' I uttered solemnly as we strolled over towards the door. 'I do hope you sleep well.'

She gave me the usual blank expression that I was reluctantly becoming use to.

'Better than me anyway.' I muttered, thinking of last night's events, when I hardly slept a wink because I was too scared to go to sleep.

Just as I was looking for the young girl who had passed me the note, something rather strange and disturbing occurred. One of the male residents suddenly appeared to be in distress, flaying their arms about and screaming wildly. It appeared the man was having a fit; he collapsed to the ground and started to foam at the mouth like some kind of rabid creature. I watched in bewilderment as Abel and Mundy frantically pushed their way through the crowd to reach him, and without uttering a single word, carried him from the hall as if it were an everyday event.

'What, what is wrong with that man?' I asked in a shaky voice. 'Where are they taking him?'

'The tonic has made him unwell.' Replied Clarice in a controlled voice. 'He'll be taken to the infirmary.' She paused. 'Just like all the rest with the condition.'

I widened my eyes in confusion. 'Is there a cure for this condition?

Clarice began to walk ahead as Proctor hurried the rest of the residents out the room.

'I do not know, no one with the condition ever returns.'

Opened mouthed, I watched as Clarice disappeared out the door. The young girl who'd given me the note briefly turned and looked at me, her eyes full of anguish.

I felt someone tightly clenching my arm, pulling me forward. It was Proctor.

'Do wake up, Miss Farraday. And get a move on.'

I nodded my head.

'I trust you can find your way back to your room now?'

'Yes.' I uttered in a grim voice.

'Splendid.'

She released her hand and marched away.

As I made my way to my room a nauseous feeling came over me, imagining what would become of that poor man, for it certainly wouldn't be pleasant. These morbid thoughts had distracted me from the daunting walk back along the passageway, and it was only when I'd reached my door that the faint sound of footsteps reached my ears. Feeling panic sweep over me, I rushed inside and slammed the door. For a minute I remained leaning up against the door, my heart thumping wildly in my chest. A gentle tapping on my door caused me to shriek in terror. I dragged the stool across the floor, desperate to lock myself in. To my alarm I heard it once more, but it was louder this time and more persistent.

'Go away, leave me alone.' I cried, covering my ears with my hands.

With the stool safely in place, I crawled onto the bed and curled up in a ball, burying my head in my arms. I'm not sure how long I remained like this, and felt brave enough to emerge

261

from my cocoon of safety, but eventually I took a deep breath and sat up on the bed. Whatever thing, whatever spectre had been tapping at my door, they had gone, for now.

Trembling, I retrieved the note from my pocket and laid it out on the bed.

### Will you be my friend?
### Lucinda

For a while I stared at the note: so short and simple though it was, it filled me with a renewed sense of hope and relief. For it seemed this Lucinda was not willing to meekly follow the absurd rules and regulations of the establishment, by turning into a docile, unthinking human. And if there was one, there must surely be others.

Lying there in bed that night I decided I would make a point of befriending Lucinda; I would do it tomorrow during breakfast.

With a yawn I closed my eyes and tried to stop thinking about the entity that had been knocking at the door, a difficult thing to do when you couldn't sleep.

'I wish I had a book to read.' I muttered quietly to myself.

For a split second I was almost tempted to creep along to the library, but the thought of bumping into someone or something was too risky, and too scary. Instead I would have to endure the endless hours of wakefulness, in the hope that I would eventually drop off into a restless sleep.

The following morning at breakfast I was served a stodgy bowl of porridge like substance, which left an odd, bitter taste on the pallet that was rather unpleasant. Discreetly I managed to sneak my newly acquired friend a note, explaining how I would love to be her friend. I asked when and where she would like to meet, so we could become acquainted. Clearly it would have to be a secret rendezvous rather than my preferred choice of tea and cakes at the local tearoom. I imagined there was a special place back home I used to frequent, where a sweet, bumbling old lady, with kindly eyes would wait upon me, eager to lap up the latest gossip. Of course, with nothing in my notebook to back this theory up, it was all merely conjecture.

Afterwards, I hurried to the study and tentatively poked my head around the door. The room appeared empty. I was loathed to go inside and wait alone, but perhaps it was safer than lingering outside in the passageway. I wandered in and made my way over to the portraits. If it hadn't been so cold and eerily quiet, I could almost have imagined it was an art gallery, a light and spacious gallery by the coast, with a quaint little tearoom and gift shop that sold postcards, depicting the paintings. Suddenly my eyes were drawn to the picture concealed under the velvet cloth. Quickly checking no one was coming, I carefully lifted the material away from the canvas. The woman in the portrait staring back at me had a kind, trustworthy face. Her thick glossy hair, coiled down her back like a dark cloak of silk. However, it was her eyes that shocked me, for they were exactly like Gideon's, dark and warm with just a fleck of blue. I knew then that it must be Sabina, the woman who had forsaken her husband Caleb and two of her sons and never returned. She had remained in another land and had Mace. And then...I tried to recall what was in my notebook but it wouldn't come to me. With a frown I returned the cloth over the portrait.

On a whim I went over to the large, wooden desk and lowered myself onto the chair. There was nothing out of the ordinary lying about, just books, ink pens and scribbled notes. Without thinking, I began rifling through the tiny drawers, situated either side at the front of the desk, and came across a knife: it was only a little larger than a penknife and had an ornate, ivory handle. Thinking it would come in handy I swiftly sneaked it into my robes only to immediately regret my actions. But it was too late to return it to its rightful home as Septimus had just walked into the room. The chair went back with a screech as I hastily got up and moved away from the desk.

'Septimius.' I breathed. 'You startled me.'

'Apparently so.' He exclaimed, looking dubiously at me and then narrowing his eyes. 'I would prefer you address me as sir, but on account of your mother I shall allow Septimius.'

I gaped at him and slowly nodded my head. 'Thank you Septimius, and please call me Effie.'

He smirked. 'For now, I shall continue to call you Miss Farraday.'

'As you wish.' I glanced behind him. 'Where is Gideon?'

'Oh, he'll be along shortly. He has various errands to attend to first.'

'Errands?' I asked curiously, wondering what they were.

'Oh, nothing of any consequence Miss Farraday.' He peered over to the windows. 'Would you mind pulling back the shutters, it really is rather dreary in here today, do you not think?'

'Yes, it is.' I uttered, reaching over and gradually heaving the wooden screens away from the windows.

'Do be careful, I've no doubt my grandson has warned you of the dangers that can occur from too much movement.'

'Yes, yes he did.' I murmured vaguely, staring out upon the trees. 'However, he didn't actually explain the history of the trees.' I swung round and faced him. 'I'd like very much to know how it all begun.'

Septimus looked at me, his face beaming. 'Why certainly Miss Farraday.' He shuffled slowly forward and sat down on the seat by the window. 'Grab a chair from the back of the study and come and sit beside me.'

I hesitated for a moment then went to fetch a chair, moving it next to his.

'That's it, now we can begin.' He uttered enthusiastically

I forced a smile, looking reluctantly into his bloodshot eyes.

'The forest trees of this land have long since exerted a deep, compelling magic, a supernatural power that still lingers in the land. The trees at the rear of the monastery are especially sacred. Many centuries ago, the monks of Hartland planted the five great trees together in a circle, as they believed that the particular spot was the centre, the core of all life. There was the Rowan, the Willow, the Oak, the Ash and the Yew; the combination of their branches was said to sweep over earth and heaven; their roots so strong that they spread deep into the ground, making a ladder between worlds, creating a link to the other worlds and underworlds.' He paused for a moment to cough. 'These great trees are known as The Elder trees and it has long since been believed that they have the power to bring upon reincarnation to those who worship them.'

In a daze I again glanced at the mammoth trees. 'Surely that is little more than myth.'

His face looked enthralled as he spoke. 'No not at all. I do believe it is possible.' He uttered in an animated voice. 'It is said that a certain monk made it his life's work to locate each and every portal that ever existed. Along with ancient manuscripts about the gateways, he detailed his entire findings in a book; thus, completely linking all worlds with one another in a precise fashion. However, whilst finishing his book the monk stumbled across a particular manuscript that revealed a shocking revelation, so incredible that many thought it not to be true, and those who did believe were so frightened of its terrible consequences that they ordered the monk to burn all his work, including the manuscripts.'

'So, I presume that didn't happen?'

'The manuscripts were destroyed but the monk's book, which held a complete, written account of the manuscript in question, apparently disappeared into thin air, along with the monk.' He looked subdued. 'For these long years I have been searching for the notes, I will never lose hope.'

I pondered over what he was telling me. Suddenly, I recalled how Isaiah had mentioned a book, a book so evil that if it got into the wrong hands the outcome could be devastating. It was clear to me now that this book and ledger were one and the same, the book my dear father had been searching for in the library and the ledger hidden in the church, were the exact same item that Septimus was desperate to possess, it was too much of a coincidence not to be.

I gulped nervously, trying to remain composed. 'So, if this book really does provide the secret to eternal life then there is a price to pay, is there not?'

His voice was smooth and controlled as he spoke. 'Apparently so. This manuscript described in detail a ritual to be performed within the circle of The Elder trees.' He coughed again. 'A ritual that would somehow activate the sacred trees here at the monastery so that they become all supreme and powerful, over every tree that ever existed in any world. Anyone who comes to pay homage to these trees shall be granted immortality.'

'But?'

'It is said that the power of The Elder's will become distorted to such a degree that they will wish to reign supreme and will therefore cause complete havoc to those who do not worship them. Their branches will reach far and wide, and little by little all other worlds will fall, leaving only Hartland in all of existence.'

For a short while we sat staring at one another, without uttering a word. However, I soon found myself erupting with laughter.

Septimus widened his eyes in astonishment. 'Pray tell me what you find so amusing?'

I placed my hand over my mouth in an attempt to stay the annoying sound that I seemed unable to control.

'This cannot be true.' I uttered in a humorous voice. 'Even if you were to find the book and go ahead with the ritual, such catastrophe would never come to pass, it is preposterous.'

'I see you too are a non-believer Miss Farraday, along with so many others that have frequented this monastery.'

I threw him a quizzical glance. 'So, where are all these non-believers?'

'They have all gone from this place.' He paused. 'One way or another.'

An uneasy feeling crept over me as I read between the lines. A frightening vision of poor, defenceless souls being dragged away by the trees filled my thoughts.

He frowned. 'To find the book would be the greatest achievement of my life; to discover the key to eternal life must surely be mankind's ultimate goal.'

My eyes became distant as I stared out the window. 'Oh, I don't think so, no one is meant to live forever; it's just not natural.'

A serious look came upon his face. 'I used to think that too, but as I...' He faltered 'As I advance in years, I find myself pondering more and more over such a phenomenon.'

'But the tonic you take here delays old age, is it not sufficient to have your life prolonged?'

Septimus looked irritated by my question. 'Yes, yes. The berries we use from the Rowan, one of the great Elder trees, is the prime ingredient in our tonic, and it has a very special and unique quality, preserving those who take it, allowing one to appear younger than their years.' He bowed his head. 'But it cannot stamp out death.' His face became pensive. 'I'm an exceedingly practical man Miss Farraday, and accept that there's a distinct possibility that I shall never find the answer I'm seeking, and therefore I will certainly perish. That is why I require an heir to take over my good work when I am gone.'

'So, Gideon will to take your place.' I muttered.

'Precisely Miss Farraday, and I have no doubt he will make a worthy successor. He has taken well to the tonic.'

'Well? I cried, clenching my hands together. 'Everyone here has had their emotions suppressed to such a degree that they trudge through the monastery in an awakened slumber.' I threw him a quizzical look. 'Everyone except you, why is that Septimius?

'How misguided you are Miss Farraday. The tonic merely redirects one's mind and placates its recipient into living a more fulfilling existence, away from the unnecessary emotions that would otherwise encumber them.' He heaved himself up out of the chair and strolled across the room. 'I am the oldest one here and have therefore taken more doses than anyone else; I can only assume that prolonged use of the medicine makes one more...'

'Normal?

He looked annoyed. 'Wiser was the word I was going to use Miss Farraday, before you rudely interrupted.' A faint smile appeared on his lips. 'Of course, all the tonic in the world cannot change certain people's attitudes and will not improve their intellect.' Coming close he stared into my eyes. 'Your father took it for years and yet still he faltered. People such as Isaiah cannot be helped.'

I winced at the mention of his name. Since arriving here I'd hardly given Isaiah a second thought. 'What will become of him?' I asked in a feeble voice.

Septimus face became grave 'Your father is being held in the dungeons below the monastery, awaiting his fate.'

'And what is his fate?'

Septimus countenance didn't change. 'Isaiah shall be executed on Midsummer's Eve, when he shall be hung from the rafters in the great hall.'

He studied my face, waiting for a reaction.

Forlornly, I lowered my eyes to the floor. 'I see.'

Septimus moved unsteadily towards the doorway, where he almost collided with a startled looking Gideon.

'Ah there you are grandson. Miss Farraday has been patiently waiting for you.' Allowing Gideon to steady him, he momentarily turned to glance at me. 'I shall take my leave now.'

Gideon caught my eye and we held each other's gaze. 'Are you ready to begin?'

'What?' I replied in a daze.

'The portrait.' He snapped, coldly. 'The one you're supposed to be painting of me.' Looking furious he stomped across the room and took the seat by the window. 'I'm not in the mood for conversation today, so I would appreciate it if you would do your job in silence.'

I gaped at him, my mouth open wide. 'Whatever you say Gideon.'

# Chapter 18

My heart was heavy that night as I made my way along the dark passageway. I found myself mulling over what Septimus had said about Isaiah, and as much as I tried, I couldn't help but feel a small amount of pity for what awaited my dear father. However, this momentary distraction from my surroundings soon vanished, as yet again I heard the ominous footsteps, walking along the passage behind me.

I began to mumble underneath my breath. 'Why can't you leave me alone.'

Hastily, I swung around to see if someone was following me, and was not at all surprised when I saw the corridor was empty.

I shivered.

Carrying along the passage I heard the same eerie sound.

'No, no.' I cried desperately

Unable to make my legs move I froze on the spot. A coldness filled the air, so acute that I could see my breath. It was only then I felt an ice-cold hand firmly gripping my arm.

I opened my mouth to scream but nothing came out.

To my horror I felt its bitter cold breath by my ear. 'Go from this place.' The voice was so distant it was less than a whisper.

Trembling uncontrollably, I shut my eyes and imagined I was somewhere else. It seemed an eternity that I stood there in utter fear, too scared to look or move. But eventually the thing released its grip.

I let out a tortured cry.

Opening my eyes, I saw the shadow of a figure disappearing through the wall up ahead.

A hysterical sound of laughter escaped from my lips as I ran to my room, eager to reach if before another spectre materialised.

It seemed to me all the long years of the past had been captured within these very walls, and the dead still lingered amongst the living, not that there was much difference between them, I thought ironically.

As I wedged the stool up against the door, I shuddered at the thought of yet another harrowing night spent at this place, it filled me with a wretched hopelessness that showed no signs of diminishing. And never before had I felt so forlorn: how I longed to be with Gideon, the old Gideon, or Mace, even if he was invariably aggravating, I loved him all the same, like a brother I'd never had. Then there was Clarice, with her unchanging demeanour, so different from the vivacious, smiling young woman she had once been. I also imagined my mother was out there somewhere, thinking of me, or even perhaps an Aunt.

A sharp pain shot through my temple, and I wearily lay back on the bed.

Glancing at my watch I saw that it was still relatively early. I'd never known time drag so slowly as in the monastery. And, unfortunately, I had nothing but time in this horrendous place, time to dwell on ridiculously unimaginable scenarios, which in ordinary life would never come to pass. However, my eerie surroundings and the strange goings on around me, made it hard not to believe they were true; all my morbid thoughts were all too frighteningly real. How I wished to be safe and cosy at home, wherever that was, reading a musty old book. I would be curled up in a big, comfy armchair, with the rain pelting against the windowpane outside. I even would have preferred one of my nightmares, as at least I would awake with a sense of relief that it had just been a bad dream.

With a deep sigh, I retrieved my notebook from the mattress and started to flick through the pages.

'Oh, yes Rawlings.' I muttered poignantly to myself.

All thoughts of returning home had all but left me now, even with the reminder of my notes, Rawlings still seemed old and forgotten; Aunt had strayed so far away from my thoughts that I had great difficulty picturing what she looked like; how I'd wished I'd slipped a photo into my precious notebook to remind me of her face.

Shivering, I huddled up against the coarse blanket and tried to sleep. And before long I felt myself slowly drifting off.

A frenzied banging on the door caused me to stir, and instinctively I leapt out of bed. I wanted to be scared, and maybe I should have been, but something snapped within me and I felt a surge of anger overtake my fear.

'Leave me be you evil spirit, you do not frighten me.'

The noise stopped momentarily and there was silence. Smiling to myself I sighed and clambered back into bed.

Then there it was again, that annoying tapping.

'Be gone.' I hissed. 'You can hammer on the door all night; I shan't open it.' I uttered determinedly.

'Hello. Effie?'

I sat, bolt upright. 'What?'

For one, idiotic minute I imagined the evil thing to have a voice. However, common sense soon took over and I realised that it was an actual person. Wrapping the blanket around myself, I crept over, removed the stool and cautiously opened the door, only to come face to face with Mace.

I gasped with delight and bafflement. 'I...I'm so glad to see you' I pulled him into the room, and gave him a hug. 'I've missed you.' Drawing back slightly I looked into his face, his blank, expressionless face. 'Mace? Mace are you, all right?

Without saying a word, he stared into my eyes, almost as if he was looking straight through me.

I grasped his shoulders and started to gently shake him. 'Wake up Mace, wake up.' My heart sank as I saw his unchanging stare. 'Mace.' I said, urgently, shaking him harder. 'Snap out of it.' Realising it wasn't working I impulsively slapped him across the face. 'Please Mace.'

He didn't respond.

I wanted to slap him again, harder this time, but I couldn't bring myself to torture him further, or myself, for it was evident that doing so would have little effect. I took a deep breath then exhaled. 'Well, I don't understand why you've come to visit.' I guided him over to the stool and sat him down.

'Now that... now that you're a fully-fledged member of the monastery, I didn't think you'd be interested in me anymore.' With a weak laugh I sat down on the bed. 'I take it you can still speak.' I said, trying to envisage him being mute, but failing miserably. 'Well? I asked, eager for a response. 'Say something.' I shook my head in despair. 'Anything.'

Unable to bear it, I leant forward and closed my eyes. 'Not you Mace, not you as well, what am I going to do?' I uttered tearfully. 'I'm all alone.'

'Gorgon.'

The sudden sound of his voice caused me to jump. I gawped at him in bewilderment. 'What, what did you say?'

'Gorgon.' He said, in a slightly louder voice. 'You asked me to say something.'

Looking at him I couldn't see a change in his manner, and was perplexed by what it was he was attempting to tell me. 'Who's a gorgon, Mace?'

'Why Proctor of course, she is a terrifying woman which therefore makes her a gorgon.' An acute look of amusement appeared in his eyes. 'A fitting name for such a horrendous woman.' He got up and began pacing round the room. 'Tried to almost force feed me that atrocious muck of a tonic, and almost made me choke on the stuff.' With a sideways glance at me he carried on chatting. 'It was all a complete waste of time anyway, they can't change who I am.' Raising his eyebrows he smiled, crookedly at me. 'Brainwashing medicines are powerless against the almighty Mace.'

I was almost tempted to strike him again for being so infuriatingly aggravating, at making me believe the worst had happened, but ultimately the only relevant point that mattered, and the only thing I cared about was having him back.

He threw me a wary look. 'You're not going to hit me again, are you E? Raising his hand, he began rubbing his left cheek. 'That really stung when you slapped me.'

Narrowing my eyes, I looked away, pretending to be deep in thought. 'I'm just debating it.' I replied. 'I have to say you deserve it.' I swung around and faced him. 'It really wasn't very funny, was it?'

He looked sheepish. 'You know I can't resist deceiving you E, and this opportunity was just too good to waste.' He began shaking with laughter. 'I don't know how I kept a straight face for so long, I suppose I've had plenty of practice over the past few days, what with spending time with the living dead, I've become rather adapt at become a fake zombie.'

I put my hand up to my mouth, unable to stop myself from giggling. Mace's humour eased me somewhat, as the conceited and flippant manner in which he was behaving reassured me that no harm had befallen my best friend. However, I couldn't understand how the tonic had such a devastating impact on some yet hardly affected others.

'How much of the tonic did they give you Mace, I mean do you think it only alters a person after several doses.'

Mace shrugged his shoulders. 'Who knows, and quite frankly Effie, who cares.' He said, impatiently pacing back and forth. 'It actually tastes like wine, and can make you feel rather intoxicated, I can see why people could become addicted.' He gazed up at the ceiling and drew in a deep breath, allowing it to escape slowly through his closed lips. 'We just need to concentrate on leaving this place, before it's too late.'

'Too late?'

He looked suddenly disgruntled. 'Never mind.' He uttered dismissively. 'There are a few others, who are still relatively normal, and obviously they want to flee as much as we do. We've been discussing an escape route that will lead us well away from the monastery.' His face looked strained. 'There's a secret passage leading from the library that takes you down to the tunnels, which are full of abnormal tree roots, just waiting to snatch any unsuspecting victim. So, to be honest, I can't see how we can go that way. And the other predicament will be persuading Clarice and Gideon to tag along.' He stared into my face and frowned. 'Because of who Gideon is, it could cause complications.' He looked apprehensive. 'I've been told Gideon's been given a higher dose of the tonic, in order for his grandfather to keep him here.'

273

Looking dismayed I nodded, staring gloomily down at the floor. 'Yes, I thought as much.' My heart began to ache. 'And what about you, how do you feel about Septimus being your grandfather, I take it you know?

'Yes, it's horrendous.' He exclaimed. 'If he had the slightest idea who I was he'd be force-feeding me gallons of the tonic, just so I would stay with him and Gideon.' An agonised expression crossed over his face. 'You have to promise me E; you'll not tell him my true identity. I don't want to end up like Gideon.' He placed his hand over his mouth. 'Sorry E, I didn't mean...'

'It's alright Mace.' I snapped at him. 'You may believe Gideon is beyond help but I'm not leaving without him, or Clarice.'

Mace was silent for a moment then sighed heavily. 'Very well then, Clarice shouldn't be too much trouble, but we may have to give Gideon some type of sleeping draught, then carry him out of here.' He turned his head towards the door. 'Where's that nasty father of yours when we need him, he's an expert on such brews.' He said, scratching his head. 'Do you...do you think he's still alive?'

'For now.' I muttered in a calm voice. 'But surely you don't expect me to go and ask him.' I exclaimed with a laugh.

The thought of sneaking down to the depths of the monastery to see my father filled me with dread. The last time I'd seen him he was distraught and unhinged, so there'd be no telling what he'd do; I feared, even if he could provide a potion it could quite possibly contain poison. However, despite all this, a small part of me wondered if I should see him, one last time, before the end....

'I saw a medicine cabinet in the infirmary, next time I'm in there I'll try and take a peek.

'You're assuming that drugging Gideon is the solution.' I said, picturing the both of us heaving Gideon along the passageway. 'Perhaps we could fool him in some way.'

Mace looked bemused. 'Well okay E, you have a think about it.' He edged towards the door. 'I should go now before I'm noticed.'

'Can we meet again tomorrow? I asked, anxiously. 'There's a young girl who wants to be friends with me; I shall tell her to come over too.' I thought for a minute. 'Shall we say the same time tomorrow night, in my room?'

'Very well.' He uttered in a whisper. 'Abel and Mundy are usually tucked up in their beds by now, so won't be a bother, but Proctor is a different matter, she wanders these passageways morning, noon and night, so tell your friend to take care.'

'Yes, yes I will.' I said, carrying the lantern up high so I could see Mace to the door. 'Take care walking back to your room.' I uttered in a cautious voice. 'There's more out there to be scared of than Proctor.' A shiver ran through me.

Mace carefully lowered my arm, so the lantern didn't shine on the ceiling. 'Don't point the lantern up too high E.' His face came close to mine. 'They don't like the light, it awakens them.'

'Yes Mace.' I said, trying my best to push the hideous thought out of my mind; since the first night I'd spent here I knew there was something above me, moving slowly across the ceiling, twisted an unnatural, but it was too horrendous for my brain to process, so to stay the madness I chose to bury my head in the sand, like a fool.

'Oh, and Mace, just knock twice on the door, there's no need to hammer persistently on it like you did last night.'

He gave me a peculiar stare. 'Effie, last night I was in the infirmary. It was only tonight I found your room.' A huge grin spread across his face. 'That evil spirit you wanted rid of earlier must have been responsible.' Reaching out he kissed the top of my head. 'Sweet dreams E.'

My face dropped.

Unable to reply, I watched him disappear into the chilling darkness of the terrifying passageway. And then I slammed the door and hastily rammed the stool up against it.

That night I slept uneasily, and when I finally drifted off into what should have been a restful sleep, I found myself plunging into a disturbing nightmare.

I was running my hands through golden corn. Feeling a tug on my dress, I looked down upon Gilbert. His twisted smile was, as always, present, and hanging from his wooden mouth was a piece of corn that he was chewing happily away upon: somehow it made him appear less sinister but all the more absurd.

'Greetings Miss Farraday, on this glorious day I have cometh to utter a little ditty.'

Before I could say a word, his shrill voice began to float across the field, bringing an unwanted disturbance to such a tranquil setting.

*'You're not going to get what you desire and the situation has become dire.*

*Take heed when I warn you about the fire, and I'm really not a little liar.*

*The book is bad as well you know and mustn't get snatched by a nasty foe.*

*So, take my advice and run for your life or things won't be a whole lot nice.'*

Standing very still he placed his hands on his hips, awaiting my response.

'Well?'

I opened my mouth to speak but my attention was drawn to the two approaching figures. It was Gideon and the madwoman.

'Can't you see it's time to flee?' Shrieked Gilbert.

But I hardly heard him as I stood, transfixed by the couple before me, as they began dancing merrily amongst the corn. Gideon was laughing as he lifted the madwoman up, swinging her around in his arms. I watched in fascination as she clung to him, her cruel eyes filled with adoration. No longer dancing they stared lovingly at each over then began to kiss, passionately.

I felt the rising sickness within my stomach. 'No, no, no.' I cried at them.

They both turned and glared at me.

'Oh, look my love it's the Farraday woman with her odd little toy dummy.' Exclaimed the madwoman, with a distinct tone of humour in her voice.

Gideon snarled at me. 'Make them burn.'

From out of nowhere the madwoman produced a lantern, which she proceeded to fling at Gilbert and myself; shattering before our feet, the lantern's flame instantly caught light to the dry corn, rapidly spreading before us. Frantically I tried to move back but I found the corn had entwined itself around my ankles.

I felt a small, rigid hand in mine. 'I'll not desert you mistress Farraday.'

Gaping down at his abnormally large, bulbous eyes I couldn't work out why Gilbert was suddenly being my friend.

'Thank you, Gilbert.'

Just as the flames engulfed us, I saw Gideon and the madwoman casually walking away, his arm was about her and they were laughing like two lovers on a summer's day.


Despite the horrendous dream of last night, I very successfully managed to shove the extremely unpleasant memory right to the back of my mind. It wouldn't be good to dwell on what had happened, and I was determined not to allow myself to succumb to the imaginary nonsense that my brain had created.

In an act of defiance to myself I decided to wear my hair loose over my shoulders, carefully concealed behind my hood, until I reached the study. It was a ploy that I'd conjured up last night whilst lying in bed before my nightmare. It's easy to come up with logical ideas and create feasible solutions when you're unable to sleep: I would entice Gideon by flaunting my mane of curly, auburn hair, in a vain attempt to make him notice me, to make him remember. However, in the cold light of day I was not so sure, it was a silly notion; I wasn't exactly used to acting provocative and had misgivings at making it credible: the likes of me would end up looking foolish, and in Gideon's present state I doubt he would even care if I shaved my head.

I paused in the doorway as I saw Mundy striding straight towards me with an armful of books.

'Good morning Mundy.' I said struggling to smile.

'Is it?' He grunted, rudely shoving passed me and out the room. 'I've too much work to be doing to have a good morning.' Without another word he marched along the corridor towards the library.

Lowering my hood, I crossed over towards the archway. I'd arrived a little earlier to allow me the opportunity to prepare myself. I pulled out my tiny compact mirror and stood by the glowing lantern to check my hair. On reflection I can see how deluded I must have been. Did I really expect to see glossy, flowing locks, cascading down my shoulders, instead of the usual disorderly mass of curls, spurting out in every direction, like some kind of wild woman? No of course not.

I groaned in frustration.

Frantically, I searched for a hair band in my robes, in the hope that I could tie it back before Gideon arrived, but as I heard the bang of the door, I realised it was too late. Flinging the mirror on the floor, I hurriedly scurried across the room and went and stood by the paints on the table.

'Good morning Miss Farraday.' He said, nodding at me as he went over to the window. 'I trust you slept well?'

'Not too bad.' I blurted out. 'Please call me Effie, Miss Farraday sounds so formal.'

He opened the shutters then turned to look at me, momentarily running his eyes over my hair. 'Very well, from this day forth, I shall call you Effie.'

I could feel the colour rising in my cheeks.

His look was unwavering as he continued to stare. Quite by surprise, a faint smile came about his lips. 'You seem somewhat flustered, did you overlay?'

I paused for a moment, taken aback by his smile. 'Yes, I did rather. My bedroom's so dark in the mornings that quite frequently I still believe it to be the dead of night.' I ran my fingers through my hair, pushing it back over my shoulders. 'I also find myself plagued with nightmares of a rather alarming nature, they're so scary at times that invariably I can't return to sleep.' I let out a laugh. 'When I do finally drift off it's time to rise.'

Momentarily he widened his eyes, as if startled by my confession.

Collecting some paints from the table, I moved nearer to where he was standing.

'Do you dream Gideon?'

He looked mystified. 'No, not at all.'

'Ever?'

His face darkened. 'Not that I am aware of.' Gradually, he moved towards the seat by the window. 'A dream is only a dream, usually forgotten once we have awoken.' A look of intrigue swept over his face. 'Why do you ask?'

I met his unfaltering gaze. 'Oh no reason. It's just that I'm rather partial to having recurring dreams. In fact, up until fairly recently, I would have the exact same dream every single night.'

There was a stunned silence, whilst we both stood staring at one another intently.

When he spoke, his voice was low and unsure. 'How is that possible? Please, do tell me about it.'

I averted my gaze, unable to maintain eye contact any longer. 'Well, they all started when I was a young girl.' Dreamily, I looked towards the window, feeling myself drifting off to the mystical forest that I knew so well, where time had no meaning and where Gideon and I had irrevocably bonded.

'Yes?' he said. 'Do carry on.'

I turned, fleetingly glancing at him. 'It was almost like I actually stepped into my dream, to the most wondrous place you could ever imagine. But I wasn't alone, every night I would be joined by the same, special person, a young boy of similar age, who over time would grow into a remarkable man.' I reached up and flicked the hair away from my face. 'It was almost as if a magical spell had been cast upon us, binding us together.' I started to tremble. 'We came to love one another.'

There was a breathless stillness.

I stared into his gleaming eyes, searching his face for a flicker of emotion.

'So, when the dreams ended, what happened then?'

'I crossed over into his land, and stayed at his home in the village of Briarwood.'

'Briarwood?' He stammered.

'Yes.' I murmured, drifting off again into a world of my own. 'The village itself is tucked away in the countryside, and to reach it you must pass over lush, green fields and cornfields that sweep up against the white clouds and the blue sky beyond. Nearby there are charming woodlands with their unique air of mystery, and meadows covered in a profusion of wild flowers, gently swaying in the warm breeze. The sun kissed lanes filled with the delicious scent of wild roses, gracefully wind through the village so faultlessly, leading you to the cobbled streets with their thatched cottages, that hold an undeniable charm of yesteryear.'

I peeked at him, to make sure he was still paying intention.'

'Do go on.' He uttered in a strange, weak voice.'

On the edge of the village, just passed the church, tucked away out of sight stands a red-bricked cottage, secluded and peaceful: sheltered in an abundance of honeysuckle, its picture postcard magnificence is too idyllic to be real.'

He was looking at me intently. 'This is where you stayed?'

'For a while, yes.' I paused, looking down at my hands. 'I was soon swept away with the whole contentment of village life, and...and I longed to remain there with this man, forever. But then fate intervened and I had to leave, and return to my home.' My voice became faint. 'And all was lost.'

'So, what happened to this love of yours?

An unexpected and unwelcome vision of Gideon and the madwoman, passionately embracing, popped into my head. I placed my hand over my eyes in attempt to push it away.

'Effie?'

I raised my head and looked into the darkness of his eyes. 'Once we were parted it set off a train of events in motion that created a wall between us, a wall so strong and impenetrable that we may never break it down.'

For a while Gideon remained silent, mulling over what I'd told him. I wondered if he was beginning to slot the pieces in the puzzle, join up the dots. I didn't know if it was the amnesia or the potion, or perhaps a mixture of the two, making him this way, but I had to believe his old memory was hiding in there somewhere, ready and waiting for a little nudge onto the right path, that oh so familiar path of realisation.

He became fidgety. 'If your love for one another is strong enough, it will find a way for you both to be reunited.'

'Yes, I replied in a croaky voice. 'I'd like to think so.'

I met his gaze and for a moment we stared at one another, then he turned away, looking solemn. 'You should leave this place and seek him out.'

Although I wanted to scream at him, I was surprised at how calm my voice sounded. 'What if he is already here in the monastery, what if I only have to reach out to touch him, and remind him of our special bond.'

Gideon flinched, swaying a little. 'Then you should go to him.' He glowered at me as he strode past, towards the archway. 'But be warned, love is not an emotion that flourishes at Hartland, if you do not grab it soon enough it will wither and die.'

'Right.' I uttered dejectedly

I turned to look at him. 'Are you leaving so soon?' I uttered, panicking 'I've not had the opportunity to paint very much. I'm afraid I'm not one of these artists that can paint from imagination.' I said feeling flustered. 'I require my subject to be present.' It was a lie of course but necessary in the circumstances. 'Besides, your grandfather seems eager for me to complete the portrait.' I looked back at the easel. 'Please, stay for a while longer.'

He scowled at me. 'We will begin again tomorrow.' Marching over towards the doorway he mumbled something under his breath that I couldn't quite hear, then left, slamming the door behind him.

Feeling subdued, I slowly made my way over to the window and sat down. Gideon's behaviour was certainly ambiguous: I couldn't decide whether he'd worked out the truth, and finally realised he was the object of my desire, a concept that had sent him scurrying off in confusion or fright. Or, was it just the tonic doing its work: his dismissive and oblivious manner certainly seemed normal. However, as I sat there, staring dreamily at the moving trees, a thought came to me, a strange, unlikely thought that was probably my over active imagination running away with me. For it appeared that Gideon's reaction to discovering the person I loved was at the monastery, had almost seemed like jealously. Beginning to laugh at how absurd this was I gathered up the brushes and put them away.

I crept out the study hoping not to bump into anyone awful, such as the formidable Proctor or Abel, whose tendency to gawp at me was becoming rather tiresome. I knew that Septimus would undoubtedly scold me for not continuing the portrait; in fact, I imagine he would be furious; just because his grandson had stormed off in a huff, would not justify a reason for me giving up and sneaking out the study.

Impulsively, I headed for the library.

There's something overwhelmingly calming about the atmosphere within a library, the wall-to-wall abundance of books that have an undeniable quality of uniqueness in each and every one of them, their ancient pages exuding an intoxicating scent that fills your senses with a peaceful contentment, seldom found elsewhere.

As I stepped further into the room, I couldn't help but marvel at the quantity of books, not just around the walls but stacked up, pile upon pile in front of the bookcases and upon the tables. Proctor had made it clear that only Septimus was permitted to visit the library, and from what I had observed, he didn't have the energy to put the books in order. Leisurely I strolled through the room, running my fingertips along a row of books and selecting one at random. Clearing some space on the desk in the corner, I put the book down and began flicking through the pages.

'Hello Effie,' said a little voice.

It was Lucinda.

I felt my heart jumping wildly in my chest at the shock. 'Oh Lucinda, you did give me a scare.' I peered into her pale face. 'You really shouldn't creep up on people.'

She looked mortified. 'I'm ever so sorry Effie. I didn't mean to.'

'It's okay.' I replied, trying to catch my breath. 'What are you doing here?'

'Meeting you of course. You...you did want to be my friend, didn't you?'

I stared into her poor, tormented face. 'Yes, yes I did. It's just that I'm surprised you knew where I was.'

'Oh, this is my most favourite room in the whole of the monastery.' She declared, looking around in adoration. 'I spend a huge amount of time in here.'

'I didn't think anyone but Septimus was allowed in the library.'

A strange, distant look filled her eyes. 'But I'm very used to not being seen.'

'You must be very accomplished at hiding.'

'Yes, yes I am.'

We both stood there laughing.

'Well...I can see why you'd want to spend time in here. It's by far the most interesting, and dare I say normal, room in the monastery.' I looked around at the books. 'I almost feel at home.'

'The library has its mysteries too, you know. Did you know of the concealed door within this room?'

'Yes, my friend Mace mentioned it.'

Her small hand, gently took mine. 'Let me show you.'

I followed her to the rear of the room, then over to the far right, where the books were shrouded in shadow.

'All you need to do Effie, is remove these books from the shelf and put your arm through the gap.' She hovered her hand over two great leather-bound books. 'At the very back you will come across a lever, pull it to the left and you shall be amazed at what happens.'

'Will you show me, Lucinda?'

She looked pensive for a moment. 'No, you must do it Effie.'

I smiled serenely at her. 'Will something grab me from the other end?' I asked, with a giggle. 'Something unnatural.'

'No,' she bent her head forward, gazing steadily at me. 'Don't be afraid.'

I pulled out the books, and then placed the length of my right arm into the gap, feeling about with my hand for the lever. It didn't take long to locate it. 'Found it.' I gritted my teeth, then moved it leftwards. My eyes widened in astonishment as a section of the bookcase, further on up suddenly sprung out, into the room. Without thinking, I moved across to the opened door and took a peek.

Lucinda lightly touched my arm. 'Be mindful of stepping inside, as once you have the door will slam shut behind you.'

'Oh.' I exclaimed peering into the dark space.

'This route is the only safe way to leave the monastery.'

'Really? I replied. 'What about the front gates?

'That way is extremely dangerous, Effie; anyone who tells you otherwise is lying.'

'I see.' An ironic laugh escaped my lips. 'So, where does this way lead?'

'The door leads to a short passageway that will take you down a steep flight of stone steps to the area underneath the monastery.' Her face became fearful. 'But beware of losing your way. There are worse things than tree roots creeping about in the depths of the caverns.'

'Do you know the right direction to take Lucinda?'

'Yes, I've ventured down there on numerous occasions.'

I looked puzzled. Why would a young girl such as Lucinda dare to set foot in such a place, and how did she manage to find her way back.

'Have you ever thought of escaping, whilst you've been down there?'

'I have no wish to leave by myself. I would much rather have an adult to accompany me.' She looked shyly down at the ground. 'Someone like you Effie.'

Curiously, I studied her face. 'I shall therefore rely on you Lucinda, to show me the way. And we shall all leave together.' My face became serious. 'But what about the tree roots, are they not everywhere within the tunnels?'

'Seldom do they stir late at night. If we are cautious and don't make too much noise, we should be able to travel a distance away from the grounds.' She looked at me intently. 'I shall lead you to safety, Effie.'

I began shaking my head in laughter. 'You show remarkable bravery for such a young girl. I wish I was more like you.'

An acute look of melancholy appeared on her face.

I smiled sadly at her. 'Don't worry Lucinda, when we are away from the monastery, I shall take you on a glorious picnic in the middle of the countryside.'

She was silent.

'Well...Perhaps we should go before Septimus decides to pay a visit to your favourite room.'

'Sickly Septimus doesn't bother me. He is too engrossed in his books to even notice anyone.'

I beamed at her. 'Sickly Septimius, is that what you call him? I like it.'

'Tell me, have you also a nickname for his acquaintances?

'Podgy Proctor, Unable Abel.' Her face clouded over. 'And Murderous Mundy.'

I looked concerned. 'Murderous Mundy?'

'Never mind. Let's not talk about him now.' She uttered, looking distressed.

'If you'd rather not, then that's fine.'

'Will you meet me here tomorrow night, Effie? We can discuss when we should leave.'

'Well, yes. But I'm not exactly sure what time I'll be able to make it. Perhaps it would be better if...'

'Don't worry.' She interrupted. 'Just come along when you can. I shall find you.'

I stood in the library, watching her in puzzlement as she wandered out the room.

# Chapter 19

The forthcoming days passed swiftly at the monastery and were rather uneventful.

Lucinda and I would frequently meet up in the library, cautious of Septimus making an appearance; we would linger in the corner, whispering to one another about escaping.

Gideon's mood grew increasingly darker and I found him completely unresponsive to any kind of discussion.

One morning, I brought it upon myself to broach the subject of the hidden portrait, the beautiful picture of the woman, shrouded in cloth. Gideon reluctantly confirmed that it was, indeed, his mother. Although his memories were hazy, his grandfather had reminded him of what she had done. Apparently, Sabina had given Septimus her vow that she would remain at her childhood home of Hartland and not return to Briarwood, where her family were waiting for her. But in the end, she had decided to do neither, and had recklessly fled with my mother, to another realm, my home. Septimus never saw his daughter again, and never recovered from her mysterious departure. Blaming Isaiah seemed the logical explanation, but there wasn't any real proof that he was actually responsible for her leaving. Not being able to cope with seeing Sabina's face gazing down from the study wall, Septimus had covered the portrait, in an attempt to ease the pain of her loss.

On returning to my room that night I examined my notes, searching for anything on Sabina. I already knew, from what Caleb had told me, that she had taken Gideon with her when she'd left Briarwood, but being a young boy, he wasn't ready for the harsh life of the monastery and was therefore shortly returned to his father. It wasn't clear why Sabina had travelled to Abercrombie with my mother, and most likely never would be. My mother and Aunt Constance had helped her get settled, and after giving birth to Mace she had struggled on for some years, but inevitably her health had failed, and she had sadly died. Despite the mystery surrounding her, it seemed to me that her urge to travel had ultimately been her undoing.

The early evenings were made bearable by the frequent visits from Mace, and very often Clarice, who would listlessly walk around the room looking lonely. I found myself constantly averting my gaze so I didn't have to see her mournful expression; instead, I pictured her beaming smile and bright eyes. Of course, Mace and I did our best to engage Clarice in the conversation: he would frequently stare into her vacant face and tell her made up stories from our past, when we were children. And although the accounts were invented, they had an element of realism about them that could almost make you believe that they had actually occurred. With our real childhood memories of home lost deep within our minds it was comforting to pretend, and it was a welcoming break to become absorbed in something other than the monastery.

Mace pulled up the stool and started munching on a piece of bread.

'Help yourself both of you.' He muttered.

I raised my eyes at the plateful of food on his lap. 'Thank you but no.' I replied, taking a sideways glance at the silent Clarice, who seemed lost in a world of her own.

'All the more for me then.'

'How is it you manage to creep down to the kitchen each night and pinch food without anyone noticing?' I asked him in amusement.

'Pure skill I guess.' He said, continuing to eat away. 'I wait until the next chime after supper then sneak down. Most of them are in the land of nod by then.' He picked up some cheese. 'Proctor's the only one to watch out for, she has a tendency to make herself a late-night sandwich.' Sniggering he began to pick a piece of mould off the cheese. 'No wonder she's so colossal.'

I watched as he continued to shove the cheese into his mouth.

'I'm sure she has a secret stash of chocolate hidden away.' He gazed dreamily up at the ceiling. 'If only I could find it, I could really do with a bar.'

'Me too.' I frowned. 'But something tells me they don't possess such a luxury here at Hartland. It would be considered too indulgent.'

He grunted and placed the empty plate on the ground, then slunk forward on the stool. 'So, how fruitful has your day been? 'Has the love of your life declared his undying love for you yet?'

I winced. 'Well, no, not exactly. 'I think with time, he will....' My words began to falter. 'I need to work on him, make him see sense.'

Mace abruptly rose from the stool and began to pace around the room.

'Please don't take offence Effie, but your powers of persuasion aren't very dynamic. And time is something we haven't got.' He peered over at Clarice, who was perched serenely on the edge of the bed. 'We can't carry on like this.' He pranced over and knelt beside her, taking her hands in his. 'We need to get some colour into those pasty cheeks of yours, don't we Clarice.' Sighing, he reached up and cupped her face with his large hand. 'Get you back to your old self.'

Her only response was to move away from him and step across the room.

I saw a fleeting look of rejection in his eyes before he composed himself. 'Well, it's getting late, Clarice and I should return before the gorgon discovers we're not in our rooms.'

I laughed.

'Yes, I'm sure that awful woman is on the prowl.' I replied. 'Come back tomorrow and we'll device a strategy for...' I hesitated, glancing at Clarice. 'Well, you know.'

Although Clarice appeared impartial to our conversations, choosing instead to remain silent, I found myself conscious of saying something I shouldn't, something that could get us into trouble. For I was under no illusions: the mysterious spell that held her within its grasp was strong and loyal to the monastery, and my dear friend Clarice would not think twice about passing messages back to Septimius. Anything to do with escaping would therefore have to be discussed without her.

'Yeah.' Giving me a hug, he moved his mouth near my ear. 'A plan to be free of this place.' He whispered.

'I shall try and get Lucinda to come over.' I bit on my lip. 'And when I see Gideon tomorrow, I will endeavour to work on my skills of persuasion.'

He beamed at me. 'The problem is E that your love for Gideon has culminated to such a degree that you feel giddy and unable to focus on anything other than kissing him.' he said, fluttering his eyelashes at me. 'For now, you need to break away from any romantic illusion you may have and concentrate on the cold, hard facts.' He widened his eyes at me. 'Yes?'

'Whatever you say Mace.' I said, laughing. 'It's hard to take you seriously when you have crumbs all over your robe.' Reaching out I brushed them away.

He pulled a face at me. 'Thanks E,' looking serious he turned to Clarice. 'Please allow me to escort you back to your quarter's madam.' Strolling over he grabbed her hand and kissed it. 'For it isn't safe to venture along the passageway without a brave, young knight, such as myself to protect you.' Gently he guided her to the doorway and turned to me and bowed.' I bid you goodnight fair maiden, I thank you for your hospitality.'

'Goodnight Mace.' I curtsied. 'Fare thee well, my knight in shining armour.'

I watched them as they disappeared out the door, leaving me alone once more, in the semi-dark room, with only the shadows for company. For it was during those, long, lonely nights that the terror took me and the scariest thoughts imaginable seemed to crowd in my mind, waiting for their opportunity to come forward and torment me; all they had to do was to be patient and wait their turn, as there was no possibility of me falling asleep for a long while.

The dull sound of the bell shook me from my thoughts. I yawned and stretched out my arms, slowly tumbling out of the bed and placing my feet on the coldness of the floor.

'I really should have packed some slippers.' I murmured. 'My poor feet are like ice.'

Hearing a commotion from somewhere up the corridor, I hurriedly dressed in my robes, slowly opened the door and stepped outside. Proctor and Abel seemed to be carrying something out of one of the rooms up ahead. Peering closer I realised it was a body.

A faint voice whispered in my ear. 'It seems the trees have taken yet another life.'

With a shudder I swung round, coming face to face with Lucinda.

I placed my hand over my chest. 'Lucinda. You startled me.'

'Keep your voice down Effie, we don't want to draw attention to ourselves.'

'I wasn't aware the trees attacked residents in their rooms.' I remarked, thinking how absurd my comment must sound.'

'Regrettably yes. However, Septimus doesn't like the other residents knowing that they could be attacked in their sleep by The Elder's and strangled by their roots. He believes it would be detrimental to their mental health.'

My reaction was to burst out into hysterical laughter, but instead I remained composed. 'Oh, I see.'

'The whole vicinity has been infested with the roots of the ever-spreading Elders. They are becoming ruthless and greedy.'

For a moment we both stood there in the shadows, watching the two of them cart the poor person off, up the passageway.

'Where will they take the body?'

'To The Elders, just like all the others.'

I gulped. 'Oh, Lucinda what a diabolical place this is.'

'That is why we must flee whilst we still can.' She warned me grimly. 'Can we meet later to talk about our escape plan?'

'Yes, yes very well then. Come to my room after supper, with Mace.' I tried to act amused. It shall make a change from our usual meetings in the library, where we can hardly see for all the books.'

She remained subdued. 'Very well, I shall see you then.' With a decisive nod she turned and paced silently down the passageway.

My resolve was gradually waning. I longed to be out of this place and in a normal environment that didn't scare me to the point of hysteria. Having to be in a continual state of awareness and constantly looking over my shoulder, wary of who might be there, was making me increasingly nervous. In the dead of night, I would constantly hear the mysterious sound of footsteps echoing throughout the building, and would lay awake in pure fright. And now I had the added terror of being attacked in my sleep. I feared that before very much longer I would fall into a deep pit of utter despair and madness, which would hold me in its evil grip for the rest of my life. There would be no going home, the monastery would keep me for its own.


As soon as I entered the study, I knew something was wrong. The room was in total disarray with pots of paints and canvases, strewn haphazardly on the stone floor. I spotted pieces of broken wood scattered about and realised it had been the easel holding my painting. I began scanning the room for the portrait, until finally my eyes came to rest upon a figure huddled in the corner, crouching down over something.

I look mystified. 'Gideon?'

My eyes widened in horror when I saw what he was doing, it appeared he was slashing my painting with a dagger. A frantic wave of panic washed over me. 'Gideon, what are you doing?'

I screamed in a rather high-pitched voice, as I stood over him.

He ignored me and carried on dragging the weapon across the canvas, ripping it to shreds.

'Stop, Gideon stop.' I demanded. 'You will destroy the painting.' But I saw it was already too late. The painting was completely ruined.

I was engulfed in sudden pain as my mind flashed back, to what seemed to be an art gallery, where I was staring down on another mutilated painting of Gideon. There had been a burglary and the proprietor had explained how nothing had been stolen but all my work, and only my work had been destroyed. The owner had been so kind, so understanding. Oh, what was his name, I said to myself, furious for not recalling and momentarily forgetting why.

'There. It is done' Gideon whispered.

To my utter dismay I saw that the cuts were so deep that the canvas was now in pieces. It appeared he had completed his handy work a little too well.

'It's completely destroyed.' He uttered, almost as if he was pleased with himself for doing so well in his task. Without a second glance he rose from the floor and strode across the study to the door. 'I shall inform my grandfather that your work was unsatisfactory and therefore your services are no longer required.'

I began stumbling over my words. 'But...but why, what was wrong with the painting?' I asked in a hoarse voice. 'I...I did my very best to...to capture your likeness.'

As Gideon turned round to face me, I was alarmed to see the crazed look in his eyes.

I stumbled backwards.

He screamed out his words. 'Shut up Effie.' Looking agitated he came a little further back into the room. 'I made a promise to myself not to look at the painting until you had completely finished it.' He clenched his hands together, digging his nails into his palms. 'However, today I foolishly decided to take a look. Now I wished I hadn't.'

'Well admittedly, it required a little more work, but it was almost finished.'

I swerved slightly as he came bounding towards me. 'Don't you understand, you've got me all wrong.' He retorted in a distressed voice. Stooping over me he screwed up his face, as if in pain. 'I'm not like that anymore.... am I?'

Looking into his bewildered face, it only then occurred to me what Gideon was trying to tell me: inadvertently I'd painted him how he used to look, with warmth and affection radiating from his dark eyes, like a beacon of light. Strange as it sounded, it gave me hope, for it seemed I had finally hit a nerve. At last, there was the tiny flicker of human emotion, something I thought was obliterated after taking that despicable potion.

I reached out and touched his arm. 'Yes Gideon, I believe you are.'

He flinched away from me.

'Look upon this as your first step to recovery.' Tentatively, I reached up and cupped his cheek. 'If we left this place, I'm sure you will become normal again, once you return home to Briarwood.'

A fleeting tenderness flooded into his eyes, then his gaze darkened and he peered at me with a bitter hatred that made me shudder. 'What?' he replied, still clenching the dagger in his hand.

My voice became shaky. 'You...you and I...we should leave together.'

With one swift movement he grabbed my shoulders and shoved me against the wall, holding the dagger to my throat. 'That will never happen. You're trying to mislead me, aren't you Effie. Grandfather warned me about you, how you'd try and weaken me, make me sway from my faith, to try and persuade me to leave the monastery.' He glowered at me. 'It seems he was correct in his assumptions.'

The tip of the dagger had pierced my skin and a droplet of blood started to trickle down my neck.

My voice was strained and weak. 'Your grandfather only wants you to stay at the monastery to carry on his work after he's gone. He's using you Gideon; he'll say anything to make you stay.'

There was a burning anger in his face. 'And you'll say anything to prevent me from killing you.' A slight snarl appeared across his lips.

Despite my circumstances, I suddenly had the desire to laugh at the absurdness of the situation. The baffling results of the potion not only changed one into a docile, ill-thinking creature; it also appeared to have a rather nasty side effect of turning its user into a potential killer. For a moment I contemplated the unlikely possibility that this was actually Gideon's doppelganger; the real Gideon was being held captive in the dark, depths of the dungeons, still as wise, affable and charming as he'd always been. If this very unlikely theory was actually true, it would therefore put my life in considerably more danger than I had anticipated: the imitation Gideon would have no misgivings in ending my life.

I gulped uncomfortably under the pressure of the dagger. 'Please Gideon, this isn't you, put the dagger down before you do harm.'

'If I kill you now my life will go on undisrupted and unchanged, by allowing you to live you will bring me nothing but endless misery and confusion.'

Tears welled up within my eyes. 'No Gideon, do not become a murderer. Allow me to live and...if you really cannot bear my company then I...I shall leave, without you.'

'Leave?' He looked perturbed. 'It is rare indeed for anyone to leave the monastery, I do not believe my grandfather will allow it.' He lessened the pressure of the dagger, but still held it firm to my neck. 'Your only other choice is volunteering to become a Giver. Sacrificing yourself to The Elder's is an honourable way to end your existence.' His eyes softened a little. 'I shall look favourably upon you if you put yourself forward.'

I gazed at him, in complete and utter horror. 'II shall never do such a thing.'

His brooding face moved close to mine, so near I thought he was going to kiss me. I felt his lips brush against my face as they moved close to my ear. For a moment they lingered there, pressed up against my neck. 'Then you shall die.'

I swallowed hard, not knowing what to do. Instinctively, I carefully tilted my head and pressed my mouth firmly over his, waiting for him to respond to my kiss. But he did not.

I felt him wrench away from me. 'No, no, stop it.' He uttered, regaining his senses. 'How dare you kiss me.' I felt the cold steel of the dagger, pressing dangerously up against my neck.

The door swung open and Septimus stood there in shock. 'Gideon, remove the dagger from Miss Farraday's neck right this instant.'

'But Grandfather Effie is a traitor, just like you predicted.'

'Yes Gideon, yes she is, but disloyalty must not be punished by murder, that is not our way.'

Gideon continued to pin me up against the wall, staring deep into my eyes.

Septimus looked infuriated. 'Grandson, please. I insist you release your hold on Miss Farraday.'

I felt his hold slacken.

'Sorry grandfather.' Gideon's expression changed to indifference.' You are right.' He removed the dagger from my neck and it clattered loudly to the floor. 'I do not know what came over me.' Without looking at me he turned glumly and headed towards the door. 'I apologise about the painting grandfather but it had to be destroyed, there was something very wrong about it.'

Septimus stared pitifully at the fragments of canvas, scattered across the floor.

'What a dreadful shame.' He took a deep breath. However, I believe in you Gideon and trust in your judgement.'

Unable to meet his gaze, Gideon nodded slightly. 'I shall go and find Abel and ask him to clear up the study.'

Seeing him disappear out the door, I let out a sigh of relief. Up until this day I had never been afraid of Gideon, but today was different, the deranged look in his eyes rather worried me, and witnessing his reaction to the portrait could be enough to put me off painting for life.

Wheezing, Septimus sat down in front of the desk. 'Come Miss Farraday, do take a seat.'

Rubbing my neck, I moved unsteadily to the nearest chair, practically collapsing upon it.

'Well Miss Farraday the prognosis is not good is it?'

'I can hardly be blamed for painting Gideon as I truly see him, it is not a crime.'

Septimus reached forward and picked up a piece of the canvas. 'You are indeed a talented artist Miss Farraday, if a little misguided, but no I will not punish you for painting from the heart.' He discarded the broken canvas amongst the other pieces. 'I am however extremely angered by how you've attempted to compel my grandson to leave the monastery by insinuating that I'm only using him to carry on my great legacy, and by saying how rosier life would be back at Briarwood.'

My face grew red with fury. 'You were listening at the door.'

'Indeed, I was, that is why I entered at the opportune moment, before Gideon had an accident with the dagger.' He moved across the study and began to tidy some books on the desk. 'Of course, I wouldn't have held him responsible if the worst had happened, if I had been delayed... It would be an unfortunate, tragic accident on your part, you tripped and fell onto the dagger and... well you can guess the rest.'

'Yes, although it's rather an unlikely theory, don't you think?' I said, in a curt tone.

He pondered for a while. 'Or perhaps I can announce you did it deliberately.' He drummed his fingers against his lips. 'But what reason would I give, and quite frankly who would even care.' He shrugged his shoulders. 'Everyone here is busy with their lives and wouldn't even pay attention if I suddenly declared that you had gone.'

I attempted to remain composed. 'I see little point discussing the ways and means of my demise when it didn't actually occur. The question is, what happens now.'

Septimus let out a laugh. 'Perhaps I should send you to the infirmary to start your treatment, it will be interesting to see the results.'

I gasped, trying to catch my breath. 'I...I really don't think that's a good idea.'

He smiled. 'Relax; I'm not being serious. Not everyone that comes here is given the medicine. I had an inkling about you as soon as you arrived and I was correct in my assumption. I have discovered how extremely incredulous you are about our way of life.'

'So how do you decide who is suitable and who is not?'

'As a general rule, I don't. Everyone who enters the monastery is evaluated to discover whether they should be allowed to take it, and in most cases, they are. I merely decided not to give it to you because I thought it would hinder your work as an artist.' An ironic laugh escaped his lips. 'Of course, now that is inconsequential.'

'So now I've served my purpose, what happens? It's clear you do not intend to give me the tonic and for that I'm thankful.' I laughed. 'Although I am very curious as to know why.'

He became immersed in his thoughts and it seemed a long while before he finally spoke. 'Not giving you the tonic goes against my better principles but I truly believe your life lies elsewhere. I was very fond of your mother, Miss Farraday, and I believe she is still out there somewhere, I'm giving you this chance to go and seek her out.'

I stared at him without uttering a word. It seemed decidedly odd that he was giving me preferential treatment, and his tale about my mother just didn't ring true.

'Well, I suppose I should be grateful.' I said, coldly. 'The tonic would more than likely not agree with me anyway.'

'Yes, as you've probably discovered, not everyone has a healthy reaction to the treatment.' His face saddened. 'Inexplicably the tonic can destroy certain residents.'

A pained expression came upon his face. 'They're just not compatible.'

'What, what happens to them, are they taken back to the infirmary?'

He avoided my eye. 'No, there is no point.'

'But why, surely they can be nursed back to health.'

'Miss Farraday, I do not run a hospital, the infirmary is purely there to administer the tonic, if it fails to work then... then.'

Coldness crept over my body. 'Where do you take them?'

'Their taken to the deep cavern under the monastery where they are laid out, there's a network of tunnels leading out to the grounds, where the Elder trees are situated.' He looked steadily at me. 'When the trees are ready, they extend their branches through the tunnels and lay their claim to the unhealthy residents.'

'But these people are still alive.'

'Yes, just like the Giver in the ceremony, each one is fed to the Elder trees, it is a worthy end.'

'How can you say that?' I shouted at him. 'The whole thing is totally barbaric.'

'No, Miss Farraday, it is not.' He screamed back at me, slamming his fists down on the desk. 'Everyone here should be willing to make sacrifices when necessary to the Elder's. Since yesteryear this has been our way of life. Without the Elder trees our world would crumble into ruin, potatoes would not survive in the icy ground, vegetables would not grow in our greenhouses and we would not have the berries to make medicine, the tonic that sustains us.'

'But that still doesn't justify....'

'Enough, Miss Farraday.' He interrupted. 'I am very tired.' He hunched forward on his chair. 'Let us return to the matter in hand. Are you going to go and find your mother?'

I sat there mulling over what he'd said.

'I find it incredulous that you would let me go, purely because you liked my mother and want me to find her. Can't you be honest with me and tell me the real reason: you wish to be rid of me, because you fear I'm becoming too close to Gideon.' I hesitated. 'And because I'm the daughter of Isaiah.'

He laughed. 'Good gracious Miss Farraday how possibly could I be afraid of your non-existence relationship with my grandson. I grant you -your persistent harassment of Gideon is a little tiresome. As you have seen he is perfectly happy here, without your interference. And as for your father, well I cannot deny that seeing you here is a constant reminder of that horrid man.'

My voice trembled as I spoke. 'Allow me to take Gideon away for a short while, if he wishes to return then I shall not stop him.' I said, trying to sound earnest.

For a moment there was silence.

'No, that will not be advisable. This is Gideon's home now and will remain so until he says otherwise. He has relinquished his old life, and set his future in motion, a bright future where he will be master of Hartland.'

'You are an extremely selfish man, Septimius.'

He looked at me with a startled look in his eyes, and for a brief moment I thought he was going to strike me. 'I will no longer listen to your incoherent ranting.' His face came close to mine. 'You don't belong here Miss Farraday, I'd like you gone by dawn, tomorrow morning.'

'So, you are allowing me to simply walk out of here?'

He scoffed. 'Absolutely.' He lowered his eyes. Proctor shall escort you to the front gates in the morning.'

I looked alarmed. 'The front gates?'

He appeared incensed. 'Yes, the front gates are the most suitable, and really the only way to exit the monastery.'

I felt myself swaying a little, as a wave of sickness swept over me. I remembered only too well what Lucinda had told me about the gates.

'Very well, I shall go and pack my things.' I muttered, heading towards the door.

'Good, good.' Septimus said, looking pleased. 'Oh, and Miss Farraday, please don't attempt to smuggle Gideon out with you, that would not be a wise move.'

Choosing to disregard what he'd just said I mumbled to him hoarsely 'Well, goodbye Septimius.'

'Farewell Miss Farraday, I wish you well on your travels.'

I faltered at the door and looked back. He was standing there with an odd smile on his face that was rather self-righteous. The expression on his face suddenly reminded me of someone I had once seen in a play, I distinctly remember the actor having the same look, just before he callously murdered his victim.

# Chapter 20

And so, the time had come to leave this place: I would gather my friends and flee whilst I still had the opportunity, before something dreadful happened, and before I became institutionalised like so many of its inhabitants. Being at the monastery made me feel stifled, unable to breath. How I longed to be in the open air once more and feel the warmth of the sun on my face. And now it seemed my wish would soon come to true; I would be free of the confines of this awful place, free to return to Briarwood, free to once again see Noble, the man with the incredible eyes. Being so preoccupied since arriving at the monastery I'd hardly given him a second thought, but that didn't mean he wasn't important to me. Gideon however had now taken priority, I had to get him away from this place, and when we were all home everything would sort itself out, one way or another.

I lay back on the bed and stared dreamily up at the ceiling. My mind began churning over the events of the day: despite Gideon's violent outburst I had a feeling I'd successfully broken down a large part of the high wall that stood between us, his steely resolve had temporarily been weakened. The words of warning from Septimus became a blur as I convinced myself that now would be an ideal time to lure Gideon away, when he was vulnerable and confused.

In a haze, I got up and began wandering around the tiny room. Every so often I become aware of a loathsome creature, portraying uncertainty, loitering like an unwanted visitor at the back door of my mind, ready to enter and invade my thoughts. And, as I stood there in the gloom, I heard the vile creature come forth. It encouraged me to severely doubt my capabilities as a woman: who was I to believe I had the power to entice Gideon; I'd become too complacent, foolishly believing it would come easy to me; who was I to think I could save him, I was just an ordinary young woman with no particular skills in the art of persuasion, and I rarely uttered anything profound that would make anyone stand up and take notice. As a shy, young schoolgirl I would somehow manage to fade into the background and become almost invisible, like a shadow-type figure, whom the teachers would almost forget existed. The creature was standing close now, urging me to face the awful, harsh reality: I wasn't strong enough to win Gideon back, I had lost him to Hartland, and he would remain at the monastery to rot away without love or contentment, for the rest of his days.

Becoming enraged I went and threw myself down on the bed, burying my face into the hard pillow. What was wrong with me, why was I allowing that niggling creature to invade my mind? My only saviour was my stubbornness; it was the only thing that would be able to stamp out the creature of my defeatist attitude, my resolve to keep on going in the face of adversity. I had this one last chance to persuade him to leave, and I would take it. And when we were away from this desolate place he would be cured, and everything would revert back to normal, whatever that meant.

With mixed feelings I began to piece together what was going to happen. Mace, Clarice, Lucinda and myself could all slip away quietly; Septimus wouldn't miss us. But Gideon, his beloved grandson was a different matter, he already suspected I would try and steal Gideon away. A peculiar notion popped up in my head – would Septimus give me Gideon in exchange for The Monk's ledger, would he trust me to go and fetch it for him from the church, that plain, ordinary- looking ledger that apparently could destroy everything with just one tiny little ritual, a spell that would cause all worlds to be ruined. But Hartland would still be there, ready to live another miserable day, with Septimus as master for all eternity. I wonder if he would ever feel remorse for his unforgivable, heinous act, would it be worth destroying humanity in its entirety just to gain immortality.

Panicking, I grabbed my notebook, reading from the page folded in the corner, and an overwhelming sensation of heartache and longing came about me. As outlandish as it all seemed, in giving Septimus the ledger could I ultimately be responsible for destroying Rawlings, my Aunt Constance and everything I held most dear? I clasped the notebook closely to my chest and tried to stop the tears from raining down my face.

I'm not sure when I exactly dozed off, but I found myself in a strange, noisy and chaotic land: I was strolling along a pavement full of people, packed together so tightly that I began to falter, unable to find my way forward without blundering into someone. Beside me lay a busy road, with rows of vehicles slowly chugging along as best they could in the constant stream of traffic; either side stood high, skyscraper type buildings that towered so tall they blocked out the sun and much of the smog filled sky.

Out of the blue I felt someone grab my hand. 'Help me, help me find the doorway out of here Effie.'

I stared into the sweetest of faces, the face of my mother. Impulsively, I reached out and clutched her other hand in mine. 'Where are you mother, what is this place?'

A tapping sound came out of nowhere but I chose to ignore; instead, I gazed at my mother, eagerly awaiting a response. But something was wrong: although she was speaking, I couldn't hear her, and her face was becoming transparent and far away.

'Mother?' I pleaded, desperately keeping my hold on her hands. 'Please don't leave.'

As the knocking noise increased everything around me began to diminish, including my mother. As she tried to cling onto me, I briefly caught the agony in her eyes, a look of utter torment, before she completely vanished into a swirl of nothingness.

With a gasp I lurched forward and opened my eyes.

'Effie, Effie open the door.'

It was the voice of Mace.

A surge of pain enveloped me as I realised I had awoken and was back in my grim room.

Rubbing my eyes, I blearily stumbled to the door and flung it open.

'Apologies on disturbing you your majesty, would you prefer me to return later when you're less preoccupied?'

'No. I'm glad you came early; we have a lot to talk about.'

'Early? E, this is the time I visit every night.'

'Oh.' I exclaimed, realising I must have slept through supper.

I scowled at him as he shoved passed me, followed by a bashful looking Lucinda.

Giving me a closer look, his expression changed to one of concern. 'Is everything all right E? You look a little dazed.'

'Yes, yes of course it is.' I snapped at him. 'I was just having a nap.' I stammered, irritated with him for waking me from my dream.

He threw me a quizzical look. 'Tired are we, too many late nights spent fending off ghouls, or was it Gideon?'

Infuriated, I slammed the door shut, then went and sat next to Lucinda.

'I really wish you would at least try and be serious for once Mace, making jokes all the time is completely exasperating and unnecessary.'

He looked put out. 'Sorry, I was just trying to lighten the situation, which you have to admit is pretty dire.' I watched as his face dropped and a sorrowful look came into his eyes. 'But if you rather I acted like a jittery wreck of a man, filled with negative thoughts of doom, then so be it.'

'No.' I yelled at him, throwing my hands up in despair. 'I just want you to act a little more normal, can you do that?'

He shrugged his shoulders. 'I'm not like you E; I can't be serious and withdrawn all of the time. And anyway, at least I don't drift off into a dream whenever the mood takes me.'

With a deep sigh I looked glumly down at the ground. 'Well, never mind. I've more pressing matters to discuss.' I looked at them both. 'Septimus informed me that I must leave the monastery by dawn tomorrow.' I nervously began biting my nails. 'By the front gate.'

Mace gave me a vacant stare. 'Wait a minute. I need food to get me through this. I'm just going to nip down to the kitchen.'

'Oh Mace. Can't you wait?'

Without answering he slipped out the room.

Lucinda and I gave each other a knowing look.

303

'If Septimus said you can leave by the front entrance then he is lying. Like I told you before, it's a death trap.' Exclaimed Lucinda in a weak voice.

I rose up from the bed and hovered over her. 'But we entered easily enough.'

'The gates are willing to let you in, but will never let you go.' Said Lucinda looking pensive. Many a time people have attempted to escape by way of climbing over the branched gates, and every time they have failed.'

'You, you mean the trees take them?'

Lucinda nodded in silence; her head bowed. 'Every time.' She looked up at me, her face full of anguish. 'A while ago Mundy ordered a group of us to sweep the grounds near to the gates. He thought it would be funny for my friend Bertram to climb up the gate, all the way to the top.' She paused for a moment and rubbed her eyes. 'Bertram didn't want to, but Mundy forced him. He'd only climbed halfway when...when the branches started to creep around his neck, and then his hands and feet. I went forward to try and help him, but Mundy pulled me back.' Tears started to stream down her face. 'He...He said this is what happens when anyone is foolish enough to leave. By then the branches had wrapped their way completely around Bertram; he cried out in desperation, but it was no good, the trees had claimed him.' She bent forward, sobbing. 'Mundy *knew* Bertram would die. He as good as murdered my friend.'

I knelt down and hugged her. 'Oh Lucinda, I'm so sorry, it must have been awful for you.' Gently, I stroked her cold hair.

Mace came bursting back in the room, empty-handed. 'That dragon woman, Proctor is creeping about in the kitchen. No doubt searching for scraps of food to stuff in her podgy mouth. You'd think she'd have had enough at supper this evening.'

'Ah ha.' I murmured, only half listening.

He frowned at me. 'So, what were you saying about leaving?'

I spoke in a clear, slow voice. 'Like I said, before you rushed off for food, I have to leave the monastery tomorrow morning.' I glanced at Lucinda. 'Having discussed exiting by the front gates; we've decided it won't be a good idea.'

He looked infuriated. 'No Effie, we haven't had a discussion. You could at least have waited for me to return.' He pushed his floppy hair away from his eyes. 'But as it happens, you're right for once. Leaving by the front gates will be suicide.' He started to drum his fingers against his lips. 'Why do you have to go so soon, what's happened?'

Glumly, I lowered my eyes. 'I won't bore you with the detail.'

'Oh, thank you E.'

I rolled my eyes at him. 'Let's just say that Septimus doesn't want me here anymore.'

'And the portrait, have you finished it?'

I hesitated. Something held me back from telling Mace the truth. If he became aware of Gideon's violent episode, he may think twice about taking him along with us.

'No, it transpires that I failed to capture Gideon's true character.' I swallowed hard. 'So, the painting was scrapped.'

He looked sceptical. 'Really?' Studying my face, he remained silent for a while. 'Too bad eh. They obviously don't know a talented artist when they see one.'

I gave an uneasy laugh.

He stared at me with his large, kind eyes, then reached out and gently squeezed my hand. 'So, what are we going to do about leaving?'

I widened my eyes and gazed at the floor. 'There's only one other route open to us.' My voice became distant. 'We shall have to face the tunnels.'

A look of dread crossed over Mace's face.' What? Are you completely insane? Those tunnels are laden with deadly tree roots, just waiting for us.' He slapped his forehead. 'We might as well end it all now.' He strode away and faced the corner of the room, deep in thought.

Going over to him I placed my hand gently on his shoulder. 'If you would rather stay at the monastery, until you find a safer way to leave, then...then I shall understand. You are not beholden to me Mace. '

He swung round, screeching at me. 'Yes, yes I am.' He grabbed my face with his hands and forced me to look at him. 'What kind of friend would I be if I made you go without me;

how would you cope without my help and guidance.' He let go of me and slunk down to the ground, onto his knees. 'How you would suffer without your best friend by your side.'

'Get up Mace, you fool.' I said sharply. 'We haven't got time to mess about.'

He began to roll about the floor in hysterical laughter.

I glared at him. 'I've come to the conclusion that your stupid side has been accentuated by that tonic.' I folded my arms in defiance. 'And to be quite honest I would've rather you'd just become like everyone else at the monastery. At least it would have removed your infantile behaviour.' I got hold of his robes and yanked him up. 'Now, are you leaving with me tomorrow, or not?'

There was an uncomfortable silence.

Scratching his head, Mace looked me in the eye.

'If you think we can just casually walk through the tunnels, and leisurely stroll away from the monastery without a hitch, then you're more deranged than I thought, Effie Farraday.' He looked puzzled. 'Are you sure you've not been sipping on that specially brewed concoction that seems to be so popular here at the monastery.' Towering over me, he winked. 'Some of us, like my good self, can obviously handle it, but it does have a tendency to send others a little loopy.' Reaching out he touched my cheek. 'You are looking rather peaky, and you have a crazed, glazed look in your eyes.'

My temper started to flare again. 'You know perfectly well I'm tonic free.' I said, tersely. Now, if you would let me speak, I was going to tell you how I knew you would think me mad, but please, if you have a more preferable option then do tell.' I glared at him. 'Either way I have to leave tonight, if you'd rather stay then that's up to you.' I turned away from him and looked at the wall. 'Gideon and Clarice will also be coming.' My voice became faint. 'I'm not leaving them here.'

'Okay E, don't get tetchy.' He reached down and kissed the top of my head. 'And yes, I am leaving with you, you silly woman. I still think going through the tunnels is totally preposterous, but if it's the only other way out, then so be it.'

I smiled sheepishly at him. 'Thank you, Mace. I can't imagine going without you.' I glanced over at Lucinda, who had been quietly sitting there, with her hands in her lap. 'We can take the secret passage leading from the library, can't we?'

She nodded. 'Yes Effie, that's the most direct route to the tunnels.'

I began pacing impatiently up and down the room. 'Well, that's settled then, we shall all leave tonight.' A thought suddenly struck me. 'What about the other's Mace, the people you mentioned wanting to leave? We should surely warn them.'

Mace gave a big sigh. 'But I don't know what rooms they're in.' He shrugged his shoulders. 'If I'd known this news earlier, I maybe could have informed them during supper. I'm not a mind reader Effie, you should have told me all of this before nightfall.'

I felt wretched. 'I'm know, I'm sorry.'

Mace's expression softened. 'Don't blame yourself Effie. They can escape at any time, if they ever pluck up the courage to. It wasn't your decision to vacate the monastery by tomorrow.' He laughed ironically. 'Anyway, I doubt there would have been a chance you could have told me before this evening. Most of the day you're locked away in the study with Gideon, and I'm working like a slave in the greenhouses, laboriously working away tending vegetables.' He pulled a face. 'I suppose I should be grateful that I wasn't chosen to be one of the berry pickers.'

'Yes.' I said solemnly.

Out of the blue he slapped his hands together. 'So, let's get this plan underway.'

Mace opened his mouth to speak again but I rushed in before him.

'You bring Clarice, and I will go and fetch Gideon.' I said, determinedly. 'Right?'

He stared endearingly into my eyes. 'I love it when you take charge E, I could almost fall in love with you when you're like this.'

Lucinda giggled.

My face broke into a smile and I went over and slapped him playfully on the arm. 'Only almost?' I exclaimed with amusement.

He closed one eye and began to shake his head from side to side. 'Well, yes, maybe if you transformed into Clarice it might help, failing that I will settle for loving you like a sister. I will leave my brothers to fight over you like two love sick puppies.'

I winced. 'I hardly think that's an issue.' I murmured quietly. 'Gideon is barely aware of my existence.' My face began to colour. 'And Noble, well, we are just friends.'

'Mm.' He said, deep in thought. 'Time will tell.' For a while he stood there studying me closely. 'Anyhow, it's evident you still believe you can save Gideon.' A short laugh escaped his lips. How on earth are you going to get your beloved to leave with you, he won't exactly be a willing participant in our escape plan.'

I frowned. 'Don't you worry about that, just leave it to me.' I snapped. 'You just concentrate on Clarice.' I smiled at Lucinda. 'Are you sure you want to come with us?

She stared at me with an agonised expression across her face, and then nodded her head. 'Yes.' She whispered.

'Good.' I replied, squeezing her hand. 'I'm glad.' I turned towards Mace and widened my eyes. 'Let's decide on a time to meet up.'

For some reason Mace gave me an odd look, then shook his head and sighed.

I pretended to listen as Mace began to babble on about how he was going to sneak down to the kitchen, one last time, and grab some food for our journey home. All I could suddenly think about was Gideon, and how it was going to be an impossible task to compel him to join us on our trip, not without using some type of brute force.

Mace gave me an almighty nudge. 'Stop dreaming Effie, we have work to do. Now's not the time to go drifting off into some fantasy world full of dancing fairies, or freakish dummies.'

I let out a strained laugh.

After Mace, Lucinda and I had finalised our plan, they left in readiness for our departure, the time of which was fast approaching. I made sure that everything was packed in my rucksack, including my notebook and Septimius's knife. I retrieved the pendant from the side pocket and placed it around my neck, so I could call for Croft when we were away from here, and he would carry us all home. Perhaps I was fooling myself that this would actually occur, but I had to believe that it would, for we must all cling to hope in desperate situations, without it we might as well give up.

Shakily, I glanced at my watch and my heart skipped a beat. It was time to leave. With a deep sigh I rose and took one more look at my dreary room. Bizarrely, I suddenly felt almost reluctant to leave, sad almost: this little room of mine, as grim as it was, had become my home, and I was safe, tucked away in the darkness. I suspect it was last minute nerves, as the course of action I was about to embark on was undoubtedly fraught with danger, and there was a high possibility we wouldn't make it out alive.

'Be strong Effie. The brave shall conquer the world.' I whispered to myself, vaguely recalling the quote from somewhere or other.

Picking up my rucksack I strode determinedly towards the door and headed out into the shadowy passageway. I assumed everyone, including Proctor, Abel and Mundy, would be fast asleep by now, in their uncomfortable beds; how anyone had a good night's sleep in this place was beyond me.

I gently tapped four times on Mace's door and it was immediately swung open.

'Full marks for punctuality E.' he whispered, pulling me inside.

Lucinda was crouching down on the floor, looking rather apprehensive; she smiled as I came in and I went over and gave her a reassuring hug.

I glanced around the room, and then threw Mace a quizzical look. 'Where's Clarice?' I asked in a worried voice. 'You were supposed to go and fetch her from her room.'

Mace scratched his forehead and laughed nervously. 'E, I know you want to save Clarice but sometimes it's best to leave well alone.' He looked plaintive. 'The Clarice we know and love has gone.' He looked glumly down at the ground and shook his head. 'And she's not coming back.'

My eyes became filled with anguish. 'How can you say that Mace, how can you just give up so easily.' I gave him a fixed stare, laying emphasis on my words. 'Clarice is our friend, and she is coming with us.'

'No Effie, she isn't.' He retorted bluntly.

A look of frustration caused my face to colour. 'But, but Mace, she has to, we can't leave her in this place.' I began pacing around the room. 'We shall have to go back to her room and drag her out forcibly.' I mumbled, deep in concentration. 'Or better still we shall coax her out with a little fib.'

'Effie.' Mace muttered.

'Come on Mace, we need to be quick.'

'Look Effie.' Mace uttered, raising his voice. 'Clarice isn't in her room.' He laughed, shaking his head. 'I've already checked, twice.'

I suddenly became flustered. 'But... but then where is she?'

Mace shrugged his shoulders. 'I don't know.'

I gaped at him in bewilderment. 'What? That doesn't make any sense, Clarice is always in her room in the evenings; everyone has to keep to their room.'

He began to fidget and avoid my eye.

A feeling of uneasiness swept over me.

'Mace, you didn't by any chance inform Clarice of our little plan, did you?'

There was silence.

'Mace?' I went over to him. 'Please look at me.' In frustration I grabbed his chin and pulled his face round to mine. 'Tell me the truth.'

He raised his eyes and looked me straight in the face. 'Clarice may have been brainwashed but she's not a traitor.' Abruptly, he moved away from me. 'I thought it would be safe to mention our plan.' Gulping, he slunk down onto the bed. 'Besides, it would give her time to pack up her belongings.'

Anger began to boil up inside of me. 'Then, where is she?' I shrieked at him. Did it not occur to you that she may go straight to Septimius, and inform him?'

310

He gawped at me.

A little voice piped up behind us. 'Perhaps she was in the bathroom.'

I swung round and gaped at Lucinda. 'The bathroom?'

'Thank you.' Exclaimed Mace jubilantly, raising his hands up in the air.' At least you're finally using your common sense.' He smiled smugly at me. 'You know what some women are like; they spend an eternity in the bathroom, doing their hair and stuff. That lovely, long flaxen hair of Clarice's must take some maintaining.' A faraway look appeared across his face. 'It frames her beautiful face so perfectly.'

I smiled poignantly at him. 'Yes, the old Clarice perhaps.' I stepped forward and took his arm. 'I don't think she's very much into pampering herself these days.'

With a look of dismay, he mumbled something under his breath, before stomping across the room and banging his fist on the door in frustration.

Lucinda and I both jumped.

'Calm down Mace.' I uttered in a steady voice.

He turned and scowled at me. 'I'm sorry, all right, what's done is done.' For a minute he remained deep in thought, then abruptly strolled towards me. 'I only told Clarice we were leaving, not how. Maybe they'll be stupid enough to think we're going out the front entrance, over the gate.' He narrowed his eyes. 'Those bunch of lunatics have no idea that we know the other way out through the library.' Reaching out, he grasped my hands in his. 'Perhaps, with luck on our side, we may still get away.'

I raised my eyebrows and frowned. 'Well.' I said, sighing. 'What are we waiting for, let's go before we run out of time.' Frantically, I hauled my rucksack over my back.

Mace grinned. 'See, your old friend may create a problem occasionally but he'll always discover a solution to it.' He exclaimed excitedly, prancing out the door. 'I'll be waiting just outside.

I shook my head.

Looking back into the room I smiled at Lucinda, who seemed reluctant to leave.

'Come on Lucinda, let's get you away from here.'

She smiled timidly and headed towards me. 'I'm scared.'

I cupped her cheek with the palm of my hand.

'I know, me too.' I uttered, my voice unsteady with emotion. 'But that's all right, it's normal to be frightened, it shows that we're still human, and it will keep us alert, and strong. Mace will take good care of you, and I'll be seeing you very soon.'

We went and joined Mace, who was crouching down on the floor, against the damp wall of the passageway.

'You should hurry to the library and go down the steps.' I murmured. 'Gideon and I will meet you at the entrance to the tunnels.' I whispered urgently. 'Oh, and Mace, why don't you check Clarice's room on the way, just in case she really was in the bathroom.' I smiled tenderly at him.

He grinned at me. 'You read my thoughts E.' Scratching his head he appeared perplexed. 'Hang on a minute, do you even know how to activate the door in the library?

'Yes, yes. Lucinda has shown me.'

'Oh.' Without another word he turned and wandered up the passageway.

'Mace, I whispered. 'Wait for Lucinda.' But it seemed he hadn't heard me. 'Quickly Lucinda, you need to keep up with him.'

She smiled warmly at me then ran to join Mace.

As I watched them disappear up the passageway a nauseous feeling began to materialise in the pit of my stomach. And, as I crept along towards the study, I became mindful of the many things that could go wrong with our last-minute plan: it wasn't just fear of the guards capturing us, after being informed by Clarice of what we were up to, no, I also found myself conjuring up the most obscure scenarios that my befuddled mind could invent.

With bated breath, I anxiously knocked on Gideon's door, and waited. It seemed to take a lifetime before the handle turned and he stood there, unperturbed by his late-night visitor.

My heart was beating rapidly as I opened my mouth to speak. 'Quickly Gideon, it's your grandfather, he's had an accident in the tunnels.'

Still his expression was unruffled.

He nodded at me and calmly shut the door behind him. 'Very well, take me to him.'

I stared into his eyes, trying not to become distracted by his steady gaze.

'Effie?'

'Mm, yes, yes of course.' I blurted out, not sure of what to make of his behaviour.

It's not that I expected him to gasp with shock, as any emotion he'd once possessed had been suppressed by the tonic, but it all seemed too easy, worryingly easy.

'Follow me.' I mumbled, as if he didn't know the way.

# Chapter 21

Venturing underneath the monastery is decidedly creepier than above it. The steep flight of stone steps leads you down into the pitch black of a sinister underworld; even with a lantern to bring you light you could see how easy it would be to trip and fall to the bottom and break your neck. There was a dank, musty odour lingering in the air, an ancient smell of long ago, where prisoners were left to rot in their cells and then taken to the dark, burial chambers, to lay in rest. Only they were not at peace: I could almost feel the presence of their spirits as they flitted about malevolently, waiting to ward off unwelcome visitors. This was the home of the dead, and the living weren't welcome.

Unbeknown to Gideon, I hadn't a clue what direction to head. Having never been under the monastery before I would have to make him show me the way, so very discreetly I lessened my pace, allowing him to go ahead. We arrived in a central passage, and I followed closely behind him as he strolled confidently eastwards, until we arrived at, what appeared to be a labyrinth of tunnels.

Gideon came to an unexpected halt. 'So, where is my grandfather?'

I froze.

'Ah.' Chuckling nervously, I began to swing my lantern from side to side in an idiotic moment of madness. It didn't make any sense to do such a thing, but it was the only thing I could think of to distract him; to bide time until Mace and Lucinda appeared. I'd told Mace to meet me at the entranceway to the tunnels, but there was no sign of him or Lucinda.

I felt a strong grip around my wrist, steadying my lantern. 'Don't do that Effie, you're asking for trouble.'

'Sorry, I uttered in a feeble voice.

He released his hold and stepped nearer to one of the tunnels. 'I see a light ahead.

This must be the tunnel we need to go down.'

Without saying another word, he went forward into the tunnel.

As I followed on behind him my head began to throb with tension. The ground was strangely uneven in the tunnels and I felt myself constantly tripping. It was only when I shone my lantern down by my boots that I realised why: the path was knotted together into a conglomeration of roots.

'My grandfather never ventures down to the tunnels.' He said in a low voice. 'How odd that he would do such a thing.'

I shrugged my shoulders. 'Perhaps he wanted a change of scenery.'

Gideon turned and gave me one of his penetrating stares. 'What a peculiar thing to say.'

'Well, I do have a tendency to speak drivel when I'm nervous, it's a characteristic I've perfected over the years.'

He looked at me as if I was deranged. 'What a strange woman you are.'

A short burst of laughter escaped from my mouth. 'But surely in a good way?' I replied, trying to make light of the situation and failing miserably.

Out of the blue a noise came from within the heart of the tunnel. It was the faint voice of Mace. 'Effie, down here.'

Coming to my senses I gestured for Gideon to come forward. 'Just a little further and you'll see your grandfather' I said, trembling with nerves. 'He's towards the end of the tunnel.'

I could see Mace now; his lanky frame was unmistakeable.

I found myself squinting as he shone his torch directly in my eyes, the torch he'd stolen from my rucksack during our journey to Hartland. 'Look, they're straight up ahead.' With renewed energy I bounded forward towards Mace. It was only then I realised I was running alone. 'Gideon?' I said in a panic, looking at him dragging behind. 'Please, we must hurry.'

'I think the time has come to stop this foolishness.'

Mace and Lucinda had joined us now and were standing either side of me.

'What?' I replied perplexed by what he meant. 'But your grandfather.'

'It seems deceitfulness is another quality you've mastered?'

'I don't know what you mean.' I stammered.

'I know perfectly well my grandfather is fast asleep in his bed. I didn't feel it necessary to disturb him after your friend Clarice alerted me to your intentions.'

Mace stumbled forward. 'Then why are you here now, why haven't you alerted the guards?

'I thought it would be amusing to go along with your little escapade.' Gideon said in a rather gruff voice. 'Just for a while.' He reached out and got hold of my arm. 'And I have alerted the guards.'

'No Gideon, no.' I cried out in desperation. 'You shouldn't have done that.'

'What did you expect Effie.' Mace uttered. 'Hartland has poisoned his mind, just like his sanctimonious grandfather.'

Gideon glared at him but didn't respond.

Still holding my arm in a vice like grip, Gideon turned away, pulling me along. 'You are to return with me Effie.'

'Oh, I don't think so.' I said, frantically trying to yank my arm away. 'Just come with us to the end of the tunnel, you may find your memory returning when you leave the confines of the monastery. Please Gideon, I can't....' There was a dull thud and my arm was released as Gideon plunged to the ground. 'Gideon,' I bent forward. 'Gideon what is it?' He was lying face down, and wasn't moving. Apprehensively, I touched the back of his head and found it to be bleeding. It was only then I realised what had happened.

Slowly, I looked up at Mace.

'Sorry E, knocking him out seemed the logical course of action.' He uttered, still clenching the torch in his hand like a weapon. 'I could have overpowered him but that might have taken longer.'

'But Mace you could have killed him, what were you thinking.' I shrieked at him. 'Don't you care that you might have murdered your own brother?'

'Oh, E don't be so melodramatic, he'll be fine. I had to do something; the man was going to drag you back to that hellhole.'

I gaped at him for a second before turning my attentions back to Gideon, who was still comatose. 'Give me a hand Mace.' I whimpered. 'I need to get Gideon into a more comfortable position.'

Sighing, Mace reluctantly helped me hoist Gideon up by his arms and haul him against the wall. I watched as his head lulled forward over his chest.

'Leave him Effie, you tried your best.' Mace reached out his hand, beckoning me forward. 'Come on, let's get out of here.'

'No, not without Gideon.' I said quietly, glancing forlornly at the still figure of the man I loved. 'I just need a few moments alone with him, one last attempt to make him leave.' I gave Mace and agonised look. 'You understand, don't you Mace?'

Mace scoffed and shook his head. 'No.'

We heard the sound of approaching footsteps.

'Quickly.' I uttered desperately. 'You have to leave now.'

He hesitated. 'I'm not going anywhere without my best friend.'

I gazed warmly at him. 'Please Mace. I need you to go on ahead' I reached for my pendant and placed it around his neck. Once you are free of the monastery grounds, you can call for Croft.' I held the wooden bird charm up to him. 'This part is a whistle, blow on it and Croft should hopefully come for you and take you back to Briarwood.'

'And what about you?' He asked in a faint voice. 'Are you going to walk all the way back?'

I wasn't very good at telling lies, Mace knew it and so did I, but there are occasions in one's life when it is the only choice; telling someone what they want or need to hear is much kinder than the alternative, and much easier.

'Why yes, I came by foot on the journey here, I can easily make my way back.' I bit hard on my lip. 'Besides, I shall be with Gideon.'

Mace gave me a knowing, sad smile, but said nothing.

Lucinda tugged on my robes. 'Effie, I'm scared.

I glanced over at Mace, who was bending down doing up the laces on his boots.

I crouched down and cupped her face. 'Everything is going to be fine Lucinda; Mace is going to take you to safety.'

'You need to leave too Effie.' She said in a low voice. 'No good will come of you remaining here.'

I did my best to smile reassuringly at her. 'I shall be along before you know it. Just you wait and see.'

Mace came bounding over and put his arms around me. 'See you soon E.' He whispered softly in my ear.'

The footsteps were becoming clearer.

'Bye for now, Mace.' I uttered shakily.

We both took one last look at one another before he turned away, and with Lucinda right behind him, they both charged up the shadowy tunnel. I watched as they ran along, Mace tripping as he went.

'If you don't show up, they'll be trouble E.' He yelled back at me. 'I'll have to come and rescue you, and that's a promise.' His voice was barely audible. 'And a promise is a promise.'

'Then I shall hold you to that promise Mace.'

I carried on watching until they were gone, disappearing into the blackness of the tunnel.

A bellowing voice came echoing down the tunnel. 'Halt, in the name of Hartland.'

I slowly turned round and came face to face with Abel and Mundy.

Mundy sneered. 'Let's get her.'

A thunderous roar reverberated along the tunnel.

How I wanted to flee, to get away, but suddenly I felt unsteady on my feet, and that's when I realised the ground was starting to move.

A soft voice called out to me and I realised it was Gideon. 'Keep still Effie, the trees have awoken.'

For a brief moment my spirits lifted – Gideon was all right; in spite of the surroundings, I found myself momentarily lost at the hint of tenderness showing within his eyes.

'Gideon? Are you alright?'

'Yes.' He exclaimed bluntly. 'Now try not to move.'

Nodding at him, I found myself lost for words. Beyond all expectations, it appeared he cared about my safety; which means he cared about me.

'Don't just stand there Abel, go and grab her.' Yelled Mundy.

Abel seemed apprehensive. 'Why don't we just leave her here, she'll not get away.'

'Proctor gave strict instructions to bring Miss Farraday back alive. Now walk forward slowly and you'll be safe.' Mundy uttered in a sly voice.

Abel started to sob, burying his face in his hands. 'I can't be doing it Mundy. Me legs have turned to jelly.'

'Mundy let out an exasperated groan. 'You're a coward Abel. You wait here, I'll get Miss Farraday.'

Mundy blundered gradually forward, every so often glaring down at his feet in alarm. A mad panic suddenly gripped him and he began charging towards me at a tremendous pace.

'No Mundy, stop running.' Demanded Gideon.

But Mundy didn't seem to hear as he trampled noisily across the ground. I was petrified, knowing all too well that he was going to put us both into the destructive clutches of the trees. In a daze, I stood there like a frozen statue, not even moving when his hot, clammy hands gripped my wrists.

'Got you.' Exclaimed Mundy, panting from the exertion. 'Those trees aren't as bad as what folk make out.' He uttered, sounding blasé, but his eyes widened in fright as a strange, deep groan echoed along the tunnel. We both remained still until the noise had ceased. 'There, they've gone back to sleep.' He chuckled. 'Best be making our way...' He stopped in mid-sentence and slowly looked down at the huge talon, wrapping itself, so skilfully around his waist. A desperate cry erupted from his throat, as it tightened its grip, continuing to make its way to Mundy's neck. 'Help me, help me Miss.' as the root towed him back, into the darkness of the tunnel, Mundy continued to hold my wrists, unwilling to let go. 'Don't let them take me.'

'Let go Mundy, I can't help you if you do not release me.' I cried, twisting my hands in every direction. 'I have a knife, if you'll just let me get it.' I said, as I felt myself being dragged along with him. 'Mundy, please.' I shouted in a grave voice.

'Somebody save me.' he shrieked.

With all my strength I yanked myself away from him, and stumbled back onto the ground. Frantically, I pulled my rucksack from my shoulders and with shaky hands, retrieved the stolen knife. Briskly standing up I looked down the tunnel, ready to run after Mundy, who was screaming desperately for me to help him. Suddenly it went silent and I realised a length of branch had wrapped itself across his mouth, slowly moving, in snake like precision. I saw how he clawed at the branch with his hands, in a last desperate attempt to break free. I knew then that all I could do was stand there and watch. The branches had captured their prey and were dragging it off to devour it.

Even though, according to Lucinda, Mundy wasn't very nice, I still felt a tinge of remorse for not being able to help him. No one deserved such a horrific end; it was something nightmares were made of. The brevity of it all scared me, and as I stood there, I wondered if they'd soon return to collect me too.

A voice in the darkness seemed to appear out of nowhere. 'Gradually move towards me Effie.'

Looking behind, I peered into the eyes of Gideon, who stood rigidly up against the wall with a terrified looking Abel, practically clinging to him. How cautious they'd both been, standing there the entire time that Mundy and I had needed their aid, how inconsequential our lives must be. I just didn't understand Gideon anymore; he didn't care about me, how could he, when it was evident my life was just as worthless as Mundy's.

I stared solemnly into Gideon's face. 'I think it's best I leave this place.'

'If you head further down the tunnel you will surely meet your peril.'

'I'll take my chances.' I replied sternly.

'Please Effie. Your home is at the monastery, everything can be as it was, and we can start all over again with my portrait.

Looking into his eyes I noticed the faint warmth within them, just like earlier when he had warned me not to move.

Although his irregular behaviour was rather confusing, I came to the conclusion that his compassion was just a façade. Septimus had achieved what he set out to do, he had moulded his grandson into a hard-hearted, monster.

'I do believe you are lying Gideon.'

An unexpected movement underneath my feet caused me to sway slightly, almost making me topple over; I put my arms out to steady myself. Looking down I could see the roots clawing their way around my ankles, and then I heard the familiar groan, creaking its way back up the tunnel. They had finished with Mundy and were coming back for me.

I gulped.

'Come back to safety and we can discuss your concerns in a relaxed atmosphere.'

Pondering for a moment I lowered my eyes. My stubborn pride was urging me to walk away, up the tunnel, even if it meant my demise, but as common sense took over, I realised my only choice was to return to the place I had been desperately trying to escape.

Effie?'

As the noise became more distinct, I started to panic. Shakily, I reached down and began cutting away at the roots with the knife, trying to free my ankles.

'Here, let me help you.'

To my shock, I realised Gideon was crouched down beside me.

'I can't get them off, what shall I do?' I cried.

Without speaking, Gideon got hold of my waist and began dragging me backwards, towards Abel. I felt the roots loosen their hold as he continued to haul me away from them, until finally I was free. Almost immediately he removed his arms from my waist.

'Quickly now, we need to be swift.' Exclaimed Gideon, taking my arm.

The ground began to shake.

'Run.' Yelled Gideon, no longer worried about being quiet.

Never before had I ran so fast, never before had I been so eager to return to the monastery. As Gideon and I ascended the steps, poor Abel was so out of breath he was trailing dangerously behind. I envisaged him suddenly crying out in utter fright as he was seized and hauled back down to the tunnels, never to be seen or heard of ever again.

Approaching the library, we lessened our pace; several books had been wedged up against the concealed door, to allow us back in. I remembered how Lucinda had said about it slamming shut behind you. I shuddered at the mere thought of being stuck behind the library bookcase, at the mercy of all the nastiness down below.

As soon as we were safely in the library, Abel collapsed onto the stone floor, accidentally kicking over a stack of nearby books.

How I wanted to laugh, but for the time being it just wasn't in me. Instead, I just felt empty and sad, sad that I was back in the precise place I had hoped to escape, and sad that Gideon continued to be in the very place he thought of as home. It had all gone so wrong, so very wrong.

'Give me the knife Effie.' Demanded Gideon, hardly out of breath.

'What?'

'The knife in your hand, the one you stole from my grandfather's study.'

Feeling numb, I glanced down and noticed the knife, held out rather threateningly in my left hand. 'Oh, I'd forgotten all about that.' Reaching out I passed him the weapon. 'I wasn't going to stab you if that's what you were afraid of.'

He looked coldly at me, but said nothing.

'I suppose I should say thank you, for helping me to become untangled from the roots. 'I sighed. 'But I don't suppose you did it because you care.'

'Grandfather will wish to talk to you. That is why I couldn't allow you to be taken away.'

'No. You wouldn't wish to displease your dear grandfather.' I reached down and pulled off a small root that had become entwined around my boot. 'So, what happens now? Shall we go to the study and re-start the portrait? I said, in a rather mocking tone.

Gideon looked morose. 'Do not taunt me Effie, I certainly do not find it amusing.'

'You weren't telling me the truth in the tunnel, were you Gideon. You have no intention of re-sitting for a portrait.' I stepped nearer to him. 'It was all a ruse to lure me back here.'

Avoiding my eye, he shuffled passed me.

'What a coward you've become.' I cried at him. 'The Gideon I knew would never be so weak and insincere.'

'If you expect me to retaliate with anger and frustration then you are sadly mistaken.' He came close and held my gaze. 'Whatever you believed about me before has indeed gone, it is in the past. Hartland has shown me the true meaning of life, to overcome unnecessary emotions, and to strengthen my beliefs in the power that this monastery possesses.'

'If your emotions are so controlled then why did you destroy my work and pin me up against the wall yesterday.' I searched his face, waiting for an answer.

For a while we both remained glaring at one another.

Abel cleared his throat. 'Do you want me to take Miss Farraday to your grandfather?'

Gideon looked away and sighed. 'No Abel, it can wait until morning.' He briefly glanced at me then lowered his eyes. 'Take Effie to her room.'

'Yes sir.'

'Oh, and Abel, make sure Effie is locked in, she cannot be allowed to wander off again.' He strolled out of the library, without another word.


Waking up, my whole body ached from the exertion from last night, and I had a slight cut on my ankle from the knife I'd used to cut away the roots, the evil roots that had been so eager to take hold of me. As I dressed, I thought of Mundy, and the look of terror on his face as he was dragged off; my only hope was that Mace and Lucinda didn't meet the same fate: for my own sanity I had to believe they escaped, as at least this would mean someone had a happy ending, unlike myself whose future had been sealed the moment I'd made the decision to lag behind, on the assumption that I could persuade Gideon to leave with me. How tormented I felt, and how I wanted to scold myself for foolishly thinking I possessed the power to lure him from the monastery.

And so, it came to pass that I finally resigned myself to the cold hard facts: I had loved Gideon and he had loved me, but it was over now, our love was lost and could never be found. His future was at Hartland, and mine...well, I decided not to dwell on where I'd end up. As strange as it might seem, accepting this reality, eased my mind, and I felt at peace......

I kept absolutely still when I heard the dull sound of the bell, sitting on the bed with my hands in my lap, feeling perfectly serene. I was already to go, with my rucksack beside me, all packed. For some peculiar reason I'd taken it upon myself to make my bed and tidy the room, perhaps I didn't want Proctor coming along and seeing how messy I was when she prepared the room for the next occupant. For I knew I wouldn't be returning.

There was a sudden loud thud on the door, followed by a continual knocking. 'Open the door Miss.'

I heard a raised voice, which I recognised as Proctor's. She was scolding Abel, calling him dopey.

'However, you came to be a guard of the monastery is beyond belief.' She uttered curtly, turning the key in the lock. 'Forgetting that you locked the door doesn't exactly feel me with confidence Abel.'

'Least I did lock it.'

'Yes, I suppose we should be thankful for small mercies.' The door swung open and Proctor strode in the room, her countenance as formidable as ever. 'Have you gathered together all your belongings?' she asked with a grim face.

Completely composed I slid off the bed and lifted my rucksack onto my shoulders.

'Yes, I'm all ready.'

She threw me a mistrustful look. 'What are you up to?'

'Nothing.' I answered, raising my eyebrows.

Her small eyes bore into me with pure loathing. 'Turn round.' She barked at me. Grabbing my shoulders, she twisted my body so it was facing away from her, then roughly taking my arms, she pulled them behind my back. 'After the commotion you caused last night it's no surprise poor Septimus is suffering.'

'What are you doing?'

'I'm binding your hands together, just in case you try any funny business.' She tugged tightly, as she tied the rope around my wrists. 'We lost a perfectly good guard last night because of your fatuous actions.' Throwing a sideways glance at Abel, she shook her head. 'Why couldn't it have been this big lump who was taken, he would have been no sad loss.' She huffed, pushing me towards the door.

I glanced at Abel, who was cowering in the entranceway. 'Why are you so awful to him, he doesn't deserve to be spoken to in such a harsh manner.'

'I speak and act as I please.'

'Yes, I have noticed.' I uttered drolly as we headed down the passageway.

'You have the delightful gift of being rude and obnoxious to everyone.' I smiled. 'Apart from the almighty Septimius, you seem to worship the ground he walks on.' I threw a look at Abel, who was plodding along beside us. 'Do you agree with me Abel?'

He glimpsed at me, looking startled then lowered his eyes to the ground.

'Do not engage in conversation with the big oaf, he can barely string two words together.' Proctor glanced at me. 'And I shall ask that you keep your ridiculous opinions to yourself, as no one is listening.' She uttered in a harsh voice. 'So, I suggest you refrain from opening your mouth.'

'Well, since you put it so politely, perhaps I shall.' I said, smiling. 'I will save my voice for Septimius, he is more important that you.'

She glimpsed at me with a cold look of disdain.

My impromptu outbursts of sarcasm suddenly reminded me of Mace, it was as though a part of him had latched itself onto me, and was egging me on, making me speak for him in his absence. However, as we arrived ever near to the study, I came to realise the real reason for my uncharacteristic behaviour, it was clear as day. There wasn't any need to pretend anymore, or to care what I said or did; I had come to the end of my journey, I had arrived at a dead end.

# Chapter 22

The study was as dark and gloomy as ever when I entered, with only the artificial light from the lanterns. Proctor gave me a push into the room and told me to behave myself, as both her and Abel would be outside, guarding the door. They made me sound like a dangerous convict, or a raving lunatic, whose violent nature would make me lash out at Septimius. I can't imagine what harm I could do to their glorious leader with my hands bound; he was after all a weak, defenceless man on the brink of death.

Stumbling under the archway I made my way over to the spot where Gideon had been posing for me. My heart lurched as I thought how painstakingly I'd tried to reclaim the man I had lost, to try and rekindle the flame, but it had all been in vain; ultimately, I had failed, Gideon was as remote and aloof as the first day I had set foot in the monastery.

Bowing my head, I closed my eyes and let out a deep, drawn out sigh.

'Hello Miss Farraday.'

I gasped as a figure emerged from the shadows, and for one surreal moment I imagined it to be Gideon, but my heart sank as my eyes rested on his grandfather. His face seemed pale and gaunt; his eyes sunken.

Unsteady on his feet, he stepped towards me. 'Here, allow me to untie you.' He came up behind me and shakily began to loosen the rope from my wrists. 'I apologise for you being bound. Although Proctor is an attentive and capable woman, she is strangely lacking in common sense. However, she means well and is only trying to protect me.' He shrugged his shoulders and laughed. 'I know you wouldn't attack me, Miss Farraday, or make a run for it. It's too late for that, isn't it?' The rope dropped to the floor. 'There, you are free.'

'Thank you.' I said in a quiet voice, rubbing my wrists.

With great difficulty he made his way to the desk and sat down. 'Do take a seat.' He mumbled in a weak voice. 'Let us get this over and done with as painlessly as possible. I need to rest.' He glanced at my heavy rucksack. 'Please, put your bag down.'

Without a word, I placed it down on the floor, and took a seat opposite him.

He winced as if in pain and rubbed his shoulder. 'Let us begin.' He gazed at me stoically. 'Miss Farraday, your chance of departing this morning has obviously been forfeited due to your actions of last night. I therefore have no choice but to detain you here at Hartland for the remainder of your life.'

A sudden surge of dread came over me.

'Have you anything to say in your defence?'

'No, not really.' I mumbled; my voice barely audible.

'Pardon? I didn't catch what you said.'

'I said, no.' I answered, raising my tone. 'You were never going to let me go. I know what happens to anyone trying to leave by the front gates, the trees snatch them. That was going to be my fate, wasn't it Septimius?'

'Oh, come Miss Farraday, whoever told you such a thing. Your gullible nature will surely be your downfall.' He smirked at me. 'Yes, there have been unfortunate incidences at the front gate, but if you're lucky you may pass through unscathed.'

'It's strange you never mentioned that Septimius, isn't it? You knew I wouldn't make it; you didn't want me to.'

He convulsed into laughter. 'I cannot predict who the trees wish to take, it is their choice to make, and obviously if they are hungry then they will feed.'

Bending forward he began to cough, violently.

I frowned. 'You haven't just got a bad cough, have you Septimius? You're dying. That's why you were in a rush for me to complete the portrait, so you could see the finished product before you went.' I cried. 'How apt that the subject of the painting should ultimately rip it to shreds.' I eyed him intently. 'Doesn't that tell you how confused Gideon has become?'

'Gideon was merely reacting as he saw fit, that does not make him confused. I have confidence in my grandson, he will maintain the monastery as it should be.'

'But why?' I said feeling exasperated. 'It's all so meaningless.' I got up and went over to where he was huddled in his chair, and stared him straight in the eye. 'In your heart you must know that you have forced Gideon to be away from his true home. You've poisoned his mind against anyone he's ever loved. He will never be truly happy; he will never have a family and he will no longer have a life worth living. Is that really what a grandfather would wish for their grandson?'

'You talking utter nonsense Miss Farraday.'

I scoffed. 'Am I? That precious tonic of yours has ruined your faith in mankind, and made you blind to anything good and decent in this world.' In a sudden rage I spontaneously stormed over to the windows and dragged back the gigantic shutters on the windows, allowing the soft light to flood the room. 'This once beautiful monastery has been taken over by those monstrous trees out there.' I yelled, pointing out the window. 'They are responsible for the evil way of life here at Hartland.' I turned back to Septimius. 'Can you not see what the monastery has become? It's a prison. I closed my eyes for a second and sighed. 'The destruction of the trees is the only solution to this mess. Once they have gone it will set everyone free, and allow them to live their lives away from this place of death.'

Septimus shook his head violently 'No, no. That will never happen. Those trees are the life force of these lands, if they were taken away then...' He gulped. 'I cannot imagine the mayhem that would occur.' Unexpectedly he convulsed into a fit of laughter. 'And how do you intend to demolish them, with an axe.' He sniggered. 'They are no ordinary trees Miss Farraday, you cannot simply chop them down.'

I glared blankly at him. 'We would find a way.' I said, in an uncertain voice. 'There is an answer to everything.'

He screwed up his face. 'How is it a solution when the outcome will deprive the good people of Hartland of our beneficial tonic, without it they would fall by the wayside.'

I went over to him and slammed my hands on the desk. 'It is clearly evident that your selfishness is at the root of all this.' My voice was strangely controlled. 'The trees provide the berries that make up the tonic, the medicine that is prolonging your life.' I sighed. 'Has it ever occurred to you that your cherished tonic could be why your health is failing?' My face softened. 'Perhaps you've simply been greedy and taken too much.'

He rose shakily from his desk. 'I've heard enough of your drivel, and I will listen to you no more.' His eyes drifted passed me, in the direction of the entranceway. 'Abel, Abel, come here this instance.'

The door swung open and Abel came striding in.

'Take Miss Farraday away.'

'Yes Sir.' Abel gave me a brief glimpse before grabbing my arm. 'Where should I take her sir?'

'Miss Farraday is to join her father in the cells.'

I wrenched my arm free. 'Is that what happens to anyone who defies you Septimius, you lock them away so you don't have to hear the truth.'

'Oh, do be silent, Miss Farraday. You should have left when you had the chance. If you'd not been so persistent in dragging my poor grandson along with you, there would have been a remote possibility you'd be on your way home by now.' He sniggered. 'However, by the amount of commotion your rowdy friend Mace must have made, I'd be surprised if he managed to make it to the end of the tunnel without...well without rousing The Elders.' He shook his head in despair. 'I cannot see it being a happy ending for your poor, blundering friend.'

Abel grasped me once more, his large hands firmly holding my arms.

I pondered for a moment if he knew Mace hadn't fled alone: had Lucinda's departure, so far, gone unnoticed; had her presence at the monastery been so insignificant that no one was aware of her disappearance? Maybe I should have become invisible and faded effortlessly into the background, it was something that should have come so easily to me, being so quiet. When I had made the decision to save Gideon that was the moment I had ultimately ruined any chances of slipping away without a sound. He had been my downfall.

Septimus began to cough, violently.

'Perhaps you underestimate the strength of the human spirit, their will to survive. Both my mother, and your daughter Sabina, managed to get away. And you don't know Mace, if anyone can escape, he can.'

'I admire your optimistic outlook Miss Farraday; however, no one has ever left the monastery without my permission.' A look of disdain crossed over his face. 'Allowing your odious father to talk his way out of here with a string of lies was by far my biggest mistake. But as for your mother and Sabina, well.... they never actually left the premises.'

'But that doesn't make any sense.' I cried at him. 'Are you sure that tonic hasn't harmed your brain?' I dragged myself forward, trying to release myself from Abel's grip. 'They must have left the monastery, how else did they arrive at the... at the other world, where I was born?'

Septimus glowered at me. 'Puzzling isn't it? He snapped his fingers at Abel. 'Take Miss Farraday to her new home, where she will have time to think things over before the end.'

'The end?'

He titled his head and raised his eyebrows. 'Yes Miss Farraday, the end is now in sight.' With difficulty, he rose from his seat and slowly moved over to where I was standing. 'I have achieved what I set out to do, I have proved that Gideon no longer loves you.'

I threw him a quizzical look. 'Wait a minute, you've known all along haven't you, about Gideon and I?'

Slightly unsteady on his feet, Septimus came closer. 'Oh yes Miss Farraday, I've been on to you since the start. That woman, Verity told me all about you, how you callously deserted my grandson and left him heartbroken. Gideon of course was completely unaware, after the blow to the head. Imagine my dilemma when you turned up here, ready to snatch him away. So, I decided to perform a little test on Gideon, to see if his memories returned when he saw you again, and to see if spending time in your company would make him remember.' He gave a light laugh. 'To my joy he passed with flying colours.'

I nodded at him, acknowledging his confession. 'Yes, I understand now, how silly of me not to have discovered your little game. Anyhow, with the amount of tonic and his amnesia, Gideon didn't really have a fighting chance, did he?' I exclaimed, looking deep into Septimius's bloodshot eyes.

He stood there for a while, deliberating his next words.

'No amount of tonic or loss of memory would be enough to expunge you from his life if he truly loved you. I can only assume you were insignificant, a momentarily distraction that meant nothing to him. You are but a ghost of a thought in the furthest most reaches of his mind.'

My eyes widened in astonishment.

A knowing smile crossed over his face. 'You know I speak the truth.'

Without realising Abel had released me, I turned away from Septimius, and placed my hand across my chest in an attempt to prevent the acute feeling of melancholy and hopelessness from sweeping over my heart. A sensation of light-headedness caused me to sway slightly, and I felt arms steadying me from behind. Turning a little I saw Septimius, his face full of compassion.

He took my hand in his and began to whisper in my ear. 'You are nothing anymore; life has become meaningless. Your love has forsaken you; your friends have all gone and your home is far away out of reach. What's the point of carrying on?' Slowly he guided me over to the large window and nudged me gently forward. 'All you have to do is open the window and climb out, the trees want you; they need you. Isn't that a worthy end to a sad life?' Reaching up he pulled the latch on the window. 'That's it, clamber up, you only need to beckon them and they'll come and take you away to their home, they will become your family.'

Feeling the cool breeze from the open window, I breathed in the welcoming air, and in a dreamy state I put my hand on the sill and moved onto the window ledge. It wouldn't be so horrible, I thought, it would be over swiftly and the pain in my heart would be no more.

With his face close to mine he spoke softly in my ear. 'They are coming for you.'

I'm not sure if it was the chilling words he spoke or the sight of the approaching branches that made me abruptly come to my senses, but with inhuman speed I secured the window, moved off the ledge and heaved the shutters back across.

He burst into a hysterical laughter. 'On Miss Farraday, how very amusing that was.' Pity filled his face. 'Perhaps it would have been wiser to have ended it all, quickly and quietly. Now your suffering will endure, until the time is right.'

I gulped. 'Right for what?'

Without answering, he turned away and shouted over to where Abel was resting up against the table of paints, in a world of his own. 'Come here you confounded boy.'

'Yes sir, sorry sir.' He plodded over, giving me one of his unnerving stares.'

Septimus glared at him. 'For the last time of asking will you please take Miss Farraday away, she is now ready to spend time in the company of her delightful father.' He glanced towards the desk. 'Don't forget her rucksack.'

'Yes sir.' Uttered Abel, grabbing my bag from the floor and slinging it over his shoulder. 'Come now Miss.' He took a firm grip of my arm, and gently led me towards the door. Pausing for a second, he turned and peered at Septimius. 'When shall Miss Farraday be going back to her room sir?'

Septimus voice was clear and calm. 'Miss Farraday will be staying in the cell until the end. Clear her room of any possessions and deliver them to her temporary home.' He casually turned away and began to gather some books from the desk.

Abel nodded silently and guided me out the room.

I didn't struggle; I didn't see the point, after all, where would I go.

Marching through the library, Proctor released the door that led downwards, underneath the building, and gestured for us to enter.

'Be sure to take Miss Farraday directly to the cells. I shall be along shortly to see that everything is in order.'

'Thank you Proctor.' I replied, rather drolly. 'That's awfully decent of you.'

She pursed her lips. 'Enjoy your new accommodation, won't you Miss Farraday. The rats are particularly friendly.' Briskly turning on her heel she disappeared back into the library, and the concealed door creaked shut rather ominously, leaving us stranded on the other side of the bookcase.

I felt Abel tremble and for a moment I thought he was going to take my hand.

'I truly hate coming down here Miss.'

'Me too Abel.' I murmured with a big sigh.

As we began the long descent, down the narrow steps, I found myself wondering if I'd ever return to the building above: would I spend my remaining days held in a grimy cell, with only the rats and Isaiah for company? If this was to be I would certainly, slowly but surely, lose my marbles. A bleak picture came to mind of a deranged woman, smeared in dirt, huddled in a corner, rocking back and forth, and chanting. Is this what I would become, was this my destiny?

'Come on now Miss, don't dawdle.' Exclaimed Abel as he hauled my rucksack further over his shoulder. 'Not much further to go now.'

He reminded me of a tour guide, directing tourists to a historical sight. I visualised them looking around with interest and listening intently to Abel talking, but then it would dawn on them his knowledge was sadly lacking, and their eyes would gradually glaze over.

'I'm sorry Abel, but I'm not exactly in a rush.'

He grunted. 'Hmm, me neither Miss.'

As I followed on behind him, I was almost tempted to give him a small push: I imagined his bulky frame tumbling forward into the darkness. This could be my final opportunity to flee, my last chance to be brave and reckless. All I would have to do is carefully step over the unconscious Abel and sneak into the tunnels. The question of course was did I really want to, did I still have the capability.

'Why have you stopped Miss? He asked, looking suspiciously into my face. 'There be no place to go but the one I'm leading you to.' Grinning, he waved his finger at me. 'You don't want to be going into those scary tunnels again, they'll be the death of you.' His face became pale. 'And those caves aren't a nice place, they be bad.'

I swallowed hard. 'That's where the victims are left isn't it, the ones that have had an adverse reaction to the tonic.'

Abel stood there with his mouth gaping wide. 'That be right Miss.' He glanced around, just to check no one was listening. 'I be the one that helps bring them down, foaming at the mouth and all they are.'

'Poor mites.'

'Nothing poor about them Miss, they deserve all they get.'

I looked perplexed. 'What?'

He looked around again, and then leant in close.

'Septimus told me the truth, confided in me he did. Told me how they all be traitors, bad people who are trying to kill him.' He laughed. 'The tonic don't work on them, you see. It knows.'

I threw him a blank stare. 'So, let me get this right, Septimus has told you the tonic has the ability to work out what people are supposedly plotting to do away with him, and therefore makes them ill.'

He gawped at me and scratched his head. 'Well, yeah. 'Sir would only get rid of bad people, people who deserve to be taken away by them trees.' Bowing his head, he looked glumly towards the ground. 'Mundy was unlucky; he was a good person; he was always looking out for me and Sir.'

My mind drifted back to what Lucinda had said about her friend, how he'd died following orders from Mundy.

'And what about making people climb the front gate, for no reason, knowing full well they'll never reach the other side. That doesn't make Mundy very kind now does it?'

'All of them were planning to scarper, to leave our great home that Septimus has made for them. They show no loyalty to Hartland.' He shook his head violently. 'No loyalty at all.'

We both stared at one another.

I ran my tongue over my lips. 'I see.' My voice was but a murmur. 'Abel, I tried to escape but that doesn't make me an evil person, I just wanted to go home.' My voice began to break up. 'I just wanted to be happy.'

To my astonishment he reached out and patted my shoulder. 'I know Miss, I like you.' He lowered his gaze, looking bashful. ''Tis not right you're being dragged down here, with all the rats and all.'

'I like you too Abel.' It seemed odd to utter such words to such a man.

'I asked Sir I did, begged him not to put you with that father of yours. He's an evil man. I knew it the moment I set eyes on him, remembered I did.'

'Remembered what?'

Abel looked dazed. 'Well, I don't rightly know exactly, it's just that one thing you see.' He appeared deep in concentration. 'There be a time he hurt me, kept pinching me, really hard. Said I deserved a taste of me own medicine. Never forgotten it I haven't.'

I gawped at him in bewilderment.

My mind drifted back to the mean, chubby schoolboy who would cruelly taunt me, pulling my hair and pinching me. It was now evident that the man standing before me was my childhood bully; the one Isaiah had taken from his home as a young boy, throwing him out of his safe world.

Intense pain, shot through my head.

'Oh my god, Abel.'

'Miss?'

Having not written anything in my notebook, I was amazed at how I was suddenly able to recall this particular memory from my childhood, I suppose Abel mentioning being pinched had triggered it. Nevertheless, I still felt inane for not seeing what had been staring me right in the face. It explained the odd stares he would constantly give me, he must half suspect who I was.

'Miss, what's wrong?'

I stared into his red face, unable to say anything. Despite the circumstances, it seemed he had changed; he wasn't that nasty

336

little boy anymore. Hartland had somehow managed to mend his personality.

'Help me Abel, help me get away.' I began stuttering over my words. 'You, you could come... come with me.'

'No Miss, they'll be no leaving my only home.'

'But Abel, you have another home, a home where you have a family who love you.' I gazed pleadingly into his eyes. 'Wouldn't you like to see them again?'

He flickered his eyes and sighed. 'Well I be damned.' His face became animated. 'You bet I would.' He began jumping up and down. 'Would you come with me to meet them?'

I hesitated. 'Yes, yes of course.' Smiling nervously, I averted my eyes from his gaze. 'Come on let's get out of here why we've still got the chance.' Apprehensively, I took his hand and we ran down the remainder of the steps. 'If luck is on our side the tress should be resting.' My voice echoed throughout the long, twisting tunnels before us and I felt a mixture of nerves and excitement wash over me like a cold wave of awareness. 'We must keep our voices down Abel.' I whispered. 'And we must keep to the sides.' I said, as if I'd taken the route many times. It was only when he wrenched his hand from mine that I realised something wasn't right. Turning to face him I could just make out the furious scowl on his face. 'Abel?' My voice was weak and uncertain. 'Abel, what is it?'

'It's you Miss, you be tricking me.' He said in a troubled voice. 'And trying to confuse me.' He reached up and rubbed his hands across his brow. 'Well Abel don't take no nonsense.' With one swift movement he got hold of my arm and yanked me in the other direction. 'My orders are to take you to your father, and that be what I must do.'

'Try to remember Abel, try to remember how you used to pinch me and pull my hair at school.'

Looking dumbfounded, Abel took a few steps backwards.

'You and I come from the same place, from the same town.' I shook my head in frustration. 'I know it's hard but do try and think.'

'You think I'm thick don't you, just like Proctor.'

'No, no Abel, I didn't mean you're not capable of thinking.' I paused, trying to phrase my words carefully, without offending him. 'You see our memories are lost when we leave a particular world, and without a reminder can be gone forever; the only way to totally regain them is to return to our past lives.' I put my hand on his shoulder. 'That makes you and I very much alike Abel.'

His face softened. 'It does Miss?'

'Yes Abel, now let's go home.'

We smiled at one another.

'Right you are Miss.' He reached forward and hugged me.

A screeching sound could suddenly be heard, close to where we were standing, but it wasn't the trees.

'What in the name of Hartland is going on here?' It was the harsh voice of Proctor. 'Release Miss Farraday this instant you imbecile.' She hit out with her hand, striking Abel across the back of the head. 'That tonic is wasted on stupid men like you Abel. We should have put you out in the caves long ago, the trees would have a hearty meal feeding on your bulk.' She pushed him forward then took a firm hold of my arm. 'Come on Miss Farraday, your father is waiting for you.'

'See how cruel she is to you Abel; you don't have to put up with it.' I yelled as she guided me roughly forward. 'We can still leave together.' With a great force I brought my boot down onto Proctor's foot, then dug my fingernails into her hand that was clenching my arm. With a cry she released me. 'Quickly Abel, follow me.' I started to run into one of the tunnels.

'Stop this very second.' Roared Proctor, her voice bellowing up the tunnel after me. 'You take one more step and I shall scream so loud that the entire tunnel will be filled with a mass of roots eager to drag your body back to their hungry masters.' She stood there sternly; her arms folded.'

There was silence, as we all stood there glaring at one another.

Proctor spoke first. 'Go and grab her Abel.'

He remained still, looking troubled. 'Miss Farraday was going to take me home, my proper home, where I belong. She don't deserve to be locked away like a prisoner.'

I watched as Proctor took a deep breath then exhaled, in an apparent attempt to remain calm. 'Oh Abel, this woman doesn't care about you.' With an evil scowl she pointed to where I was standing. 'This woman is the reason you came to Hartland in the first place, this woman asked your father to dispose of you.' She turned to Abel looking sympathetic. 'And all because you were a little mean to her at school.' A light laugh escaped her lips. 'That's all, nothing major. And because of that you were taken from your loving family, your safe, secure home and thrown through a black hole that took you to another world, a new scary world where you knew no one, and where you were all alone. You wouldn't be living anymore if it had not been for the kindness of Septimius.' She faltered for a moment. 'He, he took you in and treated you like a son.' Her eyes narrowed. 'Would you rather run off with the very woman who was responsible for placing your life in peril, or remain loyal to Hartland, and to our great leader Septimius, the man who saved you?'

'Proctor is lying to you Abel, until recently I knew nothing of what my father had done; I totally condone his actions and would have stopped him had I known what he was up to.' My expression was filled with sorrow. 'I'm sorry Abel; sorry my father took you away. You do not deserve to live so dismally, so alone and without love.'

'Huh.' Proctor remarked. 'Well, even if that were true it's still all your fault.'

Seeing it was pointless arguing with her I turned to go. 'I'm going now Abel, with or without you.'

'No miss, there's only death that way.' He leapt forward and took hold of my hands. 'Best we do as Proctor says.' His face came close to mine. 'I don't want you to die.' With a deep sigh he pulled me away from the tunnel. 'Least we be safe now, away from those nasty tree roots.'

'Yes Abel.' I muttered in a sad voice. 'At least we are safe.'

As we moved away from the tunnels a cold sensation of complete dread crept over my body, a feeling that I was being led to my doom. My heart was filled with the deepest of sorrow, a grief I had never known before. Seldom had I felt so despondent and helpless: I likened it to taking the tonic, only I hadn't needed that awful medicine to make me stop feeling anything, other than wretchedness, I had managed that all by myself. The sense of foreboding had been my constant shadow during my time here, but now it had finally possessed me.

# Chapter 23

Proctor rather roughly shoved me into the cell. felt completely numb - nothing could touch me anymore, and I barely noticed as she and Abel left, leaving me in my new home.

As I became aware of my surroundings, I noticed how the cell was dark and foul smelling, with the constant dripping of water. I walked along the straw scattered floor noticing various shackles along the walls -no doubt many a tortured soul had been chained up here, awaiting their fate. The fact that I was free to wander brought me little comfort; I was after all caged up, waiting for the end…

At first, I didn't recognise the poor, pathetic creature huddled in the far corner, but as I crept nearer, I saw that it was indeed my father.

'Isaiah, Isaiah, it's me Effie.' I whispered in monotone voice.

Muttering to himself he glanced up, but barely acknowledged me.

'Isaiah?' I said in a somewhat louder voice.

He jumped at the noise and looked up, directly into my face. 'What?'

I was struck by how awful he looked: His pallid complexion highlighted the dark circles underneath his eyes, and his face was half hidden under a rather unruly beard, with his spectacles nowhere to be seen. His usual immaculate hair was greasy and bedraggled, and his grubby clothes hung from him. I observed he'd not been given robes and guessed it was because of his forthcoming execution.

A look of terror crossed over his face and he began to babble, burying his face in his hands. 'No, no, go away.' He whimpered. 'You're not real.'

I crouched down beside him and took a firm grip of his arms. 'Yes, I am Isaiah, I've come to join you.' I noticed how my voice had a hint of hysteria, a madness of some sorts. 'I too am a prisoner now.' An ironic laugh escaped my lips.

I was surprised to feel a single tear rolling down my cheek. Wiping it swiftly away I rose and stumbled away from him.

'Effelia? Is it really you?' He croaked. 'Or is my mind playing tricks on me.'

I swung round to face him. 'No Isaiah, it's the real me.'

He got up and staggered towards me. 'But why, why are you here in this hovel?'

'My plan didn't exactly work out as expected.' I mumbled, not caring about sounding foolish. 'Basically, I've ruined any hope I had of getting away from the monastery.' Sullenly, I stared deep into his eyes. 'I'm just like you now Isaiah, a traitor of Hartland.'

For a while his countenance was reticent, but very gradually a look of empathy crept over his face.

'I'm sure your intentions were honourable my daughter, however Hartland does not take kindly to those who neglect their hospitality.' He started to pace around the cell. 'Being locked in this prison I hear nothing of what's going on; however, I imagine you tried to sneak away with your little friends, and it all backfired.' He sniggered. 'The probability of which could have been achievable, had it not been for that chap of yours, the one known as Gideon. Did you really think Septimus would stand by and allow you to steal away his grandson?'

I went over and sat down on my rucksack. 'Please Isaiah, it's too late to dwell on such things, and too painful.' My eyes glazed over. 'None of it matters anymore.

'What about the boy, did he make it out?'

'If you're referring to Mace, then yes I believe he did.' I began to brush the straw off my boots. 'I have to have faith that something good has come of all this.'

I shuddered as Isaiah stomped over and yelled in my ear. 'How is it right that the idiotic boy should escape the clutches of the monastery when my beloved daughter has not.' He began to mumble under his breath. 'There is no justice in this world.'

My head began to throb. 'Please Isaiah calm down.

He laughed. 'Do not try and placate me Effelia. As much as I despise that creepy little village of Briarwood, I do wish you'd stayed there and not gone gallivanting off in search of Gideon and that other friend of yours. Your actions have put both of our lives in jeopardy.'

I allowed my thoughts to momentarily linger on Briarwood, the country village that had captivated me in its tight embrace. I recall how my yearning to stay had been overwhelmingly tempting. And then there was the allure of Noble, whose charismatic personality and appealing eyes would be more than enough to prevent me from leaving. But my steely determination and foolhardiness had overridden all of this when I went on my little quest to Hartland, and the end result? I had gained absolutely nothing, and lost everything.

Isaiah cleared his throat. 'I see you still have the ability to drift off into a dream world whenever it suits you.'

With a deep sigh I looked up at him. 'Yes, well sorry about that, dreaming seems the favourable option in our current situation.'

He sat down beside me. 'For once I'm inclined to agree with you.'

We both looked at one another and smiled poignantly.

'It's probably a poor consolation but at least we are together.' He paused. 'At the end.'

All my instincts were telling me no but still I reached out and placed my hand over his, squeezing it softly.

'I would like to make amends with you Effelia. If there are any misdeeds that I have committed in the past, then I am truly sorry.' I heard him take a deep breath. 'Will you forgive me Effelia, will you forgive your father?'

I looked into his woebegone face searching for whether his remorse was genuine. Without grabbing my notebook any knowledge of his misdemeanours back home was somewhat hazy; my instincts told me he had not been a paragon of virtue, but irrespective of that my conscience and my heart told me to let it go, it was too late to hold grudges and I was to weary to argue.

Trying to appear sincere I smiled sweetly. 'Yes Isaiah, I forgive you.'

His face broke into a smile, and his eyes brightened. 'Thank you, dear daughter.' He thought for a second. 'I do hope you can also find it in your heart to address me as father.' A spasm of nervous laughter erupted from his throat. 'It would mean the world to me, to hear you say that precious word before...' He gulped, 'before it's too late.'

I found myself nodding at him blankly.

He stared at me intently. 'In time eh?' Sighing, he gazing ahead. 'And you must know that I forgive you too.'

I automatically withdrew my hand from his. 'Pardon?'

'I forgive you for dragging me across to this contemptible world; I'm willing to overlook it. You did it for Gideon didn't you? Being in love is such an affliction; it has the ability to smother all other emotions so entirely that we become blind to the world around us, and all our common sense goes by the wayside.'

My eyes glazed over. 'It wasn't just for Gideon; I came to this world for Mace and Clarice too.' I faltered for a moment. 'And I wanted to ensure Noble got home safe and sound.'

'Oh yes the audacious Noble who stayed at Briarwood with his father rather than face the perils of Hartland with the woman he loves.'

My cheeks started to burn.

'Tell me Effelia, are these two brothers worthy of your love, would they go to the ends of the earth to find you, would they die for you?' His voice was resolute. 'No, I think not.'

I felt unable to answer.

'Love got you into this mess, but I fear it won't get you out.'

Isaiah's voice faded into the background as he continued to jabber on about how the men in my life were completely inadequate and that I deserved better. But as his tone became louder my head began to pound and a sudden surge of fury took over.

'Shut up Isaiah, just shut up.' I exclaimed loudly. 'Why is it you feel the overwhelming need to punish me so.' As he went to grab my hand I swiftly rose and walked away from him. 'My only crime was falling in love, and as you've said, it's an emotion that can't be controlled.' Looking directly at him my words were clear and precise. 'You must know Isaiah, you loved my mother, didn't you?' I folded my arms. 'Then there was your previous wife, the one who was bludgeoned to death, or was Sabina your one true love?'

He looked dumfounded.

'Now is not the time Isaiah to go over what I should have done or who you really loved. If you wish to mend our fragile relationship, I suggest you decide if you want to be amicable to me, in which case we can at least chat, or if you want to carry on criticising me, and if that is so then I suggest you hold your tongue.'

He looked pensive. 'The latter of the two sounds rather more appealing. I apologise for my rather ambiguous behaviour; my only defence is being trapped in this cell; it has a tendency to give me mood swings.'

'Yes, I can see why that would be so.' I uttered candidly. 'I would envisage even the ghosts are too frightened to venture down here.'

We both laughed.

'Come Effelia do take a seat, I would offer you tea but we've run out. Can I suggest a delicious drink of ice-cold water?' I watched as he went over to a tiny table and began pouring from a jug. 'Sadly, there's no biscuits or cake, but if we're lucky we may be served soup and bread later.' He smiled, rather ingratiatingly as he handed me a goblet. 'Here, I'm afraid we've run out of ice, so the water is a little tepid.'

I strode over and took the goblet from him, then sat down on the straw floor.

Cautiously I took a sip. 'Mm, delicious, I exclaimed, playing along with him. 'Much more preferable than tea.' Narrowing my eyes, I pointed over to the right. 'I think I spy a few slices of lemon cake over there, you must have forgotten about, I would love some of that.'

Isaiah clapped his hands together. 'Certainly, and I do believe I have some freshly bakes scones, we will eat them next, with clotted cream and jam.'

I giggled. 'Sounds scrumptious.'

As he sat down beside me, we pretended to eat our cake; I imagined we were two children at a make-believe tea party, on a bright summer's day, when everything was right with the world and our heads were filled with the carefree thoughts of a child.

The spray from the sea splashed delicately across my face and I closed my eyes, breathing in the fresh, sea air. I could hear the muffled thud of the stones as they moved rhythmically in unison with the flow of the incoming tide; it made an inexplicable soothing sound that was so powerfully evocative that it had the unique gift of transporting one back across the ages, when the sights and sounds of the waves were precisely as they were now.

I suddenly became aware of the dulcet sound of music drifting along on the light sea breeze; feeling curious I wandered up the beach, my bare feet crunching down on the pebbles. I meandered towards the pier, where hordes of people were enjoying their day; children were laughing, holding balloons, as they ran ahead of their parents. The music was louder now and I realised it was coming from the bandstand by the pier where a brass band were playing: a crowd had assembled there, sitting on deckchairs and drinking tea. Joining them I allowed myself to become absorbed in the moment, drifting off on a cloud of melodious abandonment.

My attention was drawn to one particular family who were moving away from the bandstand. The mother, who was dressed in a full ground length skirt with a cape-like garment about her shoulders, was pushing an elegant looking pram, which although I couldn't see, I assumed held a baby. A young girl of about seven was skipping alongside them, her long auburn hair squashed, rather messily under a wide- brimmed bonnet.

I can't really say what possessed me to follow them, but as is often the way in dreams, we have little choice but to see where they may lead. On and on I followed them, passed the little gift shops and down the shady, tree lined avenues filled with rows of imposing looking dwellings with their immaculate lawns and pretty rose-covered borders. We'd passed into countryside now, making our way along a winding pathway with freshly planted trees.

The young girl looked up at the woman. 'Mama, can I play with my new dolls when we arrive home?'

I heard the mother gently murmur something to the girl, who began to giggle with delight.

And that's when I saw it, the house: so grand and impressive in its entirety that it was hard for me to tear my eyes away. My heart skipped a beat as I realised where I was- it was my home, it was Rawlings, and it was all brand new. How strange to see the exposed brickwork, bare from the creeping ivy and wisteria, and the freshly painted porch, so clean and tidy. The wide expanse of the front garden was laid to lawn without any flowers; I thought how stark it all appeared, so empty of life, and of colour. And I realised then, that although I was home, I didn't belong here, it was before my time.

A high-pitched voice made me jolt.

Shivering slightly, I turned to see the auburn-haired girl on a rug. It was a typical scene of a child playing with her dolls and having a tea party.

'Now, now Adriana, play nicely with Anna.' She uttered, talking to the dolls.

Deciding to try and make contact with the girl I moved towards her. However, as I watched her playing with the toys, something struck me rather odd. One particular doll, which I could only see from the back, was dressed rather differently from the rest: instead of a lacy dress it wore a vibrant red jumper and green checked breeches.

'Gilbert, you devil. You've taken your cravat off.' Exclaimed the girl, pretending to scold him.

I watched in fascinated awe as she diligently tied the cravat around his wooden neck.

'Now, all of you behave yourself whilst I fetch some more milk for our tea.' She scrambled up from the grass and raced inside the house, yelling out as she went. 'Your mummy Florentine will be back in a jiffy.'

A tiny spark flared up in my mind. Florentine, the little girl was named Florentine.

I screwed up my face, trying desperately to recall where I'd heard that name before.

Turning my attention back to the tea party I stared in a daze at the dummy.

'Gilbert, my old friend.' I muttered in a rather ironic tone. 'I didn't think it would take you long to rear your ugly head.'

An unexpected cold breeze blew across my face and I heard a sinister whisper.

'Miss Farraday.'

I should have been aghast at hearing the dummy talk; however, Gilbert was no ordinary toy. As his wooden -head began to move round to face me I didn't shudder or gasp, instead I tentatively stepped closer. I was struck how his large bulbous eyes seemed vividly brighter than usual and how his rouge cheeks stood out against the colour of his freshly painted flesh. The mid-afternoon sun glistened down onto his full head of jet-black hair. Yes, Gilbert was all shiny and new.

'What are you doing here Gilbert?'

He smiled at me with his crooked grin. 'Miss Florentine received me as a birthday present this very day.' Jumping up, he nimbly trotted along the lawn to where I was standing. 'I'm part of the family now.' Although his voice was jolly there was a hint of foreboding in his tone. 'Come join me in the attic.'

Before I had a chance to respond he was darting across the garden, towards the house.

'The attic, why did it have to be the attic.' I mumbled to myself.

Following after him, I picked up the pace in an attempt to keep up. The moment I entered Rawlings a potent smell of beeswax filled my senses. Just before ascending the staircase I fleetingly glanced at the elaborate teak dresser in the spacious hallway, displaying two marble busts, and a coat stand with flamboyant looking hats, lavishly decorated with bows and flowers. Reaching the landing I spotted an oak table full of impressive looking vases and potted plants, but Gilbert was nowhere in sight.

I shook my head in disbelief.

This was my home and yet somehow, I'd become muddled as to where the attic room was: perhaps it was the unfamiliar furnishings of the house, or simply that I wasn't supposed to be here, it wasn't my time yet.

Hearing a mischievous giggle over to the right, I followed the direction of the noise. Once I had veered sharply around the corner, I came upon an open door, so tiny that I had to crouch down low to enter, and once inside I made my way to the top of the spiral stairway. And there I was...in the attic. I gasped with surprise at how capacious it seemed, with hardly any items apart from a pile of trunks, hatboxes and vintage type boots, neatly arranged by the far wall. I had never seen it so empty. There was, however, no difference in the atmosphere, it was still as unsettling as ever. And, as I happened to glance over to the shadowy corner of the room, I spotted a tall object, swathed in a dustsheet. Slowly, I shakily stepped towards it and with one hand, pulled away the cloth, half expecting to see Gilbert hiding beneath it, or worse an apparition.

Breathing a sigh of relief, I laughed out loud.

It was a mirror, just a tall, elegant looking mirror. But as I stood there, admiring the flawless, cherub carvings around the frame, I noticed something: becoming visible within the glass was a distant, swirling mist. Frozen, I stood transfixed, barely having time to jump as two spindly wooden arms reached out from within the mirror and dragged me in.

I cried out in terror.

'Welcome Miss Farraday, so glad you could join me.'

Gulping, I stared around at the devastation.

'This is what havoc one little book can create.' He started to chuckle, wickedly. 'Welcome to the end of all worlds.'

Powerless to do anything but stare, I looked on as the huge trees ripped up the earth, pulling it apart as if it were made of paper, until there was nothing left, nothing but space.

I began to fall...

Awaking in a panic, I could hear the quickened beat of my heart. Feeling disorientated I blearily glanced around the semi-darkness of the room, trying to recall where I was, and the familiar sensation of dread crept rapidly over my body as I slowly became aware of my bleak surroundings.

Rising swiftly from the straw covered floor, I sat bolt upright. 'Isaiah, where are you?' I cried.

I felt a cold hand on my cheek. 'I'm right here Effelia.' He yawned. 'I assume it's morning?'

'I do hope so, I wouldn't wish to sleep again after the nightmare I just had.'

'Ah, I did wonder, you were murmuring in your sleep.'

I gawped at him. 'Oh.'

'Care to enlighten me on what you dreamt about.' He hesitated. 'It may help discussing it.'

Trying to keep warm, I rubbed my hands up and down my arms. 'I'd rather not, if it's all the same with you.'

I reflected on how Gilbert had pulled me through the mirror, and how I'd felt myself falling, endlessly into oblivion.

Impulsively, I grabbed Isaiah's arm. 'Actually, there was something in my dream, something that struck me rather odd. It involved a mirror, but it was no ordinary mirror, it was a door, a type of portal.' I took a sideways glance at Isaiah. 'It seemed to me that...' I paused, not wishing to mention Gilbert. 'It was almost like the dream was trying to give me a hint.' I turned to glance at his reaction. 'Do you know of any magical mirrors Isaiah?'

I watched as he stretched and got up. 'As it so happens, yes I do. Strange as it may seem there was once such a mirror here at the monastery.' He peered out of the bars on the prison door. 'Your mother and Sabina used it when they left.'

'They did?'

'In their delicate conditions it would have been fatal to use anything but.'

I looked perplexed. 'Wasn't that taking rather a risk, how would they know where they would end up.'

He bellowed with laughter. 'My dear Effelia, any such forms of transportation are risky and hazardous, as you well know.' Slowly he ran his finger over an ancient carving in the door. 'Sabina had always been fascinated with supernatural power; in fact, such an interest was ultimately her downfall. She would spend hours researching the subject and was especially interested in ancient portals.' He smiled weakly. 'Sabina was an astute woman; when both of them left that day I'm sure they would have arrived safely through another mirror portal.' Moving away from the door, he stared at me. 'You and that boy are living proof that they made it through alive.' He frowned. 'Although I envisage there would have been complications for Sabina and your mother on arrival at the other side.'

I nodded without saying a word.

Crouching down in front of me, he tilted my chin so I was looking into his face.

'Where was this mirror, the one you saw in your nightmare?'

I lowered my eyes and shifted back, away from him. 'I didn't recognise the place.' I murmured quietly, not wishing him to know it was in the attic at my home, the home I had already forgotten the name of. 'What happened to the mirror that was here in the monastery?'

He sighed and slightly unsteadily rose to his feet. 'Oh, that is long gone. Septimus smashed the portal in a rage when he'd realised Sabina and your mother had travelled through it.'

'He must have been furious with my mother and Sabina for leaving without his permission.'

'Yes, most certainly, but I have an inkling it was more out of frustration than anything else. You see Sabina knew how to activate the mirror, if Septimus had known how to open it, he would have followed them.' He grunted. 'And my journey too would have been quick and relatively painless.'

I pondered over what he'd said. 'So am I correct in thinking that to travel by this method one must exit through another magical mirror, otherwise'

He interrupted. 'Otherwise, one would be lost in limbo forever, rather like the place we were stranded in before we arrived in Briarwood, a lost soul, doomed to wander between worlds for all eternity.'

I shuddered at the mere thought of it.

'So how many of these mirrors exist?'

'It is said there are many, but very few people have the key required to open them, and without it a mirror is just a mirror.'

Nodding, I stared down at my boots.

Suddenly, I thought of the Monk's ledger and remembered some vague mention of mirrored gateways.

I bit down hard on my lip.

'Where's the ledger Effelia, the one you hid.'

Looking shifty, I shrugged my shoulders. 'I...I can't recall.' I stammered, shocked that he seemingly knew what I was thinking. 'I really don't believe it's relevant anyway, it was just full of illegible scribblings.'

His face became sceptical. 'Perhaps, but its whereabouts could be crucial to us.' A sickly smile appeared on his face. 'Do try and recollect Effelia, that ledger is our salvation.' Slowly, he came over and knelt beside me again. 'If we gave Septimus the ledger, or even told him we'd found it, he would set us both free.'

I swallowed hard. 'You would risk the endings of worlds just to save yourself?'

He roared with laughter. 'Don't tell me you really believe that preposterous story, it is just a fable, made up to scare people, such as yourself.' He glared deep into my eyes. 'Effelia you must tell me where it is, before it is too late.'

An uneasy sensation crept over me, a desperate confused feeling of what to do for the best. I knew that time was against me, it was running out fast; it would be so easy to tell Septimus the location of the ledger, but I was apprehensive if he'd even believe me. My recent nightmare had caused the niggling doubt in my mind to grow; perhaps the story may be true, however ridiculously farcical it may be. And, if it did result in the endings of worlds, it would be entirely my fault. No, I thought determinedly, I would pretend I'd forgotten...for now.

'Well? He exclaimed in an impatient voice.

'I told you, I cannot remember.' I shouted, wearily getting up from the ground and going over to the shackles. 'And even if I could there's no certainty that our outcome would be different. Septimus may think we're making it up in desperation.'

Isaiah became agitated. 'Please, just think.' He bellowed at me. 'If you have any clue at all then I beg of you, please say.'

My eyes travelled to my rucksack, lying amongst the straw, containing all my worldly possessions: the contents were rather mundane, just toiletries, clothing and so forth, the only remotely interesting item was my notebook, my invaluable notebook that I'd meticulously detailed important facts, including the location of The Monk's ledger. The purpose of my notebook had originally been meant for making notes on things I'd forgotten, from my life back at home, yet somehow, I'd become carried away with myself and jotted down more than was needed, including where I'd hidden the ledger. How easy it would be for Isaiah to open my rucksack, flick through the pages and find my brief reminder –

**The Monk's Ledger is hidden behind the portrait in Briarwood church.**

Trying to act normal, I casually made my way over to my bag and sat down beside it.

'I shall do my very best Isaiah.' Sighing, I rubbed my forehead. 'I'm sure with a little rest I shall remember where I've hidden it.' Pretending to yawn I lay back on the straw, resting my head on the bag. 'I'm still very rather tired.' I muttered, closing my eyes. 'A little sleep may clear my head.'

He made a huffing noise but said nothing.

Less than a minute passed when I heard a clinking sound coming from the cell door, and Proctor entered looking as fearsome as usual.

'Get up Miss Farraday, you are to come along with me.'

I was bewildered. 'Am I being freed?'

She pursed her lips. 'Not exactly, Septimus wants you to be present when we have today's ceremony.'

Isaiah started to become agitated, crossing over in front of me. 'Why? What is that man up to?'

'Now Isaiah, I don't want any trouble.' She barked at him. 'You are to remain here.'

Abel came up behind her and gave me a coy smile.

Proctor's eyes widened. 'Otherwise, Abel will be forced to chain you up again.'

'You wicked old goat. Those trees should have had you years ago.' He glared at her with pure hatred. 'Although they most likely would have spat you out.'

With a knowing smile, she stepped forward. 'What a scornful man you have become Isaiah, how the mighty have fallen.' She gestured for Abel, who came plodding over to Isaiah. 'Shackle him up.'

Isaiah attempted to push past Abel, but his hefty arms grabbed him with ease.

'Come now Mr Isaiah, you know misbehaving isn't allowed.' He dragged him to the chains and expertly secured the metal rings around his wrists.

I heard Isaiah mumble something underneath his breath.

As Proctor beckoned me forward, I noticed the unnatural twist of her lips.

'You're going to love the ceremony, Miss Farraday.'

Taking a deep breath, I made my way towards the door, closely followed by Abel.

Isaiah's voice came booming into my ear. 'The ledger, tell them about the Monk's ledger Effelia.' His face was white with fear. 'It is your only hope.'

Proctor threw Isaiah a stern look before hurrying me out of the cell. 'We will ignore your father; he has a tendency to rant and rave about nothing at all.'

On reaching the door, I briefly looked across at him, and when I spoke my voice was calm and controlled. 'It will be all right...father. I shall see you again soon.'

A glimmer of joy appeared in his eyes. 'So, you shall, my dear daughter.'

Nodding, I smiled sincerely at him.

# Chapter 24

In a dream-like state I allowed myself to be led away, out of the monastery and along the back, down a side path that snaked onwards, then past the great greenhouses and barns. A dank fog had closed in around us, making it difficult to see.

I was filled with acute apprehension, aware that the Elder trees must now be within a close proximity, a horrifying realisation that caused me to shudder involuntary.

Mindful of Proctor, I discretely whispered to Abel. 'Are…are we near the trees?'

'No miss, they be far behind us now. This be the only safe path to get past them.' He briefly glanced at Proctor, who was striding ahead of us. 'You see, the ceremony site is right at the back of the grounds, way behind the monastery and The Elder trees. It is where everyone waits, and when The Giver stands in the correct spot… well that be when the trees make their way over. And…' He hesitated. 'Well, you can guess the rest.'

I gulped.

Proctor swung round and huffed. 'Do stop whittling on Abel, you really have the dreariest of voices.' She narrowed her eyes and glared at me. 'Walk in front Miss Farraday, so we can keep an eye on you. And in case it has escaped your notice the whole perimeter of Hartland has a towering fence of branches that can just as easily reach out and grab you as our ancient Elder trees behind the monastery.' She smirked. 'I therefore suggest you move a little to the left Miss Farraday, so you are out of harm's way.'

In alarm, I swiftly did as she said.

The mist was lifting now and I could make out the Harts in the nearby fields; they were such magnificent creatures, full of spirit and dignity. How I wished at that moment that I could become one of them, free to roam across the land without any restraints.

We were in a frost-covered field now and I could feel an icy chill in the air. Trudging wearily on I noticed, what appeared to be, several barrows rising up from the ground, shrouded in an eerie wreath of mist; they reminded me of historical burial mounds of long ago, and at the back of my mind I had a dim recollection of visiting a similar site as a child. But I knew, all too well, that I wasn't a mere visitor who would be allowed to leisurely meander my way round and then go home for tea. No, there was a more menacing reason for me being here, a petrifying event was about to take place, and it involved death.

I drew in a deep breath as I saw the mass of figures congregated nearby. It seemed the entire occupants of the monastery were standing there patiently. And in my state of confusion I convinced myself they were waiting for me.

Proctor jabbed me rather cruelly in the back. 'Keep moving Miss Farraday, we are to join the others.'

I looked into her dispassionate face then turned to glance at Abel, who was trailing a little behind. He had a plaintive expression in his eyes that was so woeful that I almost wanted to reach out and give him a reassuring hug. It struck me then how somehow, in his own unique way, he had managed to mask the fact that the tonic hadn't been effective; his emotions hadn't been cruelly snatched away like so many of the others, and by some small miracle he'd managed to survive life in this bleak environment. But what was most evident was how much he'd changed since we were children; it seemed miraculous that being brought here as a boy had oddly altered his character for the better; my childhood bully had disappeared and grownup into a compassionate and amicable young man, be it a little simple.

We were all standing together now, with the entire occupants of Hartland.

Carefully, I passed my eyes over their staid faces, until I reached Gideon. Despite everything, my heart still fluttered when I met his gaze, those deep, brown eyes bore into me with an intensity that was so profound that it didn't matter that they were filled with a cold detachment; he still possessed the power to draw me in.

A bent figure stepped forward, dressed in long grey robes, and as he came nearer, I peered into the pallid face of Septimius. I watched as he hovered there for a moment, collecting his thoughts, and then in deep concentration he moved forward.

His voice was hoarse when he spoke. 'Welcome one and all to The Giver Ceremony. The time has come once again to celebrate our joyous existence in the sacred land of our forefathers, who in their infinite wisdom bestowed upon us the almighty Elders.' He bowed his head and began to pray. 'Let us give our thanks to the perpetual bounty of fruit that sustains us so completely, allowing us the wisdom to carry on the great legacy of the monastery.' Stumbling slightly, Proctor rushed forward and steadied him. 'We have true faith in The Elder's ability to keep us strong and would like to show them our gratitude by providing offerings.' Pausing, he took a few paces towards the crowd. 'Let our first Giver be selected.' A bowl was passed to Septimus from one of the residents and he delved into it, producing a small piece of paper. 'Cuthbert Larkfield, please come forth.'

A young man walked confidently forward across the field and began clambering up to the largest barrow, which was situated in the precise centre to the others. On reaching the top he stood, motionless.

Septimus gazed at The Giver, with a beaming smile on his face. 'Cuthbert, you have honourably volunteered to be a Giver, do you still freely offer yourself as a sacrifice to our beloved Elders?

The Giver turned directly to Septimius. 'Yes sir, I will proudly and willingly give my life for such a great cause.'

'I congratulate you Cuthbert. Your body and soul will therefore become forever part of our trees. The essence of The Elders will enfold you in their arms and their spirits will welcome you.'

Cuthbert nodded at Septimus - his face full of appreciation. 'Thank you, sir.'

357

Calmly, he outstretched his arms, gazed up to the sky, and waited.

At first nothing happened, and we all stood there at the side of the field in complete and utter silence. Then the gentle rumbling came forth, from the earth beneath our feet; like the galloping hooves of almighty beasts, gradually making their way towards us. When the ground began to shake violently and I heard the ghoulishly familiar groan that had reverberated in the tunnel, I knew they were coming; they were coming for Cuthbert.

Instinctively, we all edged our way backwards as the huge branches came crashing down onto the icy field, moving rapidly towards the barrow, the great gnarled branches ran greedily to Cuthbert. Thick roots twisted up through the ground and joined the race to reach the poor, wretched man. I watched in morbid fascination as the branches and roots eagerly stretched out to where he was standing. With his face still reaching up to the heavens, Cuthbert swiftly became obscured by a mass of dense branches, expertly wrapping themselves about him. Within but a moment they were carting him off, taking him to their heart.

I shivered, watching them retreat with their prey, until they had disappeared up ahead, near to the monastery. A cold chill blew across the field, carried on a wave of dank, rolling mist. Standing there trembling, I looked upon the blank faces amongst me: in their eyes nothing unordinary had taken place, they were used to this, it was part of their life. I wondered when these abhorrent rituals first came about, how soon were they introduced after the original monks initially planted The Elder trees, what possessed them to bring such death to their door; had some dangerous magical power been unleashed from the trees, that emitted a substance so compelling that the monks were powerless to resist it, and henceforth they were servants to the trees, toiling away in the monastery to create a potion, a special tonic to bestow upon unsuspecting guests. Whatever the hypothesis, there was no doubt in my mind that man was ultimately responsible for the ruination of Hartland,

and in doing so humanity had been lost, along with their reason for being.

Septimus began to applaud, followed by the crowd. 'Excellent that was excellent. Now, for our final Giver.' he exclaimed jubilantly as he selected another name from the bowl. 'Clara Damson, please come forth.'

A woman of about my age began to walk, unfalteringly towards the barrow, bowing her head when she'd reached the top. As I peered closer, I noticed she was shaking.

Fleetingly, I glanced at Abel. 'There are only two sacrifices?'

'Yep, until the next time.'

Relief flooded over me, followed by pity for the unfortunate woman.

Hearing raised voices, I glimpsed across to see a displeased Septimus and Proctor in deep discussion. Something was wrong.

'Move out the way.' Demanded Proctor, as she barged her way through the crowd and walked briskly to the barrow. She signalled for the woman to come down, then pulled her away.

Turning to face the crowd Septimus began to chuckle. 'It seems there has been a mix up. The second Giver is not, at present, a suitable candidate. Therefore, a fresh offering will be requested.'

There was a deathly silence.

'Rather than have a volunteer, I would like to take this opportunity to personally select a Giver, from all of you good people here at Hartland.' Septimus scanned the crowd, pretending to look for the right person. 'After careful consideration, I have made my choice.' His voice suddenly bellowed out. 'Effie Farraday, please step forward.'

As the mass of people sought me out, a sinister chill ran through my body as I realised the apprehension of earlier was well founded.

Slowly, I stumbled back.

Strong hands clasped my shoulders. 'I congratulate you, Miss Farraday. Septimus has made a wise choice.' Proctor exclaimed with a triumphant laugh.

I flinched, wrenching myself away from her.

Abel took my hand, his expression full of sorrow. 'Sorry Miss, I'm really sad to see...to see you go.' He moved his mouth close to my ear. 'Forgive me for those pranks I played on you as a child, for pinching you and all. It weren't nice, was it?'

I stared up into his face. 'You remember all that?

'Everything.' He whispered tearfully. 'I was too ashamed to admit it before.'

Proctor took hold of my arm, dragging me roughly forward.

'Miss? Abel cried.

I called out to him. 'I forgive you Abel. And please don't worry, everything's going to be fine.'

It wasn't of course; everything was going completely wrong. Ever since leaving the cell this morning, my eerie sense of foreboding had prepared me a little for what was about to happen, so it wasn't really much of a surprise when Septimus called out my name. I wasn't however quite yet ready to succumb to my rather unfortunate fate.

With a violent yank, I wrenched my arm free from Proctor's grip.

'At least let me go to my doom with dignity.' I said tersely to her. 'I really don't need to be escorted.'

She glared sternly at me and nodded.

Trying to act calm I strode forward, then rapidly changed course, running quickly through the crowd of people, shoving them out the way as I went, knowing they wouldn't have it in them to hold me back. By now, I had no idea where Septimus or Proctor were and had no desire to stop and find out, as long as I kept away from them, I had a chance, slim as it may be. Finally, having reached the back of the crowd, I began to sprint across the field, not having the slightest idea what direction I was heading. But, to my alarm, I unexpectedly tripped, landing flat on my face on the icy ground.

I cried out in pain.

Sensing a figure hovering over me, I apprehensively looked up into the unmistakable face of Gideon.

'Time to go Effie.'

The soft murmur of his words was so comforting that I imagined I was in a dream within a dream. I was back in the forest, where the trees were dark and shadowy; where Gideon was waiting for me, my beloved Gideon.

'Come to me Effie.'

Feeling decidedly disorientated I attempted to stand up, only to find myself collapsing to the ground.

Strong arms caught me, lifting me up. 'I got you.' Murmured Gideon, as he started carrying me across the field.

'How sad we couldn't remain in our forest Gideon, we were so happy there, in our dreams.' I said, transfixed by his remarkable face. 'If only you and I could return there; the forest would bring you back to me.' I whimpered, burying my face in the crook of his neck. 'I will always love you Gideon.'

Abruptly, he placed me down, staring strangely into my eyes. 'What?' A look of confusion was etched across his face.

Before I had a chance to respond I heard Septimus shouting nearby. 'Leave her now Gideon.' Slowly, he shuffled forward with Proctor beside him, and then reached out to ruffle Gideon's hair. 'Well done Gideon, now move away and allow the trees to do their job.' As the ground began to shake his voice rose in panic. 'Quickly Gideon, they are returning. Gideon please, what are you doing.'

Their voices became a blur as I realised where I was standing.

'No.' I cried. 'No.'

I was standing right on top of the barrow.

There was something of a commotion behind me, but I was only vaguely aware of it as I tried to come to terms with my situation.

'Please do not run Miss Farraday, it is futile.' Septimus croaked in a weak voice.

As I stood there, wobbling slightly I thought how fate had indeed dealt me a curious blow. Up until a while ago any cherished hopes or happy prospects had still seemed achievable, in my somewhat deluded mind. But recent events had forced me to accept my grim destiny, making the end a little easier to tolerate.

An icy rain was falling now, causing a bone chilling coldness to my entire body. I took in a deep breath then exhaled, reaching my arms out wide, ready for the inevitable.

I had always been in awe of the beauty of trees, how dignified and serene they appeared; whenever I am near them, I am filled with a sense of complete peace and abandonment. As I peered through the mist and gazed upon the great trees up ahead, I came to a sudden realisation; even though they were something of an unnatural monstrosity, I couldn't help but be inspired by how vital and powerful they were, ruthless in their domination of this land, they held the mysteries of life and death in the very depths of their roots that grew so powerfully from the earth. I couldn't drag my eyes away from their magnificence, from their great strength as they approached me.

'I'm ready, come and take me.' I declared in a shaky voice.

Someone was screaming my name, but I didn't allow it to disturb me, such things no longer troubled me. In a daze I observed the branches drawing nearer, then felt the clawing of roots around my ankles, and a gentle murmur, like the wind in the trees, seemed to whisper my name. A wondrous electric sensation ran through my body as I became aware of the vitality of the living thing creeping around my waist and winding upwards to my face. I was being lifted up now, transported across the land to the heart of The Elders, where immediately I sensed the warm support of the trunk; a great energy passed through me as I felt myself sinking into the dark, woody depths of the bark. Closing my eyes, I fell into a delirious dream where great birds were swooping close overhead; they fought the trees with the aid of men, then took me away, high up into the sky, away from my new, warm home, away from my fate. The dream was over now, and I had awoken....

Printed in Great Britain
by Amazon